PENGUIN BOOKS

DRAGONLANCE LEGENDS™
Volume 3

Margaret Weis was born and grew up in Independence, Missouri. Her first book, a biography of Frank and Jesse James, was inspired by her childhood fascination with their graves at a local cemetery. She graduated in creative writing from the University of Missouri and worked for a publisher for fourteen years, during which time she advanced to the position of editor. She then accepted a job as fiction editor with TSR, Inc., where she now works. Besides the *Dragonlance Chronicles* and the *Dragonlance Legends*, she has published a great many books for younger readers and is working on her own science fantasy trilogy as well as a fantasy trilogy, with Tracy Hickman, called *The Necroclast*. She lives in Wisconsin with her husband and three cats.

Tracy Hickman was born in Salt Lake City, Utah, in 1955. He served as a missionary in Indonesia for two years before returning to the United States to pursue his art. He now combines his skills as a writer and games designer with TSR, Inc., as the author of the complete Dragonlance™ package, including games, books and miniatures. The *Dragonlance Chronicles*, written with Margaret Weis, were his first novels. He lives in Wisconsin with his wife and their two children.

Margaret Weis and Tracy Hickman

LEGENDS

Volume 3

TEST OF THE TWINS

Poetry by Michael Williams

Illustrations by Valerie Valusek

PENGUIN BOOKS

Penguin Books Ltd, Harmondsworth, Middlesex, England
Viking Penguin Inc., 40 West 23rd Street, New York, New York 10010, U.S.A.
Penguin Books Australia Ltd, Ringwood, Victoria, Australia
Penguin Books Canada Ltd, 2801 John Street, Markham, Ontario, Canada L3R 1B4
Penguin Books (N.Z.) Ltd, 182–190 Wairau Road, Auckland 10, New Zealand

First published by TSR, Inc. 1986
Distributed to the book trade in the U.S.A. by Random House, Inc.,
and in Canada by Random House of Canada Ltd
Distributed in the U.K. by TSR U.K. Ltd
Distributed to the toy and hobby trade by regional distributors
Published in Penguin Books 1987

Printed and bound in Great Britain by
Cox & Wyman Ltd, Reading

the world of krynn
the continent of ansalon

BOOK 1

The Hammer of the Gods

Like sharp steel, the clarion call of a trumpet split the autumn air as the armies of the dwarves of Thorbardin rode down into the Plains of Dergoth to meet their foe—their kinsmen. Centuries of hatred and misunderstanding between the hill dwarves and their mountain cousins poured red upon the plains that day. Victory became meaningless—an objective no one sought. To avenge wrongs committed long ago by grandfathers long since dead was the aim of both sides. To kill and kill and kill again—this was the Dwarfgate War.

True to his word, the dwarven hero, Kharas, fought for his King Beneath the Mountain. Clean-shaven, his beard sacrificed to shame that he must fight those he called kin, Kharas was at the vanguard of the army, weeping even as he killed. But as he fought, he suddenly came to see that the word *victory* had become twisted to mean annihilation. He saw the standards of both armies fall, lying trampled and forgotten upon the bloody plain as the madness of revenge engulfed both armies in a fearsome red wave. And when he saw that no matter who won there would be no victor, Kharas threw down his Hammer—the Hammer forged with the help of Reorx, god of the dwarves—and left the field.

Many were the voices that shrieked "coward." If Kharas heard, he paid them no heed. He knew his worth in his own heart, he knew it better than any. Wiping the bitter tears from his eyes, washing the blood of his kinsmen from his hands, Kharas searched among the dead until he found the bodies of King Duncan's two beloved sons. Throwing the hacked and mutilated corpses of the young dwarves over the back of a horse, Kharas left the Plains of Dergoth, returning to Thorbardin with his burden.

Kharas rode far, but not far enough to escape the sound of hoarse voices crying for revenge, the clash of steel, the screams

---

of the dying. He did not look back. He had the feeling he would hear those voices to the end of his days.

The dwarven hero was just riding into the first foothills of the Kharolis Mountains when he heard an eerie rumbling sound begin. Kharas's horse shied nervously. The dwarf checked it and stopped to soothe the animal. As he did so, he looked around uneasily. What was it? It was no sound of war, no sound of nature.

Kharas turned. The sound came from behind him, from the lands he had just left, lands where his kinsmen were still slaughtering each other in the name of justice. The sound increased in magnitude, becoming a low, dull, booming sound that grew louder and louder. Kharas almost imagined he could see the sound, coming closer and closer. The dwarven hero shuddered and lowered his head as the dreadful roar came nearer, thundering across the Plains.

It is Reorx, he thought in grief and horror. It is the voice of the angry god. We are doomed.

The sound hit Kharas, along with a shock wave—a blast of heat and scorching, foul-smelling wind that nearly blew him from the saddle. Clouds of sand and dust and ash enveloped him, turning day into a horrible, perverted night. Trees around him bent and twisted, his horses screamed in terror and nearly bolted. For a moment, it was all Kharas could do to retain control of the panic-stricken animals.

Blinded by the stinging dustcloud, choking and coughing, Kharas covered his mouth and tried—as best he could in the strange darkness—to cover the eyes of the horses as well. How long he stood in that cloud of sand and ash and hot wind, he could not remember. But, as suddenly as it came, it passed.

The sand and dust settled. The trees straightened. The horses grew calm. The cloud drifted past on the gentler winds of autumn, leaving behind a silence more dreadful than the thunderous noise.

Filled with dreadful foreboding, Kharas urged his tired horses on as fast as he could and rode up into the hills, seeking desperately for some vantage site. Finally, he found it—an outcropping of rock. Tying the pack animals with their sorrowful burden to a tree, Kharas rode his horse out onto the rock and looked out over the Plains of Dergoth. Stopping, he stared down below him in awe.

Nothing living stirred. In fact, there was nothing there at all; nothing except blackened, blasted sand and rock.

Both armies were completely wiped out. So devastating was the explosion that not even corpses remained upon the ash-covered Plain. Even the very face of the land itself had changed. Kharas's horrified gaze went to where the magical fortress of Zhaman had once stood, its tall, graceful spires ruling the Plains. It, too, had been destroyed—but not totally. The fortress had collapsed in upon itself and now—most horribly—its ruins resembled a human skull sitting, grinning, upon the barren Plain of Death.

"Reorx, Father, Forger, forgive us," murmured Kharas, tears blurring his vision. Then, his head bowed in grief, the dwarven hero left the site, returning to Thorbardin.

The dwarves would believe—for so Kharas himself would report—that the destruction of both armies on the Plains of Dergoth was brought about by Reorx. That the god had, in his anger, hurled his hammer down upon the land, smiting his children.

But the Chronicles of Astinus truly record what happened upon the Plains of Dergoth that day:

Now at the height of his magical powers, the archmage, Raistlin, known also as Fistandantilus, and the White-robed cleric of Paladine, Crysania, sought entry into the Portal that leads to the Abyss, there to challenge and fight the Queen of Darkness.

Dark crimes of his own this archmage had committed to reach this point—the pinnacle of his ambition. The Black Robes he wore were stained with blood; some of it his own. Yet this man knew the human heart. He knew how to wrench it and twist it and make those who should have reviled him and spurned him come to admire him instead. Such a one was Lady

Crysania, of the House of Tarinius. A Revered Daughter of the church, she possessed one fatal flaw in the white marble of her soul. And that flaw Raistlin found and widened so that the crack would spread throughout her being and eventually reach her heart. . . .

Crysania followed him to the dread Portal. Here she called upon her god and Paladine answered, for, truly, she was his chosen. Raistlin called upon his magic and he was successful, for no wizard had yet lived as powerful as this young man.

The Portal opened.

Raistlin started to enter, but a magical, time-traveling device being operated by the mage's twin brother, Caramon, and the kender, Tasslehoff Burrfoot, interfered with the archmage's powerful spell. The field of magic was disrupted . . .

. . . with disastrous and unforeseen consequences.

"Oops," said Tasslehoff Burrfoot.

Caramon fixed the kender with a stern eye.

"It's not my fault! Really, Caramon!" Tas protested.

But, even as he spoke, the kender's gaze went to their surroundings, then he glanced up at Caramon, then back to their surroundings again. Tas's lower lip began to tremble and he reached for his handkerchief, just in case he felt a snuffle coming. But his handkerchief wasn't there, his pouches weren't there. Tas sighed. In the excitement of the moment, he'd forgotten—they'd all been left behind in the dungeons of Thorbardin.

And it had been a truly exciting moment. One minute he and Caramon had been standing in the magical fortress of Zhaman, activating the magical time-traveling device; the next minute Raistlin had begun working *his* magic and, before Tas knew it, there had been a terrible commotion—stones singing and rocks cracking and a horrible feeling of being pulled in six different directions at once and then—WHOOSH—here they were.

———

Wherever here was. And, wherever it was, it certainly didn't seem to be where it was supposed to be.

He and Caramon were on a mountain trail, near a large boulder, standing ankle-deep in slick ash-gray mud that completely covered the face of the land below them for as far as Tas could see. Here and there, jagged ends of broken rock jutted from the soft flesh of the ash covering. There were no signs of life. Nothing could be alive in that desolation. No trees remained standing; only fire-blackened stumps poked through the thick mud. As far as the eye could see, clear to the horizon, in every direction, there was nothing but complete and total devastation.

The sky itself offered no relief. Above them, it was gray and empty. To the west, however, it was a strange violet color, boiling with weird, luminous clouds laced with lightning of brilliant blue. Other than the distant rumble of thunder, there was no sound . . . no movement . . . nothing.

Caramon drew a deep breath and rubbed his hand across his face. The heat was intense and, already, even though they had been standing in this place only a few minutes, his sweaty skin was coated with a fine film of gray ash.

"Where are we?" he asked in even, measured tones.

"I—I'm sure I haven't any idea, Caramon," Tas said. Then, after a pause, "Have you?"

"*I* did everything the way you told me to," Caramon replied, his voice ominously calm. "You said Gnimsh said that all we had to do was *think* of where we wanted to go and there we'd be. I know *I* was thinking of Solace—"

"I was too!" Tas cried. Then, seeing Caramon glare at him, the kender faltered. "At least I was thinking of it *most* of the time. . . ."

"*Most* of the time?" Caramon asked in a dreadfully calm voice.

"Well"—Tas gulped—"I—I did th-think once, just for an instant, mind you, about how—er—how much fun and interesting and, well, unique, it would be to—uh—visit a—uuh . . . um . . ."

"Um what?" Caramon demanded.

"A . . . mmmmmm."

"A what?"

"Mmmmm," Tas mumbled.

Caramon sucked in his breath.

"A moon!" Tas said quickly.

"Moon!" repeated Caramon incredulously. "Which moon?" he asked after a moment, glancing around.

"Oh"—Tas shrugged—"any of the three. I suppose one's as good as another. Quite similar, I should imagine. Except, of course, that Solinari would have all glittering silver rocks and Lunitari all bright red rocks, and I guess the other one would be all black, though I can't say for sure, never having seen—"

Caramon growled at this point, and Tas decided it might be best to hold his tongue. He did, too, for about three minutes during which time Caramon continued to look around at their surroundings with a solemn face. But it would have taken more holding than the kender had inside him (or a sharp knife) to keep his tongue from talking longer than that.

"Caramon," he blurted out, "do—do you think we actually *did* it? Went to a—uh—moon, that is? I mean, this certainly doesn't look like anyplace I've ever been before. Not that these rocks are silver or red or even black. They're more of a rock color, but—"

"I wouldn't doubt it," Caramon said gloomily. "After all, you did take us to a seaport city that was sitting squarely in the middle of a desert—"

"That wasn't my fault either!" Tas said indignantly. "Why even Tanis said—"

"Still"—Caramon's face creased in puzzlement—"this place certainly *looks* strange, but it *seems* familiar somehow."

"You're right," said Tas after a moment, staring around again at the bleak, ash-choked landscape. "It does remind me of somewhere, now that you mention it. Only"—the kender shivered—"I don't recall ever having been anyplace quite this awful . . . except the Abyss," he added, but he said it under his breath.

The boiling clouds surged nearer and nearer as the two

———

spoke, casting a further pall over the barren land. A hot wind sprang up, and a fine rain began to fall, mingling with the ash drifting through the air. Tas was just about to comment on the slimy quality of the rain when suddenly, without warning, the world blew up.

At least that was Tas's first impression. Brilliant, blinding light, a sizzling sound, a crack, a boom that shook the ground, and Tasslehoff found himself sitting in the gray mud, staring stupidly at a gigantic hole that had been blasted in the rock not a hundred feet away from him.

"Name of the gods!" Caramon gasped. Reaching down, he dragged Tas to his feet. "Are you all right?"

"I—I think so," said Tas, somewhat shaken. As he watched, lightning streaked again from the cloud to ground, sending rock and ash hurtling through the air. "*My!* That certainly was an interesting experience. Though nothing I'd care to repeat right away," he added hastily, fearful that the sky, which was growing darker and darker by the minute, might decide to treat him to that interesting experience all over again.

"Wherever we are, we better get off this high ground," Caramon muttered. "At least there's a trail. It must lead somewhere."

Glancing down the mud-choked trail into the equally mud-choked valley below, Tas had the fleeting thought that Somewhere was likely to be every bit as gray and yucky as Here, but, after a glimpse of Caramon's grim face, the kender quickly decided to keep his thoughts to himself.

As they slogged down the trail through the thick mud, the hot wind blew harder, driving specks of blackened wood and cinders and ash into their flesh. Lightning danced among the trees, making them burst into balls of bright green or blue flame. The ground shook with the concussive roar of the thunder. And still, the storm clouds massed on the horizon. Caramon hurried their pace.

As they labored down the hillside they entered what must once have been, Tas imagined, a beautiful valley. At one time, he guessed, the trees here must have been ablaze with autumn oranges and golds, or misty green in the spring.

Here and there, he saw spirals of smoke curling up, only to be whipped away immediately by the storm wind. Undoubtedly from more lightning strikes, he thought. But, in an odd sort of way, that reminded him of something, too. Like Caramon, he was becoming increasingly convinced that he knew this place.

Wading through the mud, trying to ignore what the icky stuff was doing to his green shoes and bright blue leggings, Tas decided to try an old kender trick To Use When Lost. Closing his eyes and blotting everything from his mind, he ordered his brain to provide him with a picture of the landscape before him. The rather interesting kender logic behind this being that since it was likely that some kender in Tasslehoff's family had undoubtedly been to this place before, the memory was somehow passed on to his or her descendants. While this was never scientifically verified (the gnomes are working on it, having referred it to committee), it certainly is true that—to this day—no kender has ever been reported lost on Krynn.

At any rate, Tas, standing shin-deep in mud, closed his eyes and tried to conjure up a picture of his surroundings. One came to him, so vivid in its clarity that he was rather startled—certainly his ancestors' mental maps had never been so perfect. There were trees—giant trees—there were mountains on the horizon, there was a lake. . . .

Opening his eyes, Tas gasped. There *was* a lake! He hadn't noticed it before, probably because it was the same gray, sludge color as the ash-covered ground. Was there water there, still? Or was it filled with mud?

I wonder, Tas mused, if Uncle Trapspringer ever visited a moon. If so, that would account for the fact that I recognize this place. But surely he would have told someone. . . . Perhaps he would have if the goblins hadn't eaten him before he had the chance. Speaking of food, that reminds me . . .

"Caramon," Tas shouted over the rising wind and the boom of the thunder. "Did you bring along any water? I didn't. Nor any food, either. I didn't suppose we'd need any, what with

19

going back home and all. But—"

Tas suddenly saw something that drove thoughts of food and water and Uncle Trapspringer from his mind.

"Oh, Caramon!" Tas clutched at the big warrior, pointing. "Look, do you suppose *that's* the sun?"

"What else would it be?" Caramon snapped gruffly, his gaze on a watery, greenish-yellow disk that had appeared through a rift in the storm clouds. "And, no, I didn't bring any water. So just keep quiet about it, huh?"

"Well, you needn't be ru—" Tas began. Then he saw Caramon's face and quickly hushed.

They had come to a halt, slipping in the mud, halfway down the trail. The hot wind blew about them, sending Tas's topknot streaming out from his head like a banner and whipping Caramon's cloak out. The big warrior was staring at the lake—the same lake Tas had noticed. Caramon's face was pale, his eyes troubled. After a moment, he began walking again, trudging grimly down the trail. With a sigh, Tas squished along after him. He had reached a decision.

"Caramon," he said, "let's get out of here. Let's leave this place. Even if it *is* a moon like Uncle Trapspringer must have visited before the goblins ate him, it isn't much fun. The moon, I mean, not being eaten by goblins which I suppose wouldn't be much fun either, come to think of it. To tell you the truth, this moon's just about as boring as the Abyss and it certainly smells as bad. Besides, there I wasn't thirsty. . . . Not that I'm thirsty now," he added hastily, remembering too late that he wasn't supposed to talk about it, "but my tongue's sort of dried out, if you know what I mean, which makes it hard to talk. We've got the magical device." He held the jewel-encrusted sceptre-shaped object up in his hand, just in case Caramon had forgotten in the last half-hour what it looked like. "And I *promise* . . . I solemnly vow . . . that I'll think of Solace with *all* my brain this time, Caramon. I— Caramon?"

"Hush, Tas," Caramon said.

They had reached the valley floor, where the mud was ankle-deep on Caramon, which made it about shin-deep on Tas. Caramon had begun to limp again from when he'd fallen and wrenched his knee back in the magical fortress of Zhaman. Now, in addition to worry, there was a look of pain on his face.

There was another look, too. A look that made Tas feel all prickly inside—a look of true fear. Tas, startled, glanced about quickly, wondering what Caramon saw. It seemed pretty much the same at the bottom as it had at the top, he thought— gray and yucky and horrible. Nothing had changed, except that it was growing darker. The storm clouds had obliterated the sun again, rather to Tas's relief, since it was an unwholesome-looking sun that made the bleak, gray landscape appear worse than ever. The rain was falling harder as the storm clouds drew nearer. Other than that, there certainly didn't appear to be anything frightening.

The kender tried his best to keep silent, but the words just sort of leaped out of his mouth before he could stop them.

"What's the matter, Caramon? I don't see anything. Is your knee bothering you? I—"

"Be quiet, Tas!" Caramon ordered in a strained, tight voice. He was staring around him, his eyes wide, his hands clenching and unclenching nervously.

Tas sighed and clapped his hand over his mouth to bottle up the words, determined to keep quiet if it killed him. When he was quiet, it suddenly occurred to him that it was so *very* quiet around here. There was no sound at all when the thunder wasn't thundering, not even the usual sounds he was used to hearing when it rained—water dripping from tree leaves and plopping onto the ground, the wind rustling in the branches, birds singing their rain songs, complaining about their wet feathers. . . .

Tas had a strange, quaking feeling inside. He looked at the stumps of the burned trees more closely. Even burned, they were huge, easily the largest trees he had ever seen in his life except for—

Tas gulped. Leaves, autumn colors, the smoke of cooking fires curling up from the valley, the lake—blue and smooth as crystal . . .

Blinking, he rubbed his eyes to clear them of the gummy film of mud and rain. He stared around him, looking back up at the trail, at that huge boulder. . . . He stared at the lake that he could see quite clearly through the burned tree stumps. He stared at the mountains with their sharp, jagged peaks.

It wasn't Uncle Trapspringer who'd been here before. . . .

"Oh, Caramon!" he whispered in horror.

Chapter 2

What is it?" Cara-
mon turned, looking at Tas so strangely that the kender felt his
inside prickly feeling spread to his outside. Little bumps
appeared all up and down his arms.

"N-nothing," Tas stammered. "Just my imagination. Caramon," he added urgently, "let's leave! Right now. We can go
anywhere we want to! We can go back in time to when we were
all together, to when we were all happy! We can go back to
when Flint and Sturm were alive, to when Raistlin still wore the
red robes and Tika—"

"Shut up, Tas," snapped Caramon warningly, his words
accented by a flash of lightning that made even the kender
flinch.

The wind was rising, whistling through the dead tree stumps
with an eerie sound, like someone drawing a shivering breath
through clenched teeth. The warm, slimy rain had ceased. The
clouds above them swirled past, revealing the pale sun shimmering in the gray sky. But on the horizon, the clouds continued to mass, continued to grow blacker and blacker.

Multicolored lightning flickered among them, giving them a distant, deadly beauty.

Caramon started walking along the muddy trail, gritting his teeth against the pain of his injured leg. But Tas, looking down that trail that he now knew so well—even though it was appallingly different—could see to where it rounded a bend. Knowing what lay beyond that bend, he stood where he was, planted firmly in the middle of the road, staring at Caramon's back.

After a few moments of unusual silence, Caramon realized something was wrong and glanced around. He stopped, his face drawn with pain and fatigue.

"C'mon, Tas!" he said irritably.

Twisting his topknot of hair around his finger, Tas shook his head.

Caramon glared at him.

Tas finally burst out, "Those are vallenwood trees, Caramon!"

The big man's stern expression softened. "I know, Tas," he said wearily. "This is Solace."

"No, it isn't!" Tas cried. "It—it's just some place that has vallenwoods! There must be lots of places that have vallenwoods—"

"And are there lots of places that have Crystalmir Lake, Tas, or the Kharolis Mountains or that boulder up where you and I've both seen Flint sitting, carving his wood, or this road that leads to the—"

"You don't know!" Tas yelled angrily. "It's possible!" Suddenly, he ran forward, or he tried to run forward, dragging his feet through the oozing, clinging mud as fast as possible. Stumbling into Caramon, he grabbed the big man's hand and tugged on it. "Let's go! Let's get out of here!" Once again, he held up the time-traveling device. "We—we can go back to Tarsis! Where the dragons toppled a building down on top of me! That was a fun time, very interesting. Remember?" His shrill voice screeched through the burned-out trees.

Reaching out, his face grim, Caramon grabbed the magical device from the kender's hand. Ignoring Tas's frantic protests, he took the device and began twisting and turning the jewels, gradually transforming it from a sparkling sceptre into a plain, nondescript pendant. Tas watched him miserably.

"Why won't we go, Caramon? This place is horrible. We don't have any food or water and, from what I've seen, there's not much likelihood of us finding either. Plus, we're liable to get blasted right out of our shoes if one of those lightning bolts hits us, and that storm's getting closer and closer and you *know* this isn't Solace—"

"I *don't* know, Tas," Caramon said quietly. "But I'm going to find out. What's the matter? Aren't you curious? Since when did a kender ever turn down the chance for an adventure?" He began to limp down the trail again.

"I'm just as curious as the next kender," Tas mumbled, hanging his head and trudging along after Caramon. "But it's one thing to be curious about some place you've never been before, and quite another to be curious about home. You're not *supposed* to be curious about home! Home isn't supposed to change. It just stays there, waiting for you to come back. Home is someplace you say 'My, this looks just like it did when I left!' *not* 'My, this looks like six million dragons flew in and wrecked the joint!' Home is *not* a place for adventures, Caramon!"

Tas peered up into Caramon's face to see if his argument had made any impression. If it had, it didn't show. There was a look of stern resolution on the pain-filled face that rather surprised Tas, surprised and startled him as well.

Caramon's changed, Tas realized suddenly. And it isn't just from giving up dwarf spirits. There's something different about him—he's more serious and . . . well, responsible-looking, I guess. But there's something else. Tas pondered. Pride, he decided after a minute of profound reflection. Pride in himself, pride and determination.

This isn't a Caramon who will give in easily, Tas thought with a sinking heart. This isn't a Caramon who needs a kender to keep him out of mischief and taverns. Tas sighed bleakly. He rather missed that old Caramon.

They came to the bend in the road. Each recognized it, though neither said anything—Caramon, because there wasn't anything to be said, and Tas, because he was steadfastly refusing to admit he recognized it. But both found their footsteps dragging.

Once, travelers coming around that bend would have seen the Inn of the Last Home, gleaming with light. They would have smelled Otik's spiced potatoes, heard the sounds of laughter and song drift from the door every time it opened to admit the wanderer or regular from Solace. Both Caramon and Tas stopped, by unspoken agreement, before they rounded that corner.

Still they said nothing, but each looked around him at the desolation, at the burned and blasted tree stumps, at the ash-covered ground, at the blackened rocks. In their ears rang a silence louder and more frightening than the booming thunder. Because both knew that they should have heard Solace, even if they couldn't see it yet. They should have heard the sounds of the town—the sounds of the smithy, the sounds of market day, the sounds of hawkers and children and merchants, the sounds of the Inn.

But there was nothing, only silence. And, far off in the distance, the ominous rumble of thunder.

Finally, Caramon sighed. "Let's go," he said, and hobbled forward.

Tas followed more slowly, his shoes so caked with mud that he felt as if he were wearing iron-shod dwarf boots. But his shoes weren't nearly as heavy as his heart. Over and over he muttered to himself, "This isn't Solace, this isn't Solace, this isn't Solace," until it began to sound like one of Raistlin's magical incantations.

Rounding the bend, Tas fearfully raised his eyes—

—and heaved a vast sigh of relief.

"What did I tell you, Caramon?" he cried over the wailing of the wind. "Look, nothing there, nothing there at all. No Inn, no town, nothing." He slipped his small hand into Caramon's large one and tried to pull him backward. "Now, let's go. I've got an idea. We can go back to the time when Fizban made the golden span come out of the sky—"

But Caramon, shaking off the kender, was limping ahead, his face grim. Coming to a halt, he stared down at the ground. "What's this then, Tas?" he demanded in a voice taut with fear.

Chewing nervously on the end of his topknot, the kender came up to stand beside Caramon. "What's what?" he asked stubbornly.

Caramon pointed.

Tas sniffed. "So, it's a big cleared-off space on the ground. All right, maybe something *was* there. Maybe a big building was there. But it isn't there now, so why worry about it? I-Oh, Caramon!"

The big man's injured knee suddenly gave way. He staggered, and would have fallen if Tas hadn't propped him up. With Tas's help, Caramon made his way over to the stump of what had been an unusually large vallenwood, on the edge of the empty patch of mud-covered ground. Leaning against it, his face pale with pain and dripping with sweat, Caramon rubbed his injured knee.

"What can I do to help?" Tas asked anxiously, wringing his hands. "I know! I'll find you a crutch! There must be lots of broken branches lying about. I'll go look."

Caramon said nothing, only nodded wearily.

Tas dashed off, his sharp eyes scouring the gray, slimy ground, rather glad to have something to do and not to have to answer questions about stupid cleared-off spaces. He soon found what he was looking for—the end of a tree branch sticking up through the mud. Catching hold of it, the kender gave it a yank. His hands slipped off the wet branch, sending him toppling over backward. Getting up, staring ruefully at the gunk on his blue leggings, the kender tried unsuccessfully to wipe it off. Then he sighed and grimly took hold of the branch again. This time, he felt it give a little.

"I've almost got it, Caramon!" he reported. "I—"

A most unkenderlike shriek rose above the screaming wind. Caramon looked up in alarm to see Tas's topknot disappearing into a vast sink hole that had apparently opened up beneath his feet.

"I'm coming, Tas!" Caramon called, stumbling forward. "Hang on—"

But he halted at the sight of Tas crawling back out of the hole. The kender's face was like nothing Caramon had ever seen. It was ashen, the lips white, the eyes wide and staring.

"Don't come any closer, Caramon," Tas whispered, gesturing him away with a small, muddy hand. "Please, stay back!"

But it was too late. Caramon had reached the edge of the hole and was staring down. Tas, crouched beside him on the ground, began to shake and sob. "They're all dead," he whimpered. "All dead." Burying his face in his arms, he rocked back and forth, weeping bitterly.

At the bottom of the rock-lined hole that had been covered by a thick layer of mud lay bodies, piles of bodies, bodies of men, women, children. Preserved by the mud, some were still pitifully recognizable—or so it seemed to Caramon's feverish gaze. His thoughts went to the last mass grave he had seen—the plague village Crysania had found. He remembered his brother's angry, grief-stricken face. He remembered Raistlin calling down the lightning, burning everything, burning the village to ash.

Gritting his teeth, Caramon forced himself to look into that grave—forced himself to look for a mass of red curls. . . .

He turned away with a shuddering sob of relief, then, looking around wildly, he began to run back toward the Inn. "Tika!" he screamed.

Tas raised his head, springing up in alarm. "Caramon!" he cried, slipped in the mud, and fell.

"Tika!" Caramon yelled hoarsely above the howl of the wind and the distant thunder. Apparently oblivious to the pain of his injured leg, he staggered down a wide, clear area, free of tree stumps—the road leading past the Inn, Tas's mind registered, though he didn't think it clearly. Getting to his feet again, the kender hurried after Caramon, but the big man was making rapid headway, staggering through the mud, his fear and hope giving him strength.

Tas soon lost sight of him amid the blackened stumps, but he could hear his voice, still calling Tika's name. Now Tas knew where the big man was headed. His footsteps slowed. His head ached with the heat and the foul smells of the place, his heart ached with what he had just seen. Dragging his heavy, mud-caked shoes, fearful of what he would find ahead, the kender stumbled on.

Sure enough, there was Caramon, standing in a barren space next to another vallenwood stump. In his hand, he held something, staring at it with the look of one who is, at last, defeated.

Mud-covered, bedraggled, heartsick, the kender went to stand before him. "What?" he asked through trembling lips, pointing to the object in the big man's hand.

"A hammer," Caramon said in a choked voice. "*My* hammer."

Tas looked at it. It was a hammer, all right. Or at least appeared to have been one. The wooden handle had been burned about three-fourths of the way off. All that was left was a charred bit of wood and the metal head, blackened with flame.

"How—how can you be sure?" he faltered, still fighting, still refusing to believe.

"I'm sure," Caramon said bitterly. "Look at this." The handle wiggled, the head wobbled when he touched it. "I made it when I was—was still drinking." He wiped his eyes with his hand. "It isn't made very well. The head used to come off about half the time. But then"—he choked—"I never did much work with it anyway."

Weakened from the running, Caramon's injured leg suddenly gave out. This time, he didn't even try to catch himself, but just slumped down into the mud. Sitting in the clear patch of ground that had once been his home, he clutched the hammer in his hand and began to cry.

Tas turned his head away. The big man's grief was sacred, too private a thing for even his eyes. Ignoring his own tears, which were trickling past his nose, Tas stared around bleakly. He had never felt so helpless, so lost and alone. *What had happened? What had gone wrong?* Surely there must be a clue, an answer.

"I—I'm going to look around," he mumbled to Caramon, who didn't hear him.

With a sigh, Tas trudged off. He knew where he was now, of course. He could refuse to admit it no longer. Caramon's house had been located near the center of town, close to the Inn. Tas continued walking along what had once been a street running between rows of houses. Even though there was nothing left now—not the houses, not the street, not the vallenwoods that held the houses—he knew exactly where he was. He wished he didn't. Here and there he saw branches poking up out of the mud, and he shivered. For there was nothing else. Nothing except . . .

"Caramon!" Tas called, thankful to have something to investigate and to, hopefully, take Caramon's mind off his sorrow. "Caramon, I think you should come see this!"

But the big man continued to ignore him, so Tas went off to examine the object by himself. Standing at the very end of the street, in what had once been a small park, was a stone obelisk. Tas remembered the park, but he didn't remember the obelisk. It hadn't been there the last time he'd been in Solace, he realized, examining it.

Tall, crudely carved, it had, nevertheless, survived the ravages of fire and wind and storm. Its surface was blackened and charred but, Tas saw as he neared it, there were letters carved into it, letters that, once he had cleaned away the muck, he thought he could read.

Tas brushed away the soot and muddy film covering the stone, stared at it for a long moment, then called out softly, "Caramon."

The odd note in the kender's voice penetrated Caramon's haze of grief. He lifted his head. Seeing the strange obelisk and seeing Tas's unusually serious face, the big man painfully heaved himself up and limped toward it.

"What is it?" he asked.

Tas couldn't answer, he could only shake his head and point.

Caramon came around to the front and stood, silently reading the roughly carved letters and unfinished inscription.

Hero of the Lance

Tika Waylan Majere

Death Year 358

Your life's tree felled too soon.
I fear, lest in my hands the axe be found.

"I—I'm sorry, Caramon," Tas murmured, slipping his hand into the big man's limp, nerveless fingers.

Caramon's head bowed. Putting his hand on the obelisk, he stroked its cold, wet surface as the wind whipped around them. A few raindrops splattered against the stone. "She died alone," he said. Doubling his fist, he bashed it into the rock, cutting his flesh on the sharp edges. "I left her alone! I should have been here! Damn it, I should have been here!"

His shoulders began to heave with sobs. Tas, looking over at the storm clouds and realizing that they were moving again, and coming closer, held Caramon's hand tightly.

"I don't think there would have been anything you could have done, Caramon, if you had been here—" the kender began earnestly.

Suddenly, he bit his words off, nearly biting his tongue in the process. Withdrawing his hand from Caramon's—the big man never even noticed—the kender knelt down in the mud. His quick eyes had caught sight of something shining in the sickly rays of the pale sun. Reaching down with a trembling hand, Tas hurriedly scooped away the muck.

"Name of the gods," he said in awe, leaning back on his heels. "Caramon, you *were* here!"

"What?" he growled.

Tas pointed.

Lifting his head, Caramon turned and looked down.

There, at his feet, lay his own corpse.

t least it appeared
to be Caramon's corpse. It was wearing the armor he had
acquired in Solamnia—armor he had worn during the
Dwarfgate War, armor he had been wearing when he and Tas
left Zhaman, armor he was wearing now. . . .

But, beyond that, there was nothing specific that identified
the body. Unlike the bodies Tas had discovered that had been
preserved beneath layers of mud, this corpse lay relatively
close to the surface and had decomposed. All that was left was
the skeleton of what had obviously been a large man lying at
the foot of the obelisk. One hand, holding a chisel, rested
directly beneath the stone monument as if his final act had been
to carve out that last dreadful phrase.

There was no sign of what had killed him.

"What's going on, Caramon?" Tas asked in a quivering
voice. "If that's you and you're dead, how can you be here at
the same time?" A sudden thought occurred to him. "Oh, no!
What if you're *not* here!" He clutched at his topknot, twisting it
round and round. "If you're *not* here, then I've made you up.

33

My!" Tas gulped. "I never knew I had such a vivid imagination. You certainly *look* real." Reaching out a trembling hand, he touched Caramon. "You *feel* real and, if you don't mind my saying so, you even smell real!" Tas wrung his hands. "Caramon! I'm going crazy," he cried wildly. "Like one of those dark dwarves in Thorbardin!"

"No, Tas," Caramon muttered. "This is real. All too real." He stared at the corpse, then at the obelisk that was now barely visible in the rapidly fading light. "And it's starting to make sense. If only I could—" He paused, staring intently at the obelisk. "That's it! Tas, look at the date on the monument!"

With a sigh, Tas lifted his head. "358," he read in a dull voice. Then his eyes opened wide. "358?" he repeated. "Caramon—it was 356 when we left Solace!"

"We've come too far, Tas," Caramon murmured in awe. "We've come into our own future."

The boiling black clouds they had been watching mass along the horizon like an army gathering its full strength for the attack surged in just before nightfall, mercifully obliterating the final few moments of the shrunken sun's existence.

The storm struck swiftly and with unbelievable fury. A blast of hot wind blew Tas off his feet and slammed Caramon back against the obelisk. Then the rain hit, pelting them with drops like molten lead. Hail beat on their heads, battering and bruising flesh.

More dreadful, though, than wind or rain was the deadly, multicolored lightning that leaped from cloud to ground, striking the tree stumps, shattering them into brilliant balls of flame visible for miles. The booming rumble of thunder was constant, shaking the very ground, numbing the senses.

Desperately trying to find shelter from the storm's violence, Tas and Caramon huddled beneath a fallen vallenwood, crouching in a hole Caramon dug in the gray, oozing mud. From this scant cover, they watched in disbelief as the storm wreaked further destruction upon the already dead land. Fires swept the sides of the mountains; they could smell the stench of burning wood. Lightning struck near, exploding trees, sending great chunks of ground flying. Thunder hit their ears with concussive force.

The only blessing the storm offered was rainwater. Caramon left his helmet out, upturned, and almost immediately collected water enough to drink. But it tasted horrible—like rotten eggs, Tas shouted, holding his nose as he drank—and it did little to ease their thirst.

Neither mentioned, though both thought of it, that they had no way to store water, nor was there anything to eat.

Feeling more like himself since he now knew where he was and when he was (if not exactly why he was or how he got here), Tasslehoff even enjoyed the storm for the first hour or so.

"I've never seen lightning that color," he shouted above the booming thunder, and he watched it with rapt interest. "It's as good as a street illusionist's show!" But he soon grew bored with the spectacle.

"After all," he yelled, "even watching trees get blasted right out of the ground loses something after about the fiftieth time you've seen it. If you won't be lonely, Caramon," he added with a jaw-cracking yawn, "I think I'll take a little nap. You don't mind keeping watch, do you?"

Caramon shook his head, about to reply when a shattering blast made him start. A tree stump not a hundred feet from them disappeared in a blue-green ball of flame.

That could have been us, he thought, staring at the smoldering ashes, his nose wrinkling at the smell of sulphur. We could be next! A wild desire to run came into his head, a desire so strong that his muscles twitched and he had to force himself to stay where he was.

It's certain death out there. At least here, in this hole, we're below ground level. But, even as he watched, he saw lightning blow a gigantic hole in the ground itself, and he smiled bitterly. No, nowhere was safe. We'll just have to ride it out and trust in the gods.

He glanced over at Tas, prepared to say something comforting to the kender. The words died on his lips. Sighing, he shook his head. Some things never changed—kender among them. Curled up in a ball, completely oblivious to the horrors raging around him, Tas was sound asleep.

Caramon crouched down farther into the hole, his eyes on the churning, lightning-laced clouds above him. To take his mind off his fear, he began to try to sort out what had happened, how they had landed in this predicament. Closing his eyes to the blinding lightning, he saw—once again—his twin standing before the dread Portal. He could hear Raistlin's voice, calling on the five dragon's heads that guarded the Portal to open it and permit his entry into the Abyss. He saw Crysania, cleric of Paladine, praying to her god, lost in the ecstasy of her faith, blind to her brother's evil.

Caramon shuddered, hearing Raistlin's words as clearly as if the archmage were standing beside him.

She will enter the Abyss with me. She will go before me and fight my battles. She will face dark clerics, dark magic-users, spirits of the dead doomed to wander in that cursed land, plus the unbelievable torments that my Queen can devise. All these will wound her in body, devour her mind, and shred her soul. Finally, when she can endure no more, she will slump to the ground to lie at my feet . . . bleeding, wretched, dying.

She will, with her last strength, hold out her hand to me for comfort. She will not ask me to save her. She is too strong for that. She will give her life for me willingly, gladly. All she will ask is that I stay with her as she dies. . . .

But I will walk past her without a look, without a word. Why? Because I will need her no longer. . . .

It was after hearing these words that Caramon had understood at last that his brother was past redemption. And so he had left him.

Let him go into the Abyss, Caramon had thought bitterly. Let him challenge the Dark Queen. Let him become a god. It doesn't matter to me. I don't care what happens to him any longer. I am finally free of him—as he is free of me.

Caramon and Tas had activated the magical device, reciting

the rhyme Par-Salian had taught the big man. He had heard the stones singing, just as he had heard them sing during the two other times he had been present at the casting of the time-travel spell.

But then, something had happened. Something that was different. Now that he had time to think and consider, he remembered wondering in sudden panic if something was wrong, but he couldn't think what.

Not that I could have done anything about it anyway, he thought bitterly. I never understood magic—never trusted it either, for that matter.

Another nearby lightning strike shattered his concentration and even caused Tas to jump in his sleep. Muttering in irritation, the kender covered his eyes with his hands and slept on, looking like a dormouse curled up in its burrow.

With a sigh, Caramon forced his thoughts away from storms and dormice back to those last few moments when the magical spell had been activated.

I remember feeling pulled, he realized suddenly, pulled out of shape, as if some force were trying to drag me one way while another was tugging at me from the opposite direction. What was Raistlin doing then? Caramon struggled to recall. A dim image of his brother came to his mind. He saw Raistlin, his face twisted in horror, staring at the Portal in shock. He saw Crysania, standing in the Portal, but she was no longer praying to her god. Her body seemed wracked by pain, her eyes were wide with terror.

Caramon shivered and licked his lips. The bitter-tasting water had left some kind of film behind that made his mouth taste as if he'd been chewing on rusty nails. Spitting, he wiped his mouth with his hand and leaned back wearily. Another blast made him flinch. And so did the answer.

His brother had failed.

The same thing had happened to Raistlin that had happened to Fistandantilus. He had lost control of the magic. The magical field of the time-travel device had undoubtedly disrupted the spell he was casting. That was the only probable explanation—

Caramon frowned. No, surely Raistlin must have foreseen the possibility of that happening. If so, he would have stopped them from using the device, killed them just as he had killed Tas's friend, the gnome.

Shaking his head to clear it, Caramon started over, working through the problem much as he had worked through the hated ciphering his mother'd taught him when he was a child. The magical field had been disrupted, that much was obvious. It had thrown him and the kender too far forward in time, sending them into their future.

Which means, I suppose, that all I have to do is activate the device and it will take us back to the present, back to Tika, back to Solace. . . .

Opening his eyes, he looked around. But would they face this same future when they returned?

Caramon shivered. He was soaked through from the torrential rain. The night was growing chill, but it wasn't the cold that was tormenting him. He knew what it was to live knowing what was going to happen in the future. He knew what it was to live without hope. How could he go back and face Tika and his friends, knowing that this awaited them? He thought of the corpse beneath the monument. How could he go back knowing what awaited him?

If that had *been* him. He remembered the last conversation between himself and his brother. Tas had altered time—so Raistlin had said. Because kender, dwarves, and gnomes were races created by accident, not design, they were not in the flow of time as were the human, elf, and ogre races. Thus kender were prohibited from traveling back in time because they had the power to alter it.

But Tas had been send back by accident, leaping into the magical field just as Par-Salian, head of the Tower of High Sorcery, was casting the spell to send back Caramon and Crysania. Tas had altered time. Therefore, Raistlin knew he wasn't locked into the doom of Fistandantilus. He had the power to change the outcome. Where Fistandantilus had died, Raistlin might live.

Caramon's shoulders slumped. He felt suddenly sick and dizzy. What did it mean? What was he doing here? How could he be dead and alive at the same time? Was that even his corpse? Since Tas had altered time, it could be someone else. But—most importantly—what had happened to Solace?

"Did Raistlin cause this?" Caramon muttered to himself, just to hear the sound of his voice amid the flashing light and concussive blasts. "Does this have something to do with him? Did this happen because he failed or—"

Caramon caught his breath. Beside him, Tas stirred in his sleep and whimpered and cried out. Caramon patted him absently. "A bad dream," he said, feeling the kender's small body twitch beneath his hand. "A bad dream, Tas. Go back to sleep."

Tas rolled over, pressing his small body close against Caramon's, his hands still covering his eyes. Caramon continued to pat him soothingly.

A bad dream. He wished that were all this was. He wished, most desperately, that he would wake up in his own bed, his head pounding from drinking too much. He wished he could hear Tika slamming plates around in the kitchen, cursing him for being a lazy, drunken bum even while she fixed his favorite breakfast. He wished that he could have gone on in that wretched, spirit-soaked existence because then he would have died, died without knowing. . . .

Oh, please let it be a dream! Caramon prayed, lowering his head to his knees and feeling bitter tears creep beneath his closed eyelids.

He sat there, no longer even affected by the storm, crushed by the weight of his sudden understanding. Tas sighed and shivered, but continued to sleep quietly. Caramon did not move. He did not sleep. He couldn't. The dream he walked in was a waking dream, a waking nightmare. He needed only one thing to confirm the knowledge that he knew, in his heart, needed no confirmation.

———

The storm passed gradually, moving on to the south. Caramon could literally feel it go, the thunder walking the land like the feet of giants. When it was ended, the silence rang in his ears louder than the blasts of the lightning. The sky would be clear now, he knew. Clear until the next storm. He would see the moons, the stars. . . .

The stars . . .

He had only to raise his head and look up into the sky, the clear sky, and he would know.

For another moment he sat there, willing the smell of spiced potatoes to come to him, willing Tika's laughter to banish the silence, willing a drunken aching in his head to replace the terrible ache in his heart.

But there was nothing. Only the silence of this dead, barren land, broken by the distant, faraway rumble of thunder.

With a small sigh, barely audible even to himself, Caramon raised his head and looked up into the heavens.

He swallowed the bitter saliva in his mouth, nearly choking. Tears stung his eyes, but he blinked them back so that he could see clearly.

There it was—the confirmation of his fears, the sealing of his doom.

A new constellation in the sky.

An hourglass. . . .

"What does it mean?" asked Tas, rubbing his eyes and staring sleepily up at the stars, only half awake.

"It means Raistlin succeeded," Caramon answered with an odd mixture of fear, sorrow, and pride in his voice. "It means he entered the Abyss and challenged the Queen of Darkness and—defeated her!"

"Not defeated her, Caramon," said Tas, studying the sky intently and pointing. "There's *her* constellation, but it's in the wrong place. It's over there when it should be over here. And there's Paladine." He sighed. "Poor Fizban. I wonder if he had to fight Raistlin. I don't think he'd like that. I always had the feeling that he understood Raistlin, perhaps better than any of the rest of us."

"So maybe the battle is still going on," Caramon mused. "Perhaps that's the reason for the storms." He was silent for a moment, staring up at the glittering shape of the hourglass. In his mind, he could see his brother's eyes as they had been when he emerged—so long ago—from the terrible test in the Tower of High Sorcery—the pupils of the eyes had become the shape of hourglasses.

"Thus, Raistlin, you will see time as it changes all things," Par-Salian had told him. "Thus, hopefully, you will gain compassion for those around you."

But it hadn't worked.

"Raistlin won," Caramon said with a soft sigh. "He's what he wanted to be—a god. And now he rules over a dead world."

"Dead world?" Tas said in alarm. "D-do you mean the whole world's like *this*? Everything in Krynn—Palanthas and Haven and Qualinesti? K-kendermore? Everything?"

"Look around," Caramon said bleakly. "What do you think? Have you seen any other living being since we've been here?" He waved a hand that was barely visible by the pale light of Solinari, visible now that the clouds were gone, shining like a staring eye in the sky. "You watched the fire sweep the mountainside. I can see the lightning now, on the horizon." He pointed east. "And there, another storm coming. No, Tas. Nothing can live through this. We'll be dead ourselves before long—either blown to bits or—"

"Or . . . or something else . . ." Tas said miserably. "I—I really don't feel good, Caramon. And it—it's either the water or I'm getting the plague again." His face twisting in pain, he put his hand on his stomach. "I'm beginning to feel all funny inside, like I swallowed a snake."

"The water," said Caramon with a grimace. "I'm feeling it, too. Probably some kind of poison from those clouds."

"Are—are we just going to die here then, Caramon?" Tas asked after a minute of silent contemplation. "Because, if we are, I really think I'd like to go over and lie down next to Tika, if you don't mind. It—it would make me feel more at home. Until I got to Flint and his tree." Sighing, he rested his head against Caramon's strong arm. "I'll certainly have a lot to tell Flint, won't I, Caramon? All about the Cataclysm and the fiery mountain and me saving your life and Raistlin becoming a god. I'll bet he won't believe that part. But maybe you'll be there with me, Caramon, and you can tell him I'm truly *not*, well—er—exaggerating."

"Dying would certainly be easy," Caramon murmured, looking wistfully over in the direction of the obelisk.

Lunitari was rising now, its blood-red light blending with the deathly white light of Solinari to shed an eerie purplish radiance down upon the ash-covered land. The stone obelisk, wet with rain, glistened in the moonlight, its crudely carved black letters starkly visible against the pallid surface.

"It would be easy to die," Caramon repeated, more to himself than to Tas. "It would be easy to lie down and let the darkness take me." Then, gritting his teeth, he staggered to his feet. "Funny," he added as he drew his sword and began to hack a branch off the fallen vallenwood they had been using as shelter. "Raist asked me that once. 'Would you follow me into darkness?' he said."

"What are you doing?" Tas asked, staring at Caramon curiously.

But Caramon didn't answer. He just kept hacking away at the tree branch.

"You're making a crutch!" Tas said, then jumped to his feet in sudden alarm. "Caramon! You can't be thinking that! That—that's crazy! *I* remember when Raistlin asked you that question and I remember his answer when you told him yes! He said it would be the death of you, Caramon! As strong as you are, it would kill you!"

Caramon still did not reply. Wet wood flew as he sawed at the tree branch. Occasionally he glanced behind him at the new storm clouds that were approaching, slowly obliterating the constellations and creeping toward the moons.

"Caramon!" Tas grabbed the big man's arm. "Even if you

went . . . there"—the kender found he couldn't speak the name—"what would you do?"

"Something I should have done a long time ago," Caramon said resolutely.

———

ou're going after
him, aren't you?" Tas cried, scrambling out of the hole—a
move which, more or less, put him at eye-level with Caramon,
who was still chopping away at the branch. "That's crazy, just
crazy! How will you get there?" A sudden thought struck him.
"Where is *there* anyway? You don't even know where you're
going! You don't know where *he* is!"

"I have a way to get there," Caramon said coolly, putting his
sword back in its sheath. Taking the branch in his strong hands,
he bent and twisted it and finally succeeded in breaking it off.
"Lend me your knife," he muttered to Tas.

The kender handed it over with a sigh, starting to continue
his protest as Caramon trimmed off small twigs, but the big
man interrupted him.

"I have the magical device. As for where *there* is"—he eyed
Tas sternly—"*you* know that!"

"The—the Abyss?" Tas faltered.

A dull boom of thunder made them both look apprehen-
sively at the approaching storm, then Caramon returned to his

work with renewed vigor while Tas returned to his argument. "The magical device got Gnimsh and me *out* of there, Caramon, but I'm positive it won't get you *in*. You don't want to go there anyway," the kender added resolutely. "It is *not* a nice place."

"Maybe it can't get me in," Caramon began, then motioned Tas over to him. "Let's see if this crutch I've made works before another storm hits. We'll walk over to Tika's— the obelisk."

Slashing off a part of his muddy wet cloak with his sword, the warrior bundled it over the top of the branch, tucked it under his arm and leaned his weight on it experimentally. The crude crutch sank into the mud several inches. Caramon yanked it out and took another step. It sank again, but he managed to move forward at least a little and keep his weight off his injured knee. Tas came over to help him walk and, hobbling along slowly, they inched their way across the wet, slimy ground.

Where are we going? Tas longed to ask, but he was afraid to hear the answer. For once, he didn't find it hard to keep quiet. Unfortunately, Caramon seemed to *hear* his thoughts, for he answered his unspoken question.

"Maybe that device can't get me into the Abyss," Caramon repeated, breathing heavily, "but I know someone who can. The device'll take us to him."

"Who?" the kender asked dubiously.

"Par-Salian. He'll be able to tell us what has happened. He'll be able to send me . . . wherever I need to go."

"Par-Salian?" Tas looked almost as alarmed as if Caramon had said the Queen of Darkness herself. "That's even crazier!" he started to say, only he was suddenly violently sick instead. Caramon paused to wait for him, looking pale and ill in the moonlight himself.

Convinced that he had thrown up everything inside him from his topknot down to his socks, Tas felt a little better. Nodding at Caramon, too tired to talk just yet, he managed to stagger on.

Trudging through the slime and the mud, they reached the

obelisk. Both slumped down on the ground and leaned against it, exhausted by the exertion even that short journey of only twenty or so paces had cost them. The hot wind was rising again, the sound of thunder getting nearer. Sweat covered Tas's face and he had a green tinge around his lips, but he managed nonetheless, to smile at Caramon with what he hoped was innocent appeal.

"Us going to see Par-Salian?" he said offhandedly, mopping his face with his topknot. "Oh, I don't think that would be a good idea at all. You're in no shape to walk all that way. We don't have any water or food and—"

"I'm not going to walk." Caramon took the pendant out of his pocket and begin the transformation process that would turn it into a beautiful, jeweled sceptre.

Seeing this and gulping slightly, Tas continued on talking more rapidly.

"I'm certain Par-Salian is—uh—is . . . busy. Busy! That's it!" He gave a ghastly grin. "Much too busy to see us now. Probably lots of things to do, what with all this chaos going on around him. So let's just forget this and go back to someplace in time where we had fun. How about when Raistlin put the charm spell on Bupu and she fell in love with him? That was really funny! That disgusting gully dwarf following him around. . . ."

Caramon didn't reply. Tas twisted the end of his topknot around his finger.

"Dead," he said suddenly, heaving a mournful sigh. "Poor Par-Salian. Probably dead as a doorknob. After all," the kender pointed out cheerfully, "he was *old* when we saw him back in 356. He didn't look at all well then, either. This must have been a real shock to him—Raistlin becoming a god and all. Probably too much for his heart. Bam—he probably just keeled right over."

Tas peeped up at Caramon. There was a slight smile on the big man's lips, but he said nothing, just kept turning and twisting the pieces of the pendant. A bright flash of lightning made him start. He glanced at the storm, his smile vanishing.

"I'll bet the Tower of High Sorcery's not even there any-more!" Tas cried in desperation. "If what you say is right and the whole world is . . . is like this"—he waved his small hand as the foul-smelling rain began to fall—"then the Tower must have been one of the first places to go! Struck by lightning! Blooey! After all, the Tower's much taller than most trees I've seen—"

"The Tower'll be there," Caramon said grimly, making the final adjustment to the magical device. He held it up. Its jewels caught the rays of Solinari and, for an instant, gleamed with radiance. Then the storm clouds swept over the moon, devour-ing it. The darkness was now intense, split only by the brilliant, beautiful, deadly lightning.

Gritting his teeth against the pain, Caramon grabbed his crutch and struggled to his feet. Tas followed more slowly, gaz-ing at Caramon miserably.

"You see, Tas, I've come to know Raistlin," Caramon contin-ued, ignoring the kender's woebegone expression. "Too late, maybe, but I know him now. He hated that Tower, just as he hated those mages for what they did to him there. But even as he hates it, he loves it all the same—because it is part of his Art, Tas. And his Art, his magic, means more to him than life itself. No, the Tower will be there."

Lifting the device in his hands, Caramon began the chant, " 'Thy time is thine own. Though across it you travel—' "

But he was interrupted.

"Oh, Caramon!" Tas wailed, clutching at him. "Don't take me back to Par-Salian! He'll do something *awful* to me! I know it! He might turn me into a—a bat!" Tas paused. "And, while I suppose it might be interesting being a bat, I'm not certain I could get used to sleeping upside down, hanging by my feet. And I *am* rather fond of being a kender, now that I think of it, and—"

"What are you talking about?" Caramon glared at him, then glanced up at the storm clouds. The rain was increasing in fury, the lightning striking nearer.

"Par-Salian!" cried Tas frantically. "I—I messed up his magi-cal time-traveling spell! I went when I wasn't supposed to go!

And then I stol—er—found a magical ring that someone had left lying about and it turned me into a mouse! I'm certain he must be rather peeved over that! And then I—I broke the magical device, Caramon. Remember? Well, it wasn't exactly my fault, Raistlin made me break it! But a really strict person might take the unfortunate attitude that if I had left it alone in the first place—like I knew I was supposed to—then that wouldn't have happened. And Par-Salian seems an *awfully* strict sort of person, don't you think? And while I *did* have Gnimsh fix it, he didn't fix it quite right, you know—"

"Tasslehoff," said Caramon tiredly, "shut up."

"Yes, Caramon," Tas said meekly, with a snuffle.

Caramon looked at the small dejected figure reflected in the bright lightning and sighed. "Look, Tas, I won't let Par-Salian do anything to you. I promise. He'll have to turn *me* into a bat first."

"Truly?" asked Tas anxiously.

"My word," said Caramon, his eyes on the storm. "Now, give me your hand and let's get out of here."

"Sure," said Tas cheerfully, slipping his small hand into Caramon's large one.

"And Tas . . ."

"Yes, Caramon?"

"This time—think of the Tower of High Sorcery in Wayreth! No moons!"

"Yes, Caramon," Tas said with a profound sigh. Then he smiled again. "You know," he said to himself as Caramon began to recite the chant again, "I'll bet Caramon would make a whopping big bat—".

They found themselves standing at the edge of a forest.

"It's not my fault, Caramon!" Tas said quickly. "I thought about the Tower with all my heart and soul. I'm certain I never thought once about a forest."

Caramon stared intently into the woods. It was still night, but the sky was clear, though storm clouds were visible on the horizon. Lunitari burned a dull, smoldering red. Solinari was dropping down into the storm. And above them, the starry hourglass.

"Well, we're in the right time period. But where in the name of the gods are we?" Caramon muttered, leaning on his crutch and glaring at the magical device irritably. His gaze went back to the shadowy trees, their trunks visible in the garish moonlight. Suddenly, his expression cleared. "It's all right, Tas," he said in relief. "Don't you recognize this? It's Wayreth Forest— the magical forest that stands guard around the Tower of High Sorcery!"

"Are you sure?" Tas asked doubtfully. "It certainly doesn't look the same as the last time I saw it. Then it was all ugly, with dead trees lurking about, staring at me, and when I tried to go inside it wouldn't let me and when I tried to leave it wouldn't let me and—"

"This is it," Caramon muttered, folding the sceptre back into its nondescript pendant shape again.

"Then what happened to it?"

"The same thing that happened to the rest of the world, Tas," Caramon replied, carefully slipping the pendant back into the leather pouch.

Tas's thoughts went back to the last time he had seen the magical Forest of Wayreth. Set to guard the Tower of High Sorcery from unwelcome intruders, the Forest was a strange and eerie place. For one thing, a person didn't find the magical forest—it found you. And the first time it had found Tas and Caramon was right after Lord Soth had cast the death spell on Lady Crysania. Tas had wakened from a sound sleep to discover the Forest standing where no forest had been the night before!

The trees then had appeared to be dead. Their limbs were bare and twisted, a chill mist flowed from beneath their trunks. Inside dwelt dark and shadowy shapes. But the trees hadn't been dead. In fact, they had the uncanny habit of *following* a person. Tas remembered trying to walk away from the Forest, only to continually find himself—no matter what direction he traveled—always walking into it.

———

That had been spooky enough, but when Caramon walked into the Forest, it had changed dramatically. The dead trees began to grow, turning into vallenwoods! The Forest was transformed from a dark and forbidding wood filled with death into a beautiful green and golden forest of life. Birds sang sweetly in the branches of the vallenwoods, inviting them inside.

And now the Forest had changed again. Tas stared at it, puzzled. It seemed to be both forests he remembered—yet neither of them. The trees appeared dead, their twisted limbs were stark and bare. But, as he watched, he thought he saw them move in a manner that seemed very much alive! Reaching out, like grasping arms. . . .

Turning his back on the spooky Forest of Wayreth, Tas investigated his surroundings. All else was exactly as it had been in Solace. No other trees stood at all—living or dead. He was surrounded by nothing but blackened, blasted stumps. The ground was covered with the same slimy, gray mud. For as far as he could see, in fact, there was nothing but desolation and death. . . .

"Caramon," Tas cried suddenly, pointing.

Caramon glanced over. Beside one of the stumps lay a huddled figure.

"A person!" Tas cried in wild excitement. "Someone else is here!"

"Tas!" Caramon called out warningly, but before he could stop him, the kender was dashing over.

"Hey!" he yelled. "Hullo! Are you asleep? Wake up." Reaching down, he shook the figure, only to have it roll over at his touch, lying stiff and rigid.

"Oh!" Tas took a step backward, then stopped. "Oh, Caramon," he said softly. "It's Bupu!"

Once, long ago, Raistlin had befriended the gully dwarf. Now she stared up at the starlit sky with empty, sightless eyes. Dressed in filthy, ragged clothing, her small body was pitifully thin, her grubby face wasted and gaunt. Around her neck was a leather thong. Attached to the end of the thong was a stiff, dead lizard. In one hand, she clutched a dead rat, in the other she held a dried-up chicken leg. As death approached, she had summoned up all the magic she possessed, Tas thought sadly, but it hadn't helped.

"She hasn't been dead long," Caramon said. Limping over, he knelt down painfully beside the shabby little corpse. "Looks like she starved to death." He reached out his hand and gently closed the staring eyes. Then he shook his head. "I wonder how she came to live this long? The bodies we saw back in Solace must have been dead months, at least."

"Maybe Raistlin protected her," Tasslehoff said before he thought.

Caramon scowled. "Bah! It's just coincidence, that's all," he said harshly. "You know gully dwarves, Tas. They can live on anything. My guess is that they were the last creatures to survive. Bupu, being the smartest of the lot, just managed to survive longer than the rest. But—in the end, even a gully dwarf would perish in this god-cursed land." He shrugged. "Here, help me stand."

"What—what are we going to do with her, Caramon?" Tas asked bleakly. "Are—are we just going to leave her?"

"What else can we do?" Caramon muttered gruffly. The sight of the gully dwarf and the nearness of the Forest were bringing back painful, unwelcome memories. "Would you want to be buried in that mud?" He shivered and glanced about. The storm clouds were rushing closer; he could see the lightning streaking down to the ground and hear the roar of the thunder. "Besides, we don't have much time, not the way those clouds are moving in."

Tas continued to stare at him sorrowfully.

"There's nothing left alive to bother her anyway, Tas," he snapped irritably. Then, seeing the grieved expression on the kender's face, Caramon slowly removed his own cloak and carefully spread it over the emaciated corpse. "We better get going," he said.

"Good-bye, Bupu," Tas said softly. Patting the stiff little hand that was tightly clutching the dead rat, he started to pull the corner of the cloak over it when he saw something flash in Lunitari's red light. Tas caught his breath, thinking he recognized the object. Carefully, he pried the gully dwarf's death-stiffened fingers apart. The dead rat fell to the ground and—with it—an emerald.

Tas picked up the jewel. In his mind, he was back to . . . where had it been? Xak Tsaroth?

They had been in a sewer pipe hiding from draconian troops. Raistlin had been seized by a fit of coughing. . . .

Bupu gazed at him anxiously, then thrust her small hand into her bag, fished around for several moments, and came up with an object that she held up to the light. She squinted at it, then sighed and shook her head. "This not what I want," she mumbled.

Tasslehoff, catching sight of a brilliant, colorful flash, crept closer. "What is it?" he asked, even though he knew the answer. Raistlin, too, was staring at the object with wide glittering eyes.

Bupu shrugged. "Pretty rock," she said without interest, searching through the bag once more.

"An emerald!" Raistlin wheezed.

Bupu glanced up. "You like?" she asked Raistlin.

"Very much!" The mage gasped.

"You keep." Bupu put the jewel in the mage's hand. Then, with a cry of triumph, she brought out what she had been searching for. Tas, leaning up close to see the new wonder, drew back in disgust. It was a dead—very dead—lizard. There was a piece of chewed-on leather tied around the lizard's stiff tail. Bupu held it toward Raistlin.

"You wear around neck," she said. "Cure cough."

"So Raistlin *was* here," Tas murmured. "He gave this to her, he must have! But why? A charm . . . a gift? . . ." Shaking his head, the kender sighed and stood up. "Caramon—" he began, then he saw the big man standing, staring into the Forest of Wayreth. He saw Caramon's pale face and he guessed what he must be thinking, remembering.

Tasslehoff slipped the emerald into a pocket.

———

53

The Forest of Wayreth seemed as dead and desolate as the rest of the world around them. But, to Caramon, it was alive with memories. Nervously he stared at the strange trees, their wet trunks and decaying limbs seeming to glisten with blood in Lunitari's light.

"I was frightened the first time I came here," Caramon said to himself, his hand on the hilt of his sword. "I wouldn't have gone in at all if it hadn't been for Raistlin. I was even more frightened the second time, when we brought Lady Crysania here to try to find help for her. I wouldn't have gone in then for any reason except those birds lured me with their sweet song." He smiled grimly. " 'Easeful the forest. Easeful the mansions perfected. Where we grow and decay no longer,' they sang. I thought they promised help. I thought they promised me all the answers. But I see now what the song meant. Death, that is the only perfect mansion, the only dwelling place where we grow and decay no longer!"

Staring into the woods, Caramon shivered, despite the oppressive heat of the night air. "I'm more frightened of it this time than ever before," he muttered. "Something's wrong in there." A brilliant flash lit up sky and ground with the brightness of day, followed by a dull boom and the splash of rain upon his cheek. "But at least it's still standing," he said. "Its magic must be strong—to survive the storm." His stomach wrenched painfully. Reminded of his thirst, he licked his dry, parched lips. " 'Easeful the forest,' " he muttered.

"What did you say?" asked Tas, coming up beside him.

"I said as good one death as another," Caramon answered, shrugging.

"You know, I've died three times," said Tas solemnly. "The first was in Tarsis, where the dragons knocked a building down on top of me. The second was in Neraka, where I was poisoned by a trap and Raistlin saved me. And the last was when the gods dropped a fiery mountain on me. And, all in all"—he pondered a moment—"I think I could say that was a fair statement. One death *is* just about the same as another. You see, the poison

---

54

hurt a great deal, but it was over pretty quickly. While the building, on the other hand—"

"C'mon"—Caramon grinned wearily—"save it to tell Flint." He drew his sword. "Ready?"

"Ready," answered Tas stoutly. " 'Always save the best for last,' my father used to say. Although"—the kender paused—"I think he meant that in reference to dinner, not to dying. But perhaps it has the same significance."

Drawing his own small knife, Tas followed Caramon into the enchanted Forest of Wayreth.

CHAPTER 5

The darkness swallowed them. Light from neither moon nor stars could penetrate the night of the Forest of Wayreth. Even the brilliance of the deadly, magical lightning was lost here. And though the booming of the thunder could be heard, it seemed nothing but a distant echo of itself. Behind them, Caramon could hear, too, the drumming of the rain and the pelting of the hail. In the Forest, it was dry. Only the trees that stood on the outer fringes were affected by the rain.

"Well, this is a relief!" said Tasslehoff cheerfully. "Now, if we just had some light. I—"

His voice was cut off with a choking gurgle. Caramon heard a thud and creaking wood and a sound like something being dragged along the ground.

"Tas?" he called.

"Caramon!" Tas cried. "It's a tree! A tree's got me! Help, Caramon! Help!"

"Is this a joke, Tas?" Caramon asked sternly. "Because it's not funny—"

"No!" Tas screamed. "It's got me and it's dragging me off somewhere!"

"What . . . where?" Caramon yelled. "I can't see in this damn darkness? Tas?"

"Here! Here!" Tas screamed wildly. "It's got hold of my foot and it's trying to tear me in two!"

"Keep yelling, Tas!" Caramon cried, stumbling about in the rustling blackness. "I think I'm close—"

A huge tree limb bashed Caramon in the chest, knocking him to the ground and slamming his breath from his body. He lay there, trying to draw in air, when he heard a creaking to his right. As he slashed at it blindly with his sword, he rolled away. Something heavy crashed right where he'd been lying. He staggered to his feet, but another limb struck him in the small of his back, sending him sprawling face first onto the barren floor of the Forest.

The blow to the back caught him in the kidneys, making him gasp in pain. He tried to struggle back up, but his knee throbbed painfully, his head spun. He couldn't hear Tas anymore. He couldn't hear anything except the creaking, rustling sounds of the trees closing in on him. Something scraped along his arm. Caramon flinched and crawled out of its reach, only to feel something grab his foot. Desperately he hacked at it with his sword. Flying wood chips stung his leg, but apparently did no harm to his attacker.

The strength of centuries was in the tree's massive limbs. Magic gave it thought and purpose. Caramon had trespassed on land it guarded, land forbidden to the uninvited. It was going to kill him, he knew.

Another tree limb caught hold of Caramon's thick thigh. Branches clutched at his arms, seeking a firm grip. Within seconds, he would be ripped apart. . . . He heard Tas cry out in pain. . . .

Raising his voice, Caramon shouted desperately, "I am Caramon Majere, brother of Raistlin Majere! I must speak to Par-Salian or whoever is Master of the Tower now!"

There was a moment's silence, a moment's hesitation. Cara-

---

mon felt the will of the trees waver, the branches loosen their grip ever so slightly.

"Par-Salian, are you there? Par-Salian, you know me! I am *his* twin. I am your only hope!"

"Caramon?" came a quavering voice.

"Hush, Tas!" Caramon hissed.

The silence was as thick as the darkness. And then, slowly, he felt the branches release him. He heard the creaking and rustling sounds again, only this time they were moving slowly away from him. Gasping in relief, weak from fear and the pain and the growing sickness inside him, Caramon lay his head on his arm, trying to catch his breath.

"Tas, are you all right?" he managed to call out.

"Yes, Caramon," came the kender's voice beside him. Reaching out his hand, Caramon caught hold of the kender and pulled him close.

Though he heard the sounds of movement in the darkness and knew the trees were withdrawing, he also had the feeling the trees were watching his every move, listening to every word. Slowly and cautiously, he sheathed his sword.

"I am truly thankful you thought of telling Par-Salian who you are, Caramon," Tas said, panting for breath. "I was just imagining trying to explain to Flint how I'd been murdered by a tree. I'm not certain whether or not you're allowed to laugh in the Afterlife, but I'll bet he would have roared—"

"Shhhh," Caramon said weakly.

Tas paused, then whispered, "Are you all right?"

"Yeah, just let me catch my breath. I've lost my crutch."

"It's over here. I fell over it." Tas crawled off and returned moments later, dragging the padded tree branch. "Here." He helped Caramon stagger to his feet.

"Caramon," he asked after a moment, "how long do you think it will take us to get to the Tower? I—I'm awfully thirsty and, while my insides are a little better since I was sick a while back, I still get queer squirmy feelings in my stomach sometimes."

"I don't know, Tas." Caramon sighed. "I can't see a damn

---

thing in this darkness. I don't know where we're going or what's the right way or how we're going to manage to walk without running smack into something—"

The rustling sounds suddenly started again, as though a storm wind were tossing the branches of the trees. Caramon tensed and even Tas stiffened in alarm as they heard the trees start to close in around them once more. Tas and Caramon stood helpless in the darkness as the trees came nearer and nearer. Branches touched their skin and dead leaves brushed their hair, whispering strange words in their ears. Caramon's shaking hand closed over his sword hilt, though he knew it would do little good. But then, when the trees were pressed close around them, the movement and the whispering ceased. The trees were silent once more.

Reaching out his hand, Caramon touched solid trunks to his right and his left. He could feel them massed behind him. An idea occurred to him. He stretched his arm out into the darkness and felt around ahead of him. All was clear.

"Keep close to me, Tas," he ordered and, for once in his life, the kender didn't argue. Together, they walked forward into the opening provided by the trees.

At first they moved cautiously, fearful of stumbling over a root or a fallen branch or becoming entangled in brush or tumbling into a hole. But gradually they came to realize that the forest floor was smooth and dry, cleared of all obstacles, free from undergrowth. They had no idea where they were going. They walked in absolute darkness, kept to some irreversible path only by the trees that parted before them and closed in after them. Any deviation from the set path brought them into a wall of trunks and tangled branches and dead, whispering leaves.

The heat was oppressive. No wind blew, no rain fell. Their thirst, lost in their fear, returned to plague them. Wiping the sweat from his face, Caramon wondered at the strange, intense heat, for it was much greater here than outside the Forest. It seemed as if the heat were being generated by the Forest itself. The Forest was more alive that he had noticed the last two times he had been here. It was certainly more alive than the world outside. Amid the rustling of the trees, he could hear—or thought he heard—movements of animals or the rush of birds' wings, and sometimes he caught a glimpse of eyes shining in the darkness. But being among living beings once more brought no sense of comfort to Caramon. He felt their hatred and their anger and, even as he felt it, he realized that it wasn't directed against him. It was directed against itself.

And then he heard the birds' songs again, as he had heard them the last time he'd entered this eerie place. High and sweet and pure, rising above death and darkness and defeat, rose the song of a lark. Caramon stopped to listen, tears stinging his eyes at the beauty of the song, feeling his heart's pain ease.

> *The light in the eastern skies*
> *Is still and always morning,*
> *It alters the renewing air*
> *Into belief and yearning.*
>
> *And larks rise up like angels,*
> *Like angels larks ascend*
> *From sunlit grass as bright as gems*
> *Into the cradling wind.*

But even as the lark's song pierced his heart with its sweetness, a harsh cackle made him cringe. Black wings fluttered around him, and his soul was filled with shadows.

> *The plain light in the east*
> *Contrives out of the dark*
> *The machinery of day,*
> *The diminished song of the lark.*
>
> *But ravens ride the night*
> *And the darkness west,*
> *The wingbeat of their hearts*
> *Large in a buried nest.*

"What does it mean, Caramon?" Tas asked in awe as they continued to grope their way through the Forest, guided, always, by the angry trees.

The answer to his question came, not from Caramon, but from other voices, mellow, deep, sad with the ancient wisdom of the owl.

> *Through night the seasons ride into the dark,*
> *The years surrender in the changing lights,*
> *The breath turns vacant on the dusk or dawn*
> *Between the abstract days and nights.*
> *For there is always corpselight in the fields*
> *And corposants above the slaughterhouse,*
> *And at deep noon the shadowy vallenwoods*
> *Are bright at the topmost boughs.*

"It means the magic is out of control," Caramon said softly. "Whatever will holds this Forest in check is just barely hanging on." He shivered. "I wonder what we'll find when we get to the Tower."

"*If* we get to the Tower," Tas muttered. "How do we know that these awful, old trees aren't leading us to the edge of a tall cliff?"

Caramon stopped, panting for breath in the terrible heat. The crude crutch dug painfully into his armpit. With his weight off of it, his knee had begun to stiffen. His leg was inflamed and swollen, and he knew he could not go on much longer. He, too, had been sick, purging his system of the poison, and now he felt somewhat better. But thirst was a torment. And, as Tas reminded him, he had no idea where these trees were leading them.

Raising his voice, his throat parched, Caramon cried out harshly, "Par-Salian! Answer me or I'll go no farther! Answer me!"

The trees broke out in a clamor, branches shaking and stirring as if in a high wind, though no breeze cooled Caramon's feverish skin. The birds' voices rose in a fearful cacophony, intermingling, overlapping, twisting their songs into horrible, unlovely melodies that filled the mind with terror and foreboding.

Even Tas was a bit startled by this, creeping closer to Caramon (in case the big man needed comfort), but Caramon stood resolutely, staring into the endless night, ignoring the turmoil around him.

"Par-Salian!" he called once more.

Then he heard his answer—a thin, high-pitched scream.

At the dreadful sound, Caramon's skin crawled. The scream pierced through the darkness and the heat. It rose above the strange singing of the birds and drowned out the clashing of the trees. It seemed to Caramon as if all the horror and sorrow of the dying world had been sucked up and released at last in that fearful cry.

"Name of the gods!" Tas breathed in awe, catching hold of Caramon's hand (in case the big man should feel frightened). "What's happening?"

Caramon didn't answer. He could feel the anger in the Forest grow more intense, mingled now with an overwhelming fear and sadness. The trees seemed to be prodding them ahead, crowding them, urging them on. The screaming continued for as long as it might take a man to use up his breath, then it quit for the space of a man drawing air into his lungs, then it began again. Caramon felt the sweat chill on his body.

He kept walking, Tas close by his side. They made slow progress, made worse by the fact that they had no idea if they were making progress at all, since they could not see their destination nor even know if they were headed in the right direction. The only guide they had to the Tower was that shrill, inhuman scream.

On and on they stumbled and, though Tas helped as best he could, each step for Caramon was agony. The pain of his injuries took possession of him and soon he lost all conception of time. He forgot why they had come or even where they were going. To stagger ahead, one step at a time through the darkness that had become a darkness of the mind and soul, was Caramon's only thought.

He kept walking—

and walking—

and walking—

one step, one step, one step . . .

And all the time, shrilling in his ears, that horrible, undying scream . . .

"Caramon!"

The voice penetrated his weary, pain-numbed brain. He had a feeling he had been hearing it for some time now, above the scream, but—if so—it hadn't pierced the fog of blackness that enshrouded him.

"What?" he mumbled, and now he became aware that hands were grasping him, shaking him. He raised his head and looked around. "What?" he asked again, struggling to regain his grasp of reality. "Tas?"

"Look, Caramon!" The kender's voice came to him through a haze, and he shook his head, desperately, to clear away the fog in his brain.

And he realized he could see. It was light—moonlight! Blinking his eyes, he stared around. "The Forest?"

"Behind us," Tas whispered, as though talking about it might suddenly bring it back. "It's brought us somewhere, at least. I'm just not certain where. Look around. Do you remember this?"

Caramon looked. The shadow of the Forest was gone. He and Tas were standing in a clearing. Swiftly, fearfully, he glanced around.

At his feet yawned a dark chasm.

Behind them, the Forest waited. Caramon did not have to turn to see it, he knew it was there, just as he knew that they would never reenter it and get out alive. It had led them this far, here it would leave them. But where was here? The trees were behind them, but ahead of them lay nothing—just a vast, dark void. They might have been standing on the very edge of a cliff, as Tas had said.

Storm clouds darkened the horizon, but—for the time being—none seemed close. Up above, he could see the moons and stars in the sky. Lunitari burned a fiery red, Solinari's silver light glowed with a radiant brilliance Caramon had never seen before. And now, perhaps because of the stark contrast between darkness and light, he could see Nuitari—the black moon, the moon that had been visible only to his brother's eyes. Around the moons, the stars shone fiercely, none brighter than the strange hourglass constellation.

The only sounds he could hear were the angry mutterings of the Forest behind him and, ahead of him, that shrill, horrible scream.

They had no choice, Caramon thought wearily. There was no turning back. The Forest would not permit that. And what was death anyhow except an end to this pain, this thirst, this bitter aching in his heart.

"Stay here, Tas," he began, trying to disengage the kender's small hand as he prepared to step forward into the darkness. "I'm going to go ahead a little way and scout—"

"Oh, no!" Tas cried. "You're not going anywhere without me!" The kender's hand gripped his even more firmly. "Why, just look at all the trouble you got into by yourself in the dwarf wars!" he added, trying to get rid of an annoying choking feeling in his throat. "And when I *did* get there, I had to save your life." Tas looked down into the darkness that lay at their feet, then he gritted his teeth resolutely and raised his gaze to meet that of the big man. "I—I think it would be awfully lonely in—in the Afterlife without you and, besides, I can just hear Flint—'Well, you doorknob, what have you gone and done *this* time? Managed to lose that great hulking hunk of lard, did you? It figures. Now, I suppose *I'll* have to leave my nice soft seat here under this tree and set off in search of the muscle-bound idiot. Never did know when to come in out of the rain—"

"Very well, Tas," Caramon interrupted with a smile, having a sudden vision of the crotchety old dwarf. "It would never do to disturb Flint. I'd never hear the end of it."

"Besides," Tas went on, feeling more cheerful, "why would

they bring us all this way just to dump us in a pit?"

"Why, indeed?" Caramon said, reflecting. Gripping his crutch, feeling more confident, he took a step into the darkness, Tas following along behind.

"Unless," the kender added with a gulp, "Par-Salian's still mad at me. . . ."

CHAPTER 6

The Tower of High Sorcery loomed before them—a thing of darkness, silhouetted against the light of moon and stars, looking as though it had been created out of the night itself. For centuries it had stood, a bastion of magic, the repository of the books and artifacts of the Art, collected over the years.

Here the mages had come when they were driven from the Tower of High Sorcery in Palanthas by the Kingpriest, here they brought with them those most valued objects, saved from the attacking mobs. Here they dwelt in peace, guarded by the Forest of Wayreth. Young apprentice magic-users took the Test here, the grueling Test that meant death to those who failed it.

Here Raistlin had come and lost his soul to Fistandantilus. Here Caramon had been forced to watch as Raistlin murdered an illusion of his twin brother.

Here Caramon and Tas had returned with the gully dwarf, Bupu, bearing the comatose body of Lady Crysania. Here they had attended a Conclave of the Three Robes—Black, Red, and White. Here they had learned Raistlin's ambition—to challenge

---

the Queen of Darkness. Here they had met his apprentice and spy for the Conclave—Dalamar. Here the great archmage Par-Salian had cast a time-travel spell on Caramon and Lady Crysania, sending them back to Istar before the mountain fell.

Here, Tasslehoff had inadvertently upset the spell by jumping in to go with Caramon. Thus, the presence of the kender—forbidden by all the laws of magic—allowed time to be altered.

Now Caramon and Tas had returned—to find what?

Caramon stared at the Tower, his heart heavy with foreboding and dread. His courage failed him. He could not enter, not with the sound of that pitiful, persistent screaming echoing in his ears. Better to go back, better to face quick death in the Forest. Besides, he had forgotten the gates. Made of silver and of gold, they still stood, steadfastly blocking his way into the Tower. Thin as cobweb they seemed, looking like black streaks painted down the starlit sky. A touch of a kender's hand might have opened them. Yet magical spells were wound about them, spells so powerful an army of ogres could have hurled itself against those fragile-seeming gates without effect.

Still the screaming, louder now and nearer. So near, in fact, that it might have come from—

Caramon took another step forward, his brow creased in a frown. As he did so, the gate came clearly into view.

And revealed the source of the screaming. . . .

The gates were not shut, nor were they locked. One gate stood fast, as if still spellbound. But the other had broken, and now it swung by one hinge, back and forth, back and forth in the hot, unceasing wind. And, as it blew back and forth slowly in the breeze, it gave forth a shrill, high-pitched shriek.

"It's not locked," said Tas in disappointment. His small hand had already been reaching for his lockpicking tools.

"No," said Caramon, staring up at the squeaking hinge. "And there's the voice we heard—the voice of rusty metal." He supposed he should have been relieved, but it only deepened the mystery. "If it wasn't Par-Salian or someone up there"—his eyes went to the Tower that stood, black and apparently empty before them—"who got us through the Forest, then who was it?"

"Maybe no one," Tas said hopefully. "If no one's here, Caramon, can we leave?"

"There has to be someone," Caramon muttered. "Something made those trees let us pass."

Tas sighed, his head drooping. Caramon could see him in the moonlight, his small face pale and covered with grime. There were dark shadows beneath his eyes, his lower lip quivered, and a tear was sneaking down one side of his small nose.

Caramon patted him on the shoulder. "Just a little longer," he said gently. "Hold out just a little longer, please, Tas?"

Looking up quickly, swallowing that traitor tear and its partner that had just dripped into his mouth, Tas grinned cheerfully. "Sure, Caramon," he said. Not even the fact that his throat was aching and parched with thirst could keep him from adding, "You know me—always ready for adventure. There's bound to be lots of magical, wonderful things in there, don't you think?" he added, glancing at the silent Tower. "Things no one would miss. Not magical rings, of course. I'm finished with magical rings. First one lands me in a wizard's castle where I met a truly wicked demon, then the next turns me into a mouse. I—"

Letting Tas prattle on, glad that the kender was apparently feeling back to normal, Caramon hobbled forward and put his hand upon the swinging gate to shove it to one side. To his amazement, it broke off—the weakened hinge finally giving way. The gate clattered to the gray paving stone beneath it with a clang that made both Tas and Caramon cringe. The echoes bounded off the black, polished walls of the Tower, resounding through the hot night and shattering the stillness.

"Well, now they know we're here," said Tas.

Caramon's hand once again closed over his sword hilt, but he did not draw it. The echoes faded. Silence closed in. Nothing happened. No one came. No voice spoke.

Tas turned to help Caramon limp ahead. "At least we won't have to listen to that awful sound anymore," he said, stepping over the broken gate. "I don't mind saying so now, but that

---

shriek was beginning to get on my nerves. It certainly sounded very ungate-like, if you know what I mean. It sounded just like . . . just like . . ."

"Like that," Caramon whispered.

The scream split the air, shattering the moonlit darkness, only this time it was different. There were words in this scream—words that could be heard, if not defined.

Turning his head involuntary, though he knew what he would see, Caramon stared back at the gate. It lay on the stones, dead, lifeless.

"Caramon," said Tas, swallowing, "it—it's coming from there—the Tower. . . ."

"End it!" screamed Par-Salian. "End this torment! Do not force me to endure more!"

How much did you force me to endure, O Great One of the White Robes? came a soft, sneering voice into Par-Salian's mind. The wizard writhed in agony, but the voice persisted, relentless, flaying his soul like a scourge. *You brought me here and gave me up to him—Fistandantilus! You sat and watched as he wrenched the lifeforce from me, draining it so that he might live upon this plane.*

"It was you who made the bargain," Par-Salian cried, his ancient voice carrying through the empty hallways of the Tower. "You could have refused him—"

And what? Died honorably? The voice laughed. What kind of choice is that? I wanted to live! To grow in my Art! And I did live. And you, in your bitterness, gave me these hourglass eyes—these eyes that saw nothing but death and decay all around me. Now, you look, Par-Salian! What do you see around you? Nothing but death. . . . Death and decay . . . So we are even.

Par-Salian moaned. The voice continued, mercilessly, pitilessly.

Even, yes. And now I will grind you into dust. For, in your last tortured moments, Par-Salian, you will witness my tri-

umph. Already my constellation shines in the sky. The Queen dwindles. Soon she will fade and be gone forever. My final foe, Paladine, waits for me now. I see him approach. But he is no challenge—an old man, bent, his face grieved and filled with the sorrow that will prove his undoing. For he is weak, weak and hurt beyond healing, as was Crysania, his poor cleric, who died upon the shifting planes of the Abyss. You will watch me destroy him, Par-Salian, and when that battle is ended, when the constellation of the Platinum Dragon plummets from the sky, when Solinari's light is extinguished, when you have seen and acknowledged the power of the Black Moon and paid homage to the new and only god—to me—then you will be released, Par-Salian, to find what solace you can in death!

Astinus of Palanthas recorded the words as he had recorded Par-Salian's scream, writing the crisp, black, bold letters in slow, unhurried style. He sat before the great Portal in the Tower of High Sorcery, staring into the Portal's shadowy depths, seeing within those depths a figure blacker even than the darkness around him. All that was visible were two golden eyes, their pupils the shape of hourglasses, staring back at him and at the white-robed wizard trapped next to him.

For Par-Salian was a prisoner in his own Tower. From the waist up, he was living man—his white hair flowing about his shoulders, his white robes covering a body thin and emaciated, his dark eyes fixed upon the Portal. The sights he had seen had been dreadful and had, long ago, nearly destroyed his sanity. But he could not withdraw his gaze. From the waist up, Par-Salian was living man. From the waist down—he was a marble pillar. Cursed by Raistlin, Par-Salian was forced to stand in the topmost room of his Tower and watch—in bitter agony—the end of the world.

Next to him sat Astinus—Historian of the World, Chronicler, writing this last chapter of Krynn's brief, shining history. Palanthas the Beautiful, where Astinus had lived and where the Great Library had stood, was now nothing but a heap of ash and charred bodies. Astinus had come to this, the last place standing upon Krynn, to witness and record the world's final, terrifying hours. When all was finished, he would take the closed book and lay it upon the altar of Gilean, God of Neutrality. And that would be the end.

Sensing the black-robed figure within the Portal turning its gaze upon him, when he came to the end of a sentence, Astinus raised his eyes to meet the figure's golden ones.

As you were first, Astinus, said the figure, *so shall you be last. When you have recorded my ultimate victory, the book will be closed. I will rule unchallenged.*

"True, you will rule unchallenged. You will rule a dead world. A world your magic destroyed. You will rule alone. And you will *be* alone, alone in the formless, eternal void," Astinus replied coolly, writing even as he spoke. Beside him, Par-Salian moaned and tore at his white hair.

Seeing as he saw everything—without seeming to see—Astinus watched the black-robed figure's hands clench. *That is a lie, old friend! I will create! New worlds will be mine. New peoples I will produce—new races who will worship me!*

"Evil cannot create," Astinus remarked, "it can only destroy. It turns in upon itself, gnawing itself. Already, you feel it eating away at you. Already, you can feel your soul shrivel. Look into Paladine's face, Raistlin. Look into it as you looked into it once, back on the Plains of Dergoth, when you lay dying of the dwarf's sword wound and Lady Crysania laid healing hands upon you. You saw the grief and sorrow of the god then as you see it now, Raistlin. And you knew then, as you know now but refuse to admit, that Paladine grieves, not for himself, but for you.

"Easy will it be for us to slip back into our dreamless sleep. For you, Raistlin, there will be no sleep. Only an endless waking, endless listening for sounds that will never come, endless staring into a void that holds neither light nor darkness, endless shrieking words that no one will hear, no one will answer, endless plotting and scheming that will bear no fruit as you turn round and round upon yourself. Finally, in your madness and desperation, you will grab the tail of your existence and, like a starving snake, devour yourself whole in an effort to find food for your soul.

"But you will find nothing but emptiness. And you will continue to exist forever within this emptiness—a tiny spot of nothing, sucking in everything around itself to feed your endless hunger. . . ."

The Portal shimmered. Astinus quickly looked up from his writing, feeling the will behind those golden eyes waver. Staring past the mirrorlike surface, looking deep into their depths, he saw—for the space of a heartbeat—the very torment and torture he had described. He saw a soul, frightened, alone, caught in its own trap, seeking escape. For the first time in his existence, compassion touched Astinus. His hand marking his place in his book, he half-rose from his seat, his other hand reaching into the Portal. . . .

Then, laughter . . . eerie, mocking, bitter laughter—laughter not at him, but at the one who laughed.

The black-robed figure within the Portal was gone.

With a sigh, Astinus resumed his seat and, almost at the same instant, magical lightning flickered inside the Portal. It was answered by flaring, white light—the final meeting of Paladine and the young man who had defeated the Queen of Darkness and taken her place.

Lighting flickered outside, too, stabbing the eyes of the two men watching with blinding brilliance. Thunder crashed, the stones of the Tower trembled, the foundations of the Tower shook. Wind howled, its wail drowning out Par-Salian's moaning.

Lifting a drawn, haggard face, the ancient wizard twisted his head to stare out the windows with an expression of horror. "This is the end," he murmured, his gnarled, wasted hands plucking feebly at the air. "The end of all things."

"Yes," said Astinus, frowning in annoyance as a sudden lurching of the Tower caused him to make an error. He gripped his book more firmly, his eyes on the Portal, writing, recording the last battle as it occurred.

Within a matter of moments, all was over. The white light flickered briefly, beautifully, for one instant. Then it died.

———

Within the Portal, all was darkness.

Par-Salian wept. His tears fell down upon the stone floor and, at their touch, the Tower shook like a living thing, as if it, too, foresaw its doom and was quaking in horror.

Ignoring the falling stones and the heaving of the rocks, Astinus coolly penned the final words.

As of Fourthday, Fifthmonth, Year 358, the world ends.

Then, with a sigh, Astinus started to close the book.

A hand slammed down across the pages.

"No," said a firm voice, "it will not end here."

Astinus's hands trembled, his pen dropped a blot of ink upon the paper, obliterating the last words.

"Caramon . . . Caramon Majere!" Par-Salian cried, pitifully reaching out to the man with feeble hands. "It was you I heard in the Forest!"

"Did you doubt me?" Caramon growled. Though shocked and horrified by the sight of the wretched wizard and his torment, Caramon found it difficult to feel any compassion for the archmage. Looking at Par-Salian, seeing his lower half turned to marble, Caramon recalled all too clearly his twin's torment in the Tower, his own torment upon being sent back to Istar with Crysania.

"No, not doubted you!" Par-Salian wrung his hands. "I doubted my own sanity! Can't you understand? How can you be here? How could you have survived the magical battles that destroyed the world?"

"He didn't," Astinus said sternly. Having regained his composure, he placed the open book down on the floor at his feet and stood up. Glowering at Caramon, he pointed an accusing finger. "What trick is this? You died! What is the meaning—"

Without speaking a word, Caramon dragged Tasslehoff out from behind him. Deeply impressed by the solemnity and seriousness of the occasion, Tas huddled next to Caramon, his wide eyes fixed upon Par-Salian with a pleading gaze.

"Do—do you want me to explain, Caramon?" Tas asked in a small, polite voice, barely audible over the thunder. "I—I really

---

feel like I should tell *why* I disrupted the time-travel spell, and then there's how Raistlin gave me the wrong instructions and made me break the magical device, even though part of that *was* my fault, I suppose, and how I ended up in the Abyss where I met poor Gnimsh." Tas's eyes filled with tears. "And how Raistlin killed him—"

"All this is known to me," Astinus interrupted. "So you were able to come here because of the kender. Our time is short. What is it you intend, Caramon Majere?"

The big man turned his gaze to Par-Salian. "I bear you no love, wizard. In that, I am at one with my twin. Perhaps you had your reasons for what you did to me and to Lady Crysania back there in Istar. If so"—Caramon raised a hand to stop Par-Salian who, it seems, would have spoken—"if so, then you are the one who lives with them, not me. For now, know that I have it in my power to alter time. As Raistlin himself told me, because of the kender, we can change what has happened.

"I have the magical device. I can travel back to any point in time. Tell me when, tell me what happened that led to this destruction, and I will undertake to prevent it, if I can."

Caramon's gaze went from Par-Salian to Astinus. The historian shook his head. "Do not look to me, Caramon Majere. I am neutral in this as in all things. I can give you no help. I can only give you this warning: You may go back, but you may find you change nothing. A pebble in a swiftly flowing river, that is all you may be."

Caramon nodded. "If that is all, then at least I will die knowing that I tried to make up for my failure."

Astinus regarded Caramon with a keen, penetrating glance. "What failure is that you speak of, Warrior? You risked your life going back after your brother. You did your best, you endeavored to convince him that this path of darkness he walked would lead only to his own doom." Astinus gestured toward the Portal. "You heard me speak to him? You know what he faces?"

Wordlessly, Caramon nodded again, his face pale and anguished.

———

"Then tell me," Astinus said coolly.

The Tower shuddered. Wind battered the walls, lightning turned the waning night of the world into a garish, blinding day. The small, bare tower room in which they stood shook and trembled. Though they were alone within it, Caramon thought he could hear sounds of weeping, and he slowly came to realize it was the stones of the Tower itself. He glanced about uneasily.

"You have time," Astinus said. Sitting back down on his stool, he picked up the book. But he did not close it. "Not long, perhaps, but time, still. Wherein did you fail?"

Caramon drew a shaking breath. Then his brows came together. Scowling in anger, his gaze went to Par-Salian. "A trick, wasn't it, wizard? A trick to get me to do what you mages could not—stop Raistlin in his dreadful ambition. But you failed. You sent Crysania back to die because you feared her. But her will, her love was stronger than you supposed. She lived and, blinded by her love and her own ambition, she followed Raistlin into the Abyss." Caramon glowered. "I don't understand Paladine's purpose in granting her prayers, in giving her the power to go there—"

"It is not for you to understand the ways of the gods, Caramon Majere," Astinus interrupted coldly. "Who are you to judge them? It may be that they fail, too, sometimes. Or that they choose to risk the best they have in hopes that it will be still better."

"Be that as it may," Caramon continued, his face dark and troubled, "the mages sent Crysania back and thereby gave my brother one of the keys he needed to enter the Portal. They failed. The gods failed. And I failed." Caramon ran a trembling hand through his hair.

"I thought I could convince Raistlin with words to turn back from this deadly path he walked. I should have known better." The big man laughed bitterly. "What poor words of mine ever affected him? When he stood before the Portal, preparing to enter the Abyss, telling me what he intended, I left him. It was all so easy. I simply turned my back and walked away."

———

"Bah!" Astinus snorted. "What would you have done? He was strong then, more powerful than any of us can begin to imagine. He held the magical field together by his force of will and his strength alone. You could not have killed him—"

"No," said Caramon, his gaze shifting away from those in the room, staring out into the storm that raged ever more fiercely, "but I could have followed him—followed him into darkness— even if it meant my death. To show him that I was willing to sacrifice for love what he was willing to sacrifice for his magic and his ambition." Caramon turned his gaze upon those in the room. "Then he would have respected me. Then he might have listened. And so I will go back. I will enter the Abyss"—he ignored Tasslehoff's cry of horror—"and there I will do what must be done."

"What must be done," Par-Salian repeated feverishly. "You do not realize what that means! Dalamar—"

A blazing, blinding bolt of lightning exploded within the room, slamming those within back against the stone walls. No one could see or hear anything as the thunder crashed over them. Then above the blast of thunder rose a tortured cry.

Shaken by that strangled, pain-filled scream, Caramon opened his eyes, only to wish they had been shut forever before seeing such a grisly sight.

Par-Salian had turned from a pillar of marble to a pillar of flame! Caught in Raistlin's spell, the wizard was helpless. He could do nothing but scream as the flames slowly crept up his immobile body.

Unnerved, Tasslehoff covered his face with his hands and cowered, whimpering, in a corner. Astinus rose from where he had been hurled to the floor, his hands going immediately to the book he still held. He started to write, but his hand fell limp, the pen slipped from his fingers. Once more, he began to close the cover . . .

"No!" Caramon cried. Reaching out, he laid his hands upon the pages.

Astinus looked at him, and Caramon faltered beneath the gaze of those deathless eyes. His hands shook, but they

---

remained pressed firmly across the white parchment of the leather-bound volume. The dying wizard wailed in dreadful agony.

Astinus released the open book.

"Hold this," Caramon ordered, closing the precious volume and thrusting it into Tasslehoff's hands. Nodding numbly, the kender wrapped his arms around the book, which was almost as big as he was, and remained, crouched in his corner, staring around him in horror as Caramon lurched across the room toward the dying wizard.

"No!" shrieked Par-Salian. "Do not come near me!" His white, flowing hair and long beard crackled, his skin bubbled and sizzled, the terrible cloying stench of burning flesh mingling with the smell of sulphur.

"Tell me!" cried Caramon, raising his arm against the heat, getting as near the mage as he could. "Tell me, Par-Salian! What must I do? How can I prevent this?"

The wizard's eyes were melting. His mouth was a gaping hole in the black formless mass that was his face. But his dying words struck Caramon like another bolt of lightning, to be burned into his mind forever.

"Raistlin must not be allowed to leave the Abyss!"

BOOK 2

The Knight of the Black Rose

Lord Soth sat upon the crumbling, fire-blackened throne in the blasted, desolate ruins of Dargaard Keep. His orange eyes flamed in their unseen sockets, the only visible sign of the cursed life that burned within the charred armor of a Knight of Solamnia.

Soth sat alone.

The death knight had dismissed his attendants—former knights, like himself, who had remained loyal to him in life and so were cursed to remain loyal to him in death. He had also sent away the banshees, the elven women who had played a role in his downfall and who were now doomed to spend their lives in his service. For hundreds of years, ever since that terrible night of his death, Lord Soth had commanded these unfortunate women to relive that doom with him. Every night, as he sat upon his ruined throne, he forced them to serenade him with a song that related the story of his disgrace and their own.

That song brought bitter pain to Soth, but he welcomed the pain. It was ten times better than the nothingness that pervaded his unholy life-in-death at all other times. But tonight he did not listen to the song. He listened, instead, to his story as it whispered like the bitter night wind through the eaves of the crumbling keep.

"Once, long ago, I was a Lord Knight of Solamnia. I was everything then—handsome, charming, brave, married to a woman of fortune, if not of beauty. My knights were devoted to me. Yes, men envied me—Lord Soth of Dargaard Keep.

"The spring before the Cataclysm, I left Dargaard Keep and rode to Palanthas with my retinue. A Knights' Council was being held, my presence was required. I cared little for the Council meeting—it would drag on with endless arguments over insignificant rules. But there would be drinking, good fellowship, tales of battle and adventure. *That* was why I went.

"We rode slowly, taking our time, our days filled with song

81

and jesting. At night we'd stay in inns when we could, sleep beneath the stars when we could not. The weather was fine, it was a mild spring. The sunshine was warm upon us, the evening breeze cooled us. I was thirty-two years old that spring. Everything was going well with my life. I do not recall ever being happier.

"And then, one night—curse the silver moon that shone upon it—we were camped in the wilderness. A cry cut through the darkness, rousing us from our slumbers. It was a woman's cry, then we heard many women's voices, mingled with the harsh shouts of ogres.

"Grabbing our weapons, we rushed to battle. It was an easy victory; only a roving band of robbers. Most fled at our approach, but the leader, either more daring or more drunken than the rest, refused to be deprived of his spoils. Personally, I didn't blame him. He'd captured a lovely young elfmaiden. Her beauty in the moonlight was radiant, her fear only enhanced her fragile loveliness. Alone, I challenged him. We fought, and I was the victor. And it was my reward—ah, what bitter-sweet reward—to carry the fainting elfmaid in my arms back to her companions.

"I can still see her fine, golden hair shining in the moonlight. I can see her eyes when she wakened, looking into mine, and I can see even now—as I saw then—her love for me dawn in them. And she saw—in my eyes—the admiration I could not hide. Thoughts of my wife, of my honor, of my castle—everything fled as I gazed upon her beautiful face.

"She thanked me; how shyly she spoke. I returned her to the elven women—a group of clerics they were, traveling to Palanthas and thence to Istar on a pilgrimage. She was just an acolyte. It was on this journey that she was to be made a Revered Daughter of Paladine. I left her and the women, returning with my men to my camp. I tried to sleep, but I could still feel that lithe, young body in my arms. Never had I been so consumed with passion for a woman.

"When I did sleep, my dreams were sweet torture. When I awoke, the thought that we must part was like a knife in my heart. Rising early, I returned to the elven camp. Making up a tale of roving bands of goblins between here and Palanthas, I easily convinced the elven women that they needed my protection. My men were not averse to such pleasant companions, and so we traveled with them. But this did not ease my pain. Rather, it intensified it. Day after day I watched her, riding near me—but not near enough. Night after night I slept alone—my thoughts in turmoil.

"I wanted her, wanted her more than anything I had ever wanted in this world. And yet, I was a Knight, sworn by the strictest vows to uphold the Code and the Measure, sworn by holy vows to remain true to my wife, sworn by the vows of a commander to lead my men to honor. Long I fought with myself and, at last, I believed I had conquered. Tomorrow, I will leave, I said, feeling peace steal over me.

"I truly intended to leave, and I would have. But, curse the fates, I went upon a hunting expedition in the woods and there, far from camp, I met her. She had been sent to gather herbs.

"She was alone. I was alone. Our companions were far away. The love that I had seen in her eyes shone there still. She had loosened her hair, it fell to her feet in a golden cloud. My honor, my resolve, were destroyed in an instant, burned up by the flame of desire that swept over me. She was easy to seduce, poor thing. One kiss, then another. Then drawing her down beside me on the new grass, my hands caressing, my mouth stopping her protests, and . . . after I had made her mine . . . kissing away her tears.

"That night, she came to me again, in my tent. I was lost in bliss. I promised her marriage, of course. What else could I do? At first, I didn't mean it. How could I? I had a wife, a wealthy wife. I needed her money. My expenses were high. But then one night, when I held the elf maid in my arms, I knew I could never give her up. I made arrangements to have my wife permanently removed. . . .

"We continued our journey. By this time, the elven women had begun to suspect. How not? It was hard for us to hide our secret smiles during the day, difficult to avoid every opportunity to be together.

"We were, of necessity, separated when we reached Palan-thas. The elven women went to stay in one of the fine houses that the Kingpriest used when he visited the city. My men and I went to our lodgings. I was confident, however, that she would find a way to come to me since I could not go to her. The first night passed, I was not much worried. But then a second and a third, and no word.

"Finally, a knock on my door. But it was not her. It was the head of the Knights of Solamnia, accompanied by the heads of each of the three Orders of Knights. I knew then, when I saw them, what must have happened. She had discovered the truth and betrayed me.

"As it was, it was not she who betrayed me, but the elven women. My lover had fallen ill and, when they came to treat her, they discovered that she was carrying my child. She had told no one, not even me. They told her I was married and, worse still, word arrived in Palanthas at the same time that my wife had 'mysteriously' disappeared.

"I was arrested. Dragged through the streets of Palanthas in public humiliation, I was the object of the vulgars' crude jokes and vile names. They enjoyed nothing more than seeing a Knight fall to their level. I swore that, someday, I would have my revenge upon them and their fine city. But that seemed hopeless. My trial was swift. I was sentenced to die—a traitor to the Knighthood. Stripped of my lands and my title, I would be executed by having my throat slit with my own sword. I accepted my death. I even looked forward to it, thinking still that she had cast me off.

"But, the night before I was to die, my loyal men freed me from my prison. She was with them. She told me everything, she told me she carried my child.

"The elven women had forgiven her, she said, and, though she could never now become a Revered Daughter of Paladine, she might still live among her people—though her disgrace would follow her to the end of her days. But she could not bear the thought of leaving without telling me good-bye. She loved

---

me, that much was plain. But I could tell that the tales she had heard worried her.

"I made up some lie about my wife that she believed. She would have believed dark was light if I'd told her. Her mind at ease, she agreed to run away with me. I know now that this was why she had come in the first place. My men accompanying us, we fled back to Dargaard Keep.

"It was a difficult journey, pursued constantly by the other Knights, but we arrived, finally, and entrenched ourselves within the castle. It was an easy position to defend—perched as it was high upon sheer cliffs. We had large stores of provisions and we could easily hold out during the winter that was fast approaching.

"I should have been pleased with myself, with life, with my new bride—what a mockery that marriage ceremony was! But I was tormented by guilt and, what was worse, the loss of my honor. I realized that I had escaped one prison only to find myself in another—another of my own choosing. I had escaped death only to live a dark and wretched life. I grew moody, morose. I was always quick to anger, quick to strike, and now it was worse. The servants fled, after I'd beaten several. My men took to avoiding me. And then, one night, I struck her— her, the only person in this world who could give me even a shred of comfort.

"Looking into her tear-filled eyes, I saw the monster I had become. Taking her in my arms, I begged forgiveness. Her lovely hair fell around me. I could feel my child kicking in her womb. Kneeling there, together, we prayed to Paladine. I would do anything, I told the god, to restore my honor. I asked only that my son or daughter never grow up to know my shame.

"And Paladine answered. He told me of the Kingpriest, and what arrogant demands the foolish man planned to make of the gods. He told me that the world itself would feel the anger of the gods unless—as Huma had done before me—one man was willing to sacrifice himself for the sake of the innocent.

"Paladine's light shone around me. My tormented soul was

filled with peace. What small sacrifice it seemed to me to give my life so that my child should be raised in honor and the world could be saved. I rode to Istar, fully intent upon stopping the Kingpriest, knowing that Paladine was with me.

"But another rode beside me, too, on that journey—the Queen of Darkness. So does she wage constant war for the souls she delights in holding in thrall. What did she use to defeat me? Those very same elven women—clerics of the god whose mission I rode upon.

"These women had long since forgotten the name of Paladine. Like the Kingpriest, they were wrapped in their own righteousness and could see nothing through their veils of goodness. Filled with my own self-righteousness, I let them know what I intended. Their fear was great. They did not believe the gods would punish the world. They saw a day when only the good (meaning the elves) would live upon Krynn.

"They had to stop me. And they were successful.

"The Queen is wise. She knows the dark regions of a man's heart. I would have ridden down an army, if it had stood in my way. But the soft words of those elven women worked in my blood like poison. How clever it was for the elfmaid to have been rid of me so easily, they said. Now she had my castle, my wealth, all to herself, without the inconvenience of a human husband. Was I even certain the baby was mine? She had been seen in the company of one of my young followers. Where did she go when she left my tent in the night?

"They never once lied. They never once said anything against her directly. But their questions ate at my soul, gnawing at me. I remembered words, incidents, looks. I was certain I'd been betrayed. I would catch them together! I would kill him! I would make her suffer!

"I turned my back upon Istar.

"Arriving home, I battered down the doors of my castle. My wife, alarmed, came to meet me, holding her infant son in her arms. There was a look of despair upon her face—I took it for an admission of guilt. I cursed her, I cursed her child. And, at that moment, the fiery mountain struck Ansalon.

"The stars fell from the sky. The ground shook and split asunder. A chandelier, lit with a hundred candles, fell from the ceiling. In an instant my wife was engulfed with flame. She knew she was dying, but she held out her babe to me to rescue from the fire that was consuming her. I hesitated, then, jealous rage still filling my heart, I turned away.

"With her dying breath, she called down the wrath of the gods upon me. 'You will die this night in fire,' she cried, 'even as your son and I die. But you will live eternally in darkness. You will live one life for every life that your folly has brought to an end this night!' She perished.

"The flames spread. My castle was soon ablaze. Nothing we tried would put out that strange fire. It burned even rock. My men tried to flee. But, as I watched, they, too, burst into flame. There was no one, no one left alive except myself upon that mountain. I stood in the great hall, alone, surrounded on all sides by fire that did not yet touch me. But, as I stood there, I saw it closing in upon me, coming closer . . . closer. . . .

"I died slowly, in unbearable agony. When death finally came, it brought no relief. For I closed my eyes only to open them again, looking into a world of emptiness and bleak despair and eternal torment. Night after night, for endless years, I have sat upon this throne and listened to those elven women sing my story.

"But that ended, it ended with you, Kitiara. . . .

"When the Dark Queen called upon me to aid her in the war, I told her I would serve the first Dragon Highlord who had courage enough to spend the night in Dargaard Keep. There was only one—you, my beauty. You, Kitiara. I admired you for that, I admired you for your courage, your skill, your ruthless determination. In you, I see myself. I see what I might have become.

"I helped you murder the other Highlords when we fled Neraka in the turmoil following the Queen's defeat, I helped you reach Sanction, and there I helped you establish your power once again upon this continent. I helped you when you tried to thwart your brother, Raistlin's, plans for challenging the Queen of Darkness. No, I wasn't surprised he outwitted you. Of all the living I have ever met, he is the only one I fear.

"I have even been amused by your love affairs, my Kitiara. We dead cannot feel lust. That is a passion of the blood and no blood flows in these icy limbs. I watched you twist that weakling, Tanis Half-Elven, inside out, and I enjoyed it every bit as much as you did.

"But now, Kitiara, what have you become? The mistress has become the slave. And for what—an elf! Oh, I have seen your eyes burn when you speak his name. I've seen your hands tremble when you hold his letters. You think of him when you should be planning war. Even your generals can no longer claim your attention.

"No, we dead cannot feel lust. But we can feel hatred, we can feel envy, we can feel jealousy and possession.

"I could kill Dalamar—the dark elf apprentice is good, but he is no match for me. His master? Raistlin? Ah, now that would be a different story.

"My Queen in your dark Abyss—beware Raistlin! In him, you face your greatest challenge, and you must—in the end— face it alone. I cannot help you on that plane, Dark Majesty, but perhaps I can aid you on this one.

"Yes, Dalamar, I could kill you. But I have known what it is to die, and death is a shabby, paltry thing. Its pain is agony, but soon over. What greater pain to linger on and on in the world of the living, smelling their warm blood, seeing their soft flesh, and knowing that it can never, never be yours again. But you will come to know, all too well, dark elf. . . .

"As for you, Kitiara, know this—I would endure this pain, I would live out another century of tortured existence rather than see you again in the arms of a living man!"

The death knight brooded and plotted, his mind twisting and turning like the thorny branches of the black roses that overran his castle. The skeletal warriors paced the ruined battlements, each hovering near the place where he had met his death. The elven women wrung their fleshless hands and moaned in bitter sorrow at their fate.

Soth heard nothing, was aware of nothing. He sat upon his blackened throne, staring unseeing at a dark, charred splotch upon the stone floor—a splotch that he had sought for years with all the power of his magic to obliterate—and still it remained, a splotch in the shape of a woman. . . .

And then, at last, the unseen lips smiled, and the flame of the orange eyes burned bright in their endless night.

"You, Kitiara—you will be mine—forever. . . ."

Chapter
I

The carriage rumbled to a stop. The horses snorted and shook themselves, jingling the harness, thudding their hooves against the smooth paving stones, as if eager to get this journey over with and return to their comfortable stables.

A head poked in the carriage window.

"Good morning, sir. Welcome to Palanthas. Please state your name and business." This delivered in a bright, official voice by a bright, official young man who must have just come on duty. Peering into the carriage, the guard blinked his eyes, trying to adjust them to the cool shadows of the coach's interior. The late spring sun shone as brightly as the young man's face, probably because it, too, had just recently come on duty.

"My name is Tanis Half-Elven," said the man inside the carriage, "and I am here by invitation to see Revered Son Elistan. I've got a letter here. If you'll wait half a moment, I'll—"

"Lord Tanis!" The face outlined by the carriage window turned as crimson as the ridiculously frogged and epauletted uniform he wore. "I beg your pardon, sir. I—I didn't recognize

. . . that is, I couldn't see or I'm sure I would have recognized—"

"Damn it, man," Tanis responded irritably, "don't apologize for doing your job. Here's the letter—"

"I won't, sir. That is, I will, sir. Apologize, that is. Dreadfully sorry, sir. The letter? That really won't be necessary, sir."

Stammering, the guard saluted, cracked his head smartly on the top of the carriage window, caught the lacy sleeve of his cuff on the door, saluted again, and finally staggered back to his post looking as if he had just emerged from a fight with hobgoblins.

Grinning to himself, but a rueful grin at that, Tanis leaned back as the carriage continued on its way through the gates of the Old City Wall. The guard was his idea. It had taken a great deal of argument and persuasion on Tanis's part to convince Lord Amothus of Palanthas that the city gates should actually not only be shut but guarded as well.

"But people might not feel welcome. They might be offended," Amothus had protested faintly. "And, after all, the war *is* over."

Tanis sighed again. When would they learn? Never, he supposed gloomily, staring out the window into the city that, more than any other on the continent of Ansalon, epitomized the complacency into which the world had fallen since the end of the War of the Lance two years ago. Two years ago this spring, in fact.

That brought still another sigh from Tanis. Damn! He had forgotten! War End's Day! When was that? Two weeks? Three? He would have to put on that silly costume—the ceremonial armor of a Knight of Solamnia, the elven regalia, the dwarven trappings. There'd be dinners of rich food that kept him awake half the night, speeches that put him to sleep after dinner, and Laurana. . . .

Tanis gasped. Laurana! *She'd* remembered! Of course! How could he have been so thick-headed? They'd just returned home to Solanthus a few weeks ago after attending Solostaran's funeral in Qualinesti—and after he'd made an unsuccessful trip back to Solace in search of Lady Crysania—when a letter arrived for Laurana in flowing elven script:

"Your Presence Urgently Required in Silvanesti!"

"I'll be back in four weeks, my dear," she'd said, kissing him tenderly. Yet there had been laughter in her eyes, those lovely eyes!

She'd left him! Left him behind to attend those blasted ceremonies! And she would be back in the elven homeland which, though still struggling to escape the horrors inflicted upon it by Lorac's nightmare, was infinitely preferable to an evening with Lord Amothus. . . .

It suddenly occurred to Tanis what he had been thinking. A mental memory of Silvanesti came to mind—with its hideously tortured trees weeping blood, the twisted, tormented faces of long dead elven warriors staring out from the shadows. A mental image of one of Lord Amothus's dinner parties rose in comparison—

Tanis began to laugh. He'd take the undead warriors any day!

As for Laurana, well, he couldn't blame her. These ceremonies were hard enough on him—but Laurana was the Palanthians' darling, their Golden General, the one who had saved their beautiful city from the ravages of the war. There was nothing they wouldn't do for her, except leave her some time to herself. The last War's End Day celebration, Tanis had carried his wife home in his arms, more exhausted than she had been after three straight days of battle.

He envisioned her in Silvanesti, working to replant the flowers, working to soothe the dreams of the tortured trees and slowly nurse them back to life, visiting with Alhana Starbreeze, now her sister-in-law, who would be back in Silvanesti as well—but without her new husband, Porthios. Theirs was, so far, a chill, loveless marriage and Tanis wondered, briefly, if Alhana might not be seeking the haven of Silvanesti for the same reason. War's End Day must be difficult for Alhana, too. His thoughts went to Sturm Brightblade—the knight Alhana had loved, who was lying dead in the High Clerist's Tower and, from there, Tanis's memories wandered to other friends . . . and enemies.

As if conjured up by those memories, a dark shadow swept over the carriage. Tanis looked out the window. Down a long, empty, deserted street, he caught a glimpse of a patch of blackness—Shoikan Grove, the guardian forest of Raistlin's Tower of High Sorcery.

Even from this distance, Tanis could feel the chill that flowed from those trees, a chill that froze the heart and the soul. His gaze went to the Tower, rising up above the beautiful buildings of Palanthas like a black iron spike driven through the city's white breast.

His thoughts went to the letter that had brought him to Palanthas. Glancing down at it, he read the words over:

Tanis Half-Elven,

We must meet with you immediately. Gravest emergency. The Temple of Paladine, Afterwatch Rising 12, Fourthday, Year 356.

That was all. No signature. He knew only that Fourthday was today and, having received the missive only two days ago, he had been forced to travel day and night to reach Palanthas on time. The note's language was elven, the handwriting was elven, also. Not unusual. Elistan had many elven clerics, but why hadn't he signed it? If, indeed, it came from Elistan. Yet, who else could so casually issue such an invitation to the Temple of Paladine?

Shrugging to himself—remembering that he had asked himself these same questions more than once and had never come to a satisfactory conclusion—Tanis tucked the letter back inside his pouch. His gaze went, unwillingly, to the Tower of High Sorcery.

"I'll wager it has something to do with *you*, old friend," he murmured to himself, frowning and thinking, once again, of the strange disappearance of the cleric, Lady Crysania.

The carriage rolled to a halt again, jolting Tanis from his

---

dark thoughts. He looked out the window, catching a glimpse of the Temple, but forcing himself to sit patiently in his seat until the footman came to open the door for him. He smiled to himself. He could almost see Laurana, sitting across from him, glaring at him, daring him to make a move for the door handle. It had taken her many months to break Tanis of his old impetuous habit of flinging open the door, knocking the footman to one side, and proceeding on his way without a thought for the driver, the carriage, the horses, anything.

It had now become a private joke between them. Tanis loved watching Laurana's eyes narrow in mock alarm as his hand strayed teasingly near the door handle. But that only reminded him how much he missed her. Where was that damn footman anyway? By the gods, he was alone, he'd do it *his* way for a change—

The door flew open. The footman fumbled with the step that folded down from the floor. "Oh, forget that," Tanis snapped impatiently, hopping to the ground. Ignoring the footman's faint look of outraged sensibility, Tanis drew in a deep breath, glad to have escaped—finally—from the stuffy confines of the carriage.

He gazed around, letting the wonderful feeling of peace and well-being that radiated from the Temple of Paladine seep into his soul. No forest guarded this holy place. Vast, open lawns of green grass as soft and smooth as velvet invited the traveler to walk upon it, sit upon it, rest upon it. Gardens of bright-colored flowers delighted the eye, their perfume filling the air with sweetness. Here and there, groves of carefully pruned shade trees offered a haven from glaring sunlight. Fountains poured forth pure cool water. White-robed clerics walked in the gardens, their heads bent together in solemn discussion.

Rising from the frame of the gardens and the shady groves and the carpet of grass, the Temple of Paladine glowed softly in the morning sunlight. Made of white marble, it was a plain, unadorned structure that added to the impression of peace and tranquility that prevailed all around it.

There were gates, but no guards. All were invited to enter,

and many did so. It was a haven for the sorrowful, the weary, the unhappy. As Tanis started to make his way across the well-kept lawn, he saw many people sitting or lying upon the grass, a look of peace upon faces that, from the marks of care and weariness, had not often known such comfort.

Tanis had taken only a few steps when he remembered—with another sigh—the carriage. Stopping, he turned. "Wait for me," he was about to say when a figure emerged from the shadows of a grove of aspens that stood at the very edge of the Temple property.

"Tanis Half-Elven?" inquired the figure.

As the figure walked into the light, Tanis started. It was dressed in black robes. Numerous pouches and other spell-casting devices hung from its belt, runes of silver were embroidered upon the sleeves and the hood of its black cloak. *Raistlin!* Tanis thought instantly, having had the archmage in his mind only moments before.

But no. Tanis breathed easier. This magic-user was taller than Raistlin by at least a head and shoulders. His body was straight and well-formed, even muscular, his step youthful and vigorous. Besides, now that Tanis was paying attention, he realized that the voice was firm and deep—not like Raistlin's soft, unsettling whisper.

And, if it were not too odd, Tanis would have sworn he had heard the man speak with an elven accent.

"I am Tanis Half-Elven," he said, somewhat belatedly.

Though he could not see the figure's face, hidden as it was by the shadows of its black hood, he had the impression the man smiled.

"I thought I recognized you. You have often been described to me. You may dismiss your carriage. It will not be needed. You will be spending many days, possibly even weeks, here in Palanthas."

The man was speaking elven! Silvanesti Elven! Tanis was, for a moment, so startled that he could only stare. The driver of the carriage cleared his throat at that moment. It had been a long, hard journey and there were fine inns in Palanthas with ale that was legendary all over Ansalon. . . .

But Tanis wasn't going to dismiss his equipage on the word of a black-robed mage. He opened his mouth to question him further when the magic-user withdrew his hands from the sleeves of his robes, where he'd kept them folded, and made a swift, negating motion with one, even as he made a motion of invitation with the other.

"Please," he said in elven again, "won't you walk with me? For I am bound for the same place you go. Elistan expects us."

Us! Tanis's mind fumbled about in confusion. Since when did Elistan invite black-robed magic-users to the Temple of Paladine? And since when did black-robed magic-users voluntarily set foot upon these sacred grounds!

Well, the only way to find out, obviously, was to accompany this strange person and save his questions until they were alone. Somewhat confusedly, therefore, Tanis gave his instructions to the coachman. The black-robed figure stood in silence beside him, watching the carriage depart. Then Tanis turned to him.

"You have the advantage of me, sir," the half-elf said in halting Silvanesti, a language that was purer elven than the Qualinesti he'd been raised to speak.

The figure bowed, then cast aside his hood so that the morning light fell upon his face. "I am Dalamar," he said, returning his hands to the sleeves of his robe. Few there were upon Krynn who would shake hands with a black-robed mage.

"A dark elf!" Tanis said in astonishment, speaking before he thought. He flushed. "I'm sorry," he said awkwardly. "It's just that I've never met—"

"One of my kind?" Dalamar finished smoothly, a faint smile upon his cold, handsome, expressionless elven features. "No, I don't suppose you would have. We who are 'cast from the light,' as they say, do not often venture onto the sunlit planes of existence." His smile grew warmer, suddenly, and Tanis saw a wistful look in the dark elf's eyes as their gaze went to the grove of aspens where he had been standing. "Sometimes, though, even we grow homesick."

———

97

Tanis's gaze, too, went to the aspens—of all trees most beloved of the elves. He smiled, too, feeling much more at ease. Tanis had walked his own dark roads, and had come very near tumbling into several yawning chasms. He could understand.

"The hour for my appointment draws near," he said. "And, from what you said, I gather that you are somehow involved in this. Perhaps we should continue—"

"Certainly." Dalamar seemed to recollect himself. He followed Tanis onto the green lawn without hesitation. Tanis, turning, was considerably startled, therefore, to see a swift spasm of pain contort the elf's delicate features and to see him flinch, visibly.

"What is it?" Tanis stopped. "Are you unwell? Can I help—"

Dalamar forced his pain-filled features into a twisted smile. "No, Half-Elven," he said. "There is nothing you can do to help. Nor am I unwell. Much worse would you look, if you stepped into the Shoikan Grove that guards *my* dwelling place."

Tanis nodded in understanding, then, almost unwillingly, glanced into the distance at the dark, grim Tower that loomed over Palanthas. As he looked at it, a strange impression came over him. He looked back at the plain white Temple, then over again at the Tower. Seeing them together, it was as if he were seeing each for the first time. Both looked more complete, finished, whole, than they had when viewed separately and apart. This was only a fleeting impression and one he did not even think about until later. Now, he could only think of one thing—

"Then you live there? With Rai— With him?" Try as he might, Tanis knew he could not speak the archmage's name without bitter anger, and so he avoided it altogether.

"He is my *Shalafi*," answered Dalamar in a pain-tightened voice.

"So you are his apprentice," Tanis responded, recognizing the elven word for *Master*. He frowned. "Then what are you doing here? Did he send you?" If so, thought the half-elf, I will leave this place, if I have to walk back to Solanthas.

"No," Dalamar replied, his face draining of all color. "But it is of him we will speak." The dark elf cast his hood over his head. When he spoke, it was obviously with intense effort. "And now, I must beg of you to move swiftly. I have a charm, given me by Elistan, that will help me through this trial. But it is not one I care to prolong."

Elistan giving charms to black-robed magic-users? Raistlin's apprentice? Absolutely mystified, Tanis agreeably quickened his steps.

"Tanis, my friend!"

Elistan, cleric of Paladine and head of the church on the continent of Ansalon, reached out his hand to the half-elf. Tanis clasped the man's hand warmly, trying not to notice how wasted and feeble was the cleric's once strong, firm grip. Tanis also fought to control his face, endeavoring to keep the feelings of shock and pity from registering on his features as he stared down at the frail, almost skeletal, figure resting in a bed, propped up by pillows.

"Elistan—" Tanis began warmly.

One of the white-robed clerics hovering near their leader glanced up at the half-elf and frowned.

"That is, R-revered Son"—Tanis stumbled over the formal title—"you are looking well."

"And you, Tanis Half-Elven, have degenerated into a liar," Elistan remarked, smiling at the pained expression Tanis tried desperately to keep off his face.

Elistan patted Tanis's sun-browned hand with his thin, white fingers. "And don't fool with that 'Revered Son' nonsense. Yes, I know it's only proper and correct, Garad, but this man knew me when I was a slave in the mines of Pax Tharkas. Now, go along, all of you," he said to the hovering clerics. "Bring what we have to make our guests comfortable."

His gaze went to the dark elf who had collapsed into a chair near the fire that burned in Elistan's private chambers. "Dalamar," Elistan said gently, "this journey cannot have been an easy one for you. I am indebted to you that you have made it. But, here in my quarters you can, I believe, find ease. What will you take?"

"Wine," the dark elf managed to reply through lips that were stiff and ashen. Tanis saw the elf's hands tremble on the arm of the chair.

"Bring wine and food for our guests," Elistan told the clerics who were filing out of the room, many casting glances of disapproval at the black-robed mage. "Escort Astinus here at once, upon his arrival, then see that we are not disturbed."

"Astinus?" Tanis gaped. "Astinus, the Chronicler?"

"Yes, Half-Elven." Elistan smiled once again. "Dying lends one special significance. 'They stand in line to see me, who once would not have glanced my way.' Isn't that how the old man's poem went? There now, Half-Elven. The air is cleared. Yes, I know I am dying. I have known for a long time. My months dwindle to weeks. Come, Tanis. You have seen men die before. What was it you told me the Forestmaster said to you in Darken Wood—'we do not mourn the loss of those who die fulfilling their destinies.' My life has been fulfilled, Tanis—much more than I could ever have imagined." Elistan glanced out the window, out to the spacious lawns, the flowering gardens, and—far in the distance—the dark Tower of High Sorcery.

"It was given me to bring hope back to the world, Half-Elven," Elistan said softly. "Hope and healing. What man can say more? I leave knowing that the church has been firmly established once again. There are clerics among all the races now. Yes, even kender." Elistan, smiling, ran a hand through his white hair. "Ah," he sighed, "what a trying time *that* was for our faith, Tanis! We are still unable to determine exactly what all is missing. But they are a good-hearted, good-souled people. Whenever I started to lose patience, I thought of Fizban— Paladine, as he revealed himself to us—and the special love he bore your little friend, Tasslehoff."

Tanis's face darkened at the mention of the kender's name, and it seemed to him that Dalamar looked up, briefly, from where he had been staring into the dancing flames. But Elistan did not notice.

"My only regret is that I leave no one truly capable of taking over after me." Elistan shook his head. "Garad is a good man. Too good. I see the makings of another Kingpriest in him. But he doesn't understand yet that the balance must be maintained, that we are all needed to make up this world. Is that not so, Dalamar?"

To Tanis's surprise, the dark elf nodded his head. He had cast his hood aside and had been able to drink some of the red wine the clerics brought to him. Color had returned to his face, and his hands trembled no longer. "You are wise, Elistan," the mage said softly. "I wish others were as enlightened."

"Perhaps it is not wisdom so much as the ability to see things from all sides, not just one." Elistan turned to Tanis. "You, Tanis, my friend. Did you not notice and appreciate the view as you came?" He gestured feebly to the window, through which the Tower of High Sorcery was plainly visible.

"I'm not certain I know what you mean," Tanis hedged, uncomfortable as always about sharing his feelings.

"Yes, you do, Half-Elven," Elistan said with a return of his old crispness. "You looked at the Tower and you looked at the Temple and you thought how right it was they should be so near. Oh, there were many who argued long against this site for the Temple. Garad and, of course, Lady Crysania—"

At the mention of that name, Dalamar choked, coughed, and set the wine glass down hurriedly. Tanis stood up, unconsciously beginning to pace the room—as was his custom—when, realizing that this might disturb the dying man, he sat back down again, shifting uncomfortably in his chair.

"Has there been word of her?" he asked in a low voice.

"I am sorry, Tanis," Elistan said gently, "I did not mean to distress you. Truly, you must stop blaming yourself. What she did, she chose to do of her own free will. Nor would I have had it otherwise. You could not have stopped her, nor saved her from her fate—whatever that may be. No, there has been no word of her."

"Yes, there has," Dalamar said in a cold, emotionless voice that drew the immediate attention of both men in the room. "That is one reason I called you together—"

———

"*You* called!" Tanis repeated, standing up again. "I thought Elistan asked us here. Is your *Shalafi* behind this? Is he responsible for this woman's disappearance?" He advanced a step, his face beneath his reddish beard flushed. Dalamar rose to his feet, his eyes glittering dangerously, his hand stealing almost imperceptibly to one of the pouches he wore upon his belt. "Because, by the gods, if he has harmed her, I'll twist his golden neck—"

"Astinus of Palanthas," announced a cleric from the doorway.

The historian stood within the doorway. His ageless face bore no expression as his gray-eyed gaze swept the room, taking in everything, everyone with a minute attention to the detail that his pen would soon record. It went from the flushed and angry face of Tanis, to the proud, defiant face of the elf, to the weary, patient face of the dying cleric.

"Let me guess," Astinus remarked, imperturbably entering and taking a seat. Setting a huge book down upon a table, he opened it to a blank page, drew a quill pen from a wooden case he carried with him, carefully examined the tip, then looked up. "Ink, friend," he said to a startled cleric, who—after a nod from Elistan—left the room hurriedly. Then the historian continued his original sentence. "Let me guess. You were discussing Raistlin Majere."

"It is true," Dalamar said. "I called you here."

The dark elf had resumed his seat by the fire. Tanis, still scowling, went back to his place near Elistan. The cleric, Garad, returning with Astinus's ink, asked if they wanted anything else. The reply being negative, he left, sternly adding, for the benefit of those in the room, that Elistan was unwell and should not be long disturbed.

"I called you here, together," Dalamar repeated, his gaze upon the fire. Then he raised his eyes, looking directly at Tanis. "You come at some small inconvenience. But *I* come, knowing that I will suffer the torment all of my faith feel trodding upon this holy ground. But it is imperative that I speak to you, all of you, together. I knew Elistan could not come to me. I knew Tanis Half-Elven *would* not come to me. And so I had no choice but to—"

"Proceed," Astinus said in his deep, cool voice. "The world passes as we sit here. You have called us here together. That is established. For what reason?"

Dalamar was silent for a moment, his gaze going back once again to the fire. When he spoke, he did not look up.

"Our worst fears are realized," he said softly. "He has been successful."

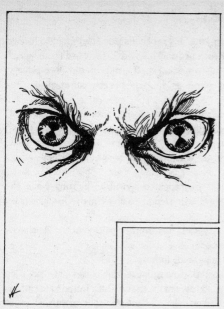

Come home . . . .

The voice lingered in his memory. Someone kneeling beside the pool of his mind, dropping words into the calm, clear surface. Ripples of consciousness disturbed him, woke him from his peaceful, restful sleep.

"Come home. . . . My son, come home."

Opening his eyes, Raistlin looked into the face of his mother.

Smiling, she reached out her hand and stroked back the wispy, white hair that fell down across his forehead. "My poor son," she murmured, her dark eyes soft with grief and pity and love. "What they did to you! I watched. I've watched for so long now. And I've wept. Yes, my son, even the dead weep. It is the only comfort we have. But all that is over now. You are with me. Here you can rest. . . ."

Raistlin struggled to sit up. Looking down at himself, he saw—to his horror—that he was covered with blood. Yet he felt no pain, there seemed to be no wound. He found it hard to take a breath, and he gasped for air.

———

"Here, let me help you," his mother said. She began to loosen the silken cord he wore around his waist, the cord from which hung his pouches, his precious spell components. Reflexively, Raistlin thrust her hand aside. His breath came easier. He looked around.

"What happened? Where am I?" He was vastly confused. Memories of his childhood came to him. Memories of *two* childhoods came to him! His . . . and someone else's! He looked at his mother, and she was someone he knew and she was a stranger.

"What happened?" he repeated irritably, beating back the surging memories that threatened to overthrow his grasp on sanity.

"You have died, my son," his mother said gently. "And now you are here with me."

"*Died!*" Raistlin repeated, aghast.

Frantically he sorted through the memories. He recalled being near death. . . . How was it that he had failed? He put his hand to his forehead and felt . . . flesh, bone, warmth . . . And then he remembered. . . .

The Portal!

"No," he cried angrily, glaring at his mother. "That's impossible."

"You lost control of the magic, my son," his mother said, reaching out her hand to touch Raistlin again. He drew away from her. With the slight, sad smile—a smile he remembered so well!—she let her hand drop back in her lap. "The field shifted, the forces tore you apart. There was a terrible explosion, it leveled the Plains of Dergoth. The magical fortress of Zhaman collapsed." His mother's voice shook. "The sight of your suffering was almost more than I could bear."

"I remember," Raistlin whispered, putting his hands to his head. "I remember the pain . . . but . . ."

He remembered something else, too—brilliant bursts of multicolored lights, he remembered a feeling of exultation and ecstasy welling up in his soul, he remembered the dragon's heads that guarded the Portal screaming in fury, he remembered wrapping his arms around Crysania.

Standing up, Raistlin looked around. He was on flat, level ground—a desert of some sort. In the distance he could see mountains. They looked familiar—of course! Thorbardin! The dwarven kingdom. He turned. There were the ruins of the fortress, looking like a skull devouring the land in its eternally grinning mouth. So, he was on the Plains of Dergoth. He recognized the landscape. But, even as he recognized it, it seemed strange to him. Everything was tinged with red, as though he were seeing all objects through blood-dimmed eyes. And, though objects looked the same as he remembered them, they were strange to him as well.

Skullcap he had seen during the War of the Lance. He didn't remember it grinning in that obscene way. The mountains, too, were sharp and clearly defined against the sky. The sky! Raistlin drew in a breath. It was empty! Swiftly he looked in all directions. No, there was no sun, yet it was not night. There were no moons, no stars; and it was such a strange color—a kind of muted pink, the reflection of a sunset.

He looked down at the woman kneeling on the ground before him.

Raistlin smiled, his thin lips pressed together grimly.

"No," he said, and this time his voice was firm and confident. "No, I did *not* die! I succeeded." He gestured. "This is proof of my success. I recognize this place. The kender described it to me. He said it was all places he had ever been. This is where I entered the Portal, and now I stand in the Abyss."

Leaning down, Raistlin grabbed the woman by the arm, dragging her to her feet. "Fiend, apparition! Where is Crysania? Tell me, whoever or whatever you are! Tell me, or by the gods I'll—"

"Raistlin! Stop, you're hurting me!"

Raistlin started, staring. It was Crysania who spoke, Crysania whose arm he held! Shaken, he loosed his grip but, within instants, he was master of himself again. She tried to pull free, but he held her firmly, drawing her near.

"Crysania?" he questioned, studying her intently.

She looked up at him, puzzled. "Yes," she faltered. "What's wrong, Raistlin? You've been talking so strangely."

The archmage tightened his grip. Crysania cried out. Yes, the pain in her eyes was real, so was the fear.

Smiling, sighing, Raistlin put his arms around her, pressing her close against his body. She was flesh, warmth, perfume, beating heart. . . .

"Oh, Raistlin!" She nestled close to him. "I was so frightened. This terrible place. I was all alone."

His hand tangled in her black hair. The softness and fragrance of her body intoxicated him, filling him with desire. She moved against him, tilting her head back. Her lips were soft, eager. She trembled in his arms. Raistlin looked down at her—

—and stared into eyes of flame.

So, you have come home at last, my mage!

Sultry laughter burned his mind, even as the lithe body in his arms writhed and twisted . . . he clasped one neck of a five-headed dragon . . . acid dripped from the gaping jaws above him . . . fire roared around him . . . sulphurous fumes choked him. The head snaked down. . . . .

Desperately, furiously, Raistlin called upon his magic. Yet, even as he formed the words of the defensive spell chant in his mind, he felt a twinge of doubt. Perhaps the magic won't work! I am weak, the journey through the Portal has drained my strength. Fear, sharp and slender as the blade of a dagger, pierced his soul. The words to the chant slipped from his mind. Panic flooded his body. The Queen! She is doing this! *Ast takar ist* . . . No! That isn't right! He heard laughter, victorious laughter. . . .

Bright white light blinded him. He was falling, falling, falling endlessly, spiraling down from darkness into day.

Opening his eyes, Raistlin looked into Crysania's face.

Her face, but it was not the face he remembered. It was aging, dying, even as he watched. In her hand, she held the platinum medallion of Paladine. Its pure white radiance shone brightly in the eerie pinkish light around them.

———

Raistlin closed his eyes to blot out the sight of the cleric's aging face, summoning back memories of how it looked in the past—delicate, beautiful, alive with love and passion. Her voice came to him, cool, firm.

"I very nearly lost you."

Reaching up, but without opening his eyes, he grabbed hold of the cleric's arms, clinging to her desperately. "What do I look like? Tell me! I've changed, haven't I?"

"You are as you were when I first met you in the Great Library," Crysania said, her voice still firm, too firm—tight, tense.

Yes, thought Raistlin, I am as I was. Which means I have returned to the present. He felt the old frailty, the old weakness, the burning pain in his chest, and with it the choking huskiness of the cough, as though cobwebs were being spun in his lungs. He had but to look, he knew, and he would see the gold-tinged skin, the white hair, the hourglass eyes. . . .

Shoving Crysania away, he rolled over onto his stomach, clenching his fists in fury, sobbing in anger and fear.

"Raistlin!" True terror was in Crysania's voice now. "What is it? Raistlin, where are we? What's wrong?"

"I succeeded," he snarled. Opening his eyes, he saw her face, withering in his sight. "I succeeded. We are in the Abyss."

Her eyes opened wide, her lips parted. Fear mingled with joy. Raistlin smiled bitterly. "And my magic is gone."

Startled, Crysania stared at him. "I don't understand—"

Twisting in agony, Raistlin screamed at her. "*My magic is gone!* I am weak, helpless, here—in her realm!" Suddenly, recollecting that *she* might be listening, watching, enjoying, Raistlin froze. His scream died in the blood-tinged froth upon his lips. He looked about, warily.

"But, no, you haven't defeated me!" he whispered. His hand closed over the Staff of Magius, lying at his side. Leaning upon it heavily, he struggled to his feet. Crysania gently put her strong arm around him, helping him stand.

"No," he murmured, staring into the vastness of the empty Plains, into the pink, empty sky, "I know where you are! I sense it! You are in Godshome. I know the lay of the land. I know how to move about, the kender gave me the key in his feverish ramblings. The land below mirrors the land above. I will seek you out, though the journey be long and treacherous.

"Yes"—he looked all around him—"I feel you probing my mind, reading my thoughts, anticipating all I say and do. You think it will be easy to defeat me! But I sense your confusion, too. There is one with me whose mind you cannot touch! She defends and protects me, do you not, Crysania?"

"Yes, Raistlin," Crysania replied softly, supporting the arch-mage.

Raistlin took a step, another, and another. He leaned upon Crysania, he leaned upon his staff. And still, each step was an effort, each breath he drew burned. When he looked about this world, all he saw was emptiness.

Inside him, all was emptiness. His magic was gone.

Raistlin stumbled. Crysania caught him and held onto him, clasping him close, tears running down her cheeks.

He could hear laughter. . . .

Maybe I should give up now! he thought in bitter despair. I am tired, so very tired. And without my magic, what am I?

Nothing. Nothing but a weak, wretched child. . . .

For long moments after Dalamar's pronouncement, there was silence in the room. Then the silence was broken by the scratching of a pen as Astinus recorded the dark elf's words in his great book.

"May Paladine have mercy," Elistan murmured. "Is she with him?"

"Of course," Dalamar snapped irritably, revealing a nervousness that all the skills of his Art could not hide. "How else do you think he succeeded? The Portal is locked to all except the combined forces of a Black-Robed wizard of such powers as his and a White-Robed cleric of such faith as hers."

Tanis glanced from one to the other, confused. "Look," he said angrily, "I don't understand. What's going on? Who are you talking about? Raistlin? What's he done? Does it have something to do with Crysania? And what about Caramon? He's vanished, too. Along with Tas! I—"

"Get a grip on the impatient human half of your nature, Half-Elven," Astinus remarked, still writing in firm, black strokes. "And you, Dark Elf, begin at the beginning instead of

———

III

in the middle."

"Or the end, as the case may be," Elistan remarked in a low voice.

Moistening his lips with the wine, Dalamar—his gaze still on the fire—related the strange tale that Tanis, up until now, had only known in part. Much the half-elf could have guessed, much astounded him, much filled him with horror.

"Lady Crysania was captivated by Raistlin. And, if the truth be told, he was attracted to her, I believe. Who can tell with him? Ice water is too hot to run in *his* veins. Who knows how long he has plotted this, dreamed of this? But, at last, he was ready. He planned a journey, back in time, to seek the one thing he lacked—the knowledge of the greatest wizard who has ever lived—Fistandantilus.

"He set a trap for Lady Crysania, planning to lure her back in time with him, as well as his twin brother—"

"Caramon?" asked Tanis in astonishment.

Dalamar ignored him. "But something unforeseen occurred. The *Shalafi's* half-sister, Kitiara, a Dragon Highlord. . . ."

Blood pounded in Tanis's head, dimming his vision and obscuring his hearing. He felt that same blood pulse in his face. He had the feeling his skin might be burning to the touch, so hot was it.

Kitiara!

She stood before him, dark eyes flashing, dark hair curling about her face, her lips slightly parted in that charming, crooked smile, the light gleaming off her armor. . . .

She looked down on him from the back of her blue dragon, surrounded by her minions, lordly and powerful, strong and ruthless. . . .

She lay in his arms, languishing, loving, laughing. . . .

Tanis sensed, though he could not see, Elistan's sympathetic but pitying gaze. He shrank from the stern, knowing look of Astinus. Wrapped up in his own guilt, his own shame, his own wretchedness, Tanis did not notice that Dalamar, too, was having trouble with *his* countenance which was pale, rather than flushed. He did not hear the dark elf's voice quiver when he spoke the woman's name.

After a struggle, Tanis regained control of himself and was able to continue listening. But he felt, once again, that old pain in his heart, the pain he had thought forever vanished. He was happy with Laurana. He loved her more deeply and tenderly than he had supposed it possible for a man to love a woman. He was at peace with himself. His life was rich, full. And now he was astonished to discover the darkness still inside of him, the darkness he thought he had banished forever.

"At Kitiara's command, the death knight, Lord Soth, cast a spell upon Lady Crysania, a spell that should have killed her. But Paladine interceded. He took her soul to dwell with him, leaving the shell of her body behind. I thought the *Shalafi* was defeated. But, no. He turned this betrayal of his sister's into an advantage. His twin brother, Caramon, and the kender, Tassle-hoff, took Lady Crysania to the Tower of High Sorcery in Way-reth, hoping that the mages would be able to cure her. They could not, of course, as Raistlin well knew. They could only send her back in time to the one period in the history of Krynn when there lived a Kingpriest powerful enough to call upon Paladine to restore the woman's soul to her body. And this, of course, was exactly what Raistlin wanted."

Dalamar's fist clenched. "I told the mages so! Fools! I told them they were playing right into his hands."

"*You* told them?" Tanis felt master of himself enough now to ask this question. "You betrayed him, your *Shalafi?*" He snorted in disbelief.

"It is a dangerous game I play, Half-Elven." Dalamar looked at him now, his eyes alight from within, like the burning embers of the fire. "I am a spy, sent by the Conclave of Mages to watch Raistlin's every move. Yes, you may well look aston-ished. They fear him—all of the Orders fear him, the White, the Red, the Black. Most especially the Black, for we know what our fate will be should he rise to power."

As Tanis stared, the dark elf lifted his hand and slowly parted the front closure of his black robes, laying bare his breast. Five oozing wounds marred the surface of the dark elf's smooth skin. "The mark of his hand," Dalamar said in an expressionless tone. "My reward for my treachery."

Tanis could see Raistlin laying those thin, golden fingers upon the young dark elf's chest, he could see Raistlin's face—without feeling, without malice, without cruelty, without any touch of humanity whatsoever—and he could see those fingers burn through the flesh of his victim. Shaking his head, feeling sickened, Tanis sank back in his chair, his gaze on the floor.

"But they would not listen to me," Dalamar continued. "They grasped at straws. As Raistlin had foreseen, their greatest hope lay in their greatest fear. They decided to send Lady Crysania back in time, ostensibly so that the Kingpriest could aid her. That is what they told Caramon, for they knew he would not go otherwise. But, in reality, they sent her back to die or to at least disappear as did all other clerics before the Cataclysm. And they hoped that Caramon, when he went back into time and learned the truth about his twin—learned that Raistlin was, in reality, Fistandantilus—that he would be forced to kill his brother."

"Caramon?" Tanis laughed bitterly, then scowled again in anger. "How could they do such a thing? The man is sick! The only thing Caramon can kill now is a bottle of dwarf spirits! Raistlin's already destroyed him. Why didn't they—"

Catching Astinus's irritated glance, Tanis subsided. His mind reeled in turmoil. None of this made sense! He looked over at Elistan. The cleric must have known much of this already. There was no look of shock or surprise on his face—even when he heard that the mages had sent Crysania back to die. There was only an expression of deep sorrow.

Dalamar was continuing. "But the kender, Tasslehoff Burrfoot, disrupted Par-Salian's spell and accidentally traveled back in time with Caramon. The introduction of a kender into the flow of time made it possible for time to be altered. What happened back there, in Istar, we can only surmise. What we do know is that Crysania did *not* die. Caramon did *not* kill his brother. And Raistlin was successful in obtaining the knowledge of Fistandantilus. Taking Crysania and Caramon with him, he moved forward in time to the one period when he would possess, in Crysania, the only true cleric in the land. He traveled to the one period in our history when the Queen of Darkness would be most vulnerable and unable to stop him.

"As Fistandantilus did before him, Raistlin fought the Dwarfgate War, and so obtained access to the Portal that stood, then, in the magical fortress of Zhaman. If history had repeated itself, Raistlin should have died at that Portal, for thus did Fistandantilus meet his doom."

"We counted on this," Elistan murmured, his hands plucking feebly at the bedclothes that covered him. "Par-Salian said that there was no way Raistlin could change history—"

"That wretched kender!" Dalamar snarled. "Par-Salian should have known, he should have realized the miserable creature would do exactly what he did—leap at a chance for some new adventure! He should have taken our advice and smothered the little bastard—"

"Tell me what's happened to Tasslehoff and Caramon," Tanis interrupted coldly. "I don't care what's become of Raistlin or— and I apologize, Elistan—Lady Crysania. She was blinded by her own goodness. I am sorry for her, but she refused to open her eyes and see the truth. I care about my friends. What has become of them?"

"We do not know," Dalamar said. He shrugged. "But if I were you, I would not look to see them again in this life, Half-Elven. . . . They would be of little use to the *Shalafi*."

"Then you have told me all I need to hear," Tanis said, rising, his voice taut with grief and fury. "If it's the last thing I do, I'll seek out Raistlin and I'll—"

"Sit down, Half-Elven," Dalamar said. He did not raise his voice, but there was a dangerous glint in his eyes that made Tanis's hand reach for the hilt of his sword, only to remember that—since he was visiting the Temple of Paladine—he had not worn it. More furious still, not trusting himself to speak, Tanis bowed to Elistan, then to Astinus, and started for the door.

"You *will* care what becomes of Raistlin, Tanis Half-Elven," Dalamar's smooth voice intercepted him, "because it affects you. It affects all of us. Do I speak truly, Revered Son?"

"He does, Tanis," Elistan said. "I understand your feelings, but you must put them aside!"

Astinus said nothing, the scratching of his pen was the only indication that the man was in the room. Tanis clenched his fists, then, with a vicious oath that caused even Astinus to glance up, the half-elf turned to Dalamar. "Very well, then. What could Raistlin possibly do that would further hurt and injure and destroy those around him?"

"I said when I began that our worst fears were realized," Dalamar replied, his slanted, elven eyes looking into the slightly slanted eyes of the half-elf.

"Yes," snapped Tanis impatiently, still standing.

Dalamar paused dramatically. Astinus, looking up again, raised his gray eyebrows in mild annoyance.

"Raistlin has entered the Abyss. He and Lady Crysania will challenge the Queen of Darkness."

Tanis stared at Dalamar in disbelief. Then he burst out laughing. "Well," he said, shrugging, "it seems I have little to worry about. The mage has sealed his own doom."

But Tanis's laughter fell flat. Dalamar regarded him with cool, cynical amusement, as if he might have expected this absurd response from a half-human. Astinus snorted and kept writing. Elistan's frail shoulders slumped. Closing his eyes, he leaned back against his pillows.

Tanis stared at all of them. "You can't consider this a serious threat!" he demanded. "By the gods, I have stood before the Queen of Darkness! I have felt her power and her majesty— and that was when she was only partially in this plane of existence." The half-elf shuddered involuntarily. "I can't imagine what it would be like to meet her on her own . . . her own . . ."

"You are not alone, Tanis," said Elistan wearily. "I, too, have conversed with the Dark Queen." He opened his eyes, smiling wanly. "Does that surprise you? I have had my trials and temptations as have all men."

"Once only has she come to me." Dalamar's face paled, and there was fear in his eyes. He licked his lips. "And that was to bring me these tidings."

Astinus said nothing, but he had ceased to write. Rock itself was more expressive than the historian's face.

Tanis shook his head in wonder. "You've met the Queen, Elistan? You acknowledge her power? Yet you still think that a frail and sickly wizard and an old-maid cleric can somehow do her harm?"

Elistan's eyes flashed, his lips tightened, and Tanis knew he had gone too far. Flushing, he scratched his beard and started to apologize, then stubbornly snapped his mouth shut. "It just doesn't make sense," he mumbled, walking back and throwing himself down in his chair.

"Well, how in the Abyss do we stop him?" Realizing what he'd said, Tanis's flush deepened. "I'm sorry," he muttered. "I don't mean to make this a joke. Everything I'm saying seems to be coming out wrong. But, damn it, I don't understand! Are we supposed to stop Raistlin or cheer him on?"

"You cannot stop him," Dalamar interposed coolly as Elistan seemed about to speak. "That we mages alone can do. Our plans for this have been underway for many weeks now, ever since we first learned of this threat. You see, Half-Elven, what you have said is—in part—correct. Raistlin knows, we all know, that he cannot defeat the Queen of Darkness on her own plane of existence. Therefore, it is his plan to draw her out, to bring her back through the Portal and into the world—"

Tanis felt as if he had been punched hard in the stomach. For a moment, he could not draw a breath. "That's madness," he managed to gasp finally, his hands curling over the armrests of his chair, his knuckles turning white with the strain. "We barely defeated her at Neraka as it was! He's going to bring her back into the world?"

"Unless he can be stopped," Dalamar continued, "which is my duty, as I have said."

"So what are *we* supposed to do?" Tanis demanded, leaning forward. "Why have you brought us here? Are we to sit around and watch? I—"

"Patience, Tanis!" Elistan interrupted. "You are nervous and

———

117

afraid. We all share these feelings."

With the exception of that granite-hearted historian over there, Tanis thought bitterly—

"But nothing will be gained by rash acts or wild words." Elistan looked over at the dark elf and his voice grew softer. "I believe that we have not yet heard the worst, is that true, Dalamar?"

"Yes, Revered Son," Dalamar said, and Tanis was surprised to see a trace of emotion flicker in the elf's slanted eyes. "I have received word that Dragon Highlord Kitiara"—the elf choked slightly, cleared his throat, and continued speaking more firmly—"Kitiara is planning a full-scale assault on Palanthas."

Tanis sank back in his chair. His first thought was one of bitter, cynical amusement—I told you so, Lord Amothus. I told you so, Porthios. I told you, all of you who want to crawl back into your nice, warm little nests and pretend the war never happened. His second thoughts were more sobering. Memories returned—the city of Tarsis in flames, the dragonarmies taking over Solace, the pain, the suffering . . . death.

Elistan was saying something, but Tanis couldn't hear. He leaned back, closing his eyes, trying to think. He remembered Dalamar talking about Kitiara, but what was it he had said? It drifted on the fringes of his consciousness. He had been thinking about Kit. He hadn't been paying attention. The words were vague. . . .

"Wait!" Tanis sat up, suddenly remembering. "You said Kitiara was furious with Raistlin. You said she was just as frightened of the Queen reentering the world as we are. That was why she ordered Soth to kill Crysania. If that's true, *why* is she attacking Palanthas? That doesn't make sense! She grows in strength daily in Sanction. The evil dragons have congregated there and we have reports that the draconians who were scattered after the war have also been regrouping under her command. But Sanction is a long way from Palanthas. The lands of the Knights of Solamnia lie in between. The good dragons will rise up and fight if the evil ones take to the skies again. Why? Why would she risk all she has gained? And for what—"

"You know Lord Kitiara I believe, Half-Elven?" Dalamar interrupted.

Tanis choked, coughed, and muttered something.

"I beg your pardon?"

"Yes, damn it, I know her!" Tanis snapped, caught Elistan's glance, and sank back into his chair once again, feeling his skin burn.

"You are right," Dalamar said smoothly, a glint of amusement in his light, elven eyes. "When Kitiara first heard about Raistlin's plan, she was frightened. Not for him, of course, but for fear that he would bring the wrath of the Dark Queen down upon her. But"—Dalamar shrugged—"this was when Kitiara believed Raistlin must lose. Now, it seems, she thinks he has a chance to win. And Kit will always try to be on the winning side. She plans to conquer Palanthas and be prepared to greet the wizard as he passes through the Portal. Kit will offer the might of her armies to her brother. If he is strong enough—and by this time, he should be—he can easily convert the evil creatures from their allegiance to the Dark Queen to serving *his* cause."

"Kit?" It was Tanis's turn to look amused. Dalamar sneered slightly.

"Oh, yes, Half-Elven. I know Kitiara every bit as well as you do."

But the sarcastic tone in the dark elf's voice faltered, twisting unconsciously to one of bitterness. His slender hands clenched. Tanis nodded in sudden understanding, feeling, oddly enough, a strange kind of sympathy for the young elf.

"So she has betrayed you, too," Tanis murmured softly. "She pledged you her support. She said she would be there, stand beside you. When Raistlin returned, she would fight at your side."

Dalamar rose to his feet, his black robes rustling around him. "I never trusted her," he said coldly, but he turned his back upon them and stared intently into the flames, keeping his face averted. "I knew what treachery she was capable of committing, none better. This came as no surprise."

But Tanis saw the hand that gripped the mantelpiece turn white.

"Who told you this?" Astinus asked abruptly. Tanis started. He had almost forgotten the historian's presence. "Surely not the Dark Queen. She would not care about this."

"No, no." Dalamar appeared confused for a moment. His thoughts had obviously been far away. Sighing, he looked up at them once more. "Lord Soth, the death knight, told me."

"Soth?" Tanis felt himself losing his grip on reality.

Frantically his brain scrambled for a handhold. Mages spying on mages. Clerics of light aligned with wizards of darkness. Dark trusting light, turning against darkness. Light turning to the dark. . . .

"Soth has pledged allegiance to Kitiara!" Tanis said in confusion. "Why would he betray her?"

Turning from the fire, Dalamar looked into Tanis's eyes. For the span of a heartbeat, there was a bond between the two, a bond forged by a shared understanding, a shared misery, a shared torment, a shared passion. And, suddenly, Tanis understood, and his soul shriveled in horror.

"He wants her dead," Dalamar replied.

CHAPTER
4

The young boy walked down the streets of Solace. He was not a comely boy, and he knew it—as he knew so much about himself that is not often given children to know. But then, he spent a great deal of time with himself, precisely because he was not comely and because he knew too much.

He was not walking alone today, however. His twin brother, Caramon, was with him. Raistlin scowled, scuffing through the dust of the village street, watching it rise in clouds about him. He may not have been walking alone, but in a way he was more alone with Caramon than without him. Everyone called out greetings to his likeable, handsome twin. No one said a word to him. Everyone yelled for Caramon to come join their games. No one invited Raistlin. Girls looked at Caramon out of the corners of their eyes in that special way girls had. Girls never even noticed Raistlin.

"Hey, Caramon, wanna play King of the Castle?" a voice yelled.

"You want to, Raist?" Caramon asked, his face lighting up

---

eagerly. Strong and athletic, Caramon enjoyed the rough, strenuous game. But Raistlin knew that if he played he would soon start to feel weak and dizzy. He knew, too, that the other boys would argue about whose team *had* to take him.

"No. You go ahead, though."

Caramon's face fell. Then, shrugging, he said, "Oh, that's all right, Raist. I'd rather stay with you."

Raistlin felt his throat tighten, his stomach clenched. "No, Caramon," he repeated softly, "it's all right. Go ahead and play."

"You don't look like you're feeling good, Raist," Caramon said. "It's no big deal. Really. C'mon, show me that new magic trick you learned—the one with the coins—"

"Don't treat me like this!" Raistlin heard himself screaming. "I don't need you! I don't want you around! Go ahead! Go play with those fools! You're all a pack of fools together! I don't need any of you!"

Caramon's face crumbled. Raistlin had the feeling he'd just kicked a dog. The feeling only made him angrier. He turned away.

"Sure, Raist, if that's what you want," Caramon mumbled.

Glancing over his shoulder, Raistlin saw his twin run off after the others. With a sigh, trying to ignore the shouts of laughter and greeting, Raistlin sat down in a shady place and, drawing one of his spellbooks from his pack, began to study. Soon, the lure of the magic drew him away from the dirt and the laughter and the hurt eyes of his twin. It led him into an enchanted land where *he* commanded the elements, *he* controlled reality. . . .

The spellbook tumbled from his hands, landing in the dust at his feet. Raistlin looked up, startled. Two boys stood above him. One held a stick in his hand. He poked the book with it, then, lifting the stick, he poked Raistlin, hard, in the chest.

You are bugs, Raistlin told the boys silently. Insects. You mean nothing to me. Less than nothing. Ignoring the pain in his chest, ignoring the insect life standing before him, Raistlin reached out his hand for his book. The boy stepped on his fingers.

Frightened, but now more angry than afraid, Raistlin rose to his feet. His hands were his livelihood. With them, he manipulated the fragile spell components, with them he traced the delicate arcane symbols of his Art in the air.

"Leave me alone," he said coldly, and such was the way he spoke and the look in his eye that, for an instant, the two boys were taken aback. But now a crowd had gathered. The other boys left their game, coming to watch the fun. Aware that others were watching, the boy with the stick refused to let this skinny, whining, sniveling bookworm have the better of him.

"What're ya going to do?" the boy sneered. "Turn me into a frog?"

There was laughter. The words to a spell formed in Raistlin's mind. It was not a spell he was supposed to have learned yet, it was an offensive spell, a hurting spell, a spell to use when true danger threatened. His Master would be furious. Raistlin smiled a thin-lipped smile. At the sight of that smile and the look in Raistlin's eyes, one of the boys edged backward.

"Let's go," he muttered to his companion.

But the other boy stood his ground. Behind him, Raistlin could see his twin standing among the crowd, a look of anger on his face.

Raistlin began to speak the words—

—and then he froze. No! Something was wrong! He had forgotten! His magic wouldn't work! Not here! The words came out as gibberish, they made no sense. Nothing happened! The boys laughed. The boy with the stick raised it and shoved it into Raistlin's stomach, knocking him to the ground, driving the breath from his body.

He was on his hand and knees, gasping for air. Somebody kicked him. He felt the stick break over his back. Somebody else kicked him. He was rolling on the ground now, choking in the dust, his thin arms trying desperately to cover his head. Kicks and blows rained in on him.

"Caramon!" he cried. "Caramon, help me!"

But there was only a deep, stern voice in answer. "You don't need me, remember."

A rock struck him in the head, hurting him terribly. And he knew, although he couldn't see, that it was Caramon who had thrown it. He was losing consciousness. Hands were dragging him along the dusty road, they were hauling him to a pit of vast darkness and cold, icy cold. They would hurl him down there and he would fall, endlessly, through the darkness and the cold and he would never, never hit the bottom, for there was no bottom. . . .

Crysania stared around. Where was she? Where was Raistlin? He had been with her only moments before, leaning weakly on her arm. And then, suddenly, he had vanished and she had found herself alone, walking in a strange village.

Or was it strange? She seemed to recall having been here once, or at least someplace like this. Tall vallenwoods surrounded her. The houses of the town were built in the trees. There was an inn in a tree. She saw a signpost.

Solace.

How strange, she marveled, looking around. It was Solace, all right. She had been here recently, with Tanis Half-Elven, looking for Caramon. But *this* Solace was different. Everything seemed tinged with red and just a tiny bit distorted. She kept wanting to rub her eyes to clear them.

"Raistlin!" she called.

There was no answer. The people passing by acted as if they neither heard her nor saw her. "Raistlin!" she cried, starting to panic. What had happened to him? Where had he gone? Had the Dark Queen—

She heard a commotion, children shouting and yelling and, above the noise, a thin, high-pitched scream for help.

Turning, Crysania saw a crowd of children gathered around a form huddled on the ground. She saw fists flailing and feet kicking, she saw a stick raised and then brought down, hard. Again, that high-pitched scream. Crysania glanced at the people around her, but they seemed unaware of anything unusual occurring.

Gathering her white robes in her hand, Crysania ran toward

the children. She saw, as she drew nearer, that the figure in the center of the circle was a child! A young boy! They were killing him, she realized in sudden horror! Reaching the crowd, she grabbed hold of one of the children to pull him away. At the touch of her hand, the child whirled to face her. Crysania fell back, alarmed.

The child's face was white, cadaverous, skull-like. Its skin stretched taut over the bones, its lips were tinged with violet. It bared its teeth at her, and the teeth were black and rotting. The child lashed out at her with its hand. Long nails ripped her skin, sending a stinging, paralyzing pain through her. Gasping, she let go, and the child—with a grin of perverted pleasure on its face—turned back to torment the boy on the ground.

Staring at the bleeding marks upon her arm, dizzy and weak from the pain, Crysania heard the boy cry out again.

"Paladine, help me," she prayed. "Give me strength."

Resolutely, she grabbed hold of one of the demon children and hurled it aside, and then she grabbed another. Managing to reach the boy upon the ground, she shielded his bleeding, unconscious body with her own, trying desperately all the while to drive the children away.

Again and again, she felt the long nails tear her skin, the poison course through her body. But soon she noticed that, once they touched her, the children drew back, in pain themselves. Finally, sullen expressions on their nightmarish faces, they withdrew, leaving her—bleeding and sick—alone with their victim.

Gently, she turned the bruised body of the young boy over. Smoothing back the brown hair, she looked at his face. Her hands began to shake. There was no mistaking that delicate facial structure, the fragile bones, the jutting chin.

"Raistlin!" she whispered, holding his small hand in her own.

The boy opened his eyes. . . .

The man, dressed in black robes, sat up.

Crysania stared at him as he looked grimly around.

"What is happening?" she asked, shivering, feeling the effects of the poison spreading through her body.

———

Raistlin nodded to himself. "This is how she torments me," he said softly. "This is how she fights me, striking at me where she knows I am weakest." The golden, hourglass eyes turned to Crysania, the thin lips smiled. "You fought for me. You defeated her." He drew her near, enfolding her in his black robes, holding her close. "There, rest a while. The pain will pass, and then we will travel on."

Still shivering, Crysania laid her head on the archmage's breast, hearing his breath wheeze and rattle in his lungs, smelling that sweet, faint fragrance of rose petals and death. . . .

CHAPTER
5

And so this is what comes of his courageous words and promises," said Kitiara in a low voice.

"Did you really expect otherwise?" asked Lord Soth. The words, accompanied with a shrug of the ancient armor, sounded nonchalant, almost rhetorical. But there was an edge to them that made Kitiara glance sharply at the death knight.

Seeing him staring at her, his orange eyes burning with a strange intensity, Kitiara flushed. Realization that she was revealing more emotion than she intended made her angry, her flush deepened. She turned from Soth abruptly.

Walking across the room, which was furnished with an odd mixture of armor, weaponry, perfumed silken sheets, and thick fur rugs, Kitiara clasped the folds of her filmy nightdress together across her breasts with a shaking hand. It was a gesture that accomplished little in the way of modesty, and Kitiara knew it, even as she wondered why she made it. Certainly she had never been concerned with modesty before, especially around a creature who had fallen into a heap of ash three hundred years ago. But she suddenly felt uncomfortable under the gaze of those blazing eyes, staring at her from a nonexistent face. She felt naked and exposed.

"No, of course not," Kitiara replied coldly.

"He is, after all, a dark elf," Soth went on in the same even, almost bored tones. "And he makes no secret of the fact that he fears your brother more than death itself. So is it any wonder that he chooses now to fight on Raistlin's side rather than the side of a bunch of feeble old wizards who are quaking in their boots?"

"But he stood to gain so much!" Kitiara argued, trying her best to match her tone to Soth's. Shivering, she picked up a fur nightrobe that lay across the end of her bed and flung it around her shoulders. "They promised him the leadership of the Black Robes. He was certain to take Par-Salian's place after that as Head of the Conclave—undisputed master of magic on Krynn."

And you would have known other rewards, as well, Dark Elf, Kitiara added silently, pouring herself a glass of red wine. Once that insane brother of mine is defeated, no one will be able to stop you. What of *our* plans? You ruling with the staff, I with the sword. We could have brought the Knights to their knees! Driven the elves from their homeland—your homeland! You would have gone back in triumph, my darling, and I would have been at your side!

The wine glass slipped from her hand. She tried to catch it— Her grasp was too hasty, her grip too strong. The fragile glass shattered in her hand, cutting into her flesh. Blood mingled with the wine that dripped onto the carpet.

Battle scars traced over Kitiara's body like the hands of her lovers. She had borne her wounds without flinching, most without a murmur. But now her eyes flooded with tears. The pain seemed unbearable.

A wash bowl stood near. Kitiara plunged her hand into the cold water, biting her lip to keep from crying out. The water turned red instantly.

"Fetch one of the clerics!" she snarled at Lord Soth, who had remained standing, staring at her with his flickering eyes.

Walking to the door, the death knight called a servant who left immediately. Cursing beneath her breath, blinking back her tears, Kitiara grabbed a towel and wound it around her hand. By the time the cleric arrived, stumbling over his black robes in his haste, the towel was soaked through with blood, and Kitiara's face was ashen beneath her tanned skin.

The medallion of the Five-Headed Dragon brushed against Kit's hand as the cleric bent over it, muttering prayers to the Queen of Darkness. Soon the wounded flesh closed, the bleeding stopped.

"The cuts were not deep. There should be no lasting harm," the cleric said soothingly.

"A good thing for you!" Kitiara snapped, still fighting the unreasonable faintness that assailed her. "That is my sword hand!"

"You will wield a blade with your accustomed ease and skill, I assure your lordship," the cleric replied. "Will there be—"

"No! Get out!"

"My lord." The cleric bowed—"Sir Knight"—and left the room.

Unwilling to meet the gaze of Soth's flaming eyes, Kitiara kept her head turned away from the death knight, scowling at the vanishing, fluttering robes of the cleric.

"What fools! I detest keeping them around. Still, I suppose they come in handy now and then." Though it seemed perfectly healed, her hand still hurt. All in my mind, she told herself bitterly. "Well, what do you propose I do about . . . about the dark elf?" Before Soth could answer, however, Kitiara was on her feet, yelling for the servant.

"Clean that mess up. And bring me another glass." She struck the cowering man across the face. "One of the golden goblets this time. You know I detest these fragile elf-made things! Get them out of my sight! Throw them away!"

"Throw them away!" The servant ventured a protest. "But they are valuable, Lord. They came from the Tower of High Sorcery in Palanthas, a gift from—"

"I said get rid of them!" Grabbing them up, Kitiara flung

them, one by one, against the wall of her room. The servant cringed, ducking as the glass flew over his head, smashing against the stone. When the last one left her fingers, she sat down into a chair in a corner and stared straight ahead, neither moving nor speaking.

The servant hastily swept up the broken glass, emptied the bloody water in the wash bowl, and departed. When he returned with the wine, Kitiara had still not moved. Neither had Lord Soth. The death knight remained standing in the center of the room, his eyes glowing in the gathering gloom of night.

"Shall I light the candles, Lord?" the servant asked softly, setting down the wine bottle and a golden goblet.

"Get out," Kitiara said, through stiff lips.

The servant bowed and left, closing the door behind him.

Moving with unheard steps, the death knight walked across the room. Coming to stand next to the still unmoving, seemingly unseeing Kitiara, he laid his hand upon her shoulder. She flinched at the touch of the invisible fingers, their cold piercing her heart. But she did not withdraw.

"Well," she said again, staring into the room whose only source of light now came from the flaming eyes of the death knight, "I asked you a question. What do we do to stop Dalamar and my brother in this madness? What do we do before the Dark Queen destroys us all?"

"You must attack Palanthas," said Lord Soth.

"I believe it can be done!" Kitiara murmured, thoughtfully tapping the hilt of her dagger against her thigh.

"Truly ingenious, my lord," said the commander of her forces with undisguised and unfeigned admiration in his voice.

The commander—a human near forty years of age—had scratched and clawed and murdered his way up through the ranks to attain his current position, General of the Dragonarmies. Stooped and ill-favored, disfigured by a scar that slashed across his face, the commander had never tasted the favors enjoyed in the past by so many of Kitiara's other captains. But he was not without hope. Glancing over at her, he saw her face—unusually cold and stern these past few days—brighten with pleasure at his praise. She even deigned to smile at him— that crooked smile she knew how to use so well. The commander's heart beat faster.

"It is good to see you have not lost your touch," said Lord Soth, his hollow voice echoing through the map room.

The commander shuddered. He should be used to the death knight by now. The Dark Queen knew, he'd fought enough battles with him and his troop of skeletal warriors. But the chill of the grave surrounded the knight as his black cloak shrouded his charred and blood-stained armor.

How does she stand him? the commander wondered. They say he even haunts her bedchambers! The thought made the commander's heartbeat rapidly return to normal. Perhaps, after all, the slave women weren't so bad. At least when one was alone with them in the dark, one was *alone* in the dark!

"Of course, I have not lost my touch!" Kitiara returned with such fierce anger that the commander looked about uneasily, hurriedly manufacturing some excuse to leave. Fortunately, with the entire city of Sanction preparing for war, excuses were not hard to find.

"If you have no further need of me, my lord," the commander said, bowing, "I must check on the work of the armory. There is much to be done, and not much time in which to do it."

"Yes, go ahead," Kitiara muttered absently, her eyes on the huge map that was inlaid in tile upon the floor beneath her feet. Turning, the commander started to leave, his broadsword clanking against his armor. At the door, however, his lord's voice stopped him.

"Commander?"

He turned. "My lord?"

Kitiara started to say something, stopped, bit her lip, then continued, "I—I was wondering if you would join me for dinner this evening." She shrugged. "But, it is late to be asking. I presume you have made plans."

The commander hesitated, confused. His palms began to

sweat. "As a matter of fact, lord, I *do* have a prior commitment, but that could easily be changed—"

"No," Kitiara said, a look of relief crossing her face. "No, that won't be necessary. Some other night. You are dismissed."

The commander, still puzzled, turned slowly and started once again to leave the room. As he did so, he caught a glimpse of the orange, burning eyes of the death knight, staring straight through him.

Now he would have to come up with a dinner engagement, he thought as he hurried down the hall. Easy enough. And he would send for one of the slave girls tonight—his favorite. . . .

"You should relax. Treat yourself to an evening of pleasure," Lord Soth said as the commander's footsteps faded away down the corridor of Kitiara's military headquarters.

"There is much to be done, and little time to do it," Kitiara replied, pretending to be totally absorbed in the map beneath her feet. She stood upon the place marked "Sanction," looking into the far northwestern corner of the room where Palanthas nestled in the cleft of its protective mountains.

Following her gaze, Soth slowly paced the distance, coming to a halt at the only pass through the rugged mountains, a place marked "High Clerist's Tower."

"The Knights will try to stop you here, of course," Soth said. "Where they stopped you during the last war."

Kitiara grinned, shook out her curly hair, and walked toward Soth. The lithe swagger was back in her step. "Now, won't that be a sight? All the pretty Knights, lined up in a row." Suddenly, feeling better than she had in months, Kitiara began to laugh. "You know, the looks on their faces when they see what we have in store for them will be almost worth waging the entire campaign."

Standing on the High Clerist's Tower, she ground it beneath her heel, then took a few quick steps to stand next to Palanthas.

"At last," she murmured, "the fine, fancy lady will feel the sword of war slit open her soft, ripe flesh." Smiling, she turned back to face Lord Soth. "I think I will have the commander to dinner tonight after all. Send for him." Soth bowed his acquiescence, the orange eyes flaming with amusement. "We have many military matters to discuss." Kitiara laughed again, starting to unbuckle the straps of her armor. "Matters of unguarded flanks, breaching walls, thrust, and penetration. . . ."

"Now, calm down, Tanis," said Lord Gunthar good-naturedly. "You are overwrought."

Tanis Half-Elven muttered something.

"What was that?" Gunthar turned around, holding in his hand a mug of his finest ale (drawn from the barrel in the dark corner by the cellar stairs). He handed the ale to Tanis.

"I said you're damn right I'm overwrought!" the half-elf snapped, which wasn't what he had said at all, but was certainly more appropriate when talking to the head of the Knights of Solamnia than what he had actually spoken.

Lord Gunthar uth Wistan stroked his long moustaches—the ages-old symbol of the Knights and one that was currently much in fashion—hiding his smile. He had heard, of course, what Tanis originally said. Gunthar shook his head. Why hadn't this matter been brought straight to the military? Now, as well as preparing for this minor flare-up of undoubtedly frustrated enemy forces, he had also to deal with black-robed wizards' apprentices, white-robed clerics, nervous heroes, and a librarian! Gunthar sighed and tugged at his moustaches gloomily. All he needed now was a kender. . . .

"Tanis, my friend, sit down. Warm yourself by the fire. You've had a long journey, and it's cold for late spring. The sailors say something about prevailing winds or some such nonsense. I trust your trip was a good one? I don't mind telling you, I prefer griffons to dragons—"

"Lord Gunthar," Tanis said tensely, remaining standing, "I did not fly all the way to Sancrist to discuss the prevailing winds nor the merits of griffons over dragons! We are in danger! Not only Palanthas, but the world! If Raistlin succeeds—" Tanis's fist clenched. Words failed him.

Filling his own mug from the pitcher that Wills, his old retainer, had brought up from the cellar, Gunthar walked over

———

to stand beside the half-elf. Putting his hand on Tanis's shoulder, he turned the man to face him.

"Sturm Brightblade spoke highly of you, Tanis. You and Laurana were the closest friends he had."

Tanis bowed his head at these words. Even now, more than two years since Sturm's death, he could not think of the loss of his friend without sorrow.

"I would have esteemed you on that recommendation alone, for I loved and respected Sturm like one of my own sons," Lord Gunthar continued earnestly. "But I have come to admire and like you myself, Tanis. Your bravery in battle was unquestioned, your honor, your nobility worthy of a Knight." Tanis shook his head irritably at this talk of honor and nobility, but Gunthar did not notice. "Those honors accorded you at the end of the war you more than merited. Your work since the war's end has been outstanding. You and Laurana have brought together nations that have been separated for centuries. Porthios has signed the treaty and, once the dwarves of Thorbardin have chosen a new king, they will sign as well."

"Thank you, Lord Gunthar," Tanis said, holding his mug of untouched ale in his hand and staring fixedly into the fire. "Thank you for your praise. I wish I felt I had earned it. Now, if you'll tell me where this trail of sugar is leading—"

"I see you are far more human than you are elven," Gunthar said, with a slight smile. "Very well, Tanis. I will skip the elven amenities and get right to the point. I think your past experiences have made you jumpy—you and Elistan both. Let's be honest, my friend. You are not a warrior. You were never trained as such. You stumbled into this last war by accident. Now, come with me. I want to show you something. Come, come . . ."

Tanis set his full mug down upon the mantelpiece and allowed himself to be led by Gunthar's strong hand. They walked across the room that was filled with the solid, plain, but comfortable furniture preferred by the Knights. This was Gunthar's war room, shields and swords were mounted on the walls, along with the banners of the three Orders of Knights—

the Rose, the Sword, and the Crown. Trophies of battles fought through the years gleamed from the cases where they were carefully preserved. In an honored place, spanning the entire length of the wall, was a dragonlance—the first one Theros Ironfeld had forged. Ranged around it were various goblin swords, a wicked saw-toothed blade of a draconian, a huge, double-bladed ogre sword, and a broken sword that had belonged to the ill-fated Knight, Derek Crownguard.

It was an impressive array, testifying to a lifetime of honored service in the Knights. Gunthar walked past it without a glance, however, heading for a corner of the room where a large table stood. Rolled-up maps were stuffed neatly into small compartments beneath the table, each compartment carefully labeled. After studying them for a moment, Gunthar reached down, pulled out a map, and spread it out upon the table's surface. He motioned Tanis nearer. The half-elf came closer, scratching his beard, and trying to look interested.

Gunthar rubbed his hands with satisfaction. He was in his element now. "It's a matter of logistics, Tanis. Pure and simple. Look, here are the Dragon Highlord's armies, bottled up in Sanction. Now I admit the Highlord is strong, she has a vast number of draconians, goblins, and humans who would like nothing better than to see the war start up again. And I also admit that our spies have reported increased activity in Sanction. The Highlord is up to something. But attacking Palanthas! Name of the Abyss, Tanis, look at the amount of territory she'd have to cover! And most of it controlled by the Knights! And even if she had the manpower to fight her way through, look how long she'd have to extend her supply lines! It would take her entire army just to guard her lines. We could cut them easily, any number of places."

Gunthar pulled on his moustaches again. "Tanis, if there was one Highlord in that army I came to respect, it was Kitiara. She is ruthless and ambitious, but she is also intelligent, and she is certainly not given to taking unnecessary risks. She has waited two years, building up her armies, fortifying herself in a place she knows we dare not attack. She has gained too much to throw it away on a wild scheme like this."

"Suppose this isn't her plan," Tanis muttered.

"What other plan could she possibly have?" Gunthar asked patiently.

"I don't know," Tanis snapped. "You say you respect her, but do you respect her enough? Do you fear her enough? I know her, and I have a feeling that she has something in mind. . . ." His voice trailed off, he scowled down at the map.

Gunthar kept quiet. He'd heard strange rumors about Tanis Half-Elven and this Kitiara. He didn't believe them, of course, but felt it better not to pursue the subject of the depth of the half-elf's knowledge of this woman further.

"You don't believe this, do you?" Tanis asked abruptly. "Any of it?"

Shifting uncomfortably, Gunthar smoothed both his long, gray moustaches and, bending down, began to roll up the map, using extreme care. "Tanis, my son, you know I respect you—"

"We've been through that."

Gunthar ignored the interruption. "And you know that there is no one in this world I hold in deeper reverence than Elistan. But when you two bring me a tale told to you by one of the Black Robes—and a dark elf at that—a tale about this wizard, Raistlin, entering the Abyss and challenging the Queen of Darkness! Well, I'm sorry, Tanis. I am not a young man anymore by any means. I've seen many strange things in my life. But this sounds like a child's bedtime story!"

"So they said of dragons," Tanis murmured, his face flushing beneath his beard. He stood, head bowed, for a moment, then, scratching his beard, he looked at Gunthar intently. "My lord, I watched Raistlin grow up. I have traveled with him, seen him, fought both with him and against him. I *know* what this man is capable of!" Tanis grasped Gunthar's arm with his hand. "If you will not accept my counsel, then accept Elistan's! We need you, Lord Gunthar! We need you, we need the Knights. You must reinforce the High Clerist's Tower. We have little time. Dalamar tells us that time has no meaning on the planes of the Dark Queen's existence. Raistlin might fight her for months or even years there, but that would seem only days to us. Dalamar believes his master's return is imminent. I believe him, and so does Elistan. Why do we believe him, Lord Gunthar? Because Dalamar is frightened. He is afraid—and so are we.

"Your spies say there is unusual activity in Sanction. Surely, that is evidence enough! Believe me, Lord Gunthar, Kitiara will come to her brother's aid. She knows he will set her up as ruler of the world if he succeeds. And she is gambler enough to risk everything for that chance! Please, Lord Gunthar, if you won't listen to me, at least come to Palanthas! Talk to Elistan!"

Lord Gunthar studied the man before him carefully. The leader of the Knights had risen to his position because he was, basically, a just and honest man. He was also a keen judge of character. He had liked and admired the half-elf since meeting him after the end of the war. But he had never been able to get close to him. There was something about Tanis, a reserved, withdrawn air that permitted few to cross the invisible barriers he set up.

Looking at him now, Gunthar felt suddenly closer than he had ever come before. He saw wisdom in the slightly slanted eyes, wisdom that had not come easily, wisdom that came through inner pain and suffering. He saw fear, the fear of one whose courage is so much a part of him that he readily admits he is afraid. He saw in him a leader of men. Not one who merely waves a sword and leads a charge in battle, but a leader who leads quietly, by drawing the best out of people, by helping them achieve things they never knew were in them.

And, at last, Gunthar understood something he had never been able to fathom. He knew now why Sturm Brightblade, whose lineage went back unsullied through generations, had chosen to follow this bastard half-elf, who—if rumors were true—was the product of a brutal rape. He knew now why Laurana, an elven princess and one of the strongest, most beautiful women he had ever known, had risked everything—even her life—for love of this man.

"Very well, Tanis." Lord Gunthar's stern face relaxed, the cool, polite tones of his voice grew warmer. "I will return to

Palanthas with you. I will mobilize the Knights and set up our defenses at the High Clerist's Tower. As I said, our spies did inform us that there is unusual activity going on in Sanction. It won't hurt the Knights to turn out. Been a long time since we've had field drill."

Decision made, Lord Gunthar immediately proceeded to turn the household upside down, shouting for Wills, his retainer, shouting for his armor to be brought, his sword sharpened, his griffon readied. Soon servants were flying here and there, his lady-wife came in, looking resigned, and insisted that he pack his heavy, fur-lined cloak even though it *was* near Spring Dawning celebration.

Forgotten in the confusion, Tanis walked back to the fireplace, picked up his mug of ale, and sat down to enjoy it. But, after all, he did not taste it. Staring into the flames, he saw, once again, a charming, crooked smile, dark curly hair. . . .

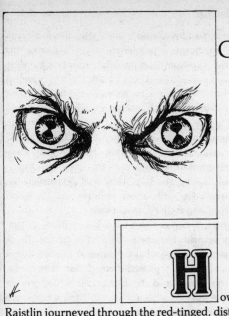

How long she and Raistlin journeyed through the red-tinged, distorted land of the Abyss, Crysania had no idea. Time ceased to have any meaning or relevance. Sometimes it seemed they had been here only a few seconds, sometimes she knew she had been walking the strange, shifting terrain for weary years. She had healed herself of the poison, but she felt weak, drained. The scratches on her arms would not close. She wrapped fresh bandages about them each day. By night, they were soaked through with blood.

She was hungry, but it was not a hunger that required food to sustain life so much as a hunger to taste a strawberry, or a mouthful of warm, fresh-baked bread, or a sprig of mint. She did not feel thirst either, and yet she dreamed of clear running water and bubbling wine and the sharp, pungent aroma of tarbean tea. In this land, all the water was tinged reddish brown and smelled of blood.

Yet, they made progress. At least so Raistlin said. He seemed to gain in strength as Crysania grew weaker. Now it was he who helped her walk sometimes. It was he who pushed them onward without rest, passing through town after town, always nearing, he said, Godshome. The mirror-image villages of this land below blurred together in Crysania's mind—Que-shu, Xak Tsaroth. They crossed the Abyss's New Sea—a dreadful journey. Looking into the water, Crysania saw the horror-filled faces of all who had died in the Cataclysm staring up at her.

They landed at a place Raistlin said was Sanction. Crysania felt her weakest here, for Raistlin told her it was the center of worship for the Dark Queen's followers. Her Temples were built far below the mountains known as the Lords of Doom. Here, Raistlin said, during the War, they had performed the evil rites that turned the unhatched children of the good dragons into the foul and twisted draconians.

Nothing further happened to them for a long while—or perhaps it was only a second. No one looked twice at Raistlin in his black robes and no one looked at Crysania at all. She might well have been invisible. They passed through Sanction easily, Raistlin growing in strength and confidence. He told Crysania they were very close now. Godshome was located somewhere to the north in Khalkist Mountains.

How he could tell any direction at all in this weird and awful land was beyond Crysania—there was nothing to guide them, no sun, no moons, no stars. It was never really night and never truly day, just some sort of dreary, reddish in-between. She was thinking of this, trudging wearily beside Raistlin, not watching where they were going since it all looked the same anyway, when, suddenly, the archmage came to a halt. Hearing his sharp intake of breath, feeling him stiffen, Crysania looked up in swift alarm.

A middle-aged man dressed in the white robes of a teacher was walking down the road toward them. . . .

"Repeat the words after me, remembering to give them the proper inflection." Slowly he said the words. Slowly the class repeated them. All except one.

"Raistlin!"

The class fell silent.

———

"Master?" Raistlin did not bother to conceal the sneer in his voice as he said the word.

"I didn't see your lips moving."

"Perhaps that is because they were not moving, Master," Raistlin replied.

If someone else in the class of young magic-users had made such a remark, the pupils would have snickered. But they knew Raistlin felt the same scorn for them that he felt for the Master, and so they glowered at him and shifted uncomfortably.

"You know the spell, do you, apprentice?"

"Certainly I know the spell," Raistlin snapped. "I knew it when I was six! When did you learn it? Last night?"

The Master glared, his face purpled with rage. "You have gone too far this time, apprentice! You have insulted me once too often!"

The classroom faded before Raistlin's eyes, melting away. Only the Master remained and, as Raistlin watched, his old teacher's white robes turned to black! His stupid, paunchy face twisted into a malevolent, crafty face of evil. A bloodstone pendant appeared, hanging around his neck.

"Fistandantilus!" Raistlin gasped.

"Again we meet, apprentice. But now, where is your magic?" The wizard laughed. Reaching up a withered hand, he began fingering the bloodstone pendant.

Panic swept over Raistlin. Where *was* his magic? Gone! His hands shook. The words of spells tumbled into his mind, only to slip away before he could grasp hold of them. A ball of flame appeared in Fistandantilus's hands. Raistlin choked on his fear.

The Staff! he thought suddenly. The Staff of Magius. Surely its magic will not be affected! Raising the staff, holding it before him, he called upon it to protect him. But the staff began to twist and writhe in Raistlin's hand. "No!" he cried in terror and anger. "Obey my command! Obey!"

The staff coiled itself around his arm and it was no longer a staff at all, but a huge snake. Glistening fangs sank into his flesh.

Screaming, Raistlin dropped to his knees, trying desperately to free himself from the staff's poisonous bite. But, battling one enemy, he had forgotten the other. Hearing the spidery words of magic being chanted, he looked up fearfully. Fistandantilus was gone, but in his place stood a drow—a dark elf. The dark elf Raistlin had fought in his final battle of the Test. And then the dark elf was Dalamar, hurling a fireball at him, and then the fireball became a sword, driven into his flesh by a beardless dwarf.

Flames burst around him, steel pierced his body, fangs dug into his skin. He was sinking, sinking into the blackness, when he was bathed in white light and wrapped in white robes and held close to a soft, warm breast. . . .

And he smiled, for he knew by the flinching of the body shielding his and the low cries of anguish, that the weapons were striking her, not him.

CHAPTER 7

ord Gunthar!" said Amothus, Lord of Palanthas, rising to his feet. "An unexpected pleasure. And you, too, Tanis Half-Elven. I assume you're both here to plan the War's End celebration. I'm so glad. Now we can get started on it *early* this year. I, that is, the committee and I believe—"

"Nonsense," said Lord Gunthar crisply, walking about Amothus's audience chamber and staring at it with a critical eye, already calculating—in his mind—what it would take to fortify it if necessary. "We're here to discuss the defense of the city."

Lord Amothus blinked at the Knight, who was peering out the windows and muttering to himself. Once he turned and snapped, "Too much glass," which statement increased the lord's confusion to such an extent that he could only stammer an apology and then stand helplessly in the center of the room.

"Are we under attack?" he ventured to ask hesitantly, after a few more moments of Gunthar's reconnaisance.

Lord Gunthar cast Tanis a sharp look. With a sigh, Tanis politely reminded Lord Amothus of the warning the dark elf,

---

Dalamar, had brought them—the probability that the Dragon Highlord, Kitiara, planned to try to enter Palanthas in order to aid her brother, Raistlin, Master of the Tower of High Sorcery, in his fight against the Queen of Darkness.

"Oh, yes!" Lord Amothus's face cleared. He waved a delicate, deprecating hand, as though brushing away gnats. "But I don't believe you need be concerned about Palanthas, Lord Gunthar. The High Clerist's Tower—"

"—is being manned. I'm doubling the strength of our forces there. That's where the major assault will come, of course. No other way into Palanthas except by sea to the north, and we rule the seas. No, it will come overland. Should matters go wrong, though, Amothus, I want Palanthas ready to defend herself. Now—"

Having mounted the horse of action, so to speak, Gunthar charged ahead. Completely riding over Lord Amothus's murmured remonstration that perhaps he should discuss this with his generals, Gunthar galloped on, and soon left Amothus choking in the dust of troop dispersements, supply requisitions, armorment caches, and the like. Amothus gave himself for lost. Sitting down, he assumed an expression of polite interest, and immediately began to think about something else. It was all nonsense anyway. Palanthas had never been touched in battle. Armies had to get past the High Clerist's Tower first and none—not even the great dragon armies of the last war—had been able to do that.

Tanis, watching all of this, and knowing well what Amothus was thinking, smiled grimly to himself and was just beginning to wonder how he, too, might escape the onslaught when there was a soft knock upon the great, ornately carved, gilt doors. With the look of one who hears the trumpets of the rescuing division, Amothus sprang to his feet, but before he could say a word, the doors opened and an elderly servant entered.

Charles had been in the service of the royal house of Palanthas for well over half a century. They could not get along without him, and he knew it. He knew everything—from the exact count of the number of wine bottles in the cellar, to which elves should be seated next to which at dinner, to when the linen had been aired last. Though always dignified and deferential, there was a look upon his face which implied that when he died, he expected the royal house to crumble down about its master's ears.

"I am sorry to disturb you, my lord," Charles began.

"*Quite* all right!" Lord Amothus cried, beaming with pleasure. "Quite all right. Please—"

"But there is an urgent message for Tanis Half-Elven," finished Charles imperturbably, with only the slightest hint of rebuke to his master for interrupting him.

"Oh." Lord Amothus looked blank and extremely disappointed. "Tanis Half-Elven?"

"Yes, my lord," Charles replied.

"Not for me?" Amothus ventured, seeing the rescuing division vanish over the horzion.

"No, my lord."

Amothus sighed. "Very well. Thank you, Charles. Tanis, I suppose you had better—"

But Tanis was already halfway across the room.

"What is it? Not from Laurana—"

"This way, please, my lord," Charles said, ushering Tanis out the door. At a glance from Charles, the half-elf remembered just in time to turn and bow to Lords Amothus and Gunthar. The knight smiled and waved his hand. Lord Amothus could not refrain from casting Tanis an envious glance, then sank back down to listen to a list of equipment necessary for the boiling of oil.

Charles carefully and slowly shut the doors behind him.

"What is it?" Tanis asked, following the servant down the hall. "Didn't the messenger say anything else?"

"Yes, my lord." Charles's face softened into an expression of gentle sorrow. "I was not to reveal this unless it became absolutely necessary to free you from your engagement. Revered Son, Elistan, is dying. He is not expected to live through the night."

The Temple lawns were peaceful and serene in the fading light of day. The sun was setting, not with fiery splendor, but with a soft, pearlized radiance, filling the sky with a rainbow of gentle color like that of an inverted sea shell. Tanis, expecting to find crowds of people standing about, waiting for news, while white-robed clerics ran here and there in confusion, was startled to see that all was calm and orderly. People rested on the lawn as usual, white-robed clerics strolled beside the flower beds, talking together in low voices or, if alone, appearing lost in silent meditation.

Perhaps the messenger was wrong or misinformed, Tanis thought. But then, as he hurried across the velvety green grass, he passed a young cleric. She looked up at him, and he saw her eyes were red and swollen with weeping. But she smiled at him, nonetheless, wiping away traces of her grief as she went on her way.

And then Tanis remembered that neither Lord Amothus, ruler of Palanthas, nor Lord Gunthar, head of the Knights of Solamnia, had been informed. The half-elf smiled sadly in sudden understanding. Elistan was dying as he had lived—with quiet dignity.

A young acolyte met Tanis at the Temple door.

"Enter and welcome, Tanis Half-Elven," the young man said softly. "You are expected. Come this way."

Cool shadows washed over Tanis. Inside the Temple, the signs of grieving were clear. An elven harpist played sweet music, clerics stood together, arms around each other, sharing solace in their hour of trial. Tanis's own eyes filled with tears.

"We are grateful that you returned in time," the acolyte continued, leading Tanis deeper into the inner confines of the quiet Temple. "We feared you might not. We left word where we could, but only with those we knew we could count upon to keep the secret of our great sorrow. It is Elistan's wish that he be allowed to die quietly and peacefully."

The half-elf nodded brusquely, glad his beard hid his tears. Not that he was ashamed of them. Elves revere life above all things, holding it to be the most sacred of the gifts from the gods. Elves do not hide their feelings, as do humans. But Tanis feared the sight of his grief might upset Elistan. He knew the good man's one regret in dying lay in the knowledge that his death would bring such bitter sorrow to those left behind.

Tanis and his guide passed through an inner chamber where stood Garad and other Revered Sons and Daughters, heads bowed, speaking words of comfort to each other. Beyond them, a door was shut. Everyone's glance strayed to that door, and Tanis had no doubt who lay beyond it.

Looking up on hearing Tanis enter, Garad himself crossed the room to greet the half-elf.

"We are so glad you could come," the older elf said cordially. He was Silvanesti, Tanis recognized, and must have been one of the first of the elven converts to the religion that they had, long ago, forgotten. "We feared you might not return in time."

"This must have been sudden," Tanis murmured, uncomfortably aware that his sword—which he had forgotten to take off—was clanking, sounding loud and harsh in such peaceful, sorrowful surroundings. He clapped his hand over it.

"Yes, he was taken gravely ill the night you left." Garad sighed. "I do not know what was said in that room, but the shock was great. He has been in terrible pain. Nothing we could do would help him. Finally, Dalamar, the wizard's apprentice"—Garad could not help but frown—"came to the Temple. He brought with him a potion that would, he said, ease pain. How he came to know of what was transpiring, I cannot guess. Strange things happen in that place." He glanced out the window to where the Tower stood, a dark shadow, defiantly denying the sun's bright light.

"You let him in?" Tanis asked, startled.

"I would have refused," Garad said grimly. "But Elistan gave orders that he should be allowed entry. And, I must admit, his potion worked. The pain left our master, and he will be granted the right to die in peace."

"And Dalamar?"

"He is within. He has neither moved nor spoken since he came, but sits silently in a corner. Yet, his presence seems to comfort Elistan, and so we permit him to stay."

I'd like to see you try to make him leave, Tanis thought privately, but said nothing. The door opened. People looked up fearfully, but it was only the acolyte who had knocked softly and who was conferring with someone on the other side. Turning, he beckoned to Tanis.

The half-elf entered the small, plainly furnished room, trying to move softly, as did the clerics with their whispering robes and padded slippers. But his sword rattled, his boots clomped, the buckles of his leather armor jingled. He sounded, to his ears, like an army of dwarves. His face burning, he tried to remedy matters by walking on tiptoe. Elistan, turning his head feebly upon the pillow, looked over at the half-elf and began to laugh.

"One would think, my friend, that you were coming to rob me," Elistan remarked, lifting a wasted hand and holding it out to Tanis.

The half-elf tried to smile. He heard the door shut softly behind him and he was aware of a shadowy figure darkening one corner of the room. But he ignored all this. Kneeling beside the bed of the man he had helped rescue from the mines of Pax Tharkas, the man whose gentle influence had played such an important role in his life and in Laurana's, Tanis took the dying man's hand and held it firmly.

"Would that I were able to fight this enemy for you, Elistan," Tanis said, looking at the shrunken white hand clasped in his own strong, tanned one.

"Not an enemy, Tanis, not an enemy. An old friend is coming for me." He withdrew his hand gently from Tanis's grasp, then patted the half-elf's arm. "No, you don't understand. But you will, someday, I promise. And now, I did not call you here to burden you with saying good-bye. I have a commission to give to you, my friend." He motioned. The young acolyte came forward, bearing a wooden box, and gave it into Elistan's hands. Then, he retired, returning to stand silently beside the door.

The dark figure in the corner did not move.

Lifting the lid of the box, Elistan removed a folded piece of pure white parchment. Taking Tanis's hand, he placed the parchment in the half-elf's palm, then closed his fingers over it.

"Give this to Crysania," he said softly. "If she survives, she is to be the next head of the church." Seeing the dubious, disapproving expression come onto Tanis's face, Elistan smiled. "My friend, you have walked in darkness—none know that better than I. We came near losing you, Tanis. But you endured the night and faced the daylight, strengthened by the knowledge that you had gained. This is what I hope for Crysania. She is strong in her faith, but, as you yourself noted, she lacks warmth, compassion, humanity. She had to see with her own eyes the lessons that the fall of the Kingpriest taught us. She had to be hurt, Tanis, and hurt deeply, before she would be able to react with compassion to the hurt of others. Above all, Tanis, she had to love."

Elistan closed his eyes, his face, drawn with suffering, filled with grief. "I would have chosen differently for her, my friend, had I been able. I saw the road she walked. But, who questions the ways of the gods? Certainly not I. Although"—opening his eyes, he looked up at Tanis, and the half-elf saw a glint of anger in them—"I might argue with them a bit."

Tanis heard, behind him, the soft step of the acolyte. Elistan nodded. "Yes, I know. They fear that visitors tire me. They do, but I will find rest soon enough." The cleric closed his eyes, smiling. "Yes, I will rest. My old friend is coming to walk with me, to guide my feeble steps."

Rising to his feet, Tanis cast a questioning glance at the acolyte, who shook his head.

"We do not know of whom he speaks," the young cleric murmured. "He has talked of little else but this old friend. We thought, perhaps, it might be you—"

But Elistan's voice rose clearly from his bed. "Farewell, Tanis Half-Elven. Give my love to Laurana. Garad and the others"— he nodded toward the doorway—"know of my wishes in this matter of the succession. They know that I have entrusted this to you. They will help you all they can. Good-bye, Tanis. May Paladine's blessing be with you."

———

Tanis could say nothing. Reaching down, he pressed the cleric's hand, nodded, struggled to speak, and at last gave up. Turning abruptly, he walked past the dark and silent figure in the corner and left the room, his vision blinded by tears.

Garad accompanied him to the front entrance of the Temple. "I know what Elistan has charged you with," the cleric said, "and, believe me, I hope with all my heart his wishes come to pass. Lady Crysania is, I understand, on some sort of pilgrimage that could prove very dangerous?"

"Yes," was all Tanis could trust himself to answer.

Garad sighed. "May Paladine be with her. We are praying for her. She is a strong woman. The church needs such youth and such strength if it is to grow. If you need any help, Tanis, please know that you can call upon us."

The half-elf could only mutter a polite reply. Bowing, Garad hurried back to be with his dying master. Tanis paused a moment near the doorway in an effort to regain control of himself before stepping outside. As he stood there, thinking over Elistan's words, he became aware of an argument being carried on near the Temple door.

"I am sorry, sir, but I cannot permit you to go inside," a young acolyte was saying firmly.

"But I tell you I'm here to see Elistan," returned a querulous, crotchety voice.

Tanis closed his eyes, leaning against the wall. He knew that voice. Memories washed over him with an intensity so painful that, for a moment, he could neither move nor speak.

"Perhaps, if you gave me your name," the acolyte said patiently, "I could ask him—"

"I am— The name is—" The voice hesitated, sounding a bit bewildered, then muttered. "I knew it yesterday . . ."

Tanis heard the sound of a wooden staff thumping irritably against the Temple steps. The voice raised shrilly. "I am a very important person, young man. And I'm not accustomed to being treated with such impertinence. Now get out of my way before you force me to do something I'll regret. I mean, you'll regret. Well, one of us will regret it."

"I'm terribly sorry, sir," the acolyte repeated, his patience obviously wearing thin, "but without a name I cannot allow—"

There was the sound of a brief scuffle, then silence, then Tanis heard a truly ominous sound—the sound of pages being turned. Smiling through his tears, the half-elf walked to the door. Looking outside, he saw an old wizard standing on the Temple stairs. Dressed in mouse-colored robes, his misshapen wizard's hat appearing ready to topple from his head at the slightest opportunity, the ancient wizard was a most disreputable sight. He had leaned the plain wooden staff he carried against the Temple wall and now, ignoring the flushed and indignant acolyte, the wizard was flipping through the pages of his spellbook, muttering "Fireball . . . Fireball. How does that dratted spell go? . . ."

Gently, Tanis placed his hand upon the acolyte's shoulder. "He truly is an important person," the half-elf said softly. "You can let him in. I'll take full responsibility."

"He is?" The acolyte looked dubious.

At the sound of Tanis's voice, the wizard raised his head and glanced about. "Eh? Important person? Where?" Seeing Tanis, he started. "Oh, there! How do you do, sir?" He started to extend his hand, became entangled in his robes, and dropped his spellbook on his foot. Bending down to pick it up, he knocked over his staff, sending it down the steps with a clatter. In the confusion, his hat tumbled off. It took Tanis and the acolyte both to get the old man back together again.

"Ouch, my toe! Confound it! Lost my place. Stupid staff! Where's my hat?"

Eventually, however, he was more or less intact. Stuffing the spellbook back in a pouch, he planted his hat firmly on his head. (Having attempted, at first, to do those two things in reverse order.) Unfortunately, the hat immediately slipped down, covering his eyes.

"Struck blind, by the gods!" the old wizard stated in awe, groping about with his hands.

This matter was soon remedied. The young acolyte—with

---

an even more dubious glance at Tanis—gently pushed the wizard's hat to the back of his white-haired head. Glaring at the acolyte irritably, the old wizard turned to Tanis. "Important person? Yes, so you are . . . I think. Have we met before?"

"Indeed, yes," Tanis replied. "But *you* are the important person I was referring to, Fizban."

"I am?" The old wizard seemed staggered for a moment. Then, with a humpf, he glared again at the young cleric. "Well, of course. Told you so! Stand aside, stand aside," he ordered the acolyte irritably.

Entering the Temple door, the old man turned to look at Tanis from beneath the brim of the battered hat. Pausing, he laid his hand on the half-elf's arm. The befuddled look left the old wizard's face. He stared at Tanis intently.

"You have never faced a darker hour, Half-Elven," the old wizard said gravely. "There is hope, but love must triumph."

With that, he toddled off and, almost immediately, blundered into a closet. Two clerics came to his rescue, and guided him on.

"Who *is* he?" the young acolyte asked, staring, perplexed, after the old wizard.

"A friend of Elistan's," Tanis murmured. "A very old friend."

As he left the Temple, Tanis heard a voice wail, "My hat!"

CHAPTER
8

"Crysania. . . ."

There was no reply, only a low moaning sound.

"Shh. It's all right. You have been hurt, but the enemy is gone. Drink this, it will ease the pain."

Taking some herbs from a pouch, Raistlin mixed them in a mug of steaming water and, lifting Crysania from the bed of blood-soaked leaves upon which she lay, he held the mug to her lips. As she drank it, her face smoothed, her eyes opened.

"Yes," she murmured, leaning against him. "That is better."

"Now," continued Raistlin smoothly, "you must pray to Paladine to heal you, Revered Daughter. We have to keep going."

"I—I don't know, Raistlin. I'm so weak and—and Paladine seems so far away!"

"Pray to Paladine?" said a stern voice. "You blaspheme, Black Robe!"

Frowning, annoyed, Raistlin glanced up. His eyes widened. "Sturm!" he gasped.

But the young knight did not hear him. He was staring at

153

Crysania, watching in awe as the wounds upon her body closed, though they did not heal completely. "Witches!" cried the knight, drawing his sword. "Witches!"

"Witches!" Crysania raised her head. "No, Sir Knight. We are not witches. I am a cleric, a cleric of Paladine! Look at the medallion I wear!"

"You lie!" Sturm said fiercely. "There are no clerics! They vanished in the Cataclysm. And, if you were, what would you be doing in the company of this dark one of evil?"

"Sturm! It's me, Raistlin!" The archmage rose to his feet. "Look at me! Don't you recognize me?"

The young knight turned his sword upon the mage, its point at Raistlin's throat. "I do not know by what sorcerous ways you have conjured up my name, Black Robe, but, speak it once more and it will go badly for you. We deal shortly with witches in Solace."

"As you are a virtuous and holy knight, bound by vows of chivalry and obedience, I beg you for justice," Crysania said, rising to her feet slowly, with Raistlin's help.

The young man's stern face smoothed. He bowed, and sheathed his sword, but not without a sideways glance at Raistlin. "You speak truly, madam. I am bound by such vows and I will grant you justice."

Even as he spoke, the bed of leaves became a wooden floor; the trees—benches; the sky above—a ceiling; the road—an aisle between the benches. We are in a Hall of Judgment, Raistlin saw, momentarily dizzied by the sudden change. His arm around Crysania still, he helped her to sit down at a small table that stood in the center of the room. Before them loomed a podium. Glancing behind them, Raistlin saw that the room was packed with people, all watching with interest and enjoyment.

He stared. He knew these people! There was Otik, the owner of the Inn of the Last Home, eating a plateful of spiced potatoes. There was Tika, her red curls bouncing, pointing at Crysania and saying something and laughing. And Kitiara! Lounging against the doorway, surrounded by admiring young men, her hand on the hilt of her sword, she looked over at

Raistlin and winked.

Raistlin glanced about feverishly. His father, a poor wood-cutter, sat in a corner, his shoulders bent, that perpetual look of worry and care on his face. Laurana sat apart, her cool elven beauty shining like a bright star in the darkest night.

Beside him, Crysania cried out, "Elistan!" Rising to her feet, she stretched out her hand, but the cleric only looked at her sadly and sternly and shook his head.

"Rise and do honor!" rang out a voice.

With much shuffling of feet and scraping of the benches, everyone in the Hall of Judgment stood up. A respectful silence descended upon the crowd as the judge entered. Dressed in the gray robes of Gilean, God of Neutrality, the judge took his place behind the podium and turned to face the accused.

"Tanis!" Raistlin cried, taking a step forward.

But the bearded half-elf only frowned at this unseemly conduct while a grumbling old dwarf—the bailiff—stumped over and prodded Raistlin in the side with the butt-end of his battle-axe. "Sit down, witch, and don't speak unless you're spoken to."

"Flint?" Raistlin grabbed the dwarf by the arm. "Don't you know me?"

"And don't touch the bailiff!" Flint roared, incensed, jerking his arm away. "Humpf," he grumbled as he stalked back to take his place beside the judge. "No respect for my age or my station. You'd think I was a sack of meal to be handled by every-one—"

"That will do, Flint," said Tanis, sternly eyeing Raistlin and Crysania. "Now, who brings the charges against these two?"

"I do," said a knight in shining armor, rising to his feet.

"Very well, Sturm Brightblade," Tanis said, "you will have a chance to present your charges. And who defends these two?"

Raistlin started to rise and reply, but he was interrupted.

"Me! Here, Tanis—uh, your honorship! Me, over here! Wait. I—I seem to be stuck. . . ."

Laughter filled the Hall of Judgment, the crowd turning and staring at a kender, loaded down with books, struggling to get through the doorway. Grinning, Kitiara reached out, grabbed him by his topknot of hair, and yanked him through the door, tossing him unceremoniously onto the floor. Books scattered everywhere, and the crowd roared with laughter. Unfazed, the kender picked himself up, dusted himself off, and, tripping over the books, managed eventually to make it up to the front.

"I'm Tasslehoff Burrfoot," the kender said, holding out his small hand for Raistlin to shake. The archmage stared at Tas in amazement and did not move. With a shrug, Tas looked at his hand, sighed, and then, turning, started toward the judge. "Hi, my name's Tasslehoff Burrfoot—"

"Sit down!" roared the dwarf. "You don't shake hands with the judge, you doorknob!"

"Well," said Tas indignantly. "I think I might if I liked. I'm only being polite, after all, something you dwarves know nothing about. I—"

"Sit down and shut up!" shouted the dwarf, thudding the butt-end of the axe on the floor.

His topknot bouncing, the kender turned and meekly made his way over to sit beside Raistlin. But, before sitting, he faced the audience and mimicked the dwarf's dour look so well that the crowd howled with glee, making the dwarf angrier than ever. But this time the judge intervened.

"Silence," called Tanis sternly, and the crowd hushed.

Tas plopped himself down beside Raistlin. Feeling a soft touch brush against him, the mage glared down at the kender and held out his hand.

"Give that back!" he demanded.

"What back? Oh, this? Is that yours? You must have dropped it," Tas said innocently, handing over one of Raistlin's spell component pouches. "I found it on the floor—"

Snatching it from the kender, Raistlin attached it once more to the cord he wore around his waist.

"You might at least have said thank you," Tas remarked in a shrill whisper, then subsided as he caught the stern gaze of the judge.

"What are the charges against these two?" Tanis asked.

Sturm Brightblade came to the front of the room. There was some scattered applause. The young knight with his high standards of honor and melancholy mien was apparently well-liked.

"I found these two in the wilderness, your honor. The Black Robed one spoke the name of Paladine"—there was angry mutterings from the crowd—"and, even as I watched, he brewed up some foul concoction and gave it to the woman to drink. She was badly hurt when I first saw them. Blood covered her robes, and her face was burned and scarred as if she had been in a fire. But when she drank that witch's brew, she was healed!"

"No!" cried Crysania, rising unsteadily to her feet. "That is wrong. The potion Raistlin gave me simply eased the pain. It was my prayers that healed me! I am a cleric of Paladine—"

"Pardon us, your honor," yelled the kender, leaping to his feet. "My client didn't mean to say she was a cleric of Paladine. *Performing a pantomime.* That's what she meant to say. Yes, that's it." Tas giggled. "Just having a little fun to lighten the journey. It's a game they play all the time. Hah, hah." Turning to Crysania, the kender frowned and said in a whisper that was audible to everyone in the room, "What *are* you doing? How can I possibly get you off if you go around telling the truth like that! I simply won't put up with it!"

"Quiet!" roared the dwarf.

The kender whirled around. "And I'm getting a bit tired of you, too, Flint!" he shouted. "Quit pounding that axe on the floor or I'll wrap it around your neck."

The room dissolved into laughter, and even the judge grinned.

Crysania sank back down beside Raistlin, her face deathly pale. "What is this mockery?" she murmured fearfully.

"I don't know, but I'm going to put an end to it." Raistlin rose to his feet.

"Silence, all of you." His soft, whispering voice brought immediate quiet to the room. "This lady *is* a holy cleric of Paladine! I am a wizard of the Black Robes, skilled in the arts of magic—"

"Oh, do something magic!" the kender cried, jumping to his feet again. "Whoosh me into a duck pond—"

"Sit down!" yelled the dwarf.

"Set the dwarf's beard on fire!" Tasslehoff laughed.

There was a round of applause for this suggestion.

"Yes, show us some magic, wizard," Tanis called out over the hilarity in the Hall.

Everyone hushed, and then the crowd began to murmur, "Yes, wizard, show us some magic. Do some magic, wizard!" Kitiara's voice rang out above the others, strong and powerful. "Perform some magic, frail and sickly wretch, if you can!"

Raistlin's tongue clove to the roof of his mouth. Crysania was staring at him, hope and terror in her gaze. His hands trembled. He caught up the Staff of Magius, which stood at his side, but, remembering what it had done to him, he dared not use it.

Drawing himself up, he cast a look of scorn upon the people around him. "Hah! I do not need to prove myself to such as you—"

"I really think it might be a good idea," Tas muttered, tugging at Raistlin's robe.

"You see!" shouted Sturm. "The witch cannot! I demand judgment!"

"Judgment! Judgment!" chanted the crowd. "Burn the witches! Burn their bodies! Save their souls!"

"Well, wizard?" Tanis asked sternly. "Can you prove you are what you claim?"

Spell words slithered from his grasp. Crysania's hands clutched at him. The noise deafened him. He couldn't think! He wanted to be alone, away from the laughing mouths and pleading, terror-filled eyes. "I—" He faltered, and bowed his head.

"Burn them."

Rough hands caught hold of Raistlin. The courtyard disappeared before his eyes. He struggled, but it was useless. The man who held him was big and strong, with a face that might once have been jovial but was now serious and intent.

"Caramon! Brother!" Raistlin cried, twisting in the big man's grasp to look into his twin's face.

But Caramon ignored him. Gripping Raistlin firmly, he dragged the frail mage up a hill. Raistlin looked around. Before him, on the top of the hill, he saw two tall, wooden stakes that had been driven into the ground. At the foot of each stake, the townspeople—his friends, his neighbors—were gleefully tossing great armloads of dry tinder onto a mound.

"Where's Crysania?" he asked his brother, hoping she might have escaped and could now return to help him. Then Raistlin caught a glimpse of white robes. Elistan was binding her to a stake. She fought, trying to escape his grasp, but she was weakened from her suffering. At last, she gave up. Weeping in fear and despair, she slumped against the stake as they tied her hands behind it and bound her feet to the base.

Her dark hair fell over the smooth bare shoulders as she wept. Her wounds had opened, blood staining her robes red. Raistlin thought he heard her cry out to Paladine, but, if she did, the words could not be heard above the howling of the mob. Her faith was weakening even as she herself weakened.

Tanis advanced, a flaming torch in his hand. He turned to look at Raistlin.

"Witness her fate and see your own, witch!" the half-elf shouted.

"No!" Raistlin struggled, but Caramon held him fast.

Leaning down, Tanis thrust the blazing torch into the oil-soaked, drying tinder. It caught. The fire spread quickly, soon engulfing Crysania's white robes. Raistlin heard her anguished scream above the roar of the flame. She managed to raise her head, seeking for one final look at Raistlin. Seeing the pain and terror in her eyes, yet, seeing, too, love for him, Raistlin's heart burned with a fire hotter than any man could create.

"They want magic! I'll give them magic!" And, before he thought, he shoved the startled Caramon away and, breaking free, raised his arms to the heavens.

And, at that moment, the words of magic entered his soul, never to leave again.

Lightning streaked from his fingertips, striking the clouds in the red-tinged sky. The clouds answered with lightning, streaking down, striking the ground before the mage's feet.

Raistlin turned in fury upon the crowd—but the people had vanished, disappeared as though they had never existed.

"Ah, my Queen!" Laughter bubbled on his lips. Joy shot through his soul as the ecstasy of his magic burned in his blood. And, at last, he understood. He perceived his great folly and he saw his great chance.

He had been deceived—by himself! Tas had given him the clue at Zhaman, but he had not bothered to think it through. *I thought of something in my mind,* the kender said, *and there it was! When I wanted to go somewhere, all I had to do was think about it, and either it came to me or I went to it, I'm not sure. It was all the cities I have ever been in and yet none.* So the kender had told him.

I assumed the Abyss was a reflection of the world, Raistlin realized. *And thus I journeyed through it. It isn't, however. It is nothing more than a reflection of my mind! All I have been doing is traveling through my own mind!*

The Queen is in Godshome because that is where I perceived her to be. And Godshome is as far away or as near as I choose! My magic did not work because I doubted it, not because she prevented it from working. I have come close to defeating myself! Ah, but now I know, my Queen! Now I know and now I can triumph! For Godshome is just a step away and it is only another step to the Portal. . . .

"Raistlin!"

The voice was low, agonized, weary, spent. Raistlin turned his head. The crowd had vanished because it had never existed. It had been his creation. The village, the land, the continent, everything he had imagined was gone. He stood upon flat, undulating nothingness. Sky and ground were impossible to tell apart, both were the same eerie, burning pink. A faint horizon line was like a knife slit across the land.

But one object had not vanished—the wooden stake. Surrounded by charred wood, it stood outlined against the pink sky, thrusting up from the nothingness below. A figure lay below it. The figure might once have worn white robes, but these were now burnt black. The smell of burned flesh was strong.

Raistlin drew closer. Kneeling down upon the still-warm ashes, he turned the figure over.

"Crysania," he murmured.

"Raistlin?" Her face was horribly burned, sightless eyes stared into the emptiness around her, she reached out a hand that was little more than a blackened claw. "Raistlin?" She moaned in agony.

His hand closed over hers. "I can't see!" she whimpered. "All is darkness! Is that you?"

"Yes," he said.

"Raistlin, I've failed—"

"No, Crysania, you have not," he said, his voice cool and even. "I am unharmed. My magic is strong now, stronger than it has ever been before in any of the times I have lived. I will go forward, now, and defeat the Dark Queen."

The cracked and blistered lips parted in a smile. The hand holding Raistlin's tightened its feeble grasp. "Then my prayers have been granted." She choked, a spasm of pain twisted her body. When she could draw breath, she whispered something. Raistlin bent close to hear. "I am dying, Raistlin. I am weakened past endurance. Soon, Paladine will take me to him. Stay with me, Raistlin. Stay with me while I die. . . ."

Raistlin gazed down at the remains of the wretched woman before him. Holding her hand, he had a sudden vision of her as he had seen her in the forest near Caergoth the one time he had come close to losing control and making her his own—her white skin, her silken hair, her shining eyes. He remembered the love in those eyes, he remembered holding her close in his arms, he remembered kissing the smooth skin. . . .

One by one, Raistlin burned those memories in his mind, setting fire to them with his magic, watching them turn to ash and blow away in smoke.

Reaching out his other hand, he freed himself from her clinging grasp.

"Raistlin!" she cried, her hand clutching out at the empty air in terror.

"You have served my purpose, Revered Daughter," Raistlin said, his voice as smooth and cold as the silver blade of the dagger he wore at his wrist. "Time presses. Even now come those to the Portal at Palanthas who will try to stop me. I must challenge the Queen, fight my final battle with her minions. Then, when I have won, I must return to the Portal and enter it before anyone has a chance to stop me."

"Raistlin, don't leave me! Please don't leave me alone in the darkness!"

Leaning upon the Staff of Magius, which now gleamed with a bright, radiant light, Raistlin rose to his feet. "Farewell, Revered Daughter," he said in a soft, hissing whisper. "I need you no longer."

Crysania heard the rustle of his black robes as he walked away. She heard the soft thud of the Staff of Magius. Through the choking, acrid smell of smoke and burned flesh, she caught the faintest scent of rose petals. . . .

And then, there was only silence. She knew he was gone.

She was alone, her life dwindling through her veins as her illusions slowly dwindled from her mind.

"The next time you will see, Crysania, is when you are blinded by darkness . . . darkness unending."

So spoke Loralon, the elven cleric, at the fall of Istar. Crysania would have cried, but the fire had burned away her tears and their source.

"I see now," she whispered into the darkness. "I see so clearly! I have deceived myself! I've been nothing to him—nothing but his gamepiece to move about the board of his great game as he chose. And even as he used me—so I used him!" She moaned. "I used him to further *my* pride, *my* ambition! My darkness only deepened his own! He is lost, and I have led him to his downfall. For if he does defeat the Dark Queen, it will be but to take her place!"

Staring up at the heavens she could not see, Crysania

screamed in agony. "I have done this, Paladine! I have brought this harm upon myself, upon the world! But, oh, my god, what greater harm have I brought upon *him?*"

Lying there, in the eternal darkness, Crysania's heart wept the tears her eyes could not. "I love you, Raistlin," she murmured. "I could never tell you. I could never admit it to myself." She tossed her head, gripped by a pain that seared her more deeply than the flames. "What might have changed, if I had?"

The pain eased. She seemed to be slipping away, losing her grasp upon consciousness.

"Good," she thought wearily, "I am dying. Let death come swiftly, then, and end my bitter torment."

She drew a breath. "Paladine, forgive me," she murmured.

Another breath. "Raistlin . . ."

Another, softer breath. ". . . forgive . . ."

CRYSANIA'S SONG

Water from dust, and dust rising out of the water
Continents forming, abstract as color or light
To the vanished eye, to the touch of Paladine's daughter
Who knows with a touch that the robe is white,
Out of that water a country is rising, impossible
When first imagined in prayer,
And the sun and the seas and the stars invisible
As gods in a code of air.

Dust from the water, and water arising from dust,
And the robe containing all colors assumed into white,
Into memory, into countries assumed in the trust
Of ever returning color and light,
Out of that dust arises a wellspring of tears
To nourish the work of our hands
In forever approaching country of yearning and years,
In due and immanent lands.

anis stood outside
the Temple, thinking about the old wizard's words. Then he
snorted. *Love must triumph!*

Brushing away his tears, Tanis shook his head bitterly. Fizban's magic wasn't going to work this time. Love didn't even
have a bit part in this play. Raistlin had long ago twisted and
used his twin's love to his own ends, finally crushing Caramon
into a sodden mass of blubbery flesh and dwarf spirits. Marble
had more capacity to love than did the marble maiden, Crysania. And, as for Kitiara. . . . Had she ever loved?

Tanis scowled. He hadn't meant to think of her, not again.
But an attempt to shove the memories of her back into the dark
closet of his soul only made the light seem to shine upon them
more brightly. He caught himself going back to the time they'd
first met, in the wilderness near Solace. Discovering a young
woman fighting for her life against goblins, Tanis had raced to
the rescue—only to have the young woman turn upon him in
anger, accusing him of spoiling her fun!

Tanis was captivated. Up until then, his only love interest

had been a delicate elven maiden, Laurana. But that had been a childish romance. He and Laurana had grown up together, her father having taken in the bastard half-elf out of charity when his mother died in childbirth. It was, in fact, partly because of Laurana's girlish infatuation with Tanis—a love her father would never have approved—that the half-elf left his elven homeland and traveled into the world with old Flint, the dwarven metalsmith.

Certainly Tanis had never met a woman like Kitiara—bold, courageous, lovely, sensual. She made no secret of the fact that she found the half-elf attractive on that first meeting. A playful battle between them ended in a night of passion beneath Kitiara's fur blankets. After that, the two had often been together, traveling by themselves or in the company of their friends, Sturm Brightblade, and Kitiara's half-brothers, Caramon and his frail twin, Raistlin.

Hearing himself sigh, Tanis shook his head angrily. No! Grasping the thoughts, he hurled them back into the darkness, shut and locked the door. Kitiara had never loved him. She had been amused by him, that was all. He had kept her entertained. When a chance came to gain what she truly wanted—power— she had left him without a second thought. But, even as he turned the key in the lock of his soul, Tanis heard, once again, Kitiara's voice. He heard the words she had spoken the night of the downfall of the Queen of Darkness, the night Kitiara had helped him and Laurana escape.

"Farewell, Half-Elven. Remember, I do this for love of you!"

A dark figure, like the embodiment of his own shadow, appeared beside Tanis. The half-elf started in a sudden, unreasonable fear that he had, perhaps, conjured up an image from his own subconscious. But the figure spoke a word of greeting, and Tanis realized it was flesh and blood. He sighed in relief, then hoped the dark elf had not noticed how abstracted his thoughts had been. He was more than half afraid, in fact, that Dalamar might have guessed them. Clearing his throat gruffly, the half-elf glanced at the black-robed mage.

"Is Elistan—"

"Dead?" said Dalamar coldly. "No, not yet. But I sensed the approach of one whose presence I would find most uncomfortable, and so, seeing that my services were no longer necessary, I left."

Stopping on the lawn, Tanis turned to face the dark elf. Dalamar had not drawn up his black hood, and his features were plainly visible in the peaceful twilight. "Why did you do it?" Tanis demanded.

The dark elf stopped walking as well, looking at Tanis with a slight smile. "Do what?"

"Come here, to Elistan! Ease his pain." Tanis waved a hand. "From what I saw last time, setting foot on this ground makes you suffer the torments of the damned." His face became grim. "I cannot believe a pupil of Raistlin's could care so much about anyone!"

"No," Dalamar replied smoothly, "Raistlin's pupil personally didn't give a cracked iron piece what became of the cleric. But Raistlin's pupil is honorable. He was taught to pay his debts, taught to be beholden to no one. Does that accord with what you know of my *Shalafi?*"

"Yes," Tanis admitted grudgingly, "but—"

"I was repaying a debt, nothing more," Dalamar said. As he resumed his walk across the lawn, Tanis saw a look of pain upon his face. The dark elf obviously wanted to leave this place as quickly as possible. Tanis had some trouble keeping pace with him. "You see," Dalamar continued, "Elistan came once to the Tower of High Sorcery to help my *Shalafi.*"

"Raistlin?" Tanis stopped again, stunned. Dalamar did not halt, however, and Tanis was forced to hurry after him.

"Yes," the dark elf was saying, as if caring little whether Tanis heard him or not, "no one knows this, not even Raistlin. The *Shalafi* grew ill once about a year ago, terribly ill. I was alone, frightened. I know nothing of sickness. In desperation, I sent for Elistan. He came."

"Did . . . did he . . . *heal* Raistlin?" Tanis asked in awe.

"No." Dalamar shook his head, his long black hair falling down around his shoulders. "Raistlin's malady is beyond the healing arts, a sacrifice made for his magic. But Elistan was able to ease the *Shalafi's* pain and give him rest. And so, I have done nothing more than discharge my debt."

"Do you . . . care about Raistlin as much as this?" Tanis asked hesitantly.

"What is this talk of caring, half-elf?" Dalamar snapped impatiently. They were near the edge of the lawn. Evening's shadows spread across it like soothing fingers, gently reaching out to close the eyes of the weary. "Like Raistlin, I care for one thing only—and that is the Art and the power that it gives. For that, I gave up my people, my homeland, my heritage. For that, I have been cast in darkness. Raistlin is the *Shalafi,* my teacher, my master. He is skilled in the Art, one of the most skilled who has ever lived. When I volunteered to the Conclave to spy upon him, I knew I might well sacrifice my life. But how little was that price to pay for the chance of studying with one so gifted! How could I afford to lose him? Even now, when I think of what I must do to him, when I think of the knowledge he has gained that will be lost when he dies, I almost—"

"Almost what?" Tanis said sharply, in sudden fear. "Almost let him through the Portal? Can you truly stop him, when he comes back, Dalamar? *Will* you stop him?"

They had reached the end of the Temple grounds. Soft darkness blanketed the land. The night was warm and filled with the smells of new life. Here and there among the aspen trees, a bird chirped sleepily. In the city, lighted candles were set in the windows to guide loved ones home. Solinari glimmered on the horizon, as though the gods had lit their own candle to brighten the night. Tanis's eyes were drawn to the one patch of chill blackness in the warm, perfumed evening. The Tower of High Sorcery stood dark and forbidding. No candles flickered in its windows. He wondered, briefly, who or what waited within that blackness to welcome the young apprentice home.

"Let me tell you of the Portals, Half-Elven," Dalamar replied. "I will tell you as my *Shalafi* told me." His gaze followed Tanis's, going to the very topmost room in Tower. When he spoke, his voice was hushed. "There is a corner in that laboratory where stands a doorway, a doorway without a lock. Five dragon's heads made of metal surround it. Look within it, you will see nothing—simply a void. The dragon's heads are cold and still. That is the Portal. Another exists beside this one—it stands in the Tower of High Sorcery at Wayreth. The only other one, as far as we know, was in Istar and it was destroyed in the Cataclysm. The one in Palanthas was originally moved to the magical fortress in Zhaman to protect it when the mobs of the Kingpriest tried to take over the Tower here. It moved again when Fistandantilus destroyed Zhaman, returning to Palanthas. Created long ago by mages who desired faster communication with each other, it led them too far—it led them onto other planes."

"The Abyss," Tanis murmured.

"Yes. Too late the mages realized what a perilous gate they had devised. For if someone from this plane entered the Abyss and returned through the Portal, the Queen would have the entrance into the world she has long sought. Thus with the help of the holy clerics of Paladine, they insured—so they thought—that none could ever use the Portals. Only one of the most profound evil, who had commited his very soul to darkness, could hope to gain the knowledge necessary to open that dread doorway. And only one of goodness and purity, with absolute trust in the one person upon this world who could never merit trust, could hold the doorway open."

"Raistlin and Crysania."

Dalamar smiled cynically. "In their infinite wisdom, those dried-up old mages and clerics never foresaw that love would overthrow their grand design. So, you see, Half-Elven, when Raistlin attempts to reenter the Portal from the Abyss, I must stop him. For the Queen will be right behind him."

None of this explanation did much to ease Tanis's doubts. Certainly the dark elf appeared cognizant of the grave danger. Certainly he appeared calm, confident. . . . "But can *you* stop him?" Tanis persisted, his gaze going—without meaning to—to the dark elf's chest where he had seen those five holes burned into his smooth skin.

———

Noticing Tanis's look, Dalamar's hand went involuntarily to his chest. His eyes grew dark and haunted. "I know my own limitations, Half-Elven," he said softly. Then, he smiled and shrugged. "I will be honest with you. If my *Shalafi* were in the full strength of his power when he tried to come through the Portal, then, no, I could not stop him. No one could. But Raistlin will not be. He will already have expended much of his power in destroying the Queen's minions and forcing her to face him alone. He will be weak and injured. His only hope—to draw the Dark Queen out here onto *his* plane. Here he can regain strength, here *she* will be the weaker of the two. And thus, yes, because he will be injured, I can stop him. And, yes, I *will* stop him!"

Noticing Tanis still looked dubious, Dalamar's smile twisted. "You see, Half-Elven," he said coolly, "I have been offered enough to make it worth my while." With that, he bowed, and—murmuring the words of a spell—vanished.

But as he left, Tanis heard Dalamar's soft, elven voice speak through the night. "You have looked upon the sun for the last time, Half-Elven. Raistlin and the Dark Queen have met. Takhisis now gathers her minions. The battle begins. Tomorrow, there will be no dawn."

And so, Raistlin, we meet again.

"My Queen."

You bow before me, wizard?

"This one last time, I do you homage."

And I bow to you, Raistlin.

"You do me too much honor, Majesty."

On the contrary, I have watched your gameplay with the keenest pleasure. For every move of mine, you had a counter move. More than once, you risked all you had to win a single turn. You have proved yourself a skilled player, and our game has brought me much amusement. But now it comes to the end, my worthy opponent. You have one gamepiece left upon the board—yourself. Ranged against you is the full might of my dark legions. But, because I have found pleasure in you, Raistlin, I will grant you one favor.

Return to your cleric. She lies dying, alone, in such torment of mind and body as only I can inflict. Return to her. Kneel down beside her. Take her in your arms and hold her close. The mantle of death will fall upon you both. Gently it will cover you, and you will drift into the darkness and find eternal rest.

"My Queen . . . "

You shake your head.

"Takhisis, Great Queen, truly I thank you for this gracious offer. But I play this game—as you call it—to win. And I will play it to the end."

And it will be a bitter end—for you! I have given you the chance your skill and daring earned for you. You would spurn it?

"Your Majesty is too gracious. I am unworthy of such attention. . . ."

And now you mock me! Smile your twisted smile while you can, mage, for when you slip, when you fall, when you make that one, small mistake—I will lay my hands upon you. My nails will sink into your flesh, and you will beg for death. But it will not come. The days are eons long here, Raistlin Majere. And every day, I will come to see you in your prison—the prison of your mind. And, since you have provided me with amusement, you will continue to provide me with amusement. You will be tortured in mind and in body. At the end of each day, you will die from the pain. At the beginning of each night, I will bring you back to life. You will not be able to sleep, but will lie awake in shivering anticipation of the day to come. In the morning, my face will be the first sight you see.

What? You grow pale, mage. Your frail body trembles, your hands shake. Your eyes grow wide with fear. Prostrate yourself before me! Beg my forgiveness! . . .

"My Queen . . ."

What, not yet on your knees?

"My Queen . . . it is your move."

Blasted overcast! If it's going to storm, I wish it would do it and be done with it," muttered Lord Gunthar.

Prevailing winds, Tanis thought sarcastically, but he kept his thoughts to himself. He also kept Dalamar's words to himself, knowing that Lord Gunthar would never believe them. The half-elf was nervous and on edge. He was finding it difficult to be patient with the seemingly complacent knight. Part of it was the strange-looking sky. That morning, as Dalamar had predicted, there came no dawn. Instead, purplish blue clouds, tinged with green and flickering with eerie, multicolored lightning, appeared, boiling and churning above them. There was no wind. No rain fell. The day grew hot and oppressive. Walking their rounds upon the battlements of the High Clerist's Tower, the knights in their heavy plate-mail armor wiped sweat from their brows and muttered about spring storms.

Only two hours ago, Tanis had been in Palanthas, tossing and turning on the silk sheets of the bed in Lord Amothus's guest room, pondering Dalamar's cryptic final words. The

---

half-elf had been up most of the night, thinking about them, and thinking, too, of Elistan.

Word had come to the palace near midnight that the cleric of Paladine had passed from this world into another, brighter realm of existence. He had died peacefully, his head cradled in the arms of a befuddled, kindly old wizard who had appeared mysteriously and left just as mysteriously. Worrying about Dalamar's warning, grieving for Elistan, and thinking he had seen too many die, Tanis had just dropped into an exhausted sleep when a messenger arrived for him.

The message was short and terse:

Your presence required immediately. High Clerist's Tower—Lord Gunthar uth Wistan.

Splashing cold water into his face, rebuffing the attempts of one of Lord Amothus's servants to help buckle him into his leather armor, Tanis dressed and stumbled out of the Palace, politely refusing Charles's offer of breakfast. Outside waited a young bronze dragon, who introduced himself as Fireflash, his secret dragon name being Khirsah.

"I am acquainted with two friends of yours, Tanis Half-Elven," the young dragon said as his strong wings carried them easily over the walls of the sleeping city. "I had the honor to fight in the Battle of the Vingaard Mountains, carrying the dwarf, Flint Fireforge, and the kender, Tasslehoff Burrfoot, into the fray."

"Flint's dead," Tanis said heavily, rubbing his eyes. He'd seen too many die.

"So I heard," the young dragon replied respectfully. "I was sorry to hear it. Yet, he led a rich, full life. Death to such a one comes as the final honor."

Sure, Tanis thought tiredly. And what of Tasslehoff? Happy, good-natured, good-hearted kender, asking nothing more of life than adventure and a pouch full of wonders? If it was true—if Raistlin had killed him, as Dalamar had intimated—what honor was there in his death? And Caramon, poor drunken Caramon—did death at the hands of his twin come as the final honor or was it the final stab of the knife to end his misery?

Brooding, Tanis fell asleep upon the dragon's back, awaking only when Khirsah landed in the courtyard of the High Clerist's Tower. Looking around grimly, Tanis's spirits did not rise. He had ridden with death only to arrive with death, for here Sturm was buried—another final honor.

Thus, Tanis was in no good humor when he was ushered into the Lord Gunthar's chambers, high in one of the tall spires of the High Clerist's Tower. It commanded an excellent view of sky and land. Staring out the window, watching the clouds with a growing feeling of ominous foreboding, Tanis only gradually became aware that Lord Gunthar had entered and was talking to him.

"I beg your pardon, lord," he said, turning around.

"Tarbean tea?" Lord Gunthar said, holding up a steaming mug of the bitter-tasting drink.

"Yes, thank you." Tanis accepted it and gulped it down, welcoming the warmth spreading through his body, ignoring the fact that he had burned his tongue.

Coming over to stand next to Tanis and stare out the window at the storm, Lord Gunthar sipped his tea with a calm that made the half-elf want to rip off the knight's moustaches.

Why did you send for me? Tanis fumed. But he knew that the knight would insist upon fulfilling the ages-old ritual of politeness before coming to the point.

"You heard about Elistan?" Tanis asked finally.

Gunthar nodded. "Yes, we heard early this morning. The knights will hold a ceremony in his honor here at the Tower . . . if we are permitted."

Tanis choked upon his tea and hastily swallowed. Only one thing would prevent the knights from holding a ceremony in honor of a cleric of their god, Paladine—war. "Permitted? Have you had some word, then? News from Sanction? What do the spies—"

"Our spies have been murdered," Lord Gunthar said evenly.

Tanis turned from the window. "What? How—"

"Their mutilated bodies were carried to the fortress of Solan-

———

175

thas by black dragons and were dropped into the courtyard last evening. Then came this strange storm—perfect cover for dragons and . . ." Lord Gunthar fell silent, staring out the window, frowning.

"Dragons and what?" Tanis demanded. A possibility was beginning to form in his mind. Hot tea sloshed over his shaking hand. Hastily, he set the cup down on the window ledge.

Gunthar tugged at his moustaches, his frown deepened. "Strange reports have come to us, first from Solanthas, then Vingaard."

"What reports. Have they seen something? What?"

"They've *seen* nothing. It's what they've heard. Strange sounds, coming from the clouds—or perhaps even from above the clouds."

Tanis's mind went back to Riverwind's description of the Siege of Kalaman. "Dragons?"

Gunthar shook his head. "Voices, laughter, doors opening and slamming, rumblings, creakings. . . ."

"I knew it!" Tanis's clenched fist smote the window ledge. "I knew Kitiara had a plan! Of course! This has to be it!" Gloomily, he stared out into the churning clouds. "A flying citadel!"

Beside him, Gunthar sighed heavily. "I told you I respected this Dragon Highlord, Tanis. Apparently, I did not respect her enough. In one fell swoop, she has solved her problems of troop movements and logistics. She has no need for supply lines, she carries her supplies with her. The High Clerist's Tower was designed to defend against ground attack. I have no idea how long we can hold out against a flying citadel. At Kalaman, draconians jumped from the citadel, floating down upon their wings, carrying death into the streets. Black-robed magic-users hurled down balls of flame, and with her, of course, are the evil dragons.

"Not that I have any doubts the knights can hold the fortress against the citadel, of course," Gunthar added sternly. "But it will be a much stiffer battle than I had at first anticipated. I've readjusted our strategy. Kalaman survived a citadel's attack by waiting until most of its troops had been dropped, then good dragons carrying men-at-arms on their backs flew up and took control of the citadel. We'll leave most of the Knights here in the fortress, of course, to fight the draconians who will drop down upon us. I have about a hundred standing by with bronze dragons ready to fly up and begin the assault on the flying citadel itself."

It made sense, Tanis admitted to himself. That much of the battle of Kalaman Riverwind had told him. But Tanis also knew that Kalaman had been unable to hold the citadel. They had simply driven it back. Kitiara's troops, giving up the battle of Kalaman, had been able to easily recapture their citadel and fly it back to Sanction where Kit had, apparently, once more put it to good use.

He was about to point this out to Lord Gunthar when he was interrupted.

"We expect the citadel to attack us almost any moment," Gunthar said, calmly staring out the window. "In fact—"

Tanis gripped Gunthar's arm. "There!" He pointed.

Gunthar nodded. Turning to an orderly by the door, he said, "Sound the alarm!"

Trumpets pealed, drums beat. The knights took their places upon the battlements of the High Clerist's Tower with orderly efficiency. "We've been on alert most of the night," Gunthar added unnecessarily.

So disciplined were the knights that no one spoke or cried out when the flying fortress dropped down from the cover of the storm clouds and floated into view. The captains walked their rounds, issuing quiet commands. Trumpets blared their defiance. Occasionally Tanis heard the clinking of armor as, here and there, a knight shifted nervously in place. And then, high above, he heard the beating of dragon wings as several flights of bronze dragons—led by Khirsah—took to the skies from the Tower.

"I am thankful you persuaded me to fortify the High Clerist's Tower, Tanis," Gunthar said, still speaking with elaborate calm. "As it was, I was able to call upon only those knights I could muster at practically a moment's notice. Still, there are well over two thousand here. We are well-provisioned. Yes," he repeated again, "we can hold the Tower—even against a citadel, I have no doubt. Kitiara could not have more than a thousand troops in that thing. . . ."

Tanis wished sourly that Gunthar would quit emphasizing that. It was beginning to sound as if the knight were trying to convince himself. Staring at the citadel as it came nearer and nearer, some inner voice was shouting at him, pummeling him, screaming that something wasn't right. . . .

And yet he couldn't move. He couldn't think. The flying citadel was now plainly visible, having dropped down completely out of the clouds. The fortress absorbed his entire attention. He recalled the first time he had seen it at Kalaman, recalled the riveting shock of the sight, at once horrifying and awe-inspiring. As before, he could only stand and stare.

Working in the depths of the dark temples of the city of Sanction, under the supervision of Lord Ariakas—the commander of the dragonarmies whose evil genuis had nearly led to the victory of his Dark Queen—black-robed magic-users and dark clerics had managed to magically rip a castle from its foundations and send it up into the skies. The flying citadels had attacked several towns during the war, the last being Kalaman in the war's final days. It had nearly defeated the walled city that had been well-fortified and expecting assault.

Drifting upon clouds of dark magic, illuminated by flashes of blinding multicolored lightning, the flying citadel came nearer and nearer. Tanis could see the lights in the windows of its three towers, he could hear the sounds that were ordinary when heard upon land but seemed sinister and appalling heard coming from the skies—sounds of voices calling orders, weapons clashing. He could continue to hear, so he thought, the chants of the black-robed magic-users preparing to cast their powerful spells. He could see the evil dragons flying about the citadel in lazy circles. As the flying citadel drew nearer still, he could see a crumbling courtyard on one side of the fortress, its broken walls lying in ruins from where it had been dragged out of its foundation.

Tanis watched in helpless fascination, and still that inner voice spoke to him. Two thousand knights! Gathered at the last moment and so ill-prepared! Only a few flights of dragons. Certainly the High Clerist's Tower might hold out, but the cost would be high. Still, they just needed to hold a few days. By that time, Raistlin would have been defeated. Kitiara would have no more need to try to attack Palanthas. By that time, too, more knights would have reached the High Clerist's Tower, along with more good dragons. Perhaps they could defeat her here, finally, once and for all.

She had broken the uneasy truce that had existed between the Dragon Highlord and the free people of Ansalon. She had left the haven of Sanction, she had come out into the open. This was their opportunity. They could defeat her, capture her perhaps. Tanis's throat constricted painfully. Would Kitiara let herself be taken alive? No. Of course not. His hand closed over the hilt of his sword. He'd be there when the knights tried to take the citadel. Perhaps *he* could persuade her to give herself up. He would see that she was treated justly, as an honorable enemy—

He could see her so clearly in his mind! Standing defiantly, surrounded by her enemies, prepared to sell her life dearly. And then she would look over, she would see him. Perhaps those glittering, hard dark eyes would soften, perhaps she would drop her sword and hold out her hands—

What *was* he thinking about! Tanis shook his head. He was daydreaming like a moon-struck youth. Still, he'd make certain he was with the knights. . . .

Hearing a commotion down on the battlements below, Tanis looked hastily outside, although he really had no need. He knew what was happening—dragonfear. More destructive than arrows, the fear generated by the evil dragons, whose black wings and blue could now be seen against the clouds, struck the knights as they stood waiting upon the battlements. Older knights, veterans of the War of the Lance, held their ground, grimly clutching their weapons, fighting the terror that filled their hearts. But younger knights, who were facing their first dragons in battle, blenched and cowered, some shaming themselves by crying out or turning from the awesome sight before them.

Seeing some of these fear-stricken young knights on the battlements below him, Tanis gritted his teeth. He, too, felt the sickening fear sweep over him, felt his stomach clench and the bile rise to his mouth. Glancing over at Lord Gunthar, he saw the knight's expression harden, and he knew he experienced the same thing.

Looking up, Tanis could see the bronze dragons who served the Knights of Solamnia flying in formation, waiting above the Tower. They would not attack until attacked—such were terms of the truce that had existed between the good dragons and the evil ones since the end of the war. But Tanis saw Khirsah, the leader, toss his head proudly, his sharp talons flaring in the reflected glare of the lightning. There was no doubt in the dragon's mind at least, that battle would soon be joined.

Still, that inner voice nagged at Tanis. All too simple, all too easy. Kitiara was up to something. . . .

The citadel flew closer and closer. It looked like the home of some foul colony of insects, Tanis thought grimly. Draconians literally covered the thing! Clinging to every available inch of space, their short, stubby wings extended, they hung from the walls and the foundation, they perched upon the battlements and dangled from the spires. Their leering, reptilian faces were visible in the windows and peered from doorways. Such awed silence reigned in the High Clerist's Tower (except for the occasional harsh weeping of some knight, overcome by fear) that there could be heard from the citadel above the rustling of the creatures' wings and, over that, faint sounds of chanting—the mingled voices of the wizards and clerics whose evil power kept the terrible device afloat.

Nearer and nearer it came, and the knights tensed. Quiet orders rang out, swords slid from scabbards, spears were set, archers nocked their arrows, buckets of water stood filled and ready to douse fires, divisions assembled within the courtyard to fight those draconians who would leap down and attack from the skies.

Above, Khirsah aligned his dragons in battle formation, breaking them into groups of twos and threes, hovering, poised to descend upon the enemy like bronze lightning.

"I am needed below," Gunthar said. Picking up his helm, he put it on and strode out the door of his headquarters to take his place at the observation tower, his officers and aides accompanying him.

But Tanis did not leave, nor even answer Gunthar's belated invitation to come with them. The voice inside him was growing louder, more insistent. Shutting his eyes, he turned from the window. Blocking out the debilitating dragonfear, blotting out the sight of that grim fortress of death, he fought to concentrate on the voice within.

And finally, he heard it.

"Name of the gods, no!" he whispered. "How stupid! How blind we've been! We've played right into her hands!"

Suddenly Kitiara's plan was clear. She might have been standing there with him, explaining it to him in detail. His chest tight with fear, he opened his eyes and leaped toward the window. His fist slammed into the carved stone ledge, cutting him. He knocked the tea mug to the floor, where it shattered. But he noticed neither the blood that flowed from his injured hand nor the spilled tea. Staring up into the eerie, cloud-darkened sky, he watched the floating citadel come nearer and nearer, draw closer and closer.

It was within long-bow-shot range.

It was within spear range.

Looking up, nearly blinded by the lightning, Tanis could see the details on the armor of the draconians, he could see the grinning faces of the mercenary humans who fought in the ranks, he could see the shining scales of the dragons flying overhead.

And then, it was gone.

Not an arrow had flown, not a spell had been cast. Khirsah and the bronze dragons circled uneasily, eyeing their evil cousins with fury, yet constrained by their oaths not to attack those who had not attacked them first. The knights stood upon the battlements, craning their necks to watch the huge, awesome creation fly over them, skimming the topmost spire of the High Clerist's Tower as it went, sending a few stones tumbling down to crash into the courtyard below.

Swearing beneath his breath, Tanis ran for the door, slamming into Gunthar as the knight, a perplexed look upon his face, was coming inside.

"I can't understand," Gunthar was saying to his aides. "Why didn't she attack us? What is she doing?"

"She's attacking the city directly, man!" Tanis gripped Gunthar by the arms, practically shaking him. "It's what Dalamar said all along! Kitiara's plan is to attack Palanthas! She's not going to fool with us and now she doesn't have to! She's going *over* the High Clerist's Tower!"

Gunthar's eyes, barely visible beneath the slits of his helm, narrowed. "That's insane," he said coldly, tugging on his moustache. Finally, irritably, he yanked his helm off. "Name of the gods, Half-Elven, what kind of military strategy's that? It leaves the rear of her army unguarded! Even if she takes Palanthas, she hasn't got strength enough to hold it. She'll be caught between the walls of the city and us. No! She has to finish us here, then attack the city! Otherwise we'll destroy her easily. There's no escape for her!"

Gunthar turned to his aides. "Perhaps this is a feint, to throw us off-guard. Better prepare for the citadel to strike from the opposite direction—"

"Listen to me!" Tanis raved. "This isn't a feint. She's going to Palanthas! And by the time you and the knights get to the city, her brother will have returned through the Portal! And she'll be waiting for him, with the city under her control!"

"Nonsense!" Gunthar scowled. "She can't take Palanthas that quickly. The good dragons will rise up to fight— Damn it, Tanis, even if the Palanthians aren't such great soldiers, they can hold her off through sheer numbers alone!" He snorted. "The knights can march at once. We'll be there within four days."

"You've forgotten one thing," Tanis snapped, firmly but politely shoving his way past the knight. Turning on his heel, he called out, "We've all forgotten one thing—the element that makes this battle even—Lord Soth!"

CHAPTER
12

Propelled by his powerful hind legs, Khirsah leaped into the air and soared over the walls of the High Clerist's Tower with graceful ease. The dragon's strong wing strokes soon caused himself and his rider to overtake the slowly moving citadel. And yet, noted Tanis grimly, the fortress is moving rapidly enough to arrive in Palanthas by dawn tomorrow.

"Not too close," he cautioned Khirsah.

A black dragon flew over, circling overhead in large, lazy spirals to keep an eye on them. Other blacks hovered in the distance and, now that he was on the same level as the citadel, Tanis could see the blue dragons as well, flying around the gray turrets of the floating castle. One particularly large blue dragon Tanis recognized as Kitiara's own mount, Skie.

Where is Kit? Tanis wondered, trying unsuccessfully to peer into the windows, crowded with milling draconians, who were pointing at him and jeering. He had a sudden fear she might recognize him, if she were watching, and he pulled his cloak hood over his head. Then, smiling ruefully, he scratched his beard. At this distance, Kit would see nothing more than a lone rider on dragonback, probably a messenger for the knights.

He could picture clearly what would be occurring within the citadel.

"We could shoot him from the skies, Lord Kitiara," one of her commanders would say.

Kitiara's remembered laughter rang in Tanis's ears. "No, let him carry the news to Palanthas, tell them what to expect. Give them time to sweat."

Time to sweat. Tanis wiped his face. Even in the chill air above the mountains, the shirt beneath his leather tunic and armor was damp and clammy. He shivered with the cold and pulled his cloak more closely about him. His muscles ached; he was accustomed to riding in carriages, not on dragons, and he briefly thought with longing of his warm carriage. Then he sneered at himself. Shaking his head to clear it (why should missing one night's sleep affect him so?), he forced his mind from his discomfort to the impossible problem confronting him.

Khirsah was trying his best to ignore the black dragon still hovering near them. The bronze increased his speed, and eventually the black, who had been sent simply to keep an eye on them, turned back. The citadel was left far behind, drifting effortlessly above mountain peaks that would have stopped an army dead.

Tanis tried to make plans, but everything he thought of doing involved doing something more important first until he felt like one of those trained mice in a fair who runs round and round upon the little wheel, getting nowhere in a tremendous hurry. At least Lord Gunthar had actually bullied and badgered Amothus's generals (an honorary title in Palanthas, granted for outstanding community service; not one general now serving had actually been in a battle) into mobilizing the local militia. Unfortunately, the mobilization had been regarded as merely an excuse for a holiday.

Gunthar and his knights had stood around, laughing and nudging each other as they watched the civilian soldiers stumble through the drills. Following this, Lord Amothus had made a two-hour speech, the militia—proud of its heroics—had drunk itself into a stupor, and everyone had enjoyed himself immensely.

Picturing in his mind the chubby tavern owners, the perspiring merchants, the dapper tailors and the ham-fisted smithies tripping over their weapons and each other, following orders that were never given, not following those that were, Tanis could have wept from sheer frustration. This, he thought grimly, is what will face a death knight and his army of skeletal warriors at the gates of Palanthas tomorrow.

"Where's Lord Amothus?" Tanis demanded, shoving his way inside the huge doors of the palace before they were open, nearly bowling over an astonished footman.

"A-asleep, sir," the footman began, "it's only midmorning—"

"Get him up. Who's in charge of the Knights?"

The footman, eyes wide, stammered.

"Damn it!" Tanis snarled. "Who's the highest ranking knight, dim-wit!"

"That would be Sir Markham, sir, Knight of the Rose," said Charles in his calm, dignified voice, emerging from one of the antechambers. "Shall I send—"

"Yes!" shouted Tanis, then, seeing everyone in the great entry hall of the palace staring at him as if he were a madman, and remembering that panic would certainly not help the situation, the half-elf put his hand over his eyes, drew a calming breath, and made himself talk rationally.

"Yes," he repeated in a quiet voice, "send for Sir Markham and for the mage, Dalamar, too."

This last request seemed to confound even Charles. He considered it a moment, then, a pained expression on his face, he ventured to protest, "I am extremely sorry, my lord, but I have no way to way to send a message to—to the Tower of High Sorcery. No living being can set foot in that accursed grove of trees, not even kender!"

"Damn!" Tanis fumed. "I *have* to talk to him!" Ideas raced

through his mind. "Surely you've got goblin prisoners? One of their kind could get through the Grove. Get one of the creatures, promise it freedom, money, half the kingdom, Amothus himself, anything! Just get it inside that blasted Grove—"

"That will be unnecessary, Half-Elven," said a smooth voice. A black-robed figure materialized within the hallway of the palace, startling Tanis, traumatizing the footmen, and even causing Charles to raise his eyebrows.

"You *are* powerful," Tanis remarked, drawing near the dark elf magic-user. Charles was issuing orders to various servants, sending one to awaken Lord Amothus and another to locate Sir Markham. "I need to talk to you privately. Come in here."

Following Tanis, Dalamar smiled coolly. "I wish I could accept the compliment, Half-Elven, but it was simply through observation that I discerned your arrival, not any magical mind-reading. From the laboratory window, I saw the bronze dragon land in the palace courtyard. I saw you dismount and enter the palace. I have need to talk to you as much as you to me. Therefore, I am here."

Tanis shut the door. "Quickly, before the others come. You know what is headed this way?"

"I knew last night. I sent word to you, but you had already left." Dalamar's smile twisted. "My spies fly on swift wings."

"If they fly on wings at all," Tanis muttered. With a sigh, he scratched his beard, then, raising his head, looked at Dalamar intently. The dark elf stood, hands folded in his black robes, calm and collected. The young elf certainly appeared to be someone who could be relied upon to perform with cool courage in a tight spot. Unfortunately, just who he would perform for was open to doubt.

Tanis rubbed his forehead. How confusing this was! How much easier it had been back in the old days—he sounded like someone's grandfather!—when good and evil had been clearly defined and everyone knew which side they were fighting for or against. Now, he was allied with evil fighting against evil. How was that possible? *Evil turns in upon itself,* so Elistan read from the Disks of Mishakal. Shaking his head angrily, Tanis realized he was wasting time. He had to trust this Dalamar—at least, he had to trust to his ambition.

"Is there any way to stop Lord Soth?"

Dalamar nodded slowly. "You are quick-thinking, Half-Elven. So you believe, too, that the death knight will attack Palanthas?"

"It's obvious, isn't it?" Tanis snapped. "That *has* to be Kit's plan. It's what equalizes the odds."

The dark elf shrugged. "To answer your question, no, there is nothing that can be done. Not now, at any rate."

"You? Can you stop him?"

"I dare not leave my post beside the Portal. I came this time because I know Raistlin is still far from it. But every breath we draw brings him nearer. This will be my last chance to leave the Tower. That was why I came to talk to you—to warn you. There is little time."

"He's winning!" Tanis stared at Dalamar incredulously.

"You have always underestimated him," Dalamar said with a sneer. "I told you, he is now strong, powerful, the greatest wizard who has ever lived. Of course, he is winning! But at what cost . . . at what great cost."

Tanis frowned. He didn't like the note of pride he heard in Dalamar's voice when he talked about Raistlin. That certainly didn't sound like an apprentice who was prepared to kill his *Shalafi* if need arose.

"But, to return to Lord Soth," said Dalamar coldly, seeing more of Tanis's thoughts on the half-elf's face than Tanis had intended. "When I first realized that he would undoubtedly use this opportunity to take his own revenge upon a city and a people he has long hated—if one believes the old legends about his downfall—I contacted the Tower of High Sorcery in Wayreth Forest—"

"Of course!" Tanis gasped in relief. "Par-Salian! The Conclave. They could—"

"There was no answer to my message," Dalamar continued, ignoring the interruption. "Something strange is transpiring there. I do not know what. My messenger found the way barred and, for one of his—shall we say—light and airy nature, that is not easy."

"But—"

"Oh"—Dalamar shrugged his black-robed shoulders—"I will continue to try. But we cannot count on them, and they are the only magic-users powerful enough to stop a death knight."

"The clerics of Paladine—"

"—are new in their faith. In Huma's day, it was said the truly powerful clerics could call down Paladine's aid and use certain holy words against death knights, but—if so—there are none now on Krynn who have that power."

Tanis pondered a moment.

"Kit's destination will be the Tower of High Sorcery to meet and help her brother, right?"

"And try to stop me," Dalamar said in a tight voice, his face paling.

"Can Kitiara get through the Shoikan Grove?"

Dalamar shrugged again, but his cool manner was, Tanis noticed, suddenly tense and forced. "The Grove is under my control. It will keep out all creatures, living and dead." Dalamar smiled again, but this time, without mirth. "Your goblin, by the way, wouldn't have lasted five seconds. However, Kitiara had a charm, given her by Raistlin. If she has it still, and the courage to use it, and if Lord Soth is with her, yes, she might get through. Once inside, however, she must face the Tower's guardians, no less formidable than those in the Grove. Still, that is my concern—not yours—" .

"Too much is your concern!" Tanis snapped. "Give *me* a charm! Let me inside the Tower! I can deal with her—"

"Oh, yes," Dalamar returned, amused, "I know how well you dealt with her in the past. Listen, Half-Elven, you will have all you can handle trying to keep control of the city. Besides, you have forgotten one thing—Soth's true purpose in this. He wants Kitiara dead. He wants her for himself. He told me as much. Of course, he must make it look good. If he can accomplish her death and avenge himself upon Palanthas, he will have succeeded in his objective. He couldn't care less about

Raistlin."

Feeling suddenly chilled to the very soul, Tanis could not reply. He had, indeed, forgotten Soth's objective. The half-elf shuddered. Kitiara had done much that was evil. Sturm had died upon the end of her spear, countless had died by her commands, countless more had suffered and still suffered. But did she deserve this? An endless life of cold and dark torment, bound forever in some type of unholy marriage to this creature of the Abyss?

A curtain of darkness shrouded Tanis's vision. Dizzy, weak, he saw himself teetering on the brink of a yawning chasm and felt himself falling. . . .

There was a dim sensation of being enfolded in soft black cloth, he felt strong hands supporting him, guiding him. . . .

Then nothing.

The cool, smooth rim of a glass touched Tanis's lips, brandy stung his tongue and warmed his throat. Groggily, he looked up to see Charles hovering over him.

"You have ridden far, without food or drink, so the dark elf tells me." Behind Charles floated the pale anxious face of Lord Amothus. Wrapped in a white dressing robe, he looked very much like a distraught ghost.

"Yes," Tanis muttered, pushing the glass away from him and trying to rise. Feeling the room sway beneath his feet, however, he decided he better remain seated. "You are right—I had better have something to eat." He glanced around for the dark elf. "Where is Dalamar?"

Charles's face grew stern. "Who knows, my lord? Fled back to his dark abode, I suppose. He said his business with you was concluded. I will, with your leave, my lord, have the cook prepare you breakfast." Bowing, Charles withdrew, first standing aside to allow young Sir Markham to enter.

"Have you breakfasted, Sir Markham?" Lord Amothus asked hesitantly, not at all certain what was going on and decidedly flustered by the fact that a dark elf magic-user felt free to simply appear and disappear in his household. "No?

Then we will have quite a threesome. How do you prefer your eggs?"

"Perhaps we shouldn't be discussing eggs right now, m'lord," Sir Markham said, glancing at Tanis with a slight smile. The half-elf's brows had knit together alarmingly and his disheveled and exhausted appearance showed that some dire news was at hand.

Amothus sighed, and Tanis saw that the lord had simply been trying to postpone the inevitable.

"I have returned this morning from the High Clerist's Tower—" he began.

"Ah," Sir Markham interrupted, seating himself negligently in a chair and helping himself to a glass of brandy. "I received a message from Lord Gunthar that he expected to engage the enemy this morning. How goes the battle?" Markham was a wealthy young nobleman, handsome, good-natured, carefree, and easy-going. He had distinguished himself in the War of the Lance, fighting under Laurana's command, and had been made a Knight of the Rose. But Tanis remembered Laurana telling him that the young man's bravery was nonchalant—almost casual—and totally undependable. ("I always had the feeling," Laurana said thoughtfully, "that he fought in the battle simply because there was nothing more interesting to do at the time.")

Remembering her assessment of the young knight, and hearing his cheerful, unconcerned tone, Tanis frowned.

"There wasn't one," he said abruptly. An almost comic look of hope and relief dawned in Lord Amothus's face. At the sight, Tanis nearly laughed, but—fearing it would be hysterical laughter—he managed to control himself. He glanced at Sir Markham, who had raised an eyebrow.

"No battle? Then the enemy didn't come—"

"Oh, they came," Tanis said bitterly, "came and went. Right by." He gestured in the air. "Whoosh."

"Whoosh?" Amothus turned pale. "I don't understand."

"A flying citadel!"

"Name of the Abyss!" Sir Markham let out a low whistle. "A flying citadel." He grew thoughtful, his hand absently smoothing his elegant riding clothes. "They didn't attack the High Clerist's Tower. They're flying over the mountains. That means—"

"They plan to throw everything they have at Palanthas," Tanis finished.

"But, I don't understand!" Lord Amothus looked bewildered. "The knights didn't stop them?"

"It would have been impossible, m'lord," Sir Markham said with a negligent shrug. "The only way to attack a flying citadel that stands a chance of succeeding is with flights of dragons."

"And by terms of the surrender treaty, the good dragons will not attack unless first attacked. All we had at the High Clerist's Tower was one flight of bronzes. It will take far greater numbers than that—silver and golden dragons, as well—to stop the citadel," Tanis said wearily.

Leaning back in his chair, Sir Markham pondered. "There are a few silver dragons in the area who will, of course, immediately rise up when the evil dragons are sighted. But there are not many. Perhaps more could be sent for—"

"The citadel is not our gravest danger," Tanis said. Closing his eyes, he tried to stop the room from spinning. What was the matter with him? Getting old, he supposed. Too old for this.

"It isn't?" Lord Amothus appeared to be on the verge of collapse from this additional blow but—nobleman that he was— he was doing his best to regain his shattered composure.

"Most assuredly Lord Soth rides with Highlord Kitiara."

"A death knight!" Sir Markham murmured with a slight smile. Lord Amothus paled so visibly that Charles, returning with the food, set it down at once and hurried to his master's side.

"Thank you, Charles," Amothus said in a stiff, unnatural voice. "A little brandy, perhaps."

"A *lot* of brandy would be more to the point," Sir Markham said gaily, draining his glass. "Might as well get good and roaring drunk. Not much use staying sober. Not against a death knight and his legions. . . ." The young knight's voice trailed off.

"You gentlemen should eat now," Charles said firmly, having made his master more comfortable. A sip of brandy brought some color back to Amothus's face. The smell of the food made Tanis realize that he *was* hungry, and so he did not protest when Charles, bustling about efficiently, brought over a table and served the meal.

"Wh-what does it all mean?" Lord Amothus faltered, spreading his napkin on his lap automatically. "I—I've heard of this death knight before. My great-great-great grandfather was one of the nobles who witnessed Soth's trial in Palanthas. And this Soth was the one who kidnapped Laurana, wasn't he, Tanis?"

The half-elf's face darkened. He did not reply.

Amothus raised his hands appealingly. "But what can he do against a city?"

Still no one replied. There was, however, no need. Amothus looked from the grim, exhausted face of the half-elf to the young knight, who was smiling bitterly as he methodically stabbed tiny holes in the lace tablecloth with his knife. The lord had his answer.

Rising to his feet, his breakfast untouched, his napkin slipping unnoticed from his lap to the floor, Amothus walked across the sumptuously appointed room to stand before a tall window made of hand-cut glass, crafted in an intricate design. A large oval pane in the center framed a view of the beautiful city of Palanthas. The sky above it was dark and filled with the strange, churning clouds. But the storm above only seemed to intensify the beauty and apparent serenity of the city below.

Lord Amothus stood there, his hand resting upon a satin curtain, looking out into the city. It was market day. People passed the palace on their way to the market square, chatting together about the ominous sky, carrying their baskets, scolding their playful children.

"I know what you're thinking, Tanis," Amothus said finally, a break in his voice. "You're thinking of Tarsis and Solace and Silvanesti and Kalaman. You're thinking of your friend who died at the High Clerist's Tower. You're thinking of all those who died and suffered in the last war while we in Palanthas remained untouched, unaffected."

Still Tanis did not respond. He ate in silence.

"And you, Sir Markham—" Amothus sighed. "I heard you and your knights laughing the other day. I heard the comments about the people of Palanthas carrying their money bags into battle, planning to defeat the enemy by tossing coins and yelling, 'Go away! Go away.'"

"Against Lord Soth, that will do quite as well as swords!" With a shrug and a short, sardonic laugh, Markham held out his brandy snifter for Charles to refill.

Amothus rested his head against the window pane. "We never thought war would come to us! It never has! Through all the Ages, Palanthas has remained a city of peace, a city of beauty and light. The gods spared us, even during the Cataclysm. And now, now that there is peace in the world, *this* comes to us!" He turned around, his pale face drawn and anguished. "Why? I don't understand?"

Tanis shoved his plate away. Leaning back, he stretched, trying to ease the cramps in his muscles. I *am* getting old, he thought, old and soft. I miss my sleep at night. I miss a meal and grow faint. I miss days long past. I miss friends long gone. And I'm sick and tired of seeing people die in some stupid, senseless war! Heaving a sigh, he rubbed his bleary eyes and then, resting his elbows on the table, let his head sink into his hands.

"You talk of peace. What peace?" he asked. "We've been behaving like children in a house where mother and father have fought constantly for days and now, at last, they're quiet and civil. We smile a lot and try to be merry and eat all our vegetables and tiptoe around, scared of making a sound. Because we know, if we do, the fighting will start all over again. And we call this peace!" Tanis laughed bitterly. "Speak one false word, my lord, and Porthios will have the elves on your neck. Stroke your beard the wrong way, and the dwarves will bar the gates to the mountain once again."

Glancing over at Lord Amothus, Tanis saw the man's head bow, he saw the delicate hand brush his eyes, his shoulders slump. Tanis's anger dwindled. Who was he angry at anyway? Fate? The gods?

Rising tiredly to his feet, Tanis walked over to stand at the window, looking out over the peaceful, beautiful, doomed city.

"I don't have the answer, my lord," he said quietly. "If I did, I'd have a Temple built to me and a whole string of clerics following me about, I suppose. All I know is that we can't give up. We've got to keep trying."

"Another brandy, Charles," said Sir Markham, holding out his glass once again. "A pledge, gentlemen." He raised his glass.

"Here's to trying. . . . Rhymes with dying."

CHAPTER 13

There came a soft knock at the door. Absorbed in his work, Tanis started. "Yes, what is it?" he called.

The door opened. "It is Charles, my lord. You asked that I call you during the changing of the watch."

Turning his head, Tanis glanced out the window. He had opened it to let in some air. But the spring night was warm and sultry and no breeze stirred. The sky was dark except for the occasional streaks of the eerie pink-tinged lightning that flashed from cloud to cloud. Now that his attention was drawn to it, he could hear the chimes striking Deepwatch, he could hear the voices of the guards newly arrived on duty, he could hear the measured tread of those departing for their rest.

Their rest would be short-lived.

"Thank you, Charles," Tanis said. "Step in for a moment, will you?"

"Certainly, my lord."

The servant entered, gently closing the door behind him. Tanis stared for a moment longer at the paper on the desk.

———

Then, his lips tightening in resolve, he wrote two more lines in a firm, elven hand. Sprinkling sand upon the ink to dry it, he began to reread the letter carefully. But his eyes misted over and the handwriting blurred in his vision. Finally, giving up, he signed his name, rolled up the parchment, and sat holding it in his hand.

"Sir," said Charles, "are you quite well?"

"Charles . . ." began Tanis, twisting a ring of steel and gold that he wore upon his finger. His voice died.

"My lord?" Charles prompted.

"This is a letter to my wife, Charles," Tanis continued in a low voice, not looking at the servant. "She is in Silvanesti. This needs to get out tonight, before—"

"I quite understand, sir," Charles said, stepping forward and taking charge of the letter.

Tanis flushed guiltily. "I know there are much more important documents than this that need to be going out—dispatches to the knights, and such—but—"

"I have just the messenger, my lord. He is elven, from Silvanesti, in fact. He is loyal and, to be quite honest, sir, will be more than pleased to leave the city on some honorable assignment."

"Thank you, Charles." Tanis sighed and ran his hand through his hair. "If something were to happen, I want her to know—"

"Of course you do, my lord. Perfectly understandable. Do not give it another thought. Your seal, perhaps, however?"

"Oh, yes, certainly." Removing the ring, Tanis pressed it into the hot wax that Charles dripped onto the parchment, imprinting in the sealing wax the image of an aspen leaf.

"Lord Gunthar has arrived, my lord. He is meeting with Lord Markham right now."

"Lord Gunthar!" Tanis's brow cleared. "Excellent. Am I—"

"They asked to meet with you, if it is convenient, my lord," Charles said imperturbably.

"Oh, it's quite convenient," Tanis said, rising to his feet. "I don't suppose there's been any sign of the cita—"

"Not yet, my lord. You will find the lords in the summer

breakfast parlor—now, officially, the war room."

"Thank you, Charles," Tanis said, amazed that he had, at last, managed to complete a sentence.

"Will there be anything else, my lord?"

"No, thank you. I know the—"

"Very good, my lord." Bowing, letter in hand, Charles held the door for Tanis, then locked it behind him. After waiting a moment to see if Tanis might have any last minute desires, he bowed again and departed.

His mind still on his letter, Tanis stood alone, thankful for the shadowy stillness of the dimly lit corridor. Then, drawing a shaking breath, he walked firmly off in search of the morning breakfast parlor—now the war room.

Tanis had his hand on the doorknob and was just about to enter the room when he caught a glimpse of movement out of the corner of his eye. Turning his head, he saw a figure of darkness materialize out of the air.

"Dalamar?" Tanis said in astonishment, leaving the unopened door to the war room and walking down the hallway toward the dark elf. "I thought—"

"Tanis. You are the one I seek."

"Do you have news?"

"None that you will like to hear," Dalamar said, shrugging. "I cannot stay long, our fate teeters on the edge of a knife's blade. But I brought you this." Reaching into a black velvet pouch hanging at his side, he took out a silver bracelet and held it out to Tanis.

Taking hold of the bracelet in his hand, Tanis examined it curiously. The bracelet was about four inches in width, made of solid silver. From its width and weight, Tanis guessed, it had been designed to fit on a man's wrist. Slightly tarnished, it was set with black stones whose polished surfaces gleamed in the flickering torchlight of the corridor. And it came from the Tower of High Sorcery.

Tanis held it gingerly. "Is it—" he hesitated, not sure he wanted to know.

"Magical? Yes," Dalamar replied.

"Raistlin's?" Tanis frowned.

"No." Dalamar smiled sardonically. "The *Shalafi* needs no such magical defenses as these. It is part of the collection of such objects in the Tower. This is very old, undoubtedly dating back to the time of Huma."

"What will it do?" Tanis studied the bracelet dubiously, still frowning.

"It makes the one wearing it resistant to magic."

Tanis raised his head. "Lord Soth's magic?"

"Any magic. But, yes, it will protect the wearer from the death knight's power words—'kill,' 'stun,' 'blind.' It will keep the wearer from feeling the effects of the fear he generates. And it will protect the wearer from both his spells of fire and of ice."

Tanis stared at Dalamar intently. "This is truly a valuable gift! It gives us a chance."

"The wearer may thank me when and if he returns alive!" Dalamar folded his hands within his sleeves. "Even without his magic, Lord Soth is a formidable opponent, not to mention those who follow him, who are sworn to his service with oaths death itself could not erase. Yes, Half-Elven, thank me *when* you return."

"Me?" Tanis said in astonishment. "But—I haven't wielded a sword in over two years!" He stared at Dalamar intently, suddenly suspicious. "Why me?"

Dalamar's smile widened. The slanted eyes glinted in amusement. "Give it to one of the knights, half-elf. Let one of them hold it. You will understand. Remember—it came from a place of darkness. It knows one of its own."

"Wait!" Seeing the dark elf prepared to leave, Tanis caught hold of Dalamar's black-robed arm. "Just one more second. You said there was news—"

"It is not your concern."

"Tell me."

Dalamar paused, his brows came together in irritation at this delay. Tanis felt the young elf's arm tense. He's frightened, Tanis realized suddenly. But even as this thought crossed his mind, he saw Dalamar regain control of himself. The handsome features grew calm, expressionless.

"The cleric, Lady Crysania, has been mortally wounded. She managed to protect Raistlin, however. He is uninjured and has gone on to find the Queen. So Her Dark Majesty tells me."

Tanis felt his throat constrict. "What about Crysania?" he said harshly. "Did he just leave her to die?"

"Of course." Dalamar appeared faintly surprised at the question. "She can be of no more use to him."

Looking down at the bracelet in his hand, Tanis longed to hurl it into the gleaming teeth of the dark elf. But, in time, he remembered that he could not afford the luxury of anger. What an insane, twisted situation! Incongruously, he remembered Elistan going to the Tower, bringing comfort to the archmage . . .

Turning on his heel, Tanis stalked angrily away. But he gripped the bracelet tightly in his hand.

"The magic is activated when you put it on," Dalamar's soft voice floated through Tanis's haze of fury. He could have sworn the dark elf was laughing.

"What's the matter, Tanis?" Lord Gunthar asked as the half-elf came into the war room. "My dear fellow, you're pale as death. . . ."

"Nothing. I—I just heard some disturbing news. I'll be all right." Tanis drew a deep breath, then glanced at the knights. "You don't look any too good yourselves."

"Another pledge?" Sir Markham said, raising his brandy snifter.

Lord Gunthar gave him a stern, disapproving glance, which the young knight ignored as he casually quaffed his drink in a gulp.

"The citadel has been sighted. It crossed the mountains. It will be here at dawn."

Tanis nodded. "About what I had figured." He scratched his beard, then wearily rubbed his eyes. Casting a glance at the brandy bottle, he shook his head. No, it would probably just send him straight to sleep.

"What's that you're holding?" Gunthar asked, reaching out his hand to take the bracelet. "Some sort of elven good-luck charm?"

"I wouldn't touch—" Tanis began.

"Damnation!" Gunthar gasped, snatching his hand back. The bracelet dropped to the floor, landing on a plush, hand-woven rug. The knight wrung his hand in pain.

Bending down, Tanis picked up the bracelet. Gunthar watched him with disbelieving eyes. Sir Markham was choking back laughter.

"The mage, Dalamar, brought it to us. It's from the Tower of High Sorcery," Tanis said, ignoring Lord Gunthar's scowl. "It will protect the wearer from the effects of magic—the one thing that will give someone a chance of getting near Lord Soth."

"Someone!" Gunthar repeated. He stared down at his hand. The fingers where he had touched the bracelet were burned. "Not only that, but it sent a jolt through me that nearly stopped my heart! Who in the name of the Abyss can wear such a thing?"

"I can, for one," Tanis returned. *It came from a place of darkness. It knows one of its own.* "It has something to do with you knights and holy vows to Paladine," he muttered, feeling his face flush.

"Bury it!" Lord Gunthar growled. "We do not need such help as those of the Black Robes would give us!"

"It seems to me we can use all the help we can get, my lord!" Tanis snapped. "I would also remind you that, odd as it may seem, we're all on the same side! And now, Sir Markham, what of the plans for defending the city?"

Slipping the bracelet into a pouch, affecting not to notice Lord Gunthar's glare, Tanis turned to Sir Markham who, though rather startled at this sudden call, quickly rode to Tanis's rescue with his report.

The Knights of Solamnia were marching from the High Clerist's Tower. It would be days, at least, before they could reach Palanthas. He had sent a messenger to alert the good dragons, but it seemed unlikely that they, too, could reach

Palanthas in time.

The city itself was on the alert. In a brief, spare speech, Lord Amothus had told the citizens what faced them. There had been no panic, a fact Gunthar found hard to believe. Oh, a few of the wealthy had tried to bribe ships' captains to take them out, but the captains had, to a man, refused to sail into the seas under the threat of such ominous-looking storm clouds. The gates to Old City were opened. Those who wanted to flee the city and risk going out in the wilderness had, of course, been allowed to go. Not many took the chance. In Palanthas, at least the city walls and the knights afforded protection.

Personally, Tanis thought that if the citizens had known what horrors they faced, they would have taken their chances. As it was, however, the women put aside their rich clothing and began filling every available container with water to have available to fight fires. Those who lived in New City (not protected by walls) were evacuated into Old City, whose walls were being fortified as best they could in the little time that remained. Children were bedded down in wine cellars and storm shelters. Merchants opened shops, handing out needed supplies. Armorers gave out weapons, and the forges were still burning, late into the night, for mending swords, shields, and armor.

Looking out over the city, Tanis saw lights in most homes— people preparing for a morning that he knew from experience could never be prepared for.

With a sigh, thinking of his letter to Laurana, he made his bitter decision. But he knew it would entail argument. He needed to lay the groundwork. Turning abruptly, he interrupted Markham. "What do you guess will be their plan of attack?" he asked Lord Gunthar.

"I think that's fairly simple." Gunthar tugged at his moustaches. "They'll do what they did at Kalaman. Bring the citadel as close as they can get. At Kalaman that wasn't very close. The dragons held them back. But"—he shrugged—"we don't have near the numbers of dragons they did. Once the citadel is over the walls, the draconians will drop from it and try to take the city from within. The evil dragons will attack—"

"And Lord Soth will sweep through the gates," Tanis finished.

"The knights should at least get here in time to keep him from looting our corpses," Sir Markham said, draining his snifter again.

"And Kitiara," Tanis mused, "will be trying to reach the Tower of High Sorcery. Dalamar says no living being can get through Shoikan Grove, but he also said Kit had a charm, given to her by Raistlin. She might wait for Soth before going, figuring he can help her, as well."

"If the Tower is her objective," Gunthar said with emphasis on the *if*. It was obvious he still believed little of the tale about Raistlin. "My guess is that she will use the battle as cover to fly her dragon over the walls and land as near the Tower as possible. Maybe we could post knights around the Grove to try to stop her—"

"They couldn't get close enough," Sir Markham interrupted, adding a belated, "m'lord. The Grove has an unnerving effect on anyone coming within miles of it."

"Besides, we'll need the knights to deal with Soth's legions," Tanis said. He drew a deep breath. ". . . I have a plan, if I may be allowed to propose it?"

"By all means, Half-Elven."

"You believe that the citadel will attack from above and Lord Soth will come through the front gates, creating a diversion that will give Kit her chance to reach the Tower. Right?"

Gunthar nodded.

"Then, mount what knights we can upon bronze dragons. Let me have Fireflash. Since the bracelet gives me the best defense against Soth, I'll take him. The rest of the knights can concentrate on his followers. I have a private score to settle with Soth anyway," Tanis added, seeing Gunthar already shaking his head.

"Absolutely not. You did very well in the last war, but you've never been trained! To go up against a Knight of Solamnia—"

"Even a dead Knight of Solamnia!" Sir Markham struck in,

with a drunken giggle.

Gunthar's moustaches quivered in anger, but he contained himself and continued coldly, "—a trained knight, as Soth is trained, and you must fall—bracelet or no bracelet."

"Without the bracelet, however, my lord, training in swordsmanship will matter very little," Sir Markham pointed out, drinking another brandy. "A chap who can point at you and say 'die' has the distinct advantage."

"Please, sir," Tanis intervened, "I admit that my formal training has been limited, but my years wearing a sword outnumber yours, my lord, by almost two to one. My elven blood—"

"To the Abyss with your elven blood," Gunthar muttered, glaring at Sir Markham, who was resolutely ignoring his superior, and lifting the brandy bottle again.

"I will, if I am forced, pull rank, my lord," Tanis said quietly.

Gunthar's face reddened. "Damn it, that was honorary!"

Tanis smiled. "The Code makes no such distinction. Honorary or not, I am a Knight of the Rose, and my age—well over one hundred, my lord—gives me seniority."

Sir Markham was laughing. "Oh, for the gods' sake, Gunthar, give him your permission to die. What the Abyss difference does it make anyway?"

"He's drunk," Gunthar muttered, casting a scathing glance at Sir Markham.

"He's young," Tanis replied. "Well, my lord?"

Lord Gunthar's eyes flashed in anger. As he glared at the half-elf, sharp words of reproval came to his lips. But they were never uttered. Gunthar knew—none better—that the one who faced Soth was placing himself in a situation of almost certain death—magical bracelet or no magical bracelet. He had first assumed Tanis was either too naive or too foolhardy to recognize this. Looking into the half-elf's dark, shadowed eyes, he realized that, once again, he had misjudged him.

Swallowing his words with a gruff cough, Lord Gunthar made a gesture at Sir Markham. "See if you can get him sobered up, Half-Elven. Then I suppose you had better get yourself into position. I'll have the knights waiting."

"Thank you, my lord," Tanis murmured.

"And may the gods go with you," Gunthar added in a low, choked voice. Gripping Tanis by the hand, he turned and stalked out of the room.

Tanis glanced over at Sir Markham, who was staring intently into the empty brandy bottle with a wry smile. He's not as drunk as he's letting on, Tanis decided. Or as he wishes he could be.

Turning from the young knight, the half-elf walked over to the window. Looking out, he waited for the dawn.

Laurana

My beloved wife, when we parted a week ago, we little thought this parting might be for a long, long time. We have been kept apart so much of our lives. But, I must admit, I cannot grieve that we are separated now. It comforts me to know that you are safe, although if Raistlin succeeds in his designs, I fear there will be no safe havens left anywhere upon Krynn.

I must be honest, my dearest. I see no hope that any of us can survive. I face without fear the knowledge that I shall probably die—I believe I can honestly say that. But I cannot face it without bitter anger. The last war, I could afford bravery. I had nothing, so had nothing to lose. But I have never wanted so much to live as I do now. I am like a miser, coveting the joy and happiness we have found, loath to give it up. I think of our plans, the children we hope for. I think of you, my beloved, and what grief my death must bring, and I cannot see this page for the tears of sorrow and fury that I cry.

I can only ask you to let this consolation be yours as it is mine—this parting will be our last. The world can never separate us again. I will wait for you, Laurana, in that realm where time itself dies.

And one evening, in that realm of eternal spring, eternal twilight, I will look down the path and see you walking toward me. I can see you so clearly, my beloved. The last rays of the setting sun shining upon your golden hair, your eyes bright with the love that fills my own heart.

You will come to me.

I will fold you in my arms.

We will close our eyes and begin to dream our eternal dream.

BOOK 3

The Return

The gate guard lounged in the dark shadows of the gatehouse of Old City. Outside, he could hear the voices of the other guards, tight and tense with excitement and fear, talking up their courage. There must be twenty of them out there, the old guard thought sourly. The night watch had been doubled, those off duty had decided to stay rather than go back home. Above him, on the wall, he could hear the slow, steady pacing of the Knights of Solamnia. High above him, occasionally, he could hear the creak and flap of a dragon's wing, or sometimes their voices, speaking to each other in the secret tongue of the dragons. These were the bronze dragons Lord Gunthar had brought from the High Clerist's Tower, keeping watch in the air as the humans kept watch upon the ground.

All around him he could hear the sounds—the sounds of impending doom.

That thought was in the gatekeeper's mind, though not in those exact words, of course—neither "impending" nor "doom" being a part of his vocabulary. But the knowledge was there, just the same. The gate guard was an old mercenary, he'd been through many of these nights. He'd been a young man like those outside, once, boasting of the great deeds he'd do in the morning. His first battle, he'd been so scared he couldn't to this day remember a thing about it.

But there'd been many battles after that. You got used to the fear. It became a part of you, just like your sword. Thinking about this battle coming up was no different. The morning would come and, if you were lucky, so would the night.

A sudden clatter of pikes and voices and a general flurry jolted the old guard out of his philosophic musings. Grumbling, but feeling a touch of the old excitement just the same, he poked his head out of the guardhouse.

"I heard something!" a young guard panted, running up,

---

nearly out of breath. "Out—out there! Sounded like armor jingling, a whole troop!"

The other guards were peering out into the darkness. Even
the Knights of Solamnia had ceased their pacing and were looking down into the broad highway that ran through the gate
from New City into Old. Extra torches had been hastily added
to those that already burned on the walls. They cast a bright
circle of light on the ground below. But the light ended about
twenty feet away, making the darkness beyond seem just that
much darker. The old guard could hear the sounds now, too,
but he didn't panic. He was veteran enough to know that darkness and fear can make one man sound like a regiment.

Stumping out of the gatehouse, he waved his hands, adding
with a snarl, "Back to yer posts."

The younger guards, muttering, returned to their positions,
but kept their weapons ready. The old guard, hand on his
sword hilt, stood stolidly in the middle of the street, waiting.

Sure enough, into the light came—not a division of
draconians—but one man (who might, however, have been big
enough for two) and what appeared to be a kender.

The two stopped, blinking in the torchlight. The old guard
sized them up. The big man wore no cloak, and the guard could
see light reflecting off armor that might once have gleamed
brightly but was now caked with gray mud and even blackened
in places, as though he had been in a fire. The kender, too, was
covered with the same type of mud—though he had apparently
made some effort to brush it off his gaudy blue leggings. The
big man limped when he walked, and both he and the kender
gave every indication of having recently been in battle.

Odd, thought the gate guard. There's been no fighting yet,
leastways none that we've heard tell of.

"Cool customers, both of 'em," the old guard muttered, not-
ing that the big man's hand rested easily on the hilt of his sword
as he looked about, taking stock of the situation. The kender
was staring around with usual kender curiosity. The gate guard
was slightly startled to see, however, that the kender held in his
arms a large, leatherbound book.

———

"State yer business," the gate guard said, coming forward to stand in front of the two.

"I'm Tasslehoff Burrfoot," said the kender, managing, after a brief struggle with the book, to free a small hand. He held it out to the guard. "And this is my friend, Caramon. We're from Sol—"

"Our business depends on where we are," said the man called Caramon in a friendly voice but with a serious expression on his face that gave the gate guard pause.

"You mean you don't know where you are?" the guard asked suspiciously.

"We're not from this part of the country," the big man answered coolly. "We lost our map. Seeing the lights of the city, we naturally headed toward it."

Yeah, and I'm Lord Amothus, thought the guard. "Yer in Palanthas."

The big man glanced behind him, then back down at the guard, who barely came to his shoulder. "So that must be New City, behind us. Where are all the people? We've walked the length and breadth of the town. No sign of anyone."

"We're under alert." The guard jerked his head. "Everyone's been taken inside the walls. I guess that's all you need to know for the present. Now, what's yer business here? And how is it you don't know what's going on? The word's over half the country by now, I reckon."

The big man ran his hand across an unshaven jaw, smiling ruefully. "A full bottle of dwarf spirits kinda blots out most everything. True enough, captain?"

"True enough," growled the guard. And also true enough that this fellow's eyes were sharp and clear and filled with a fixed purpose, a firm resolve. Looking into those eyes, the guard shook his head. He'd seen them before, the eyes of a man who is going to his death, who knows it, and who has made peace with both the gods and himself.

"Will you let us inside?" the big man asked. "I guess, from the looks of things, you could use another couple of fighters."

"We can use a man yer size," the guard returned. He scowled

down at the kender. "But I mistrust we should just leave 'im here for buzzard bait."

"I'm a fighter, too!" the kender protested indignantly. "Why, I saved Caramon's life once!" His face brightened. "Do you want to hear about it? It's the most wonderful story. We were in a magical fortress. Raistlin had taken me there, after he killed my fri— But never mind about that. Anyway, there were these dark dwarves and they were attacking Caramon and he slipped and—"

"Open the gate!" the old guard shouted.

"C'mon, Tas," the big man said.

"But I just got to the best part!"

"Oh, by the way"—the big man turned around, first deftly squelching the kender with his hand—"can you tell me the date?"

"Thirdday, Fifthmonth, 356," said the guard. "Oh, and you might be wantin' a cleric to look at that leg of yours."

"Clerics," the big man murmured to himself. "That's right, I'd forgotten. There are clerics now. Thank you," he called out as he and the kender walked through the gates. The gate guard could hear the kender's voice piping up again, as he managed to free himself from the big man's hand.

"Phew! You should really wash, Caramon. I've—blooey! Drat, mud in my mouth!— Now, where was I? Oh, yes, you should have let me finish! I'd just gotten to the part where you tripped in the blood and—"

Shaking his head, the gate guard looked after the two. "There's a story there," he muttered, as the big gates swung shut again, "and not even a kender could make up a better one, I'll wager."

CHAPTER
I

What's it say, Caramon?" Tas stood on tiptoe, trying to peer over the big man's arm.

"Shh!" Caramon whispered irritably. "I'm reading." He shook his arm. "Let loose." The big man had been leafing hurriedly through the *Chronicles* he had taken from Astinus. But he had stopped turning pages, and was now studying one intently.

With a sigh—after all, *he'd* carried the book!—Tas slumped back against the wall and looked around. They were standing beneath one of the flaming braziers that Palanthians used to light the streets at night. It was nearly dawn, the kender guessed. The storm clouds blocked the sunlight, but the city was taking on a dismal gray tint. A chill fog curled up from the bay, swirling and winding through the streets.

Though there were lights in most of the windows, there were few people on the streets, the citizens having been told to stay indoors, unless they were members of the militia. But Tas could see the faces of women, pressed against the glass, watching, waiting. Occasionally a man ran past them, clutching a weapon in his hand, heading for the front gate of the city. And once, a door to a dwelling right across from Tas opened. A man stepped out, a rusty sword in his hand. A woman followed, weeping. Leaning down, he kissed her tenderly, then kissed the small child she held in her arms. Then, turning away abruptly, he walked rapidly down the street. As he passed Tas, the kender saw tears flowing down his face.

"Oh, no!" Caramon muttered.

"What? What?" Tas cried, leaping up, trying to see the page Caramon was reading.

"Listen to this—'on the morning of Thirdday, the flying citadel appeared in the air above Palanthas, accompanied by flights of blue dragons and black. And with the appearance of the citadel in the air, there came before the Gates of Old City an apparition, the sight of which caused more than one veteran of many campaigns to blench in fear and turn his head away.

" 'For there appeared, as if created out of the darkness of the night itself, Lord Soth, Knight of the Black Rose, mounted upon a nightmare with eyes and hooves of flame. He rode unchallenged toward the city gate, the guards fleeing before him in terror.

" 'And there he stopped.

" ' "Lord of Palanthas," the death knight called in a hollow voice that came from the realms of death, "surrender your city to Lord Kitiara. Give up to her the keys to the Tower of High Sorcery, name her ruler of Palanthas, and she will allow you to continue to live in peace. Your city will be spared destruction."

" 'Lord Amothus took his place upon the wall, looking down at the death knight. Many of those around him could not look, so shaken were they by their fear. But the lord—although pale as death himself—stood tall and straight, his words bringing back courage to those who had lost it."

" ' "Take this message to your Dragon Highlord. Palanthas has lived in peace and beauty for many centuries. But we will buy neither peace nor beauty at the price of our freedom."

" ' "Then buy it at the price of your lives!" Lord Soth shouted.

Out of the air, seemingly, materialized his legions—thirteen skeletal warriors, riding upon horses with eyes and hooves of flame, took their places behind him. And, behind them, standing in chariots made of human bone pulled by wyvern, appeared banshees—the spirits of those elven women constrained by the gods to serve Soth. They held swords of ice in their hands, to hear their wailing cry alone meant death.

" 'Raising a hand made visible only by the glove of chain steel he wore upon it, Lord Soth pointed at the gate of the city that stood closed, barring his way. He spoke a word of magic and, at that word, a dreadful cold swept over all who watched, freezing the soul more than the blood. The iron of the gate began to whiten with frost, then it changed to ice, then—at another word from Soth—the ice gate shattered.

" 'Soth's hand fell. He charged through the broken gate, his legions following.

" 'Waiting for him on the other side of the gate, mounted upon the bronze dragon, Fireflash (his dragonish name being Khirsah), was Tanis Half-Elven, Hero of the Lance. Immediately upon sighting his opponent, the death knight sought to slay him instantly by shouting the magical power word, "Die!" Tanis Half-Elven, being protected by the silver bracelet of magic resistance, was not affected by the spell. But the bracelet that saved his life in this first attack, could help him no longer—' "

" 'Help him no longer!' " cried Tas, interrupting Caramon's reading. "What does that mean?"

"Shush!" Caramon hissed and went on. " '—help him no longer. The bronze dragon he rode, having no magical protection, died at Soth's command, forcing Tanis Half-Elven to fight the death knight on foot. Lord Soth dismounted to meet his opponent according to the Laws of Combat as set forth by the Knights of Solamnia, these laws binding the death knight still, even though he had long since passed beyond their jurisdiction. Tanis Half-Elven fought bravely but was no match for Lord Soth. He fell, mortally wounded, the death knight's sword in his chest—' "

"No!" Tas gasped. "No! We can't let Tanis die!" Reaching up, he tugged on Caramon's arm. "Let's go! There's still time! We can find him and warn him—"

"I can't, Tas," Caramon said quietly. "I've got to go to the Tower. I can sense Raistlin's presence drawing closer to me. I don't have time, Tas."

"You can't mean that! We can't just let Tanis die!" Tas whispered, staring at Caramon, wide-eyed.

"No, Tas, we can't," said Caramon, regarding the kender gravely. "*You're* going to save him."

The thought literally took Tasslehoff's breath away. When he finally found his voice, it was more of a squeak. "Me? But, Caramon, I'm not a warrior! Oh, I know I told the guard that I—"

"Tasslehoff Burrfoot," Caramon said sternly, "I suppose it is possible that the gods arranged this entire matter simply for your own private amusement. Possible—but I doubt it. We're part of this world, and we've got to take some responsibility for it. I see this now. I see it very clearly." He sighed, and for a moment his face was solemn and so filled with sadness that Tas felt a choking lump rise up in his throat.

"I know that I'm part of the world, Caramon," Tas said miserably, "and I'd gladly take as much responsibility as I think it likely I can handle. But—it's just that I'm such a *short* part of the world—if you take my meaning. And Lord Soth's such a tall and ugly part. And—"

A trumpet sounded, then another. Both Tas and Caramon fell silent, listening until the braying had died away.

"That's it, isn't it?" Tas said softly.

"Yes," Caramon replied. "You better hurry."

Closing the book, he shoved it carefully into an old knapsack Tas had managed to "acquire" when they were in the deserted New City. The kender had managed to acquire some new pouches for himself, as well, plus a few other interesting items it was probably just as well Caramon didn't know he had. Then, reaching out his hand, the big man laid it on Tas's head, smoothing back the ridiculous topknot.

"Good-bye, Tas. Thank you."

———

"But, Caramon!" Tas stared at him, feeling suddenly very lonely and confused. "Wh-where will you be?"

Caramon glanced up into the sky to where the Tower of High Sorcery loomed, a black rent in the storm clouds. Lights burned in the top windows of the Tower where the laboratory—and the Portal—were located.

Tas followed his gaze, looking up at the Tower. He saw the storm clouds lowering around it, the eerie lightning play around it, toying with it. He remembered his one close-up glimpse of the Shoikan Grove—

"Oh, Caramon!" he cried, catching hold of the big man's hand. "Caramon, don't . . . wait. . . ."

"Good-bye, Tas," Caramon said, firmly detaching the clinging kender. "I've got to do this. You know what will happen if I don't. And you know what you've got to do, too. Now hurry up. The citadel's probably over the gate by now."

"But, Caramon—" Tas wailed.

"Tas, you've got to do this!" Caramon yelled, his angry voice echoing down the empty street. "Are you going to let Tanis die without trying to help him?"

Tas shrank back. He'd never seen Caramon angry before, at least, not angry at him. And in all their adventures together, Caramon had never once yelled at him. "No, Caramon," he said meekly. "It's just . . . I'm not sure what I can do. . . ."

"You'll think of something," Caramon muttered, scowling. "You always do." Turning around, he walked away, leaving Tas to stare after him disconsolately.

"G-good-bye, Caramon," he called out after the retreating figure. "I—I won't let you down."

The big man turned. When he spoke, his voice sounded funny to Tas, like maybe he was choking on something. "I know you won't, Tas, no matter what happens." With a wave, he set off again down the street.

In the distance, Tas saw the dark shadows of Shoikan Grove, the shadows no day would ever brighten, the shadows where lurked the guardians of the Tower.

Tas stood for a moment, watching Caramon until he lost him

in the darkness. He *had* hoped, if the truth be told, that Caramon would suddenly change his mind, turn around and shout, "Wait, Tas! I'll come with you to save Tanis!"

But he didn't.

"Which leaves it up to me," Tas said with a sigh. "And he *yelled* at me!" Snuffling a little, he turned and trudged off in the opposite direction, toward the gate. His heart was in his mud-coated shoes, making them feel even heavier. He had absolutely no idea how he was going to go about rescuing Tanis from a death knight, and, the more he thought about it, the more unusual it seemed that Caramon would give him this responsibility.

"Still, I *did* save Caramon's life," Tas muttered. "Maybe he's coming to realize—"

Suddenly, he stopped and stood stock-still in the middle of the street.

"Caramon got rid of me!" he cried. "Tasslehoff Burrfoot, you have all the brains of a doorknob, as Flint told you many times. He got rid of me! He's going there to *die!* Sending me to rescue Tanis was just an excuse!" Distraught and unhappy, Tas stared down the street one way and up it another. "Now, what do I do?" he muttered.

He took a step toward Caramon. Then he heard a trumpet sound again, this time with a shrill, blaring note of alarm. And, rising above it, he thought he could hear a voice, shouting orders—Tanis's voice.

"But if I go to Caramon, Tanis will die!" Tas stopped. Half-turning, he took a step toward Tanis. Then he stopped again, winding his topknot into a perfect corkscrew of indecision. The kender had never felt so frustrated in his entire life.

"Both of them need me!" he wailed in agony. "How can I choose?"

Then—"I know!" His brow cleared. "That's it!"

With a great sigh of relief, Tas spun around and continued in the direction of the gate, this time at a run.

"I'll rescue Tanis," he panted as he took a short-cut through an alley, "and then I'll just come back and rescue Caramon.

Tanis might even be of some help to me."

Scuttling down the alley, sending cats scattering in a panic, Tas frowned irritably. "I wonder how many heroes this makes that I've had to save," he said to himself with a sniff. "Frankly, I'm getting just a bit fed up with all of them!"

The floating citadel appeared in the skies over Palanthas just as the trumpets sounded for the changing of the watch. The tall, crumbling spires and battlements, the towering stone walls, the lighted windows jammed with draconian troops—all could be seen quite plainly as the citadel floated downward, resting on its foundation of boiling, magical cloud.

The wall of Old City was crammed with men—townsmen, knights, mercenaries. None spoke a word. All gripped their weapons, staring upward in grim silence.

But, after all, there was one word spoken at the sight of the citadel—or several, as it were.

"Oh!" breathed Tas in awe, clasping his hands together, marveling at the sight. "Isn't it wonderful! I'd forgotten how truly magnificent and glorious the flying citadels are! I'd give anything, *anything*, to ride on one." Then, with a sigh, he shook himself. "Not now, Burrfoot," he said to himself sternly in his Flint voice. "You have work to do. Now"—he looked around— "there's the gate. There's the citadel. And there goes Lord Amothus. . . . My, he looks terrible! I've seen better looking dead people. But where's— Ah!"

A grim processional appeared, marching up the street toward Tas—a group of Solamnic Knights, walking on foot, leading their horses. There was no cheering, they did not talk. Each man's face was solemn and tense, each man knew he walked—most likely—to his death. They were led by a man whose bearded face stood out in sharp contrast to the clean-shaven, moustached faces of the knights around him. And, although he wore the armor of a Knight of the Rose, he did not wear it with the ease of the other knights.

"Tanis always hated plate-mail," Tas said, watching his friend approach. "And here he is, wearing the armor of a Knight of

---

Solamnia. I wonder what Sturm would have thought of that! I wish Sturm was here right now!" Tas's lower lip began quivering. A tear sneaked down his nose before he could stop it. "I wish *anyone* brave and clever was here right now!"

When the Knights drew near the Gate, Tanis stopped and turned to face them, issuing orders in a low voice. The creaking sound of dragon wings came from overhead. Looking up, Tasslehoff saw Khirsah, circling, leading a formation of other bronze dragons. And there was the citadel, coming closer to the wall, dropping down lower and lower.

"Sturm's not here. Caramon's not here. No one's here, Burrfoot," Tas muttered, resolutely wiping his eyes. "Once again— you're on your own. Now, what *am* I going to do?"

Wild thoughts ran through the kender's mind—everything from holding Tanis at swordpoint ("I mean it, Tanis, keep those hands in the air!") to clunking him over the head with a sharp rock ("Uh, say, Tanis, would you mind taking off your helm for a moment?"). Tas was even desperate enough to consider telling the truth ("You see, Tanis, we went back in time, then we went ahead in time, and Caramon got hold of this book from Astinus just as the world was coming to an end, and, in the next to the last chapter, it tells in there how you died, and—"). Suddenly, Tas saw Tanis raise his right arm. There was a flash of silver—

"That's it," said Tas, breathing a profound sigh of relief. "That's what I'll do—just what I do best. . . ."

"No matter what happens, leave me to deal with Lord Soth," Tanis said, looking grimly at the knights standing around him. "I want you to swear this, by the Code and the Measure."

"Tanis, my lord—" began Sir Markham.

"No, I'm not going to argue, Knight. You'll stand no chance at all against him without magical protection. Each one of you will be needed to fight his legions. Now, either swear this oath, or I will order you off the field. Swear!"

From beyond the closed gate, a deep, hollow voice spoke, calling out for Palanthas to surrender. The knights glanced at each other, feeling shivers of fear run through their bodies at the inhuman sound. There was a moment's silence, broken only by the creaking of dragons' wings overhead as the great creatures—bronze, silver, blue, and black—circled, eyeing each other balefully, waiting for the call to battle. Tanis's dragon, Khirsah, hovered in the air near his rider, ready to come down upon command.

And then they heard Lord Amothus's voice—brittle and tight, but strong with purpose—answering the death knight. "Take this message to your Dragon Highlord. Palanthas has lived in peace and beauty for many centuries. But we will buy neither peace nor beauty at the price of our freedom."

"I swear," said Sir Markham softly, "by the Code and the Measure."

"I swear," came the responses of the other knights after him.

"Thank you," Tanis said, looking at each of the young men standing before him, thinking that most wouldn't be alive much longer. . . . Thinking that he himself— Angrily, he shook his head. "Fireflash—" The words that would summon his dragon were on Tanis's lips when he heard a commotion break out at the rear of the line of knights.

"Ouch! Get off my foot, you great lummox!"

A horse whinnied. Tanis heard one of the knights cursing, then a shrill voice answering innocently, "Well, it's not my fault! Your horse *stepped* on me! Flint was right about those stupid beasts—"

The other horses, sensing battle and already affected by the tenseness of their riders, pricked their ears and snorted nervously. One danced out of line, his rider grasping at the bridle.

"Get those horses under control!" Tanis called out tensely. "What's going on—"

"Let me past! Get out of my way. What? Is that dagger yours? You must have dropped it. . . ."

Beyond the gate, Tanis heard the death knight's voice.

"You'll pay for it with your lives!"

And from the line ahead of him, another voice.

"Tanis, it's me, Tasslehoff!"

———

The half-elf's heart sank. He wasn't at all certain, at that moment, which voice chilled him more.

But there didn't seem to be time for thought or wonder. Glancing over his shoulder, Tanis saw the gate turn to ice, he saw it shatter. . . .

"Tanis!" Something had hold of his arm. "Oh, Tanis!" Tas clutched at him. "Tanis! You've got to come quickly and save Caramon! He's going into Shoikan Grove!"

Caramon? Caramon's dead! was Tanis's first thought. But then Tas is dead, too. What's going on? Am I going mad from fear?

Someone shouted. Looking around dazedly, Tanis saw the faces of the knights turn deathly white beneath their helms, and he knew Lord Soth and his legions were entering the gates.

"Mount!" he called, frantically trying to pry loose the kender, who was clinging to him tenaciously. "Tas! This is no time— Get out of here, damn it!"

"Caramon's going to die!" Tas wailed. "You've got to save him, Tanis!"

"Caramon's . . . already . . . dead!" Tanis snarled.

Khirsah landed on the ground beside him, screaming a battle cry. Evil and good—the other dragons shrieked in anger, flying at each other, talons gleaming. In an instant, battle was joined. The air was filled with the flash of lightning and the smell of acid. From above, horns sounded in the floating citadel. There were cries of glee from the draconians, who began eagerly dropping down into the city, their leathery wings spread to break their fall.

And moving closer, the chill of death flowing from his fleshless body, rode Lord Soth.

But, try as he might, Tanis couldn't shake Tas loose. Finally, swearing beneath his breath, the half-elf got a grip on the writhing kender. Catching hold of Tas around the waist, so angry he was literally choking with rage—Tanis hurled the kender into a corner of a nearby alley.

"And stay there!" he roared.

"Tanis!" Tas pleaded. "You can't go out there! You're going to die. I know!"

Giving Tas a last, furious glance, Tanis turned on his heel and ran. "Fireflash!" he shouted. The dragon swooped over to him, landing on the street beside him.

"Tanis!" Tas screamed shrilly. "You can't fight Lord Soth without the bracelet!"

CHAPTER 2

The bracelet! Tanis looked down at his wrist. The bracelet was gone! Whirling, he made a lunge for the kender. But it was too late. Tasslehoff was dashing down the street, running as if his life depended on it. (Which, after glimpsing Tanis's furious face, Tas figured it probably did.)

"Tanis!" cried out Sir Markham.

Tanis turned. Lord Soth sat upon his nightmare, framed by the shattered gates of the city of Palanthas. His flaming-eyed gaze met Tanis's and held. Even at that distance, Tanis felt his soul shrivel with the fear that shrouds the walking dead.

What could he do? He didn't have the bracelet. Without it, there'd be no chance. No chance whatsoever! Thank the gods, Tanis thought in that split second, thank the gods I'm not a knight, bound to die with honor.

"Run!" he commanded through lips so stiff he could barely speak. "Fly! There is nothing you can do against these! Remember your oath! Retreat! Spend your lives fighting the living—"

Even as he spoke, a draconian landed in front of him, its horrible reptilian face twisted in bloodlust. Remembering just in time not to stab the thing, whose foul body would turn to stone, encasing the sword of its killers, Tanis bashed it in the face with the hilt of his weapon, kicked it in the stomach, then leaped over it as it tumbled to the ground.

Behind him, he heard the sounds of horses shrieking in terror and the clattering of hooves. He hoped the knights were obeying his last command, but he could spare no time to see. There was still a chance, if he could get hold of Tas and the magical bracelet. . . .

"The kender!" he yelled to the dragon, pointing down the street at the fleeing, fleet-footed little figure.

Khirsah understood and was off at once, the tips of his wings grazing buildings as he swooped down the broad street in pursuit, knocking stone and brick to the ground.

Tanis ran behind the dragon. He did not look around. He didn't need to. He could hear, by the agonized cries and screams, what was happening.

That morning, death rode the streets of Palanthas. Led by Lord Soth, the ghastly army swept through the gate like a chill wind, withering everything that stood in its path.

By the time Tanis caught up with the dragon, Khirsah had Tas in his teeth. Gripping the kender upside down by the seat of his blue pants, the dragon was shaking him like the most efficient of jail wardens. Tas's newly acquired pouches flew open, sending a small hailstorm of rings, spoons, a napkin holder, and a half of a cheese tumbling about the street.

But no silver bracelet.

"Where is it, Tas?" Tanis demanded angrily, longing to shake the kender himself.

"Y-you'll . . . n-nev-ver . . . f-find-d-d it-t-t-t," returned the kender, his teeth rattling in his head.

"Put him down," Tanis instructed the dragon. "Fireflash, keep watch."

The floating citadel had come to a stop at the city's walls, its magic-users and dark clerics battling the attacking silver and bronze dragons. It was difficult to see in the flashes of blinding lightning and the spreading haze of smoke, but Tanis was certain he caught a quick glimpse of a blue dragon leaving the citadel. Kitiara, he thought—but he had no time to spare worrying about her.

Khirsah dropped Tas (nearly on his head), and—spreading his wings—turned to face the southern part of the city where the enemy was grouping and where the city's defenders were vailantly holding them back.

Tanis came over to stare down at the small culprit, who was staring right back at him defiantly as he stood up.

"Tasslehoff," said Tanis, his voice quivering with suppressed rage, "this time you've gone too far. This prank may cost the lives of hundreds of innocent people. Give me the bracelet, Tas, and know this—from this moment on, our friendship ends!"

Expecting some hare-brained excuse or some sniffling apology, the half-elf was not prepared to see Tas regarding him with a pale face, trembling lips, and an air of quiet dignity.

"It's very hard to explain, Tanis, and I really don't have time. But your fighting Lord Soth wouldn't have made any difference." He looked at the half-elf earnestly. "You must believe me, Tanis. I'm telling the truth. It wouldn't have mattered. All those people who are going to die would still have died, and you would have died, too, and—what's worse—the whole world would have died. But you didn't, so maybe it won't. And now," Tas said firmly, tugging and twitching his pouches and his clothes into place, "we've got to go rescue Caramon."

Tanis stared at Tas, then, wearily, he put his hand to his head and yanked off the hot, steel helm. He had absolutely no idea what was going on. "All right, Tas," he said in exhaustion. "Tell me about Caramon. He's alive? Where is he?"

Tas's face twisted in worry. "That's just it, Tanis. He may *not* be alive. At least not much longer. He's going to try to get into the Shoikan Grove!"

"The Grove!" Tanis looked alarmed. "That's impossible!"

"I know!" Tas tugged nervously at his topknot. "But he's trying to get to the Tower of High Sorcery to stop Raistlin—"

"I see," Tanis muttered. He tossed the helm down into the

street. "Or I'm beginning to, at any rate. Let's go. Which way?"

Tas's face brightened. "You're coming? You believe me? Oh, Tanis! I'm so glad! You've no idea what a major responsibility it is, looking after Caramon. This way!" he cried, pointing eagerly.

"Is there anything further I can do for you, Half-Elven?" asked Khirsah, fanning his wings, his gaze going eagerly to the battle being fought overhead.

"Not unless you can enter the Grove."

Khirsah shook his head. "I am sorry, Half-Elven. Not even dragons can enter that accursed woods. I wish you good fortune, but do not expect to find your friend alive."

Wings beating, the dragon leaped into the air and soared toward the action. Shaking his head gravely, Tanis started off down the street at a rapid pace, Tasslehoff running to keep up.

"Maybe Caramon couldn't even get that far," Tas said hopefully. "*I* couldn't, the last time Flint and I came. And kender aren't frightened of anything!"

"You say he's trying to stop Raistlin?"

Tas nodded.

"He'll get that far," Tanis predicted gloomily.

It had taken every bit of Caramon's nerve and courage to even approach the Shoikan Grove. As it was, he was able to come closer to it than any other living mortal not bearing a charm allowing safe passage. Now he stood before those dark, silent trees, shivering and sweating and trying to make himself take one more step.

"My death lies in there," he murmured to himself, licking his dry lips. "But what difference should that make? I've faced death before, a hundred times!" Hand gripping the hilt of his sword, Caramon edged a foot forward.

"No, I will not die!" he shouted at the forest. "I cannot die. Too much depends on me. And I will not be stopped by . . . by trees!"

He edged his other foot forward.

"I have walked in darker places than this." He kept talking, defiantly. "I have walked the Forest of Wayreth. I have walked Krynn when it was dying. I have seen the end of the world. No," he continued firmly. "This forest holds no terrors for me that I cannot overcome."

With that, Caramon strode forward and stepped into the Shoikan Grove.

He was immediately plunged into everlasting darkness. It was like being back in the Tower again, when Crysania's spell had blinded him. Only this time he was alone. Panic clutched him. There was life within that darkness! Horrible, unholy life that wasn't life at all but living death. . . . Caramon's muscles went weak. He fell to his hands and knees, sobbing and shivering in terror.

"You're ours!" whispered soft, hissing voices. "Your blood, your warmth, your life! Ours! Ours! Come closer. Bring us your sweet blood, your warm flesh. We are cold, cold, cold beyond endurance. Come closer, come closer."

Horror overwhelmed Caramon. He had only to turn and run and he would escape. . . . "But, no," he gasped in the hissing, smothering darkness, "I must stop Raistlin! I must . . . go . . . on."

For the first time in his life, Caramon reached far down within himself and found the same indomitable will that had led his twin to overcome frailty and pain and even death itself to achieve his goal. Gritting his teeth, unable to stand yet determined to move ahead, Caramon crawled on his hands and knees through the dirt.

It was a valiant effort, but he did not get far. Staring into the darkness, he watched in paralyzed fascination as a fleshless hand reached up through the ground. Fingers, chill and smooth as marble, closed over his hand and began dragging him down. Desperately, he tried to free himself, but other hands grasped for him, their nails tearing into his flesh. He felt himself being sucked under. The hissing voices whispered in his ears, lips of bone pressed against his flesh. The cold froze his heart.

"I have failed. . . ."

"Caramon," came a worried voice.

Caramon stirred.

"Caramon?" Then, "Tanis, he's coming around!"

"Thank the gods!"

Caramon opened his eyes. Looking up, he stared into the face of the bearded half-elf, who was looking at him with an expression of relief mingled with puzzlement, amazement, and admiration.

"Tanis!" Sitting up groggily, still numb with horror, Caramon gripped his friend in his strong arms, holding him fast, sobbing in relief.

"My friend!" Tanis said, and then was prevented from saying anything more by his own tears choking him.

"Are you all right, Caramon?" Tas asked, hovering near.

The big man drew a shivering breath. "Yes," he said, putting his head into his shaking hands. "I guess so."

"That was the bravest thing I have seen any man do," Tanis said solemnly, leaning back to rest upon his heels as he stared at Caramon. "The bravest . . . and the stupidest."

Caramon flushed. "Yeah," he muttered, "well, you know me."

"I used to," Tanis said, scratching his beard. His gaze took in the big man's splendid physique, his bronze skin, his expression of quiet, firm resolve. "Damn it, Caramon! A month ago, you passed out dead drunk at my feet! Your gut practically dragged the floor! And now—"

"I've lived years, Tanis," Caramon said, slowly getting to his feet with Tas's help. "That's all I can tell you. But, what happened? How did I get out of that horrible place?" Glancing behind him, he saw the shadows of the trees far down at the end of the street, and he could not help shuddering.

"I found you," Tanis said, rising to his feet. "They—those things—were dragging you under. You would have had an uneasy resting place there, my friend."

"How did you get in?"

"This," Tanis said, smiling and holding up a silver bracelet.

"It got you in? Then maybe—"

"No, Caramon," Tanis said, carefully tucking the bracelet back inside his belt with a sidelong glance at Tas, who was looking extremely innocent. "Its magic was barely strong enough to get me to the edge of those cursed woods. I could feel its power dwindling—"

Caramon's eager expression faded. "I tried our magical device, too," he said, looking at Tas. "It doesn't work either. I didn't much expect it to. It wouldn't even get us through the Forest of Wayreth. But I had to try. I—I couldn't even get it to transform itself! It nearly fell apart in my hands, so I left it alone." He was silent for a moment, then, his voice shaking with desperation, he burst out, "Tanis, I *have* to reach the Tower!" His hands clenched into fists. "I can't explain, but I've seen the future, Tanis! I must go into the Portal and stop Raistlin. I'm the only one who can!"

Startled, Tanis laid a calming hand on the big man's shoulder. "So Tas told me—sort of. But, Caramon, Dalamar's there . . . and . . . how in the name of the gods can you get inside the Portal anyway?"

"Tanis," Caramon said, looking at his friend with such a serious, firm expression that the half-elf blinked in astonishment, "you cannot understand and there is no time to explain. But you've got to believe me. I *must* get into that Tower!"

"You're right," Tanis said, after staring at Caramon in mystified wonder, "I don't understand. But I'll help you, if I can, if it's at all possible."

Caramon sighed heavily, his head drooping, his shoulders slumping. "Thank you, my friend," he said simply. "I've been so alone through all this. If it hadn't been for Tas—"

He looked over at the kender, but Tas wasn't listening. His gaze was fixed with rapt attention on the flying citadel, still hovering above the city walls. The battle was raging in the air around it, among the dragons, and on the ground below, as could be seen from the thick columns of smoke rising from the south part of the city, the sounds of screams and cries, the clash of arms, and the clattering of horses' hooves.

"I'll bet a person could fly that citadel to the Tower," Tas said, staring at it with interest. "Whoosh! Right over the Grove. After all, its magic is evil and the Grove's magic is evil and it's pretty big—the citadel, that is, not the Grove. It would probably take a lot of magic to stop it and—"

"Tas!"

The kender turned to find both Caramon and Tanis standing, staring at him.

"What?" he cried in alarm. "I didn't do it! It's not my fault—"

"If we could only get up there!" Tanis stared at the citadel.

"The magical device!" Caramon cried in excitement, fishing it out of the inner pocket of the shirt he wore beneath his armor. "This will take us there!"

"Take us where?" Tasslehoff had suddenly realized something was going on. "Take us . . ."—he followed Tanis's gaze— "there? There!" The kender's eyes shone as brightly as stars. "Really? Truly? Into the flying citadel! That's so wonderful! I'm ready. Let's go!" His gaze went to the magical device Caramon was holding in his hand. "But that only works for two people, Caramon. How will Tanis get up?"

Caramon cleared his throat uncomfortably, and comprehension dawned upon the kender.

"Oh, no!" Tas wailed. "No!"

"I'm sorry, Tas," Caramon said, his trembling hands hastily transforming the small, nondescript pendant into the brilliant, bejeweled sceptre, "but we're going to have a stiff fight on our hands to get inside that thing—"

"You *must* take me, Caramon!" Tas cried. "It was *my* idea! I can fight!" Fumbling in his belt, he drew his little knife. "I saved your life! I saved Tanis's life!"

Seeing by the expression on Caramon's face that he was going to be stubborn about this, Tas turned to Tanis and threw his arms around him pleadingly. "Take me with you! Maybe the device will work with three people. Or rather two people and a kender. I'm short. It may not notice me! Please!"

"No, Tas," Tanis said firmly. Prying the kender loose, he moved over to stand next to Caramon. Raising a warning finger, he cautioned—with a look Tas knew well. "And I mean it this time!"

Tas stood there with an expression so forlorn that Caramon's heart misgave him. "Tas," he said softly, kneeling down beside the distraught kender, "you saw what's going to happen if we fail! I need Tanis with me—I need his strength, his sword. You understand, don't you?"

Tas tried to smile, but his lower lip quivered. "Yes, Caramon, I understand. I'm sorry."

"And, after all, it *was* your idea," Caramon added solemnly, getting to his feet.

While this thought appeared to comfort the kender, it didn't do a lot for the confidence of the half-elf. "Somehow," Tanis muttered, "*that* has me worried." So did the expression on the kender's face. "Tas"—Tanis assumed his sternest air as Caramon moved to stand beside him once more—"promise me that you will find somewhere safe and *stay there* and that you'll keep out of mischief! Do you promise?"

Tas's face was the picture of inner turmoil—he bit his lip, his brows knotted together, he twisted his topknot clear up to the top of his head. Then—suddenly—his eyes widened. He smiled, and let go of his hair, which tumbled down his back. "Of course, I promise, Tanis," he said with expression of such sincere innocence that the half-elf groaned.

But there was nothing he could do about it now. Caramon was already reciting the magical chant and manipulating the device. The last glimpse Tanis had, before he vanished into the swirling mists of magic, was of Tasslehoff standing on one foot, rubbing the back of his leg with the other, and waving goodbye with a cheerful smile.

—

Fireflash!" said Tasslehoff to himself as soon as Tanis and Caramon had vanished from his sight.

Turning, the kender ran down the street toward the southern end of town where the fighting was heaviest. "For," he reasoned, "that's where the dragons are probably doing their battling."

It was then that the unfortunate flaw in his scheme occurred to Tas. "Drat!" he muttered, stopping and staring up into the sky that was filled with dragons snarling and clawing and biting and breathing their breath weapons at each other in rage. "Now, how am I ever going to find him in *that* mess?"

Drawing a deep, exasperated breath, the kender promptly choked and coughed. Looking around, he noticed that the air was getting extremely smoky and that the sky, formerly gray with the dawn beneath the storm clouds, was now brightening with a fiery glow.

Palanthas was burning.

"*Not* exactly a safe place to be," Tas muttered. "And Tanis told me to find a safe place. And the safest place I know is with him and Caramon and they're up there in that citadel right now, probably getting into no end of trouble, and I'm stuck here in a town that's being burned and pillaged and looted." The kender thought hard. "I know!" he said suddenly. "I'll pray to Fizban! It worked a couple of times—well, I *think* it worked. But—at any rate—it can't hurt."

Seeing a draconian patrol coming down the street and not wanting any interruption, Tas ducked down an alley where he crouched behind a refuse pile and looked up into the sky. "Fizban," he said solemnly, "this is *it!* If we don't get out of this one, then we might just as soon toss the silver down the well and move in with the chickens, as my mother used to say, and—though I'm not too certain what she had in mind—it certainly does sound dire. I need to be with Tanis and Caramon. You *know* they can't manage things without me. And to do that, I need a dragon. Now, that isn't much. I *could* have asked for a lot more—like maybe you just skipping the middle man and whooshing me up there. But I didn't. Just one dragon. That's it."

Tas waited.

Nothing happened.

Heaving an exasperated sigh, Tas eyed the sky sternly and waited some more.

Still nothing.

Tas heaved a sigh. "All right, I admit it. I'd give the contents of one pouch—maybe even two—for the chance to fly in the citadel. There, that's the truth. The rest of the truth at any rate. And I *did* always find your hat for you. . . ."

But, despite this magnanimous gesture, no dragon appeared.

Finally, Tas gave up. Realizing that the draconian patrol had passed on by, he rose up from behind the garbage heap and made his way back out of the alley onto the street.

"Well," he muttered, "I suppose you're busy, Fizban, and—"

At that instant, the ground lifted beneath Tas's feet, the air filled with broken rock and brick and debris, a sound like thunder deafened the kender, and then . . . silence.

Picking himself up, brushing the dust off his leggings, Tas peered through the smoke and rubble, trying to see what had happened. For a moment, he thought that perhaps another building had been dropped on him, like at Tarsis. But then he saw that wasn't the case.

A bronze dragon lay on its back in the middle of the street. It was covered with blood, its wings, spread over the block, had crushed several buildings, its tail lay across several more. Its eyes were closed, there were scorch marks up and down its flanks, and it didn't appear to be breathing.

"Now *this*," said Tas irritably, staring at the dragon, "was *not* what I had in mind!"

At that moment, however, the dragon stirred. One eye flickered open and seemed to regard the kender with dazed recollection.

"Fireflash!" Tas gasped, running up one of the huge legs to look the wounded dragon in the eye. "I was looking for you! Are—are you hurt badly?"

The young dragon seemed about to try to reply when a dark shadow covered both of them. Khirsah's eyes flared open, he gave a soft snarl and tried feebly to raise his head, but the effort seemed beyond him. Looking up, Tas saw a large black dragon swooping toward them, apparently intent on finishing off his victim.

"Oh, no, you don't!" Tas muttered. "This is *my* bronze! Fizban sent him to me. Now, how does one fight a dragon?"

Stories of Huma came to the kender's mind, but they weren't much help, since he didn't have a dragonlance, or even a sword. Pulling out his small knife, he looked at it hopefully, then shook his head and shoved it back in his belt. Well, he'd have to do the best he could.

"Fireflash," he instructed the dragon as he clamored up on the creature's broad, scaled stomach. "You just lie there and keep quiet, all right? Yes, I know all about how you want to die honorably, fighting your enemy. I had a friend who was a Knight of Solamnia. But right now we can't afford to be honorable. I have two other friends who are alive right now but who maybe won't be if you can't help me get to them. Besides, I saved your life once already this morning, although that's probably not too obvious at the moment, and you owe me this."

Whether Khirsah understood and was obeying orders or had simply lost consciousness, Tas couldn't be certain. Anyway, he didn't have time to worry about it. Standing on top of the dragon's stomach, he reached deep into one of his pouches to see what he had that might help and out came Tanis's silver bracelet.

"You wouldn't think he'd be so careless with this," Tas muttered to himself as he put it on his arm. "He must have dropped it when he was tending to Caramon. Lucky I picked it up. Now—" Raising his arm, he pointed at the black dragon, who was hovering above, its jaws gaping open, ready to spew its deadly acid on its victim.

"Just hold it!" the kender shouted. "This dragon corpse is mine! I found it. Well . . . it found me, so to speak. Nearly squashed me into the ground. So just clear out and don't ruin it with that nasty breath of yours!"

The black dragon paused, puzzled, staring down. She had, often enough, given over a prize or two to draconians and goblins, but never—that she could recollect—to a kender. She, too, had been injured in the battle and was feeling rather light-headed from loss of blood and a clout on the nose, but something told her this wasn't right. She couldn't recollect ever having met an evil kender. She had to admit, however, that there might be a first time. This one *did* wear a bracelet of undoubtedly black magic, whose power she could feel blocking her spells.

"Do you know what I can get for dragon's teeth in Sanction these days?" the kender shouted. "To say nothing of the claws. I know a wizard paying thirty steel pieces for one claw alone!"

The black dragon scowled. This was a stupid conversation. She was hurting and angry. Deciding to simply destroy this irritating kender along with her enemy, she opened her mouth . . . when she was suddenly struck from behind by another bronze. Shrieking in fury, the black forgot her prey as she fought for her life, clawing frantically to gain air space, the bronze following.

Heaving a vast sigh, Tas sat down on Khirsah's stomach.

"I thought we were gone for sure there," the kender muttered, pulling off the silver bracelet and stuffing it back into his pouch. He felt the dragon stir beneath him, drawing a deep breath. Sliding down the dragon's scaly side, Tas landed on the ground.

"Fireflash? Are—are you very much hurt?" How did one heal a dragon anyway? "I—I could go look for a cleric, though I suppose they're all pretty busy right now, what with the battle going on and everything—"

"No, kender," said Khirsah in a deep voice, "that will not be necessary." Opening his eyes, the dragon shook his great head and craned his long neck to look around. "You saved my life," he said, staring at the kender in some confusion.

"Twice," Tas pointed out cheerfully. "First there was this morning with Lord Soth. My friend, Caramon—you don't know him—has this book that tells what will happen in the future—or rather what *won't* happen in the future, now that we're changing it. Anyway, you and Tanis would have fought Lord Soth and you both would have died only I stole the bracelet so now you didn't. Die, that is."

"Indeed." Rolling over on his side, Khirsah extended one huge leathery wing up into the smoky air and examined it closely. It was cut and bleeding, but had not been torn. He proceeded to examine the other wing in similar fashion while Tas watched, enchanted.

"I think I would like to be a dragon," he said with a sigh.

"Of course." Khirsah slowly twisted his bronze body over to stand upon his taloned feet, first extracting his long tail from the rubble of a building it had crushed. "We are the chosen of the gods. Our life spans are so long that the lives of the elves seem as brief as the burning of a candle to us, while the lives of humans and you kender are but as falling stars. Our breath is death, our magic so powerful that only the greatest wizards outrank us."

"I know," said Tasslehoff, trying to conceal his impatience.

"Now, are you certain everything works?"

Khirsah himself concealed a smile. "Yes, Tasslehoff Burr-foot," the dragon said gravely, flexing his wings, "everything, um . . . works, as you put it." He shook his head. "I am feeling a little groggy, that is all. And so, since you have saved my life, I—"

"Twice."

"Twice," the dragon amended, "I am bound to perform a service for you. What do you ask of me?"

"Take me up to the flying citadel!" Tas said, all prepared to climb up on the dragon's back. He felt himself being hoisted in the air by his shirt collar which was hooked in one of Khirsah's huge claws. "Oh, thanks for the lift. Though I could have made it on my own—"

But he was not being placed upon the dragon's back. Rather, he found himself confronting Khirsah eye to eye.

"That would be extremely dangerous—if not fatal—for you, kender," Khirsah said sternly. "I cannot allow it. Let me take you to the Knights of Solamnia, who are in the High Clerist's Tower—"

"I've been to the High Clerist's Tower!" Tas wailed. "I must get to the flying citadel! You see, uh, you see— Tanis Half-Elven! You know him? He's up there, right now, and, uh— He left me here to get some important, uh, information for him and"—Tas finished in a rush—"I've got it and now I've got to get to him with it."

"Give me the information," Khirsah said. "I will convey it to him."

"N-no, no, that—uh—won't work at all," Tas stammered, thinking frantically. "It—it's—uh—in kenderspeak! And—and it can't be translated into—er—Common. You don't speak—uh—kenderspeak, do you, Fireflash?"

"Of course," the dragon was about to say. But, looking into Tasslehoff's hopeful eyes, Khirsah snorted. "Of course *not!*" he said scornfully. Slowly, carefully, he deposited the kender on his back, between his wings. "I will take you to Tanis Half-Elven, if that is your wish. There is no dragonsaddle, since we are not fighting using mounted riders, so hold onto my mane tightly."

"Yes, Fireflash," Tas shouted gleefully, settling his pouches about him and gripping the dragon's bronze mane with both small hands. A sudden thought occurred to him. "Say, Fireflash," he cried, "you won't be doing any adventuresome things up there—like rolling over upside down or diving straight for the ground—will you? Because, while they certainly are entertaining, it might be rather uncomfortable for me since I'm not strapped in or anything. . . ."

"No," Khirsah replied, smiling. "I will take you there as swiftly as possible so that I may return to the battle."

"Ready when you are!" Tas shouted, kicking Khirsah's flanks with his heels as the bronze dragon leaped into the air. Catching the wind currents, he rose up into the sky and soared over the city of Palanthas.

It was not a pleasant ride. Looking down, Tas caught his breath. Almost all of New City was in flames. Since it had been evacuated, the draconians swept through it unchallenged, systematically looting and burning. The good dragons had been able to keep the blue and black dragons from completely destroying Old City—as they had destroyed Tarsis—and the city's defenders were holding their own against the draconians. But Lord Soth's charge had been costly. Tas could see, from his lofty vantage point, the bodies of knights and their horses scattered about the streets like tin soldiers smashed by a vengeful child. And, while he watched, he could see Soth riding on unchecked, his warriors butchering any living thing that crossed their path, the banshees' frightful wail rising above the cries of the dying.

Tas swallowed painfully. "Oh, dear," he whispered, "suppose this *is* my fault! I don't really know, after all. Caramon never got to read any farther in the book! I just supposed— No," Tas answered himself firmly, "if I hadn't save Tanis, then Caramon would have died in the Grove. I did what I had to do and, since it's such a muddle, I won't think about it, ever again."

To take his mind off his problems—and the horrible things he

243

could see happening on the ground below—Tas looked around, peering through the smoke, to see what was happening in the skies. Catching a glimpse of movement behind him, he saw a large blue dragon rising up from the streets near Shoikan Grove. "Kitiara's dragon!" Tas murmured, recognizing the splendid, deadly Skie. But the dragon had no rider, Kitiara was nowhere to be seen.

"Fireflash!" Tas called out warningly, twisting around to watch the blue dragon, who had spotted them and was changing his direction to speed toward them.

"I am aware of him," Khirsah said coolly, glancing toward Skie. "Do not worry, we are near your destination. I will deposit you, kender, then return to deal with my enemy."

Turning, Tas saw that they were indeed very near the flying citadel. All thoughts of Kitiara and blue dragons went right out of his head. The citadel was even more wonderful up close than from down below. He could see quite clearly the huge, jagged chunks of rock hanging beneath it—what had once been the bedrock on which it was built.

Magical clouds boiled about it, keeping it afloat, lightning sizzled and crackled among the towers. Studying the citadel itself, Tas saw giant cracks snaking up the sides of the stone fortress—structural damage resulting from the tremendous force necessary to rip the building from the bones of the earth. Light gleamed from the windows of the citadel's three tall towers and from the open portcullis in front, but Tas could see no outward signs of life. He had no doubt, however, that there would be all kinds of life inside!

"Where would you like to go?" Khirsah asked, a note of impatience in his voice.

"Anywhere's fine, thank you," Tas replied politely, understanding that the dragon was eager to get back to battle.

"I don't think the main entrance would be advisable," said the dragon, swerving suddenly in his flight. Banking sharply, he circled around the citadel. "I will take you to the back."

Tas would have said "thank you" again but his stomach had, for some unaccountable reason, suddenly taken a plunge for the ground while his heart leaped into his throat as the dragon's circling motion turned them both sideways in the air. Then Khirsah leveled out and, swooping downward, landed smoothly in a deserted courtyard. Occupied for the moment with getting his insides sorted out, Tas was barely able to slide off the dragon's back and leap down into the shadows without worrying about the social amenities.

Once on the solid ground (well, sort of solid ground), however, the kender felt immensely more himself.

"Good-bye, Fireflash!" he called, waving his small hand. "Thank you! Good luck!"

But if the bronze heard him, he did not answer. Khirsah was climbing rapidly, gaining air space. Zooming up after him came Skie, his red eyes glowing with hatred. With a shrug and a small sigh, Tas left them to their battle. Turning around, he studied his surroundings.

He was standing at the back of the fortress upon half of a courtyard, the other half having apparently been left behind when the citadel was dragged from the ground. Noticing that he was, in fact, uncomfortably near the edge of the broken stone flagging, Tas hurried toward the wall of the fortress itself. He moved softly, keeping to the shadows with the unconsciously adept stealth that kender are born possessing.

Pausing, he looked around. There was a back door leading into the courtyard, but it was a huge, wooden door, banded with iron bars. And, while it *did* have a most interesting looking lock that Tas's finger itched to try, the kender figured, with a sigh, that it probably had a very interesting looking guard standing on the other side as well. He'd do much better creeping in a window, and there happened to be a lighted window, right above him.

Way above him.

"Drat!" Tas muttered. The window was at least six feet off the ground. Glancing about, Tas found a chunk of broken rock and, with much pushing and shoving, managed to maneuver it over beneath the window. Climbing up on it, he peered cautiously inside.

———

Two draconians lay in a heap of stone upon the floor, their heads smashed. Another draconian lay dead near them, its head completely severed from its body. Other than the corpses, there was no one or nothing else in the room. Standing on tip-toe, Tas poked his head inside, listening. Not too far away, he could hear the sounds of metal clashing and harsh shouts and yells and, once, a tremendous roar.

"Caramon!" said Tas. Crawling through the window, he leaped down onto the floor, pleased to notice that, as yet, the citadel was holding perfectly still and didn't seem to be going anywhere. Listening again, he could hear the familiar roaring grow louder, mingled with Tanis's swearing. "How nice of them," Tas said, nodding in satisfaction as he crept across the room. "They're waiting for me."

Emerging into a corridor with blank stone walls, Tas paused a moment to get his bearings. The sounds of battle were above him. Peering down the torchlit hall, Tas saw a staircase and headed in that direction. As a precaution, he drew his little knife, but he met no one. The corridor was empty and so were the narrow, steep stairs.

"Humpf," Tas muttered, "certainly a much *safer* place to be than the city, right now. I must remember to mention that to Tanis. Speaking of whom, where can he and Caramon be and how do I get there?"

After climbing almost straight upward for about ten min-utes, Tas stopped, staring up into the torchlit darkness. He was, he realized, ascending a narrow stair sandwiched between the inner and outer walls of one of the citadel's towers. He could still hear the battle raging—now it sounded like Tanis and Car-amon were right on the other side of the wall from him—but he couldn't see any way to get through to them. Frustrated—and with tired legs—he stopped to think.

I can either go back down and try another way, he reasoned, or I can keep going. Back down—while easier on the feet—is likely to be more crowded. And there must be a door up here somewhere, or else why have a stair?

That line of logic appealing to him, Tas decided to keep going

---

up, even though it meant that the sounds of battle seemed to be below him now instead of above him. Suddenly, just as he was beginning to think that a drunken dwarf with a warped sense of humor had built this stupid staircase, he arrived at the top and found his door.

"Ah, a lock!" he said, rubbing his hands. He hadn't had a chance to pick one in a long time, and he was afraid he might be getting rusty. Examining the lock with a practiced eye, he gingerly and delicately placed his hand upon the door handle. Much to his disappointment, it opened easily.

"Oh, well," he said with a sigh, "I don't have my lockpicking tools anyway." Cautiously pushing on the door, he peeped out. There was nothing but a wooden railing in front of him. Tas shoved the door open a bit more and stepped through it to find himself standing on a narrow balcony that ran around the inside of the tower.

The sounds of fighting were much clearer, reverberating loudly against the stone. Hurrying across the wooden floor of the balcony, Tas leaned over the edge of the railing, peering down below at the source of the sounds of wood smashing and swords clanging and cries and thuds.

"Hullo, Tanis. Hullo, Caramon!" he called in excitement. "Hey, have you figured out how to fly this thing yet?"

Chapter 4

Trapped on another balcony several flights below the one Tas leaned over, Tanis and Caramon were fighting for their lives on the opposite side of the tower from where the kender was standing. What appeared to be a small army of draconians and goblins were crammed on the stairs below them.

The two warriors had barricaded themselves behind a huge wooden bench which they had dragged across the head of the stairs. Behind them was a door, and it looked to Tas as if they had climbed up the stairs toward the door in an effort to escape but had been stopped before they could get out.

Caramon, his arms covered with green blood up to his elbows, was bashing heads with a hunk of wood he had ripped loose from the balcony—a more effective weapon than a sword when fighting these creatures whose bodies turned to stone. Tanis's sword was notched—he had been using it as a club— and he was bleeding from several cuts through the slashed chain mail on his arms, and there was a large dent in his breastplate. As far as Tas could tell from his first fevered glance, mat-

---

249

ters appeared to be at a stalemate. The draconians couldn't get close enough to the bench to haul it out of the way or climb over it. But, the moment Caramon and Tanis left their position, it would be overrun.

"Tanis! Caramon!" Tas shouted. "Up here!"

Both men glanced around in astonishment at the sound of the kender's voice. Then Caramon, catching hold of Tanis, pointed.

"Tasslehoff!" Caramon called, his booming voice echoing in the tower chamber. "Tas! This door, behind us! It's locked! We can't get out!"

"I'll be right there!" Tas called in excitement, climbing up onto the railing and preparing to leap down into the thick of things.

"No!" Tanis screamed. "Unlock it from the other side! The other side!" He pointed frantically.

"Oh," Tas said in disappointment. "Sure, no problem." He climbed back down and was just turning to his doorway when he saw the draconians on the stairs below Tanis and Caramon suddenly cease fighting, their attention apparently caught by something. There was a harsh word of command, and the draconians began shoving and pushing each other to one side, their faces breaking into fanged grins. Tanis and Caramon, startled at the lull in the battle, risked a cautious glance over the top of the bench, while Tas stared down over the railing of the balcony.

A draconian in black robes decorated with arcane runes was ascending the stairs. He held a staff in his clawed hand—a staff carved into the likeness of a striking serpent.

A Bozak magic-user! Tas felt a sinking sensation in the pit of his stomach almost as bad as the one he'd had when the dragon came in for a landing. The draconian soldiers were sheathing their weapons, obviously figuring the battle was ending. Their wizard would handle the matter, quickly and simply.

Tas saw Tanis's hand reach into his belt . . . and come out empty. Tanis's face went white beneath his beard. His hand went to another part of his belt. Nothing there. Frantically, the half-elf looked around on the floor.

"You know," said Tas to himself, "I'll bet that bracelet of magic resistance would come in handy now. Perhaps that's what he's hunting for. I guess he doesn't realize he lost it." Reaching into a pouch, he drew out the silver bracelet.

"Here it is, Tanis! Don't worry! You dropped it, but I found it!" he cried, waving it in the air.

The half-elf looked up, scowling, his eyebrows coming together in such an alaming manner that Tas hurriedly tossed the bracelet down to him. After waiting a moment to see if Tanis would thank him (he didn't), the kender sighed.

"Be there in a minute!" he yelled. Turning, he dashed back through the door and ran down the stairs.

"He certainly didn't act very grateful," Tas humpfed as he sped along. "Not a bit like the old fun-loving Tanis. I don't think being a hero agrees with him."

Behind him, muffled by the wall, he could hear the sound of harsh chanting and several explosions. Then draconian voices raised in cries of anger and disappointment.

"That bracelet will hold them off for a while," Tas muttered, "but not for long. Now, how do I get over to the other side of the tower to reach them? I guess there's no help for it but to go clear back to the bottom level."

Racing down the stairs, he reached the ground level again, ran past the room where he had entered the citadel, and continued on until he came to a corridor running at right angles to the one he was in. Hopefully, it led to the opposite side of the tower where Tanis and Caramon were trapped.

There was the sound of another explosion and, this time, the whole tower shook. Tas increased his speed. Making a sharp turn to his right, the kender hurtled around a corner.

Bam! He slammed into something squat and dark that toppled over with a "wuf."

The impact bowled Tas head over heels. He lay quite still, having the distinct impression—from the smell—that he'd been struck by a bundle of rotting garbage. Somewhat shaken, he nevertheless managed to stagger to his feet and, gripping his little knife, prepared to defend himself against the short, dark creature which was on its feet as well.

Putting a hand to its forehead, the creature said, "Ooh," in a pained tone. Then, glancing about groggily, it saw Tas standing in front of it, looking grim and determined. Torchlight flashed off the kender's knife blade. The "ooh," turned to an "AAAAAHHH." With a groan, the smelly creature fainted dead away.

"Gully dwarf!" said Tas, his nose wrinkling in disgust. He sheathed his knife and started to leave. Then he stopped. "You know, though," he said, talking to himself, "this might come in handy." Bending down, Tas grasped the gully dwarf by a handful of rag and shook it. "Hey, wake up!"

Drawing a shuddering breath, the gully dwarf opened his eyes. Seeing a stern-looking kender crouched threateningly above him, the gully dwarf went deathly white, hurriedly closed his eyes again, and attempted to look unconscious.

Tas shook the bundle again.

With a trembling sigh, the gully dwarf opened one eye, and saw Tas was still there. There was only one thing to do—look dead. This is achieved (among gully dwarves) by holding the breath and going instantly stiff and rigid.

"C'mon," play Tas irritably, shaking the gully dwarf. "I need your help."

"You go way," the gully dwarf said in deep, sepulchral tones. "Me dead."

"You're not dead yet," Tas said in the most awful voice he could muster, "but you're going to be unless you help me!" He raised the knife.

The gully dwarf gulped and quickly sat up, rubbing his head in confusion. Then, seeing Tas, he threw his arms around the kender. "You heal! Me back from dead! You great and powerful cleric!"

"No, I'm not!" snapped Tas, considerably startled by this reaction. "Now, let loose. No, you're tangled up in the pouch. Not *that* way. . . ."

After several moments, he finally managed to divest himself

of the gully dwarf. Dragging the creature to his feet, Tas glared at him sternly. "I'm trying to get to the other side of the tower. Is this the right way?"

The gully dwarf stared up and down the corridor thoughtfully, then he turned to Tas. "This right way," he said finally, pointing in the direction Tas had been heading.

"Good!" Tas started off again.

"What tower?" the gully dwarf muttered, scratching his head.

Tas stopped. Turning around, he glared at the gully dwarf, his hand straying for his knife.

"Me go with great cleric," the gully dwarf offered hurriedly. "Me guide."

"That might not be a bad idea," the kender reflected. Grabbing hold of the gully dwarf's grubby hand, Tas dragged him along. Soon they found another staircase leading up. The sounds of battle were much louder now—a fact that caused the gully dwarf's eyes to widen.

He tried to pull his hand loose. "Me been dead once," the gully dwarf cried, frantically attempting to free himself. "When you dead two times, they put you in box, throw you in big hole. Me not like that."

Although this seemed an interesting concept, Tas didn't have time to explore it. Keeping hold of the gully dwarf firmly, Tas tugged him up the stairs, the sounds of fighting on the other side of the wall getting louder every moment. As on the opposite side of the tower, the steep staircase ended at a door. Behind it, he could hear thuds and groans and Caramon's swearing. Tas tried the handle. It was locked from this side, too. The kender smiled, rubbing his hands again.

"Certainly a well-built door," he said, studying it. Leaning down, he peered through the keyhole. "I'm here!" he shouted.

"Open the"—muffled shouts—"door!" came Caramon's booming bellow.

"I'm doing the best I can!" Tas yelled back, somewhat irritably. "I don't have my tools, you know. Well, I'll just have to improvise. You—stay here!" He grabbed hold of the gully dwarf, who was just creeping back to the stairs. Taking out his knife, he held it up threateningly. The gully dwarf collapsed in a heap.

"Me stay!" he whimpered, cowering on the floor.

Turning back to the door, Tas stuck the tip of the knife into the lock and began twisting it around carefully. He thought he could almost feel the lock give when something thudded against the door. The knife jerked out of the lock.

"You're not helping!" he shouted through the door. Heaving a long-suffering sigh, Tas put the knife back in the lock again.

The gully dwarf crawled closer, staring up at Tas from the floor. "Lot *you* know. Me guess you *not* such great cleric."

"What do you mean?" Tas muttered, concentrating.

"*Knife* not open door," the gully dwarf said with vast disdain. "*Key* open door."

"I *know* a key opens the door," Tas said, glancing about in exasperation, "but I don't have— Give me that!"

Tas angrily snatched the key the gully dwarf was holding in its hand. Putting the key into the door lock, he heard it click and yanked the door open. Tanis tumbled out, practically on top of the kender, Caramon running out behind him. The big man slammed the heavy door shut, breaking off the tip of a draconian sword just entering the doorway. Leaning his back against the door, he looked down at Tas, breathing heavily.

"Lock it!" he managed to gasp.

Quickly Tas turned the key in the lock again. Behind the door, there were shouts and more thuds and the sounds of splintering wood.

"It'll hold for a while, I think," Tanis said, studying the door.

"But not long," Caramon said grimly. "Especially with that Bozak mage down there. C'mon."

"Where?" Tanis demanded, wiping sweat from his face. He was bleeding from a slash on his hand and numerous cuts on his arms, but otherwise appeared unhurt. Caramon was covered with blood, but most of it was green, so Tas assumed that it was the enemy's. "We still haven't found out where the device that flies this thing is located!"

"I'll bet he knows," Tas said, pointing to the gully dwarf. "That's why I brought him along," the kender added, rather proud of himself.

There was a tremendous crash. The door shuddered.

"Let's at least get out of here," Tanis muttered. "What's your name?" he asked the gully dwarf as they hurried back down the stairs.

"Rounce," said the gully dwarf, regarding Tanis with deep suspicion.

"Very well, Rounce," Tanis said, pausing on a shadowy landing to catch his breath, "show us the room where the device is that flies this citadel."

"The Wind Captain's Chair," Caramon added, glaring at the gully dwarf sternly. "That's what we heard one of the goblins call it."

"That secret!" Rounce said solemnly. "Me not tell! Me make promise!"

Caramon growled so fiercely that Rounce went dead white beneath the dirt on his face, and Tas, afraid he was going to faint again, hurriedly interposed. "Pooh! I'll bet he doesn't know!" Tas said, winking at Caramon.

"Me do too know!" Rounce said loftily. "And you try trick to make me tell. Me not fall for stupid trick."

Tas slumped back against the wall with a sigh. Caramon growled again, but the gully dwarf, cringing slightly, still stared at him with brave defiance. "Cross pigs not drag secret out of me!" Rounce declared, folding his filthy arms across a grease-covered, food-spattered chest.

There was a shattering crash from above, and the sound of draconian voices.

"Uh, Rounce," Tanis murmured confidentially, squatting down beside the gully dwarf, "what is it exactly that you're not supposed to tell?"

Rounce assumed a crafty look. "Me not supposed to tell that the Wind Captain's Chair in top of middle tower. *That's* what me not supposed to tell!" He scowled at Tanis viciously and raised a small, clenched fist. "And you can't make me!"

They reached the corridor leading to the room where the Wind Captain's Chair *wasn't* located (according to Rounce, who had been guiding them the entire way by saying, "This *not* door that lead to stair that lead to secret place"). They entered it cautiously, thinking that things had been just a little too quiet. They were right. About halfway down the corridor, a door burst open. Twenty draconians, followed by the Bozak magic-user, lunged out at them.

"Get behind me!" Tanis said, drawing his sword. "I've still got the bracelet—" Remembering Tas was with them, he added, "I think," and glanced hurriedly at his arm. The bracelet was still there.

"Tanis," said Caramon, drawing his sword and falling back slowly as the draconians, waiting for instructions from the Bozak, hesitated, "we're running out of time! I know! I can sense it! I've got to get to the Tower of High Sorcery! Someone's got to get up there and fly this thing!"

"One of us can't hold off this many!" Tanis returned. "That doesn't leave anyone to operate the Wind Captain—" The words died on his lips. He stared at Caramon. "Oh, you're not serious—"

"We don't have any choice," Caramon growled as the sound of chanting filled the air. He glanced back at Tasslehoff.

"No," Tanis began, "absolutely not—"

"There's no other way!" Caramon insisted.

Tanis sighed, shaking his head.

The kender, watching both of them, blinked in confusion. Then, suddenly, he understood.

"Oh, Caramon!" he breathed, clasping his hands together, barely avoiding skewering himself with his knife. "Oh, Tanis! How wonderful! I'll make you proud of me! I'll get you to the Tower! You won't be sorry! Rounce, I'm going to need your help."

Grabbing the gully dwarf by the arm, Tas raced along the corridor toward a spiral staircase Rounce was pointing out, insisting that, "This stair *not* take you to secret place!"

Designed by Lord Ariakas, formerly head of the Dark Queen's forces during the War of the Lance, the Wind Captain's Chair that operates a floating citadel has long since passed into history as one of the most brilliant creations of Ariakas's brilliant, if dark and twisted, mind.

The Chair is located in a room specially built for it at the very top of the citadel. Climbing a narrow flight of spiral steps, the Wind Captain ascends an iron ladder leading to a trap door. Upon opening the trap door, the Captain enters a small, circular room devoid of windows. In the center of the room is a raised platform. Two pedestals, positioned about three feet apart, stand on the platform.

At the sight of these pedestals, Tas—pulling Rounce up after him—drew in a deep breath. Made of silver, standing about four feet tall, the pedestals were the most beautiful things he had ever seen. Intricate designs and magical symbols were etched into their surfaces. Every tiny line was filled with gold that glittered in the torchlight streaming up from the stairway below. And, on top of each pedestal, was poised a huge globe, made of shining black crystal.

"You *not* get up on platform," Rounce said severely.

"Rounce," said Tas, climbing up onto the platform, which was about three feet off the floor, "do you know how to make this work?"

"No," said Rounce coolly, folding his arms across his chest and glaring at Tas. "Me never been here lots. Me never run errand for big boss wizard. Me never put into this room and me never told fetch whatever wizard want. Me never watch big boss wizard fly many times."

"Big boss wizard?" Tas said, frowning. He glanced hastily about the small room, peering into the shadows. "Where *is* the big boss wizard?"

"Him not down below," Rounce said stubbornly. "Him not getting ready to blow friends to tiny bits."

"Oh, that big boss wizard," Tas said in relief. Then the kender paused. "But—if he's not here—who's flying this thing?"

"I see," said Tas, stepping into the black circles set into the floor between the pedestals. They appeared to be made of the same type of black crystal as the glass globes. From the corridor below, he heard another explosion and, again, shouts of the angry draconians. Apparently Tanis's bracelet was still fending off the wizard's magic.

"Now," said Rounce, "you not s'pose to look up at circle in ceiling."

Looking up, Tas gasped in awe. Above him, a circle the same size and diameter as the platform upon which he stood was beginning to glow with an eerie blue-white light.

"All right, Rounce," Tas said, his voice shrill with excitement, "what is it I'm not supposed to do next?"

"You not put hands on black crystal globes. You not tell globes which way we go," Rounce replied, sniffing. "Pooh. You never figure out big magic like this!"

"Tanis," Tas yelled down through the opening in the floor, "which direction is the Tower of High Sorcery from here?"

For a moment, all he could hear was the clatter of swords and a few screams. Then, Tanis's voice, sounding gradually closer as he and Caramon backed their way down the corridor, floated up. "Northwest! Almost straight northwest!"

"Right!" Planting his feet firmly in the black crystal depressions, Tas drew a shaking breath, then raised his hands to place them upon the crystal globes—

"Drat!" he cried in dismay, staring up. "I'm too short!"

Looking down at Rounce, he motioned. "I suppose your hands don't have to be on the globe and your feet don't have to be in the black circles at the same time?"

Tas had the unfortunate feeling that he already knew the answer to this, which was just as well. The question had thrown Rounce into such a state of confusion that he could only stare at Tas, his mouth gaping open.

Glaring at the gully dwarf simply because he had to have something to glare at in his frustration, Tas decided to try to jump up to touch the globes. He could reach them then, but—when his feet left the black crystal circles—the blue-white light went dim.

"Now what?" he groaned. "Caramon or Tanis could reach it easily, but they're down there and, from the sounds of things, they're not going to be coming up here for a while. What can I do? I— Rounce!" he said suddenly, "come up here!"

Rounce's eyes narrowed suspiciously. "Me not allowed," he said, starting to back away from the platform.

"Wait! Rounce! Don't leave!" Tas cried. "Look, you come help me! We'll fly this together!"

"Me!" Rounce gasped. His eyes opened round as teacups. "Fly like big boss wizard?"

"Yes, Rounce! C'mon. Just climb up, stand on my shoulders, and—"

A look of wonder came into Rounce's face. "Me," he breathed with a gusty sigh of ecstasy, "fly like big boss wizard!"

"Yes, Rounce, yes," said Tas impatiently, "now, hurry up before—before the big boss wizard catches us."

"Me hurry," Rounce said, crawling up onto the platform and from there onto Tas's shoulders, "Me hurry. Me always want to fly—"

"Here, I've got hold of your ankles. Now, ouch! Let go of my hair! You're pulling! I'm not going to drop you. No, stand up. Stand up, Rounce. Just stand up slowly. You'll be all right. See, I have your ankles. I won't let you fall. No! No! You've got to balan—"

Kender and gully dwarf tumbled over in a heap.

"Tas!" Caramon's warning voice came up the stairs.

"Just a minute! Almost got it!" Tas cried, yanking Rounce to his feet and shaking him soundly. "Now, balance, balance!"

259

"Balance, balance," Rounce muttered, his teeth clicking together.

Tas took his place upon the black crystal circles once again and Rounce crawled up onto his shoulders again. This time, the gully dwarf, after a few tense moments of wobbling, managed to stand up. Tas heaved a sigh. Reaching out his dirty hands, Rounce—after a few false starts—gingerly placed them upon the black crystal globes.

Immediately, a curtain of light dropped down from the glowing circle in the ceiling, forming a brilliant wall around Tas and the gully dwarf. Runes appeared on the ceiling, glowing red and violet.

And, with a heart-stopping lurch, the flying citadel began to move.

Down the stairs in the corridor below the Wind Captain's Chair, the jolt sent draconians and their magic-user crashing to the floor. Tanis fell backward against a wall, and Caramon slammed into him.

Screaming and cursing, the Bozak wizard struggled to his feet. Stepping on his own men, who littered the corridor, and completely ignoring Tanis and Caramon, the draconian began to run toward the staircase leading up to the Wind Captain's room.

"Stop him!" Caramon growled, pushing himself away from the wall as the citadel canted to one side like a sinking ship.

"I'll try," Tanis wheezed, having had the breath knocked out of him, "but I think this bracelet is about used up."

He made a lunge for the Bozak, but the citadel suddenly tipped in the opposite direction. Tanis missed and tumbled to the floor. The Bozak, intent only on stopping the thieves who were stealing his citadel, stumbled on toward the stairs. Drawing his dagger, Caramon hurled it at the Bozak's back. But it struck a magical, invisible barrier around the black robes, and fell harmlessly to the floor.

The Bozak had just reached the bottom of the spiral stairs leading up to the Wind Captain's room, the other draconians were finally regaining their feet, and Tanis was just nearing the

Bozak once again when the citadel leaped straight up into the air. The Bozak fell backward on top of Tanis, draconians went flying everywhere, and Caramon, just barely managing to keep his feet, jumped on the Bozak wizard.

The sudden gyrations of the tower broke the mage's concentration—the Bozak's protection spell failed. The draconian fought desperately with its clawed hands, but Caramon—dragging the creature off Tanis—thrust his sword into the Bozak just as the wizard began shrieking another chant.

The draconian's body dissolved instantly in a horrible yellow pool, sending clouds of foul, poisonous smoke billowing through the chamber.

"Get away!" Tanis cried, stumbling toward an open window, coughing. Leaning out, he took a deep breath of fresh air, then gasped.

"Tas!" he shouted, "we're going the wrong way! I said north-west!"

He heard the kender's shrill voice cry, "Think *northwest*, Rounce! Northwest."

"Rounce?" Caramon muttered, coughing and glancing at Tanis in sudden alarm.

"How me think of two direction same time?" demanded a voice. "You want go north or you want go west? Make up mind."

"Northwest!" cried Tas. "It's *one* direc— Oh, never mind. Look, Rounce, you think north and I'll think west. That might work."

Closing his eyes, Caramon sighed in despair and slumped against a wall.

"Tanis," he said, "Maybe you better—"

"No time," Tanis answered grimly, his sword in his hand. "Here they come."

But the draconians, thrown into confusion by the death of their leader and completely unable to comprehend what was happening to their citadel, were eyeing each other—and their enemy—askance. At that moment, the flying citadel changed

———

direction again, heading off northwest and dropping down about twenty feet at the same time.

Turning, tripping, shoving and sliding, the draconians ran down the corridor and disappeared back through the secret way they had come.

"We're finally going in the right direction," Tanis reported, staring out the window. Joining him, Caramon saw the Tower of High Sorcery drawing nearer and nearer.

"Good! Let's see what's going on," Caramon muttered, starting to climb the stairs.

"No, wait"—Tanis stopped him—"Tas can't see, apparently. We're going to have to guide him. Besides, those draconians might come back any moment."

"I guess you're right," Caramon said, peering up the stairs dubiously.

"We should be there in a few minutes," Tanis said, leaning against the window ledge wearily. "But I think we've got time enough for you to tell me what's going on."

"It's hard to believe," said Tanis softly, looking out the window again, "even of Raistlin."

"I know," Caramon said, his voice edged with sorrow. "I didn't want to believe it, not for a long time. But when I saw him standing before the Portal and when I heard him tell what he was going to do to Crysania, I knew that the evil had finally eaten into his soul."

"You are right, you must stop him," Tanis said, reaching out to grip the big man's hand in his own. "But, Caramon, does that mean you have to go into the Abyss after him? Dalamar is in the Tower, waiting at the Portal. Surely, the two of you together can prevent Raistlin from coming through. You don't need to enter the Portal yourself—"

"No, Tanis," Caramon said, shaking his head. "Remember—Dalamar failed to stop Raistlin the first time. Something must be going to happen to the dark elf—something that will prevent him from fulfilling his assignment." Reaching into his knapsack, Caramon pulled out the leatherbound *Chronicles*.

"Maybe we can get there in time to stop it," Tanis suggested, feeling strange talking about a future that was already described.

Turning to the page he had marked, Caramon scanned it hurriedly, then drew in his breath with a soft whistle.

"What is it?" Tanis asked, leaning over to see. Caramon hastily shut the book.

"Something happens to him, all right," the big man muttered, avoiding Tanis's eyes. "Kitiara kills him."

CHAPTER 5

Dalamar sat alone in the laboratory of the Tower of High Sorcery. The guardians of the Tower, both living and dead, stood at their posts by the entrance, waiting . . . watching.

Outside the Tower window, Dalamar could see the city of Palanthas burning. The dark elf had watched the progress of the battle from his vantage point high atop the Tower. He had seen Lord Soth enter the gate, he had seen the knights scatter and fall, he had seen the draconians swoop down from the flying citadel. All the while, up above, the dragons battled, the dragon blood falling like rain upon the city streets.

The last glimpse he had, before the rising smoke obscured his vision, showed him the flying citadel starting to drift in his direction, moving slowly and erratically, once even seeming to change its mind and head back toward the mountains. Puzzled, Dalamar watched this for several minutes, wondering what it portended. Was this how Kitiara planned to get into the Tower?

The dark elf felt a moment of fear. Could the citadel fly over the Shoikan Grove? Yes, he realized, it might! His hand clenched. Why hadn't he foreseen that possibility? He stared out the window, cursing the smoke that increasingly blocked his vision. As he watched, the citadel changed direction again, stumbling through the skies like a drunkard searching for his dwelling.

It was once more headed for the Tower, but at a snail's pace. What was going on? Was the operator wounded? He stared at it, trying to see. And then thick, black smoke rolled past the windows, completely blotting out his vision of the citadel. The odor of burning hemp and pitch was strong. The warehouses, Dalamar thought. As he was turning from the window with a curse, his attention was caught by the sight of a brief flare of firelight coming from a building almost directly opposite him—the Temple of Paladine. He could see, even through the smoke, the glow brightening, and he could picture, in his mind, the white robed clerics, wielding mace and stick, calling upon Paladine as they slew their enemies.

Dalamar smiled grimly, shaking his head as he walked swiftly across the room, past the great stone table with its bottles and jars and beakers. He had shoved most of these aside, making room for his spellbooks, his scrolls and magical devices. He glanced over them for the hundredth time, making certain all was in readiness, then continued on, hurrying past the shelves lined with the nightblue-bound spellbooks of Fistandantilus, past the shelves lined with Raistlin's own black-bound spellbooks. Reaching the door of the laboratory, Dalamar opened it and spoke one word into the darkness beyond.

Instantly, a pair of eyes glimmered before him, the spectral body shimmering in and out of his vision as if stirred by hot winds.

"I want guardians at the top of the Tower," Dalamar instructed.

"Where, apprentice?"

Dalamar thought. "The doorway, leading down from the Death Walk. Post them there."

The eyes flickered closed in brief acknowledgement, then

vanished. Dalamar returned to the laboratory, closing the door behind him. Then he hesitated, stopped. He could lay spells of enchantment upon the door, spells that would prevent anyone from entering. This had been a common practice of Raistlin's in the laboratory when performing some delicate magical experiment in which the least interruption could prove fatal. A breath drawn at the wrong moment could mean the unleashing of magical forces that would destroy the Tower itself. Dalamar paused, his delicate fingers on the door, the words upon his lips.

Then, no, he thought. I might need help. The guardians must be free to enter in case I am not able to remove the spells. Walking back across the room, he sat down in the comfortable chair that was his favorite—the chair he'd had brought from his own quarters to help ease the weariness of his vigil.

In case I am not able to remove the spells. Sinking down into the chair's soft, velvet cushions, Dalamar thought about death, about dying. His gaze went to the Portal. It looked as it had always looked—the five dragon heads, each a different color, facing inward, their five mouths open in five silent shouts of tribute to their Dark Queen. It looked the same as always—the heads dark and frozen, the void within the Portal empty, unchanging. Or was it? Dalamar blinked. Perhaps it was his imagination, but he thought the eyes of each of the heads were beginning to glow, slightly.

The dark elf's throat tightened, his palms began to sweat and he rubbed his hands upon his robes. Death, dying. Would it come to that? His fingers brushed over the silver runes embroidered on the black fabric, runes that would block or dispel certain magical attacks. He looked at his hands, the lovely green stone of a ring of healing sparkled there—a powerful magical device. But its power could only be used once.

Hastily, Dalamar went over in his mind Raistlin's lessons on judging whether a wound was mortal and required immediate healing or if the healing device's power should be saved.

Dalamar shuddered. He could hear the *Shalafi's* voice coldly discussing varying degrees of pain. He could feel those fingers, burning with that strange inner heat, tracing over the different portions of his anatomy, pointing out the vital areas. Reflexively, Dalamar's hand went to his breast, where the five holes Raistlin had burned into his flesh forever bled and festered. At the same time, Raistlin's eyes burned into his mind— mirrorlike, golden, flat, deadly.

Dalamar shrank back. Powerful magic surrounds me and protects me, he told himself. I am skilled in the Art, and, though not as skilled as he, the *Shalafi* will come through that Portal injured, weak, upon the point of death! It will be easy to destroy him! Dalamar's hands clenched. Then why am I literally suffocating with fear? he demanded.

A silver bell sounded, once. Startled, Dalamar rose from the chair, his fear of the imaginings of his mind replaced by a fear of something very real. And with the fear of something concrete, tangible, Dalamar's body tensed, his blood ran cool in his veins, the dark shadows in his mind vanished. He was in control.

The silver bell meant an intruder. Someone had won his way through the Shoikan Grove and was at the Tower entrance. Ordinarily, Dalamar would have left the laboratory instantly, on the words of a spell, to confront the intruder himself. But he dared not leave the Portal. Glancing back at it, the dark elf nodded to himself slowly. No, it had not been his imagination, the eyes of the dragon's heads *were* glowing. He even thought he saw the void within stir and shift, as if a ripple had passed across its surface.

No, he dared not leave. He must trust to the guardians. Walking to the door, he bent his head, listening. He thought he heard faint sounds down below—a muffled cry, a clash of steel. Then nothing but silence. He waited, holding his breath, hearing only the beating of his own heart.

Nothing else.

Dalamar sighed. The guardians must have handled the matter. Leaving the door, he crossed the laboratory to look out the window, but he could see nothing. The smoke was as thick as fog. He heard a distant rumble of thunder, or perhaps it was an

---

explosion. Who had it been down there? he found himself wondering. Some draconian, perhaps? Eager for more killing, more loot. One of them might have won through—

Not that it mattered, he told himself coldly. When all this was over, he would go down, examine the corpse. . . .

"Dalamar!"

Dalamar's heart leaped, both fear and hope surging through him at the sound of that voice.

"Caution, caution, my friend," he whispered to himself. "She betrayed her brother. She betrayed you. Do not trust her."

Yet he found his hands shaking as he slowly crossed the laboratory toward the door.

"Dalamar!" Her voice again, quivering with pain and terror. There was a thud against the door, the sound of a body sliding down it. "Dalamar," she called again weakly.

Dalamar's hand was on the handle. Behind him, the dragon's eyes glowed red, white, blue, green, black.

"Dalamar," Kitiara murmured faintly, "I—I've come . . . to help you."

Slowly, Dalamar opened the laboratory door.

Kitiara lay on the floor at his feet. At the sight of her, Dalamar drew in his breath. If she had once worn armor, it had now been torn from her body by inhuman hands. He could see the marks of their nails upon her flesh. The black, tight-fitting garment she wore beneath her armor was ripped almost to shreds, exposing her tan skin, her white breasts. Blood oozed from a ghastly wound upon one leg, her leather boots were in tatters. Yet, she looked up at him with clear eyes, eyes that were not afraid. In her hand, she held the nightjewel, the charm Raistlin had given her to protect her in the Grove.

"I was strong enough, barely," she whispered, her lips parting in the crooked smile that made Dalamar's blood burn. She raised her arms. "I've come to you. Help me stand."

Reaching down, Dalamar lifted Kitiara to her feet. She slumped against him. He could feel her body shivering and shook his head, knowing what poison worked in her blood. His arm around her, he half-carried her into the laboratory and shut the door behind them.

Her weight upon him increased, her eyes rolled back. "Oh, Dalamar," she murmured, and he saw she was going to faint. He put his arms completely around her. She leaned her head against his chest, breathing a thankful sigh of relief.

He could smell the fragrance of her hair—that strange smell, a mixture of perfume and steel. Her body trembled in his arms. His grasp around her tightened. Opening her eyes, she looked up into his. "I'm feeling better now," she whispered. Her hands slid down. . . .

Too late, Dalamar saw the brown eyes glitter. Too late, he saw the crooked smile twist. Too late he felt her hand jerk, and the quick stabbing thrust of pain as her knife entered his body.

"Well, we made it," Caramon yelled, staring down from the crumbling courtyard of the flying citadel as it floated above the tops of the dark trees of the Shoikan Grove.

"Yes, at least this far," Tanis muttered. Even from this vantage point, high above the cursed forest, he could feel the cold waves of hatred and bloodlust rising up to grasp at them as if the guardians could, even now, drag them down. Shivering, Tanis forced his gaze to where the top of the Tower of High Sorcery loomed near. "If we can get close enough," he shouted to Caramon above the rush of the wind in his ears, "we can drop down on that walkway that circles around the top."

"The Death Walk," Caramon returned grimly.

"What?"

"The Death Walk!" Caramon edged closer, watching his footing as the dark trees drifted beneath them like the waves of a black ocean. "That's where the evil mage stood when he called down the curse upon the Tower. So Raistlin told me. That's where he jumped from."

"Nice, cheerful place," Tanis muttered into his beard, staring at it grimly. Smoke rolled around them, blotting out the sight of the trees. The half-elf tried not to think about what was happening in the city. He'd already caught a glimpse of the Temple of Paladine in flames.

"You know, of course," he yelled, grabbing hold of Caramon's shoulder as the two stood on the edge of the courtyard of the citadel, "there's every possibility Tasslehoff is going to crash right into that thing!"

"We've come this far," Caramon said softly. "The gods are with us."

Tanis blinked, wondering if he'd heard right. "That doesn't sound like the old jovial Caramon," he said with a grin.

"That Caramon's dead, Tanis," Caramon replied flatly, his eyes on the approaching Tower.

Tanis's grin softened to a sigh. "I'm sorry," was all he could think of to say, putting a clumsy hand on Caramon's shoulder.

Caramon looked at him, his eyes bright and clear. "No, Tanis," he said. "Par-Salian told me, when he sent me back in time, that I was going back to 'save a soul. Nothing more. Nothing less.'" Caramon smiled sadly. "I thought he meant Raistlin's soul. I see now he didn't. He meant my own." The big man's body tensed. "C'mon," he said, abruptly changing the subject. "We're close enough to jump for it."

A balcony that encircled the top of Tower appeared beneath them, dimly seen through the swirling smoke. Looking down, Tanis felt his stomach shrivel. Although he knew it was impossible, it seemed that the Tower itself was lurching around beneath him, while he was standing perfectly still. It had looked so huge, as they were nearing it. Now, he might have been planning to leap out of a vallenwood to land upon the roof of a child's toy castle.

To make matters worse, the citadel continued to fly closer and closer to the Tower. The blood-red tips of the black minarets that topped it danced in Tanis's vision as the citadel lurched back and forth and bobbed up and down.

"Jump!" shouted Caramon, hurling himself into space.

An eddy of smoke swirled past Tanis, blinding him. The citadel was still moving. Suddenly, a huge, black rock column loomed right before him. It was either jump or be squashed. Frantically, Tanis jumped, hearing a horrible crunching and grinding sound right above him. He was falling into nothingness, the smoke swirled about him, and then he had one split second to brace himself as the stones of the Death Walk materialized beneath his feet.

He landed with a jarring thud that shook every bone in his body and left him stunned and breathless. He had just sense enough to roll over onto his stomach, covering his head with his arms as showers of rock tumbled down around him.

Caramon was on his feet, roaring, "North! Due north!"

Very, very faintly, Tanis thought he heard a shrill voice screaming from the citadel above, "North! North! North! We've got to head off straight north!"

The grinding, crunching sound ceased. Raising his head cautiously, Tanis saw, through a ripple in the smoke, the flying citadel drifting off on its new tack, wobbling slightly, and heading straight for the palace of Lord Amothus.

"You all right?" Caramon helped Tanis to his feet.

"Yeah," said the half-elf shakily. He wiped blood from his mouth. "Bit my tongue. Damn, that hurts!"

"The only way down is over here," Caramon said, leading the way around the Death Walk. They came to an archway carved into the black stone of the Tower. A small wooden door stood closed and barred.

"There'll probably be guards," Tanis pointed out as Caramon, backing off, prepared to hurl his weight against the door.

"Yeah," the big man grunted. Making a short run, he threw himself forward, smashing into the door. It shivered and creaked, wood splintered along the iron bars, but it held. Rubbing his shoulder, Caramon backed off. Eyeing the door, concentrating all his strength and effort on it, he crashed into it once again. This time, it gave with a shattering boom, carrying Caramon with it.

Hurrying inside, peering around in the smoke-filled darkness, Tanis found Caramon lying on the floor, surrounded by shards of wood. The half-elf started to reach a hand down to his friend when he stopped, staring.

"Name of the Abyss!" he swore, his breath catching in his throat.

Hurriedly, Caramon got to his feet. "Yeah," he said warily. "I've run into these before."

Two pairs of disembodied eyes, glowing white with an eerie, cold light, floated before them.

"Don't let them touch you," Caramon warned in a low voice. "They drain the life from your body."

The eyes floated nearer.

Hurriedly Caramon stepped in front of Tanis, facing the eyes. "I am Caramon Majere, brother of Fistandantilus," he said softly. "You know me. You have seen me before, in times long past."

The eyes halted, Tanis could feel their chill scrutiny. Slowly, he lifted his arm. The cold light of the guardian's eyes was reflected in the silver bracelet.

"I am a friend of your master's, Dalamar," he said, trying to keep his voice firm. "He gave me this bracelet." Tanis felt, suddenly, a cold grip on his arm. He gasped in pain that seemed to bore straight to his heart. Staggering, he almost fell. Caramon caught hold of him.

"The bracelet's gone!" Tanis said through clenched teeth.

"Dalamar!" Caramon yelled, his voice booming and echoing through the chamber. "Dalamar! It is Caramon! Raistlin's brother! I've got to get into the Portal! I can stop him! Call off the guardians, Dalamar!"

"Perhaps it's too late," Tanis said, staring at the pallid eyes, which stared back at them. "Maybe Kit got here first. Perhaps he's dead. . . ."

"Then so are we," Caramon said softly.

Chapter 6

Damn you, Kitiara!"
Dalamar gagged in pain. Staggering backward, he pressed his hand against his side, feeling his own blood flow warm through his fingers.

There was no smile of elation on Kitiara's face. Rather, there was a look of fear, for she saw that the stroke that should have killed had missed. Why? she asked herself in fury. She had slain a hundred men that way! Why should she miss now? Dropping her knife, she drew her sword, lunging forward in the same motion.

The sword whistled with the force of her stroke, but it struck against a solid wall. Sparks crackled as the metal connected with the magical shield Dalamar had conjured up around him, and a paralyzing shock sizzled from the blade, through the handle, and up her arm. The sword fell from her nerveless hand. Gripping her arm, the astonished Kitiara stumbled to her knees.

Dalamar had time to recover from the shock of his wound. The defensive spells he had cast had been reflexive, a result of

---

275

years of training. He had not really even needed to think about them. But now he stared grimly at the woman on the floor before him, who was reaching for her sword with her left hand, even as she flexed the right, trying to regain feeling in it.

The battle had just begun.

Like a cat, Kitiara twisted to her feet, her eyes burning with battle rage and the almost sexual lust that consumed her when fighting. Dalamar had seen that look in someone's eyes before—in Raistlin's, when he was lost in the ecstasy of his magic. The dark elf swallowed a choking sensation in his throat and tried to banish the pain and fear from his mind, seeking to concentrate only on his spells.

"Don't make me kill you, Kitiara," he said, playing for time, feeling himself grow stronger every moment. He had to conserve that strength! It would avail him little to stop Kitiara, only to die at her brother's hands.

His first thought was to call for the guardians. But he rejected that. She had won past them once, probably using the nightjewel. Falling backward before the Dragon Highlord, Dalamar edged his way nearer the stone desk, where lay his magical devices. From the corner of his eye, he caught the gleam of gold—a magical wand. His timing must be precise, he would have to dispel the magical shield to use the wand against Kit. And he saw in Kitiara's eyes that she knew this. She was waiting for him to drop the shield, biding her time.

"You have been deceived, Kitiara," Dalamar said softly, hoping to distract her.

"By you!" She sneered. Lifting a silver, branched candlestand, she hurled it at Dalamar. It bounced harmlessly off the magical shield to fall at his feet. A curl of smoke rose from the carpet, but the small fire died almost instantly, drowned in the melting candlewax.

"By Lord Soth," Dalamar said.

"Hah!" Kitiara laughed, hurling a glass beaker against the magical shield. It broke into a thousand, glittering shards. Another candlestand followed. Kitiara had fought magic-users before. She knew how to defeat them. Her missiles were not intended to hurt, only to weaken the mage, force him to spend his strength maintaining the shield, make him think twice about lowering it.

"Why do you suppose you found Palanthas fortified?" Dalamar continued, backing up, creeping nearer the stone table. "Had you expected that? Soth told me your plans! He told me you were going to attack Palanthas to try to help your brother! 'When Raistlin comes through the Portal, drawing the Dark Queen after him, Kitiara will be here to greet him like a loving sister!' "

Kitiara paused, her sword lowered a fraction of an inch. "Soth told you that?"

"Yes," Dalamar said, sensing with relief her hesitation and confusion. The pain of his injury had eased somewhat. He ventured a glance down at the wound. His robes had stuck to it, forming a crude bandage. The bleeding had almost stopped.

"Why?" Kitiara raised her eyebrows mockingly. "Why would Soth betray me to you, dark elf?"

"Because he wants you, Kitiara," Dalamar said softly. "He wants you the only way he can have you. . . ."

A cold sliver of terror pierced Kitiara to her very soul. She remembered that odd edge in Soth's hollow voice. She remembered it was he who had advised her to attack Palanthas. Her rage seeping from her, Kitiara shuddered, convulsed with chills. *The wounds are poisoned* she realized bitterly, seeing the long scratches upon her arms and legs, feeling again the icy claws of those who made them. *Poison. Lord Soth.* She couldn't think. Glancing up dizzily, she saw Dalamar smile.

Angrily, she turned from him to conceal her emotions, to get hold of herself.

Keeping an eye on her, Dalamar moved nearer the stone table, his glance going to the wand he needed.

Kitiara let her shoulders slump, her head droop. She held the sword weakly in her right hand, balancing the blade with her left, feigning to be seriously hurt. All the while, she felt strength returning to her numb sword arm. *Let him think he has won. I'll hear him when he attacks. At the first magical* word he utters, I'll slice him in two! Her hand tightened on the sword hilt.

Listening carefully, she heard nothing. Only the soft rustle of black robes, the painful catch in the dark elf's breath. Was it true, she wondered, about Lord Soth? If it were, did it matter? Kitiara found the thought rather amusing. Men had done more than that to gain her. She was still free. She would deal with Soth later. What Dalamar said about Raistlin intrigued her more. Could he, perhaps, win?

Would he bring the Dark Queen into this plane? The thought appalled Kitiara, appalled and frightened her. "I was useful to you once, wasn't I, Dark Majesty?" she whispered. "Once, when you were weak and only a shadow upon this side of the glass. But when you are strong, what place will there be for me in this world? None! Because you hate me and you fear me even as I hate and fear you.

"As for my sniveling worm of a brother, there will be one waiting for him—Dalamar! You belong to your *Shalafi* body and soul! You're the one who means to help, not hinder, him when he comes through the Portal! No, dear lover. I do not trust you! Dare not trust you!"

Dalamar saw Kitiara shiver, he saw the wounds upon her body turning a purplish blue. She was weakening, certainly. He had seen her face pale when he mentioned Soth, her eyes dilate for an instant with fear. Surely she must realize she had been betrayed. Surely she must now see her great folly. Not that it mattered, not now. He did not trust her, dare not trust her. . . .

Dalamar's hand snaked backward. Grasping the wand, he swung it up, speaking the word of magic that diffused the magical shield guarding him. At that instant, Kitiara whirled around. Her sword grasped in both hands, she wielded it with all her strength. The blow would have severed Dalamar's head from his neck, had he not twisted his body to use the wand.

As it was, the blade caught him across the back of the right shoulder, plunging deep into his flesh, shattering the shoulderblade, nearly slicing his arm off. He dropped the wand with a scream, but not before it had unleashed its magical power. Lightning forked, its sizzling blast striking Kitiara in the chest, knocking her writhing body backward, slamming her to the floor.

Dalamar slumped over the table, reeling from pain. Blood spurted rhythmically from his arm. He watched it dully, uncomprehending for an instant, then Raistlin's lessons in anatomy returned. That was the heartblood pouring out. He would be dead within minutes. The ring of healing was on his right hand, his injured arm. Feebly reaching across with his left, he grasped the stone and spoke the simple word that activated the magic. Then he lost consciousness, his body slipping to the floor to lie in a pool of his own blood.

"Dalamar!" A voice called his name.

Drowsily, the dark elf stirred. Pain shot through his body. He moaned and fought to sink back into the darkness. But the voice shouted again. Memory returned, and with memory came fear.

Fear brought him to consciousness. He tried to sit up, but pain tore through him, nearly making him pass out again. He could hear the broken ends of bones crunching together, his right arm and hand hung limp and lifeless at his side. The ring had stopped the bleeding. He would live, but would it be only to die at the hands of his *Shalafi*?

"Dalamar!" the voice shouted again. "It's Caramon!"

Dalamar sobbed in relief. Lifting his head—a move that required a supreme effort—he looked at the Portal. The dragon's eyes glowed brighter still, the glow even seeming to spread along their necks. The void was definitely stirring now. He could feel a hot wind upon his cheek, or perhaps it was the fever in his body.

He heard a rustling in a shadowed corner across the room, and another fear gripped Dalamar. No! It was impossible she should be alive! Gritting his teeth against the pain, he turned his head. He could see her armored body, reflecting the glow of the dragon's eyes. She lay still, unmoving in the shadows. He could smell the stench of burned flesh. But that sound . . .

279

Wearily, Dalamar shut his eyes. Darkness swirled in his head, threatening to drag him down. He could not rest yet! Fighting the pain, he forced himself to consciousness, wondering why Caramon didn't come. He could hear him callling again. What was the matter? And then Dalamar remembered—the guardians! Of course, they would never let him pass!

"Guardians, hear my words and obey," Dalamar began, concentrating his thoughts and energies, murmuring the words that would help Caramon pass the dread defenders of the Tower and enter the chamber.

Behind Dalamar, the dragon's heads glowed brighter yet, while before him, in the shadowed corner, a hand reached into a blood-drenched belt and, with its dying strength, gripped the handle of a dagger.

"Caramon," said Tanis softly, watching the eyes watching him, "we could leave. Go up the stairs again. Maybe there's another way—"

"There isn't. I'm not leaving," Caramon said stubbornly.

"Name of the gods, Caramon! You can't fight the damn things!"

"Dalamar!" Caramon called again desperately. "Dalamar, I—"

As suddenly as if they had been snuffed out, the glowing eyes vanished.

"They're gone!" said Caramon, starting forward eagerly. But Tanis caught hold of him.

"A trick—"

"No." Caramon drew him on. "You can sense them, even when they're not visible. And I can't sense them anymore. Can you?"

"I sense something!" Tanis muttered.

"But it's not *them* and it's not concerned about *us!*" Caramon said, heading down the winding stairs of the top of the Tower at a run. Another door at the bottom of the steps stood open. Here, Caramon paused, peering inside the main part of the building cautiously.

It was dark inside, as dark as if light had not yet been created. The torches had been extinguished. No windows permitted even the smoke-clouded light from outside the Tower to seep into it. Tanis had a sudden vision of stepping into that darkness and vanishing forever, falling into the thick, devouring evil that permeated every rock and stone. Beside him, he could hear Caramon's breathing quicken, and feel the big man's body tense.

"Caramon—what's out there?"

"Nothing's out there. Just a long drop to the bottom. The center of the Tower's hollow. There are stairs that run around the edge of the wall, rooms branch off from the stairs. I'm standing on a narrow landing now, if I remember right. The laboratory's about two flights down from here." Caramon's voice broke. "We've got to go on! We're losing time! He's getting nearer!" Clutching at Tanis, he continued more calmly. "C'mon. Just keep close to the wall. This stairway leads down to the laboratory—"

"One false step in this blasted darkness and it won't matter to us anymore what your brother does!" Tanis said. But he knew his words were useless. Blind as he was in the smothering endless night, he could almost see Caramon's face tighten with resolve. He heard the big man take a shuffling step forward, trying to feel his way along the wall. With a sigh, Tanis prepared to follow. . . .

And then the eyes were back, staring at them.

Tanis reached for his sword—a stupid, futile gesture. But the eyes only continued to stare at them, and a voice spoke. "Come. This way."

A hand wavered in the darkness.

"We can't see, damn it!" Tanis snarled.

A ghostly light appeared, held in that wasted hand. Tanis shuddered. He preferred the darkness, after all. But he said nothing, for Caramon was hurrying ahead, running down a long winding flight of stairs. At the bottom, the eyes and the hand and the light came to halt. Before them was an open door and a room beyond. Inside the room, light shone brightly, beaming into the corridor. Caramon dashed ahead, and Tanis followed, hastily slamming the door shut behind him so that the horrible eyes wouldn't follow.

Turning, he stopped, staring around the room, and he realized, suddenly, where he was—Raistlin's laboratory. Standing numbly, pressed against the door, Tanis watched as Caramon hurried forward to kneel beside a figure huddled in a pool of blood upon the floor. Dalamar, Tanis registered, seeing the black robes. But he couldn't react, couldn't move.

The evil in the darkness outside the door had been smothering, dusty, centuries old. But the evil in here was alive; it breathed and throbbed and pulsed. Its chill flowed from the nightblue-bound spellbooks upon the shelves, its warmth rose from a new set of black-bound spellbooks, marked with hourglass runes, that stood beside them. His horrified gaze looked into beakers and saw tormented eyes staring back at him. He choked on the smells of spices and mold and fungus and roses and, somewhere, the sweet smell of burned flesh.

And then, his gaze was caught and held by glowing light radiating from a corner. The light was beautiful, yet it filled him with awe and terror, reminding him vividly of his encounter with the Dark Queen. Mesmerized, he stared at the light. It seemed to be of every color he had ever seen whirling into one. But, as he watched, horrified, fascinated, unable to look away, he saw the light separate and become distinct, forming into the five heads of a dragon.

A doorway! Tanis realized suddenly. The five heads rose from a golden dais, forming an oval shape with their necks. Each craned inward, its mouth open in a frozen scream. Tanis looked beyond them into the void within the oval. Nothing was there, but that nothing moved. All was empty, and alive. He knew suddenly, instinctively, where the doorway led, and the knowledge chilled him.

"The Portal," said Caramon, seeing Tanis's pale face and staring eyes. "Come here, give me a hand."

"You're going in there?" Tanis whispered savagely, amazed at the big man's calm. Crossing the room, he came to stand beside his friend. "Caramon, don't be a fool!"

"I have no choice, Tanis," Caramon said, that new look of quiet decision on his face. Tanis started to argue, but Caramon turned away from him, back to the injured dark elf.

"I've seen what will happen!" he reminded Tanis.

Swallowing his words, choking on them, Tanis knelt down beside Dalamar. The dark elf had managed to drag himself to a sitting position, so that he could face the Portal. He had lapsed into unconsciousness again, but, at the sound of their voices, his eyes flared open.

"Caramon!" He gasped, reaching out a trembling hand. "*You* must stop—"

"I know, Dalamar," Caramon said gently. "I know what I must do. But I need your help! Tell me—"

Dalamar's eyes fluttered shut, his skin was ashen. Tanis reached across Dalamar's chest to feel for the lifebeat in the young elf's neck. His hand had just touched the mage's skin when there was a ringing sound. Something jarred his arm, striking the armor and bouncing off, falling to the floor with a clatter. Looking down, Tanis saw a blood-stained dagger.

Startled, he whirled around, twisting to his feet, sword in hand.

"Kitiara!" Dalamar whispered with a feeble nod of his head.

Staring into the shadows of the laboratory, Tanis saw the body in the corner.

"Of course," Caramon murmured. "*That's* how she killed him." He lifted the dagger in his hand. "This time, Tanis, you blocked her throw."

But Tanis didn't hear. Sliding his sword back into his sheath, he crossed the room, stepping unheedingly on broken glass, kicking aside a silver candlestand that rolled beneath his feet.

Kitiara lay on her stomach, her cheek pressed against the bloody floor, her dark hair falling across her eyes. The dagger throw had taken her last energy, it seemed. Tanis, approaching her, his emotions in turmoil, was certain she must be dead.

But the indomitable will that had carried one brother

through darkness and another into light, burned still within Kitiara.

She heard footsteps . . . her enemy. . . .

Her hand grasped feebly for her sword. She raised her head, looking up with eyes fast dimming.

"Tanis?" She stared at him, puzzled, confused. Where was she? Flotsam? Were they together there again? Of course! He had come back to her! Smiling, she raised her hand to him.

Tanis caught his breath, his stomach wrenching. As she moved, he saw a blackened hole gaping in her chest. Her flesh had been burned away, he could see white bone beneath. It was a gruesome sight, and Tanis, sickened and overwhelmed by a surge of memories, was forced to turn his head away.

"Tanis!" she called in a cracked voice. "Come to me."

His heart filled with pity, Tanis knelt down beside her to lift her in his arms. She looked up into his face . . . and saw her death in his eyes. Fear shook her. She struggled to rise.

But the effort was too much. She collapsed.

"I'm . . . hurt," she whispered angrily. "How . . . bad?" Lifting her hand, she started to touch the wound.

Snatching off his cloak, Tanis wrapped it around Kitiara's torn body. "Rest easy, Kit," he said gently. "You'll be all right."

"You're a damn liar!" she cried, her hands clenching into fists, echoing—if she had only known it—the dying Elistan. "He's killed me! That wretched elf!" She smiled, a ghastly smile. Tanis shuddered. "But I fixed him! He can't help Raistlin now. The Dark Queen will slay him, slay them all!"

Moaning, she writhed in agony and clutched at Tanis. He held her tightly. When the pain eased, she looked up at him. "You weakling," she whispered in a tone that was part bitter scorn, part bitter regret, "we could have had the world, you and I."

"I *have* the world, Kitiara," Tanis said softly, his heart torn with revulsion and sorrow.

Angrily, she shook her head and seemed about to say more when her eyes grew wide, her gaze fixed upon something at the far end of the room.

"No!" she cried in a terror that no torture or suffering could have ever wrenched from her. "No!" Shrinking, huddling against Tanis, she whispered in a frantic, strangled voice. "Don't let him take me! Tanis, no! Keep him away! I always loved you, half-elf! Always . . . loved . . . you . . ."

Her voice faded to a gasping whisper.

Tanis looked up, alarmed. But the doorway was empty. There was no one there. Had she meant Dalamar? "Who? Kitiara! I don't understand—"

But she did not hear him. Her ears were deaf forever to mortal voices. The only voice she heard now was one she would hear forever, through all eternity.

Tanis felt the body in his arms go limp. Smoothing back the dark, curly hair, he searched her face for some sign that death had brought peace to her soul. But the expression on her face was one of horror—her brown eyes fixed in a terrified stare, the crooked, charming smile twisted into a grimace.

Tanis glanced up at Caramon. His face pale and grave, the big man shook his head. Slowly, Tanis laid Kitiara's body back down upon the floor. Leaning over, he started to kiss the cold forehead, but he found that he couldn't. The look on the corpse's face was too grim, too ghastly.

Pulling his cloak up over Kitiara's head, Tanis remained for a moment, kneeling beside her body, surrounded by darkness. And then he heard Caramon's step, he felt a hand upon his arm. "Tanis—"

"I'm all right," the half-elf said gruffly, rising to his feet. But, in his mind, he could still hear her dying plea—

"Keep him away!"

———

"I'm glad you're here with me, Tanis," Caramon said.

He stood before the Portal, staring into it intently, watching every shift and wave of the void within. Near him sat Dalamar, propped up by pillows in his chair, his face pale and drawn with pain, his arm bound in a crude sling. Tanis paced the floor restlessly. The dragon's heads now glowed so brightly it hurt the eye to look at them directly.

"Caramon, " he began, "please—"

Caramon looked over at him, his same grave, calm expression unchanged.

Tanis was baffled. How could you argue with granite? He sighed. "All right. But just how are you going to get in there?" he asked abruptly.

Caramon smiled. He knew what Tanis had been about to say, and he was grateful to him for not having said it.

Giving the Portal a grim look, Tanis gestured toward the opening. "From what you told me earlier, Raistlin had to study years and become this Fistandantilus and entrap Lady Crysania into going with him, and even then he barely made it!" Tanis shifted his gaze to Dalamar. "Can you enter the Portal, dark elf?"

Dalamar shook his head. "No, As you say, it takes one of great power to cross that dread threshold. I do not have such power, perhaps I never will. But, do not glower, Half-Elven. We do not waste our time. I am certain Caramon would not have undertaken this if he did not know how he could enter." Dalamar looked at the big warrior intently. "For enter he must, or we are doomed."

"When Raistlin fights the Dark Queen and her minions in the Abyss," Caramon said, his voice even and expressionless, "he will need to concentrate upon them completely, to the exclusion of all else. Isn't that true, Dalamar?"

"Most assuredly." The dark elf shivered and pulled his black robes about him closer with his good hand. "One breath, one blink, one twitch, and they will rend him limb from limb and devour him."

Caramon nodded.

How can he be so calm? Tanis wondered. And a voice within him replied, it is the calm of one who knows and accepts his fate.

"In Astinus's book," Caramon continued, "he wrote that Raistlin, knowing he would have to concentrate his magic upon fighting the Queen, opened the Portal to make sure of his escape route before he went into battle. Thus, when he arrived, he would find it ready for him to enter when he returned to this world."

"He also knew undoubtedly that he would be too weakened by that time to open it himself," Dalamar murmured. "He would need to be at the height of his strength. Yes, you are right. He will open it, and soon. And when he does, anyone with the strength and courage necessary to pass the boundary may enter."

The dark elf closed his eyes, biting his lip to keep from crying out. He had refused a potion to ease the pain. "If you fail," he had said to Caramon, "I am our last hope."

Our last hope, thought Tanis—a dark elf. This is insane! It can't be happening. Leaning against the stone table, he let his head sink into his hands. Name of the gods, he was tired! His body ached, his wounds burned and stung. He had removed the breast plate of his armor—it felt as heavy as a gravestone, slung around his neck. But as much as his body hurt, his soul hurt worse.

Memories flitted about him like the guardians of the Tower, reaching out to touch him with their cold hands. Caramon sneaking food off Flint's plate while the dwarf had his back turned. Raistlin conjuring up visions of wonder and delight for the children of Flotsam. Kitiara, laughing, throwing her arms around his neck, whispering into his ear. Tanis's heart shrank within him, the pain brought tears to his eyes. No! It was all wrong! Surely it wasn't supposed to end this way!

A book swam into his blurred vision—Caramon's book, resting upon the stone table, the last book of Astinus. Or is *that* how it was going to end? He became aware, then, of Caramon looking at him in concern. Angrily, he wiped his eyes and his face and stood up with a sigh.

But the spectres remained with him, hovering near him. Near him . . . and near the burned and broken body that lay in the corner beneath his cloak.

Human, half-elf, and dark elf watched the Portal in silence. A water clock on the mantle kept track of time, the drops falling one by one with the regularity of a heartbeat. The tension in the room stretched until it seemed it must snap and break, whipping around the laboratory with stinging fury. Dalamar began muttering in elven. Tanis glanced at him sharply, fearing the dark elf might be delirious. The mage's face was pale, cadaverous, his eyes surrounded by deep, purple shadows had sunken into their sockets. Their gaze never shifted, they stared always into the swirling void.

Even Caramon's calm appeared to be slipping. His big hands clenched and unclenched nervously, sweat covered his body, glistening in the light of the five heads of the dragon. He began to shiver, involuntarily. The muscles in his arms twitched and bunched spasmodically.

And then Tanis felt a strange sensation creep over him. The air was still, too still. Sounds of battle raging in the city outside the Tower—sounds that he had heard without even being aware of it—suddenly ceased. Inside the Tower, too, sound hushed. The words Dalamar muttered died on his lips.

The silence blanketed them, as thick and stifling as the darkness in the corridor, as the evil within the room. The dripping of the water clock grew louder, magnified, every drop seeming to jar Tanis's bones. Dalamar's eyes jerked open, his hand twitched, nervously grasping his black robes between white-knuckled fingers.

Tanis moved closer to Caramon, only to find the big man reaching out for him.

Both spoke at once. "Caramon . . ."

"Tanis . . ."

Desperately, Caramon grasped hold of Tanis's arm. "You'll take care of Tika for me, won't you?"

"Caramon, I can't let you go in there alone!" Tanis gripped him. "I'll come—"

"No, Tanis." Caramon's voice was firm. "If I fail, Dalamar will need your help. Tell Tika good-bye, and try to explain to her, Tanis. Tell her I love her very much, so much I—" His voice broke. He couldn't go on. Tanis held onto him tightly.

"I know what to tell her, Caramon," he said, remembering a letter of good-bye of his own.

Caramon nodded, shaking the tears from his eyes and drawing a deep, quivering breath. "And say good-bye to Tas. I—I don't think he ever did understand. Not really." He managed a smile. "Of course, you'll have to get him out of that flying castle first."

"I think he knew, Caramon," Tanis said softly.

The dragon's heads began to make a shrill sound, a faint scream that seemed to come from far away.

Caramon tensed.

The screaming grew louder, nearer, and more shrill. The

Portal burned with color, each head of the dragon glistened brilliantly.

"Make ready," Dalamar warned, his voice cracking.

"Good-bye, Tanis." Caramon held onto his hand tightly.

"Good-bye, Caramon."

Releasing his hold on his friend, Tanis stepped back.

The void parted. The Portal opened.

Tanis looked into it—he knew he looked into it, for he could not turn away. But he could never recall clearly what he saw. He dreamed of it, even years later. He knew he dreamed of it because he would wake in the night, drenched in sweat. But the image was always just fading from his consciousness, never to be grasped by his waking mind. And he would lie, staring into the darkness, trembling, for hours after.

But that was later. All he knew now was that he *had* to stop Caramon! But he couldn't move. He couldn't cry out. Transfixed, horror-stricken, he watched as Caramon, with a last, quiet look, turned and mounted the golden platform.

The dragons shrieked in warning, triumph, hatred. . . . Tanis didn't know. His own cry, wrenched from his body, was lost in the shrill, deafening sound.

There was a blinding, swirling, crashing wave of many-colored light.

And then it was dark.

Caramon was gone.

"May Paladine be with you," Tanis whispered, only to hear, to his discomfiture, Dalamar's cool voice, echo, "Takhisis, my Queen, go with you."

"I see him," said Dalamar, after a moment. Staring intently into the Portal, he half-rose, to see more clearly. A gasp of pain, forgotten in the excitement, escaped him. Cursing, he sank back down into the chair, his pale face covered with sweat.

Tanis ceased his restless pacing and came to stand beside Dalamar. "There," the dark elf pointed, his breath coming from between clenched teeth.

Reluctantly, still feeling the effects of the shock that lingered from when he had first looked into the Portal, Tanis looked into it again. At first he could see nothing but a bleak and barren landscape stretching beneath a burning sky. And then he saw red-tinged light glint off bright armor. He saw a small figure standing near the front of the Portal, sword in hand, facing away from them, waiting. . . .

"How will he close it?" Tanis asked, trying to speak calmly though grief choked his voice.

"He cannot," Dalamar replied.

Tanis stared at him in alarm. "Then what will stop the Queen from entering again?"

"She cannot come through unless one comes through ahead of her, half-elf," Dalamar answered, somewhat irritably. "Otherwise, she would have entered long before this. Raistlin keeps it open. If he comes through it, she will follow. With his death, it will close."

"So Caramon must kill him—his brother?"

"Yes."

"And he must die as well," Tanis murmured.

"Pray that he dies!" Dalamar licked his lips. The pain was making him dizzy, nauseated. "For he cannot return through the Portal either. And though death at the hands of the Dark Queen can be very slow, very unpleasant, believe me, Half-Elven, it is far preferable to life!"

"He knew this—"

"Yes, he knew it. But the world will be saved, Half-Elven," Dalamar remarked cynically. Sinking back into his chair, he continued staring into the Portal, his hand alternately crumpling, then smoothing, the folds of his black, rune-covered robes.

"No, not the world, a soul," Tanis started to reply bitterly, when he heard, behind him, the laboratory door creak.

Dalamar's gaze shifted instantly. Eyes glittering, his hand moved to a spell scroll he had slipped into his belt.

"No one can enter," he said softly to Tanis, who had turned at the sound. "The guardians—"

"Cannot stop *him*," Tanis said, his gaze fixed upon the door with a look of fear that mirrored, for an instant, the look of frozen fear upon Kitiara's dead face.

Dalamar smiled grimly, and relapsed back into his chair. There was no need to look around. The chill of death flowed through the room like a foul mist.

"Enter, Lord Soth," Dalamar said. "I've been expecting you."

———

Caramon was
blinded by the dazzling light that seared even through his
closed eyelids. Then darkness wrapped around him and, when
he opened his eyes, for an instant he could not see, and he pan-
icked, remembering the time he had been blind and lost in the
Tower of High Sorcery.

But, gradually, the darkness, too, lifted, and his eyes became
accustomed to the eerie light of his surroundings. It burned
with a strange, pinkish glow, *as if the sun had just set*, Tasslehoff had told him. And the land was just as the kender had
described—vast, empty terrain beneath a vast, empty sky. Sky
and land were the same color everywhere he looked, in every
direction.

Except in one direction. Turning his head, Caramon saw the
Portal, now behind him. It was the only swatch of colors in the
barren land. Framed by the oval door of the five heads of the
dragon, it seemed small and distant to him even though he
knew he must be very near. Caramon fancied it looked like a
picture, hung upon a wall. Though he could see Tanis and

Dalamar quite clearly, they were not moving. They might well have been painted subjects, captured in arrested motion, forced to spend their painted eternity staring into nothing.

Firmly turning his back upon them, wondering, with a pang, if they could see him as he could see them, Caramon drew his sword from its sheath and stood, feet firmly planted on the shifting ground, waiting for his twin.

Caramon had no doubts, no doubts at all, that a battle between himself and Raistlin must end in his own death. Even weakened, Raistlin's magic would still be strong. And Caramon knew his brother well enough to know that Raistlin would never—if he could help it—allow himself to become totally vulnerable. There would always be one spell left, or—at least—the silver dagger on his wrist.

But, even though I will die, my objective will be accomplished, Caramon thought calmly. I am strong, healthy, and all it will take is one sword thrust through that thin, frail body.

He could do that much, he knew, before his brother's magic withered him as it had withered him once, long ago, in the Tower of High Sorcery. . . .

Tears stung in his eyes, ran down his throat. He swallowed them, forcing his thoughts to something else to take his mind from his fear . . . his sorrow.

Lady Crysania.

Poor woman. Caramon sighed. He hoped, for her sake, she had died quickly . . . never knowing. . . .

Caramon blinked, startled, staring ahead of him. What was happening? Where before there had been nothing to the pinkish, glowing horizon—now there was an object. It stood starkly black against the pink sky, and appeared flat, *as if it had been cut out of paper.* Tas's words came to him again. But he recognized it—a wooden stake. The kind . . . the kind they had used in the old days to burn witches!

Memories flooded back. He could see Raistlin tied to the stake, see the heaps of wood stacked about his brother, who was struggling to free himself, shrieking defiance at those whom he had attempted to save from their own folly by exposing a charlatan cleric. But they had believed him to be a witch.

"We got there just in time, Sturm and I," Caramon muttered, remembering the knight's sword flashing in the sun, its light alone driving back the superstitious peasants.

Looking closer at the stake—which seemed, of its own accord, to move closer to him—Caramon saw a figure lying at the foot. Was it Raistlin? The stake slid closer and closer—or was he walking toward it? Caramon turned his head again. The Portal was farther back, but he could still see it.

Alarmed, fearing he might be swept away, he fought to stop himself and did so, immediately. Then, he heard the kender's voice again. *All you have to do to go anywhere is* think *yourself there. All you have to do to have anything you want is think of it, only be careful, because the Abyss can twist and distort what you see.*

Looking at the wooden stake, Caramon thought himself there and instantly was standing right beside it. Turning once again, he glanced in the direction of the Portal and saw it, hanging like a miniature painting in between the sky and ground. Satisfied that he could return at any second, Caramon hurried toward the figure lying below the stake.

At first, he had thought it was garbed in black robes, and his heart lurched. But now he saw that it had only appeared as a black silhouette against the glowing ground. The robes it wore were white. And then he knew.

Of course, he had been thinking of her. . . .

"Crysania," he said.

She opened her eyes and turned her head toward the sound of his voice, but her eyes did not fix on him. They stared past him, and he realized she was blind.

"Raistlin?" she whispered in a voice filled with such hope and longing that Caramon would have given anything, his life itself, to have confirmed that hope.

But, shaking his head, he knelt down and took her hand in his. "It is Caramon, Lady Crysania."

She turned her sightless eyes toward the sound of his voice, weakly clasping his hand with her own. She stared toward him, confused. "Caramon? Where are we?"

"I entered the Portal, Crysania," he said.

She sighed, closing her eyes. "So you are here in the Abyss, with us. . . ."

"Yes."

"I have been a fool, Caramon," she murmured, "but I am paying for my folly. I wish . . . I wish I knew. . . . Has harm come to . . . to anyone . . . other than myself? And him?" The last word was almost inaudible.

"Lady—" Caramon didn't know how to answer.

But Crysania stopped him. She could hear the sadness in his voice. Closing her eyes, tears streaming down her cheeks, she pressed his hand against her lips. "Of course. I understand!" she whispered. "That is why you have come. I'm sorry, Caramon! So sorry!"

She began to weep. Gathering her close, Caramon held her, rocking her soothingly, like a child. He knew, then, that she was dying. He could feel her life ebbing from her body even as he held it. But what had injured her, what wounds she had suffered he could not imagine, for there was no mark upon her skin.

"There is nothing to be sorry for, my lady," he said, smoothing back the thick, shining black hair that tumbled over her deathly pale face. "You loved him. If that is your folly, then it is mine as well, and I pay for it gladly."

"If that were only true!" She moaned. "But it was my pride, my ambition, that led me here!"

"Was it, Crysania?" Caramon asked. "If so, why did Paladine grant your prayers and open the Portal for you when he refused to grant the demands of the Kingpriest? Why did he bless you with that gift if not because he saw truly what was in your heart?"

"Paladine has turned his face from me!" she cried. Taking the medallion in her hand she tried to wrench it from her neck. But she was too weak. Her hand closed over the medallion and remained there. And, as she did so, a look of peace filled her face. "No," she said, talking softly to herself, "he is here. He holds me. I see him so clearly. . . ."

Standing up, Caramon lifted her in his arms. Her head sank back against his shoulder, she relaxed in his firm grasp. "We are going back to the Portal," he told her.

She did not answer, but she smiled. Had she heard him, or was she listening to another voice?

Facing the Portal that glimmered like a multicolored jewel in the distance, Caramon thought himself near it, and it moved rapidly forward.

Suddenly the air around him split and cracked. Lightning stabbed from the sky, lightning such as he had never seen. Thousands of purple, sizzling branches struck the ground, penning him for a spectacular instant in a prison whose bars were death. Paralyzed by the shock, he could not move. Even after the lightning vanished, he waited, cringing, for the explosive blast of thunder that must deafen him forever.

But there was only silence, silence and, far away, an agonized, piercing scream.

Crysania's eyes opened. "Raistlin," she said. Her hand tightened around the medallion.

"Yes," Caramon replied.

Tears slid down her cheeks. She closed her eyes and clung to Caramon. He moved on, toward the Portal, traveling slowly now, a disturbing, disquieting idea coming to his mind. Lady Crysania was dying, certainly. The lifebeat in her neck was weak, fluttering beneath his fingers like the heart of a baby bird. But she was not dead, not yet. Perhaps, if he could get her back through the Portal, she might live.

Could he get her through, though, without taking her through himself?

Holding her in his arms, Caramon drew nearer the Portal. Or rather, it drew nearer him, leaping up at him as he approached, growing in size, the dragon's heads staring at him with their glittering eyes, their mouths open to grasp and devour him.

He could still see through it, he could see Tanis and Dalamar—one standing, the other sitting; neither moving, both frozen in time. Could they help him? Could they take Crysania?

"Tanis!" he called out. "Dalamar!"

But if either heard him shouting, they did not react to his cries.

Gently, he lowered Lady Crysania to the shifting ground before the Portal. Caramon knew then that it was hopeless. He had known all along. He could take her back and she would live. But that would mean Raistlin would live and escape, drawing the Queen after him, dooming the world and its people to destruction.

He sank down to the strange ground. Sitting beside Crysania, he took hold of her hand. He was glad she was here with him, in a way. He didn't feel so alone. The touch of her hand was comforting. If only he could save her. . . .

"What are you going to do to Raistlin, Caramon?" Crysania asked softly, after a moment.

"Stop him from leaving the Abyss," Caramon replied, his voice even, without expression.

She nodded in understanding, her hand holding his firmly, her sightless eyes staring up at him.

"He'll kill you, won't he?"

"Yes," Caramon answered steadily. "But not before he himself falls."

A spasm of pain contorted Crysania's face. She gripped Caramon's hand. "I'll wait for you!" She choked, her voice weakening. "I'll wait for you. When it is over, you will be my guide since I cannot see. You will take me to Paladine. You will lead me from the darkness."

Her eyes closed. Her head sank back slowly, as though she rested upon a pillow. But her hand still held Caramon's. Her breast rose and fell with her breathing. He put his fingers on her neck, her life pulsed beneath them.

He had been prepared to condemn himself to death, he was prepared to condemn his brother. It had all been so simple!

But—could he condemn her? . . .

Perhaps he still had time. . . . Perhaps he could carry her

through the Portal and return. . . .

Filled with hope, Caramon rose to his feet and started to lift Crysania in his arms again. Then he caught a glimpse of movement out of the corner of his eye.

Turning, he saw Raistlin.

Chapter 9

"Enter, Knight of the Black Rose," repeated Dalamar.

Eyes of flame stared at Tanis, who put his hand on the hilt of his sword. At the same instant, slender fingers touched his arm, making him start.

"Do not interfere, Tanis," Dalamar said softly. "He does not care about us. He comes for one thing only."

The flickering, flaming gaze passed over Tanis. Candlelight glinted on the ancient, old-fashioned, ornate armor that bore still, beneath the blackened scorch-marks and the stains of his own blood—long since turned to dust—the faint outlines of the Rose, symbol of the Knights of Solamnia. Booted feet that made no sound crossed the room. The orange eyes had found their object in the shadowed corner—the huddled form lying beneath Tanis's cloak.

Keep him away! Tanis hear Kitiara's frantic voice. *I have always loved you, half-elf!*

Lord Soth stopped and knelt beside the body. But he appeared unable to touch it, as though constrained by some unseen force. Rising to his feet, he turned, his orange eyes flaming in the empty darkness beneath the helm he wore.

"Release her to me, Tanis Half-Elven," said the hollow voice. "Your love binds her to this plane. Give her up."

Tanis, gripping his sword, took a step forward.

"He'll kill you, Tanis," Dalamar warned. "He'll slay you without hesitation. Let her go to him. After all, I think perhaps he was the only one of us who ever truly understood her."

The orange eyes flared. "Understood her? Admired her! Like I myself, she was meant to rule, destined to conquer! But she was stronger than I was. She could throw aside love that threatened to chain her down. But for a twist of fate, she would have ruled all of Ansalon!"

The hollow voice resounded in the room, startling Tanis with its passion, its hatred.

"And there she was!" The chain mail fist clenched. "Penned up in Sanction like a caged beast, making plans for a war she could not hope to win. Her courage and resolve were beginning to weaken. She had even allowed herself to become chained like a slave to a dark-elf lover! Better she should die fighting than let her life burn out like a guttered candle."

"No!" Tanis muttered, his hand clenching his sword. "No—"

Dalamar's fingers closed over his wrist. "She never loved you, Tanis," he said coldly. "She used you as she used us all, even him." The dark elf glanced toward Soth. Tanis seemed about to speak, but Dalamar interrupted. "She used you to the end, Half-Elven. Even now, she reaches from beyond, hoping you will save her."

Still Tanis hesitated. In his mind burned the image of her horror-filled face. The image burned, flames rose. . . .

Flames filled Tanis's vision. Staring into them, he saw a castle, once proud and noble, now black and crumbling, falling into flame. He saw a lovely, delicate elf maid, a little child in her arms, falling into flame. He saw warriors, running, dying, falling into flame. And out of the flame, he heard Soth's voice.

"You have life, Half-Elven. You have much to live for. There are those among the living who depend upon you. I know, because all that you have was once mine. I cast it away, choosing to live in darkness instead of light. Will you follow me? Will you throw all you have aside for one who chose, long ago, to walk the paths of night?"

I have the world, Tanis heard his own words. Laurana's face smiled upon him.

He closed his eyes . . . Laurana's face, beautiful, wise, loving. Light shone from her golden hair, glistened in her clear, elven eyes. The light grew brighter, like a star. Purely, brilliantly, it gleamed, shining upon him with such radiance that he could no longer see in his memory the cold face beneath the cloak.

Slowly, Tanis withdrew his hand from his sword.

Lord Soth turned. Kneeling down, he lifted the body wrapped in the cloak, now stained dark with blood, in his unseen arms. He spoke a word of magic. Tanis had a sudden vision of a dark chasm yawning at the death knight's feet. Soul-piercing cold swept through the room, the blast forcing him to avert his head, as if against a bitter wind.

When he looked, the shadowed corner was empty.

"They are gone." Dalamar's hand released his wrist. "And so is Caramon."

"Gone?" Turning unsteadily, shivering, his body drenched in chill sweat, Tanis faced the Portal once again. The burning landscape was empty.

A hollow voice echoed. *Will you throw all you have aside for one who chose, long ago, to walk the paths of night?*

LORD SOTH'S SONG

Set aside the buried light
Of candle, torch, and rotting wood,
And listen to the turn of night
Caught in your rising blood.

How quiet is the midnight, love,
How warm the winds where ravens fly,
Where all the changing moonlight, love,
Pales in your fading eye.

How loud your heart is calling, love,
How close the darkness at your breast,
How hectic are the rivers, love,
Drawn through your dying wrist.

And love, what heat your frail skin hides,
As pure as salt, as sweet as death,
And in the dark the red moon rides
The foxfire of your breath.

CHAPTER
10

Ahead of him, the Portal.

Behind him, the Queen. Behind him, pain, suffering . . .

Ahead of him—victory.

Leaning upon the Staff of Magius, so weak he could barely
stand, Raistlin kept the image of the Portal ever in his mind. It
seemed he had walked, stumbled, crawled mile after endless
mile to reach it. Now he was close. He could see its glittering,
beautiful colors, colors of life—the green of grass, blue of sky,
white of clouds, black of night, red of blood. . . .

Blood. He looked at his hands, stained with blood, his own
blood. His wounds were too numerous to count. Struck by
mace, stabbed by sword, scorched by lightning, burned by fire,
he had been attacked by dark clerics, dark wizards, legions of
ghouls and demons—all who served Her Dark Majesty. His
black robes hung about him in stained tatters. He did not draw
a breath that was not wrenching agony. He had, long ago,
stopped vomiting blood. And though he coughed, coughed
until he could not stand but was forced to sink to his knees,

———

retching, there was nothing there. Nothing inside him.

And, through it all, he had endured.

Exultation ran like fever through his veins. He had endured, he had survived. He lived . . . just barely. But he lived. The Queen's fury thrummed behind him. He could feel the ground and sky pulsate with it. He had defeated her best, and there were none left now to challenge him. None, except herself.

The Portal shimmered with myriad colors in his hourglass vision. Closer, closer he came. Behind him—the Queen, rage making her careless, heedless. He would escape the Abyss, she could not stop him now. A shadow crossed over him, chilling him. Looking up, he saw the fingers of a gigantic hand darkening the sky, the nails glistening blood red.

Raistlin smiled, and kept advancing. It was a shadow, nothing more. The hand that cast the shadow reached for him in vain. He was too close, and she, having counted upon her minions to stop him, was too far away. Her hand would grasp the skirts of his tattered black robes when he crossed over the threshold of the Portal, and, with his last strength, he would drag it through the door.

And then, upon his plane, who would prove the stronger?

Raistlin coughed, but even as he coughed, even as the pain tore at him, he smiled—no, grinned—a thin-lipped, blood-stained grin. He had no doubts. No doubts at all.

Clutching his chest with one hand, the Staff of Magius with the other, Raistlin moved ahead, carefully measuring out his life to himself as he needed it, cherishing every burning breath he drew like a miser gloating over a copper piece. The coming battle would be glorious. Now it would be his turn to summon legions to fight for him. The gods themselves would answer his call, for the Queen appearing in the world in all her might and majesty would bring down the wrath of the heavens. Moons would fall, planets shift in their orbits, stars change their courses. The elements would do his bidding—wind, air, water, fire—all under his command.

And now, ahead of him—the Portal, the dragon's heads shrieking in impotent fury, knowing they lacked the power to stop him.

Just one more breath, one more lurching heartbeat, one more step. . . .

He lifted his hooded head, and stopped.

A figure, unseen before, obscured by a haze of pain and blood and the shadows of death, rose up before him, standing before the Portal, a gleaming sword in its hand. Raistlin, looking at it, stared for a moment in complete and total incomprehension. Then, joy surged through his shattered body.

"Caramon!"

He stretched out a trembling hand. What miracle this was, he didn't know. But his twin was here, as he had ever been here, waiting for him, waiting to fight at his side. . . .

"Caramon!" Raistlin panted. "Help me, my brother."

Exhaustion was overtaking him, pain claiming him. He was rapidly losing the power to think, to concentrate. His magic no longer sparkled through his body like quicksilver, but moved sluggishly, congealing like the blood upon his wounds.

"Caramon, come to me. I cannot walk alone—"

But Caramon did not move. He just stood there, his sword in his hand, staring at him with eyes of mingled love and sorrow, a deep, burning sorrow. A sorrow that cut through the haze of pain and exposed Raistlin's barren, empty soul. And then he knew. He knew why his twin was here.

"You block my way, brother," Raistlin said coldly.

"I know."

"Stand aside, then, if you will not help me!" Raistlin's voice, coming from his raw throat, cracked with fury.

"No."

"You fool! You will die!" This was a whisper, soft and lethal.

Caramon drew a deep breath. "Yes," he said steadily, "and this time, so will you."

The sky above them darkened. Shadows gathered around them, as if the light were slowly being sucked away. The air grew chill as the light dimmed, but Raistlin could feel a vast, flaming heat behind him, the rage of his Queen.

Fear twisted his bowels, anger wrenched his stomach. The

words of magic surged up, tasting like blood upon his lips. He started to hurl them at his twin, but he choked, coughed, and sank to his knees. Still the words were there, the magic was his to command. He would see his twin burn in flames as he had once, long ago, seen his twin's illusion burn in the Tower of High Sorcery. If only, if only he could catch his breath. . . .

The spasm passed. The words of magic seethed in his brain. He looked up, a grotesque snarl twisting his face, his hand raised. . . .

Caramon stood before him, his sword in his hand, staring at him with pity in his eyes.

Pity! The look slammed into Raistlin with the force of a hundred swords. Yes, his twin would die, but not with that look upon his face!

Leaning upon his staff, Raistlin pulled himself to his feet. Raising his hand, he cast the black hood from his head so that his brother could see himself—doomed—reflected in his golden eyes.

"So you pity me, Caramon," he hissed. "You bumbling harebrained slob. You who are incapable of comprehending the power that I have achieved, the pain I have overcome, the victories that have been mine. You dare to pity *me*? Before I kill you—and I *will* kill you, my brother—I want you to die with the knowledge in your heart that I am going forth into the world to become a god!"

"I know, Raistlin," Caramon answered steadily. The pity did not fade from his eyes, it only deepened. "And that is why I pity you. For I have seen the future. I know the outcome."

Raistlin stared at his brother, suspecting some trick. Above him, the red-tinged sky grew darker still, but the hand that was outstretched had paused. He could feel the Queen hesitating. She had discovered Caramon's presence. Raistlin sensed *her* confusion, *her* fear. The lingering doubt that Caramon might be some apparition conjured up to stop him vanished. Raistlin drew a step nearer his brother.

"You have seen the future? How?"

"When you went through the Portal, the magical field

affected the device, throwing Tas and me into the future."

Raistlin devoured his brother eagerly with his eyes. "And? What will happen?"

"You will win," Caramon said simply. "You will be victorious, not only over the Queen of Darkness, but over all the gods. Your constellation alone will shine in the skies . . . for a time—"

"For a time?" Raistlin's eyes narrowed. "Tell me! What happens? Who threatens? Who deposes me?"

"You do," Caramon replied, his voice filled with sadness. "You rule over a dead world, Raistlin—a world of gray ash and smoldering ruin and bloated corpses. You are alone in those heavens, Raistlin. You try to create, but there is nothing left within you to draw upon, and so you suck life from the stars themselves until they finally burst and die. And then there is nothing around you, nothing inside you."

"No!" Raistlin snarled. "You lie! Damn you! You lie!" Hurling the Staff of Magius from him, Raistlin lurched forward, his clawing hands catching hold of his brother. Startled, Caramon raised his sword, but it fell to the shifting ground at a word from Raistlin. The big man's grip tightened on his twin's arms convulsively. He could break me in two, Raistlin thought, sneering. But he won't. He is weak. He hesitates. He is lost. And I will know the truth!

Reaching up, Raistlin pressed his burning blood-stained hand upon his brother's forehead, dragging Caramon's visions from his mind into his own.

And Raistlin saw.

He saw the bones of the world, the stumps of trees, the gray mud and ash, the blasted rock, the rising smoke, the rotting bodies of the dead. . . .

He saw himself, suspended in the cold void, emptiness around him, emptiness within. It pressed down upon him, squeezed him. It gnawed at him, ate at him. He twisted in upon himself, desperately seeking nourishment—a drop of blood, a scrap of pain. But there was nothing there. There would never be anything there. And he would continue to twist, snaking inward, to find nothing . . . nothing . . . nothing.

———

Raistlin's head slumped, his hand slipped from his brother's forehead, clenching in pain. He knew this would come to pass, knew it with every fiber of his shattered body. He knew because the emptiness was already there. It had been there, within him, for so long, so long now. Oh, it had not consumed him utterly—not yet. But he could almost see his soul, frightened, lonely, crouched in a dark and empty corner.

With a bitter cry, Raistlin shoved his brother away from him. He looked around. The shadows deepened. His Queen hesitated no longer. She was gathering her strength.

Raistlin lowered his gaze, trying to think, trying to find the anger inside him, trying to kindle the burning flame of his magic— But even that was dying. Gripped by fear, he tried to run, but he was too feeble. Taking a step, he stumbled and fell on his hands and knees. Fear shook him. He sought for help, stretching out his hand. . . .

He heard a sound, a moan, a cry. His hand closed over white cloth, he felt warm flesh!

"Bupu," Raistlin whispered. With a choked sob, he crawled forward.

The body of the gully dwarf lay before him, her face pinched and starved, her eyes wide with terror. Wretched, terrified, she shrank away from him.

"Bupu!" Raistlin cried, grasping hold of her in desperation, "Bupu, don't you remember me? You gave me a book, once. A book and an emerald." Fishing around in one of his pouches, he pulled out the shimmering, shining green stone. "Here, Bupu. Look, 'the pretty rock.' Take it, keep it! It will protect you!"

She reached for it, but as she did, her fingers stiffened in death.

"No!" Raistlin cried, and felt Caramon's hand upon his arm.

"Leave her alone!" Caramon cried harshly, catching hold of his twin and hurling him backward. "Haven't you done enough to her already?"

Caramon held his sword in his hand once more. Its bright light hurt Raistlin's eyes. By its light, Raistlin saw—not Bupu—but Crysania, her skin blackened and blistered, her eyes staring at him without seeing him.

Empty . . . empty. Nothing within him? Yes. . . . Something there. Something, not much, but something. His soul stretched forth its hand. His own hand reached out, touched Crysania's blistered skin. "She is not dead, not yet," he said.

"No, not yet," Caramon replied, raising his sword. "Leave her alone! Let her at least die in peace!"

"She will live, if you take her through the Portal."

"Yes, she will live," Caramon said bitterly, "and so will you, won't you, Raistlin? I take her through the Portal and you come right after us—"

"Take her."

"No!" Caramon shook his head. Though tears glimmered in his eyes, and his face was pale with grief and anguish, he stepped toward his brother, his sword ready.

Raistlin raised his hand. Caramon couldn't move, his sword hung suspended in the hot, shifting air.

"Take her, and take this as well."

Reaching out, Raistlin's frail hand closed around the Staff of Magius that lay at his side. The light from its crystal glowed clear and strong in the deepening darkness, shedding its magical glow over the three of them. Lifting the staff, Raistlin held it out to his twin.

Caramon hesitated, his brow furrowing.

"Take it!" Raistlin snapped, feeling his strength dwindling. He coughed. "Take it!" he whispered, gasping for breath. "Take it and her and yourself back through the Portal. Use the staff to close it behind you."

Caramon stared at him, uncomprehending, then his eyes narrowed.

"No, I'm not lying," Raistlin snarled. "I've lied to you before, but not now. Try it. See for yourself. Look, I release you from the enchantment. I cannot cast another spell. If you find I am lying, you may slay me. I will not be able to stop you."

Caramon's swordarm was freed. He could move it. Still holding his sword, his eyes on his twin, he reached out his other hand, hesitantly. His fingers touched the staff and he looked

313

fearfully at the light in the crystal, expecting it to blink out and leave them all in the gathering, chilling darkness.

But the light did not waver. Caramon's hand closed around the staff, above his brother's hand. The light gleamed brightly, shedding its radiance upon the torn and bloody black robes, the dull and mud-covered armor.

Raistlin let go of the staff. Slowly, almost falling, he staggered to his feet and drew himself up, standing without aid, standing alone. The staff, in Caramon's hand, continued to glow.

"Hurry," Raistlin said coldly, "I will keep the Queen from following you. But my strength will not last long."

Caramon stared at him a moment, then at the staff, its light still burning brightly. Finally, drawing a ragged breath, he sheathed his sword.

"What will happen . . . to you?" he asked harshly, kneeling down to lift up Crysania in his arms.

You will be tortured in mind and in body. At the end of each day, you will die from the pain. At the beginning of each night, I will bring you back to life. You will not be able to sleep, but will lie awake in shivering anticipation of the day to come. In the morning, my face will the first sight you see.

The words curled about Raistlin's brain like a snake. Behind him, he could hear sultry, mocking laughter.

"Be gone, Caramon," he said. "She comes."

Crysania's head rested against Caramon's broad chest. The dark hair fell across her pale face, her hand still clasped the medallion of Paladine. As Raistlin looked at her, he saw the ravages of the fire fade, leaving her face unscarred, softened by a look of sweet, peaceful rest. Raistlin's gaze lifted to his brother's face, and he saw that same stupid expression Caramon always wore—that look of puzzlement, of baffled hurt.

"You blubbering fool! What do you care what becomes of me?" Raistlin snarled. "Get out!"

Caramon's expression changed, or maybe it didn't change. Maybe it had been this way all the time. Raistlin's strength was dwindling very fast, his vision dimmed. But, in Caramon's eyes, he thought he saw understanding. . . .

"Good-bye . . . my brother," Caramon said.

Holding Crysania in his arms, the Staff of Magius in one hand, Caramon turned and walked away. The light of the staff formed a circle around him, a circle of silver that shone in the darkness like the moonbeams of Solinari glistening upon the calm waters of Crystalmir Lake. The silver beams struck the dragon's heads, freezing them, changing them to silver, silencing their screams.

Caramon stepped through the Portal. Raistlin, watching him with his soul, caught a blurred glimpse of colors and life and felt a brief whisper of warmth touch his sunken cheek.

Behind him, he could hear the mocking laughter gurgle into harsh, hissing breath. He could hear the slithering sounds of a gigantic scaled tail, the creaking of wing tendons. Behind him, five heads whispered words of torment and terror.

Steadfastly, Raistlin stood, staring into the Portal. He saw Tanis run to help Caramon, he saw him take Crysania in his arms. Tears blurred Raistlin's vision. He wanted to follow! He wanted Tanis to touch his hand! He wanted to hold Crysania in his arms . . . He took a step forward.

He saw Caramon turn to face him, the staff in his hand.

Caramon stared into the Portal, stared at his twin, stared beyond his twin. Raistlin saw his brother's eyes grow wide with fright.

Raistlin did not have to turn to know what his brother saw. Takhisis crouched behind him. He could feel the chill of the loathsome reptile body flow about him, fluttering his robes. He sensed her behind him, yet her thoughts were not on him. She saw her way to the world, standing open. . . .

"Shut it!" Raistlin screamed.

A blast of flame seared Raistlin's flesh. A taloned claw stabbed him in the back. He stumbled, falling to his knees. But he never took his eyes from the Portal, and he saw Caramon, his twin's face anguished, take a step forward, toward him!

"Shut it, you fool!" Raistlin shrieked, clenching his fists. "Leave me alone! I don't need you any more! I don't need you!"

And then the light was gone. The Portal slammed shut, and blackness pounced upon him with raging, slathering fury. Talons ripped his flesh, teeth tore through muscle, and crunched bone. Blood flowed from his breast, but it would not take with it his life.

He screamed, and he would scream, and he would keep on screaming, unendingly. . . .

Something touched him . . . a hand. . . . He clutched at it as it shook him, gently. A voice called, "Raist! Wake up! It was only a dream. Don't be afraid. I won't let them hurt you! Here, watch . . . I'll make you laugh."

The dragon's coils tightened, crushing out his breath. Glistening black fangs ate his living organs, devoured his heart. Tearing into his body, they sought his soul.

A strong arm encircled him, holding him close. A hand raised, gleaming with silver light, forming childish pictures in the night, and the voice, dimly heard, whispered, "Look, Raist, bunnies. . . ."

He smiled, no longer afraid. Caramon was here.

The pain eased. The dream was driven back. From far away, he heard a wail of bitter disappointment and anger. It didn't matter. Nothing mattered anymore. Now he just felt tired, so very, very tired. . . .

Leaning his head upon his brother's arm, Raistlin closed his eyes and drifted into a dark, dreamless, endless sleep.

CHAPTER
II

The drops of water in the water clock dripped steadily, relentlessly, echoing in the silent laboratory. Staring into the Portal with eyes that burned from the strain, Tanis believed the drops must be falling, one by one, upon his taut, stretched nerves.

Rubbing his eyes, he turned from the Portal with a bitter snarl and walked over to look out the window. He was astonished to see that it was only late afternoon. After what he had been through, he would not have been much surprised to find that spring had come and gone, summer had bloomed and died, and autumn was setting in.

The thick smoke no longer swirled past the window. The fires, having eaten what they fed upon, were dying. He glanced up into the sky. The dragons had vanished from sight, both good and evil. He listened. No sound came from the city beneath him. A haze of fog and storm and smoke still hung over it, further shadowed by the darkness of the Shoikan Grove.

The battle is over, he realized numbly. It has ended. And we

317

have won. Victory. Hollow, wretched victory.

And then, a flutter of bright blue caught his eye. Looking out over the city, Tanis gasped.

The flying citadel had suddenly drifted into view. Dropping down from the storm clouds, it was careening along merrily, having somewhere acquired a brilliant blue banner that streamed out in the wind. Tanis looked closer, thinking he recognized not only the banner but the graceful minaret from which it flew and which was now perched drunkenly on a tower of the citadel.

Shaking his head, the half-elf could not help smiling. The banner—and the minaret—had once both been part of the palace of Lord Amothus.

Leaning against the window, Tanis continued watching the citadel, which had acquired a bronze dragon as honor guard. He felt his bleakness and grief and fear ease and the tension in his body relax. No matter what happened in the world or on the planes beyond, some things—kender among them—never changed.

Tanis watched as the flying castle wobbled out over the bay, then he was, however, considerably startled to see the citadel suddenly flip over and hang in the air, upside down.

"What is Tas doing?" he muttered.

And then he knew. The citadel began to bob up and down rapidly, like a salt shaker. Black shapes with leathery wings tumbled out of the windows and from doorways. Up and down, up and down bobbed the citadel, more and more black shapes dropping out. Tanis grinned. Tas was clearing out the guards! Then, when no more draconians could be seen spilling out into the water, the citadel righted itself again and continued on its way . . . then, as it skipped merrily along, its blue flag fluttering in the wind, it dove in a wild, unfortunate plunge, right into the ocean!

Tanis caught his breath, but almost immediately the citadel appeared again, leaping out of the water like a blue-bannered dolphin to soar up into the sky once more—water now streaming out of every conceivable opening—and vanish amidst the storm clouds.

Shaking his head, smiling, Tanis turned to see Dalamar gesture toward the Portal. "There he is. Caramon has returned to his position."

Swiftly, the half-elf crossed the room and stood before the Portal once again.

He could see Caramon, still a tiny figure in gleaming armor. This time, he carried someone in his arms.

"Raistlin?" Tanis asked, puzzled.

"Lady Crysania," Dalamar replied.

"Maybe she's still alive!"

"It would be better for her were she not," Dalamar said coldly. Bitterness further hardened his voice and his expression. "Better for all of us! Now Caramon must make a difficult choice."

"What do you mean?"

"It will inevitably occur to him that he could save her by bringing her back through the Portal himself. Which would leave us all at the mercy of either his brother or the Queen or both."

Tanis was silent, watching. Caramon was drawing closer and closer to the Portal, the white-robed figure of the woman in his arms.

"What do you know of him?" Dalamar asked abruptly. "What decision will he make? The last I saw of him he was a drunken buffoon, but his experiences appear to have changed him."

"I don't know," Tanis said, troubled, talking more to himself than to Dalamar. "The Caramon I once knew was only half a person, the other half belonged to his brother. He is different now. He has changed." Tanis scratched his beard, frowning. "Poor man. I don't know . . ."

"Ah, it seems his choice has been made for him," Dalamar said, relief mixed with fear in his voice.

Looking into the Portal, Tanis saw Raistlin. He saw the final meeting between the twins.

———

Tanis never spoke to anyone of that meeting. Though the visions seen and words heard were indelibly etched upon his memory, he found he could not talk about them. To give them voice seemed to demean them, to take away their terrible horror, their terrible beauty. But often, if he was depressed or unhappy, he would remember the last gift of a benighted soul, and he would close his eyes and thank the gods for his blessings.

Caramon brought Lady Crysania through the Portal. Running forward to help him, Tanis took Crysania in his arms, staring in wonder at the sight of the big man carrying the magical staff, its light still glowing brightly.

"Stay with her, Tanis," Caramon said, "I must close the Portal."

"Do it quickly!" Tanis heard Dalamar's sharp intake of breath. He saw the dark elf staring into the Portal in horror. "Close it!" he cried.

Holding Crysania in his arms, Tanis looked down at her and realized she was dying. Her breath faltered, her skin was ashen, her lips were blue. But he could do nothing for her, except take her to a place of safety.

Safety! He glanced about, his gaze going to the shadowed corner where another dying woman had lain. It was farthest from the Portal. She would be safe there—as safe as anywhere, he supposed sorrowfully. Laying her down, making her as comfortable as possible, he hastily returned to the opening in the void.

Tanis halted, mesmerized by the sight before his eyes.

A shadow of evil filled the Portal, the metallic dragon's heads that formed the gate howled in triumph. The living dragon's heads beyond the Portal writhed above the body of their victim as the archmage fell to their claws.

"No! Raistlin!" Caramon's face twisted in anguish. He took a step toward the Portal.

"Stop!" Dalamar screamed in fury. "Stop him, Half-Elven! Kill him if you must! Close the Portal!"

———

A woman's hand lunged for the opening and, as they watched in stunned terror, the hand became a dragon's claw, the nails tipped with red, the talons stained with blood. Nearer and nearer the Portal the hand of the Queen came, intent upon keeping this door to the world open so that, once more, she could gain entry.

"Caramon!" Tanis cried, springing forward. But, what could he do? He was not strong enough to physically overpower the big man. He'll go to him, Tanis thought in agony. He will not let his brother die. . . .

No, spoke a voice inside the half-elf. He will not . . . and therein lies the salvation of the world.

Caramon stopped, held fast by the power of that blood-stained hand. The grasping dragon's claw was close, and behind it gleamed laughing, triumphant, malevolent eyes. Slowly, struggling against the evil force, Caramon raised the Staff of Magius.

Nothing happened!

The dragon's heads of the oval doorway split the air with their trumpeting, hailing the entry of their Queen into the world.

Then, a shadowy form appeared, standing beside Caramon. Dressed in black robes, white hair flowing down upon his shoulders, Raistlin raised a golden-skinned hand and, reaching out, gripped the Staff of Magius, his hand resting near his twin's.

The staff flared with a pure, silver light.

The multicolored light within the Portal whirled and spun and fought to survive, but the silver light shone with the steadfast brilliance of the evening star, glittering in a twilight sky.

The Portal closed.

The metallic dragon's heads ceased their screaming so suddenly that the new silence rang in their ears. Within the Portal, there was nothing, neither movement nor stillness, neither darkness nor light. There was simply nothing.

Caramon stood before the Portal alone, the Staff of Magius in his hand. The light of the crystal continued to burn brightly for a moment.

Then glimmered.

Then died.

The room was filled with darkness, a sweet darkness, a darkness restful to the eyes after the blinding light.

And there came through the darkness a whispering voice.

"Farewell, my brother."

stinus of Palanthas
sat in his study in the Great Library, writing his history in the
clear, sharp black strokes that had recorded all the history of
Krynn from the first day the gods had looked upon the world
until the last, when the great book would forever close. Astinus
wrote, oblivious to the chaos around him, or rather—such was
the man's presence—that it seemed as if he forced the chaos to
be oblivious of him.

It was only two days after the end of what Astinus referred to
in the *Chronicles* as the "Test of the Twins" (but which everyone
else was calling the "Battle of Palanthas"). The city was in
ruins. The only two buildings left standing were the Tower of
High Sorcery and the Great Library, and the Library had not
escaped unscathed.

The fact that it stood at all was due, in large part, to the heroics of the Aesthetics. Led by the rotund Bertrem, whose courage was kindled, so it was said, by the sight of a draconian
daring to lay a clawed hand upon one of the sacred books, the
Aesthetics attacked the enemy with such zeal and such a wild,

reckless disregard for their own lives that few of the reptilian creatures escaped.

But, like the rest of Palanthas, the Aesthetics paid a grievous price for victory. Many of their order perished in the battle. These were mourned by their brethren, their ashes given honored rest among the books that they had sacrificed their lives to protect. The gallant Bertrem did *not* die. Only slightly wounded, he saw his name go down in one of the great books itself beside the names of the other Heroes of Palanthas. Life could offer nothing further in the way of reward to Bertrem. He never passed that one particular book upon the shelf but that he didn't surreptitiously pull it down, open it to The Page, and bask in the light of his glory.

The beautiful city of Palanthas was now nothing more than memory and a few words of description in Astinus's books. Heaps of charred and blackened stone marked the graves of palatial estates. The rich warehouses with their casks of fine wines and ales, their stores of cotton and of wheat, their boxes of wonders from all parts of Krynn, lay in a pile of cinder. Burned-out hulks of ships floated in the ash-choked harbors. Merchants picked through the rubble of their shops, salvaging what they could. Families stared at their ruined houses, holding on to each other, and thanking the gods that they had, at least, survived with their lives.

For there were many who had not. Of the Knights of Solamnia within the city, they had perished almost to a man, fighting the hopeless battle against Lord Soth and his deadly legions. One of the first to fall was the dashing Sir Markham. True to his oath to Tanis, the knight had not fought Lord Soth, but had, instead, rallied the knights and led them in a charge against Soth's skeletal warriors. Though pierced with many wounds, he fought vailiantly still, leading his bloody, exhausted men time and again in charges against the foe until finally he fell from his horse, dead.

Because of the knights' courage, many lived in Palanthas who otherwise would have perished upon the ice-cold blades of the undead, who vanished mysteriously—so it was told—

when their leader appeared among them, bearing a shrouded corpse in his arms.

Mourned as heroes, the bodies of the Knights of Solamnia were taken by their fellows to the High Clerist's Tower. Here they were entombed in a sepulcher where lay the body of Sturm Brightblade, Hero of the Lance.

Upon opening the sepulcher, which had not been disturbed since the Battle of the High Clerist's Tower, the knights were awed to find Sturm's body whole, unravaged by time. An elven jewel of some type, gleaming upon his breast, was believed accountable for this miracle. All those who entered the sepulcher that day in mourning for their fallen loved ones looked upon that steadily beaming jewel and felt peace ease the bitter sting of their grief.

The knights were not the only ones who were mourned. Many ordinary citizens had died in Palanthas as well. Men defending city and family, women defending home and children. The citizens of Palanthas burned their dead in accordance with ages-old custom, scattering the ashes of their loved ones in the sea, where they mingled with the ashes of their beloved city.

Astinus recorded it all as it was occurring. He had continued to write—so the Aesthetics reported with awe—even as Bertrem single-handedly bludgeoned to death a draconian who had dared invade the master's study. He was writing still when he gradually became aware—above the sounds of hammering and sweeping and pounding and shuffling—that Bertrem was blocking his light.

Lifting up his head, he frowned.

Bertrem, who had not blenched once in the face of the enemy, turned deathly pale, and backed up instantly, letting the sunlight fall once more upon the page.

Astinus resumed his writing. "Well?" he said.

"Caramon Majere and a—a kender are here to see you, Master." If Bertrem had said a demon from the Abyss was here to see Astinus, he could hardly have infused more horror into his voice than when he spoke the word "kender."

"Send them in," replied Astinus.

"*Them*, Master?" Bertrem could not help but repeat in shock.

Astinus looked up, his brow creased. "The draconian did not damage your hearing, did it, Bertrem? You did not receive, for example, a blow to the head?"

"N-no, Master." Bertrem flushed and backed hurriedly out of the room, tripping over his robes as he did so.

"Caramon Majere and . . . and Tassle-f-foot B-burr-hoof," announced the flustered Bertrem, moments later.

"Tasslehoff Burrfoot," said the kender, presenting a small hand to Astinus, who shook it gravely. "And you're Astinus of Palanthas," Tas continued, his topknot bouncing with excitement. "I've met you before, but you don't remember because it hasn't happened yet. Or, rather, come to think of it, it never will happen, will it, Caramon?"

"No," the big man replied. Astinus turned his gaze to Caramon, regarding him intently.

"You do not resemble your twin," Astinus said coolly, "but then Raistlin had undergone many trials that marked him both physically and mentally. Still, there is something of him in your eyes. . . ."

The historian frowned, puzzled. He did not understand, and there was nothing on the face of Krynn that he did not understand. Consequently, he grew angry.

Astinus rarely grew angry. His irritation alone sent a wave of terror through the Aesthetics. But he was angry now. His graying brows bristled, his lips tightened, and there was a look in his eyes that made the kender glance about nervously, wondering if he hadn't left something outside in the hall that he needed—now!

"What is it?" The historian demanded finally, slamming his hand down upon his book, causing his pen to jump, the ink to spill, and Bertrem—waiting in the corridor—to run away as fast as his flapping sandals could take him.

"There is a mystery about you, Caramon Majere, and there are no mysteries for me! I know everything that transpires upon the face of Krynn. I know the thoughts of every living being! I see their actions! I read the wishes of their hearts! Yet I cannot read your eyes!"

"Tas told you," Caramon said imperturbably. Reaching into a knapsack he wore, the big man produced a huge, leatherbound volume which he set carefully down upon the desk in front of the historian.

"That's one of mine!" Astinus said, glancing at it, his scowl deepening. His voice rose until he actually shouted. "Where did it come from? None of my books leave without my knowledge! Bertrem—"

"Look at the date."

Astinus glared furiously at Caramon for a second, then shifted his angry gaze to the book. He looked at the date upon the volume, prepared to shout for Bertrem again. But the shout rattled in his throat and died. He stared at the date, his eyes widening. Sinking down into his chair, he looked from the volume to Caramon, then back to the volume again.

"It is the future I see in your eyes!"

"The future that is this book," Caramon said, regarding it with grave solemnity.

"We were there!" said Tas, bouncing up eagerly. "Would you like to hear about it? It's the most wonderful story. You see, we came back to Solace, only it didn't look like Solace. I thought it was a moon, in fact, because I'd been thinking about a moon when we used the magical device and—"

"Hush, Tas," Caramon said gently. Standing up, he put his hand on the kender's shoulder and quietly left the room. Tas— being steered firmly out the door—glanced backward. "Goodbye!" he called, waving his hand. "Nice seeing you again, er, before, uh, after, well, whatever."

But Astinus neither heard nor noticed. The day he received the book from Caramon Majere was the only day that passed in the entire history of Palanthas that had nothing recorded for it but one entry:

This day, as above Afterwatch rising 14, Caramon Majere brought me the Chronicles of Krynn, *Volume 2000. A volume written by me that I will never write.*

327

The funeral of Elistan represented, to the people of Palanthas, the funeral of their beloved city as well. The ceremony was held at daybreak as Elistan had requested, and everyone in Palanthas attended—old, young, rich, poor. The injured who were able to be moved were carried from their homes, their pallets laid upon the scorched and blackened grass of the once-beautiful lawns of the Temple.

Among these was Dalamar. No one murmured as the dark elf was helped across the lawn by Tanis and Caramon to take his place beneath a grove of charred, burned aspens. For rumor had it that the young apprentice magic-user had fought the Dark Lady—as Kitiara was known—and defeated her, thereby bringing about the destruction of her forces.

Elistan had wanted to be buried in his Temple, but that was impossible now—the Temple being nothing but a gutted shell of marble. Lord Amothus had offered his family's tomb, but Crysania had declined. Remembering that Elistan had found his faith in the slave mines of Pax Tharkas, the Revered Daughter—now head of the church—decreed that he be laid to rest beneath the Temple in one of the underground caverns that had formerly been used for storage.

Though some were shocked, no one questioned Crysania's commands. The caverns were cleaned and sanctified, a marble bier was built from the remains of the Temple. And hereafter, even in the grand days of the church that were to come, all of the priests were laid to rest in this humble place that became known as one of the most holy places on Krynn.

The people settled down on the lawn in silence. The birds, knowing nothing of death or war or grief, but knowing only that the sun was rising and that they were alive in the bright morning, filled the air with song. The sun's rays tipped the mountains with gold, driving away the darkness of the night, bringing light to hearts heavy with sorrow.

One person only rose to speak Elistan's eulogy, and it was deemed fitting by everyone that she do so. Not only because she was now taking his place—as he had requested—as head of the church, but because she seemed to the people of Palanthas to epitomize their loss and their pain.

That morning, they said, was the first time she had risen from her bed since Tanis Half-Elven brought her down from the Temple of High Sorcery to the steps of the Great Library, where the clerics worked among the injured and the dying. She had been near death herself. But her faith and the prayers of the clerics restored her to life. They could not, however, restore her sight.

Crysania stood before them that morning, her eyes looking straight into the sun she would never see again. Its rays glistened in her black hair that framed a face made beautiful by a look of deep, abiding compassion and faith.

"As I stand in darkness," she said, her clear voice rising sweet and pure among the songs of the larks, "I feel the warmth of the light upon my skin and I know my face is turned toward the sun. I can look into the sun, for my eyes are forever shrouded by darkness. But if you who can see look too long in the sun, you will lose your sight, just as those who live too long in the darkness will gradually lose theirs.

"This Elistan taught—that mortals were not meant to live solely in sun or in shadow, but in both. Both have their perils, if misused, both have their rewards. We have come through our trials of blood, of darkness, of fire—" Her voice quavered and broke at this point. Those nearest her saw tears upon her cheeks. But, when she continued, her voice was strong. Her tears glistened in the sunlight. "We have come through these trials as Huma came through his, with great loss, with great sacrifice, but strong in the knowledge that our spirit shines and that we, perhaps, gleam brightest among all the stars of the heavens.

"For though some might choose to walk the paths of night, looking to the black moon to guide them, while others walk the paths of day, the rough and rock-strewn trails of both can be made easier by the touch of a hand, the voice of a friend. The capacity to love, to care, is given to us all—the greatest gift of the gods to all the races.

———

"Our beautiful city has perished in flame." Her voice softened. "We have lost many whom we loved, and it seems perhaps that life is too difficult a burden for us to bear. But reach out your hand, and it will touch the hand of someone reaching out to you, and—together—you will find the strength and hope you need to go on."

After the ceremonies, when the clerics had borne the body of Elistan to its final resting place, Caramon and Tas sought out Lady Crysania. They found her among the clerics, her arm resting upon the arm of the young woman who was her guide.

"Here are two who would speak with you, Revered Daughter," said the young cleric.

Lady Crysania turned, holding out her hand. "Let me touch you," she said.

"It's Caramon," the big man began awkwardly, "and—"

"Me," said Tas in a meek, subdued voice.

"You have come to say good-bye." Lady Crysania smiled.

"Yes. We're leaving today," Caramon said, holding her hand in his.

"Do you go straight home to Solace?"

"No, not—not quite yet," Caramon said, his voice low. "We're going back to Solanthas with Tanis. Then, when—when I feel a little more myself, I'll use the magical device to get back to Solace."

Crysania gripped his hand tightly, drawing him near to her.

"Raistlin is at peace, Caramon," she said softly. "Are you?"

"Yes, my lady," Caramon said, his voice firm and resolute. "I am at peace. At last." He sighed. "I just need to talk to Tanis and get things sorted out in my life, put back in order. For one thing," he added with a blush and a shame-faced grin, "I need to know how to build a house! I was dead drunk most of the time I worked on ours, and I haven't the faintest notion what I was doing."

He looked at her, and she—aware of his scrutiny though she could not see it—smiled, her pale skin tinged with the faintest rose. Seeing that smile, and seeing the tears that fell around it,

Caramon drew her close, in turn. "I'm sorry. I wish I could have spared you this—"

"No, Caramon," she said softly. "For now I see. I see clearly, as Loralon promised." She kissed his hand, pressing it to her cheek. "Farewell, Caramon. May Paladine go with you."

Tasslehoff snuffled.

"Good-bye, Crysani— I mean, Rev-revered Daughter," said Tas in a small voice, feeling suddenly lonely and short. "I—I'm sorry about the mess I made of things—"

But Lady Crysania interrupted him. Turning from Caramon, she reached out her hand and smoothed back his topknot of hair. "Most of us walk in the light and the shadow, Tasslehoff," she said, "but there are the chosen few who walk this world, carrying their own light to brighten both day and night."

"Really? They must get awfully tired, hauling around a light like that? Is it a torch? It can't be a candle. The wax would melt all over and drip down into their shoes and—say—do you suppose I could meet someone like that?" Tas asked with interest.

"You are someone like that," Lady Crysania replied. "And I do not think you ever need worry about your wax dripping into your shoes. Farewell, Tasslehoff Burrfoot. I need not ask Paladine's blessing on you, for I know you are one of his close, personal friends. . . ."

"Well," asked Caramon abruptly as he and Tas made their way through the crowd. "Have you decided what you're going to do yet? You've got the flying citadel, Lord Amothus gave it to you. You can go anywhere on Krynn. Maybe even a moon, if you want."

"Oh, that." Tas, looking a little awestruck after his talk with Lady Crysania, seemed to have trouble remembering what Caramon was referring to. "I don't have the citadel anymore. It was awfully big and boring once I got around to exploring it. And it wouldn't go to the moon. I tried. Do you know," he said, looking at Caramon with wide eyes, "that if you go up high enough, your nose starts to bleed? Plus it's extremely cold and uncomfortable. Besides, the moons seem to be a lot farther

away than I'd imagined. Now, if I had the magical device—"
He glanced at Caramon out of the corner of his eye.

"No," said Caramon sternly. "Absolutely not. That's going
back to Par-Salian."

"I could take it to him," Tas offered helpfully. "That would
give me a chance to explain about Gnimsh fixing it and my dis-
rupting the spell and— No?" He heaved a sigh. "I guess not.
Well, anyway, I've decided to stick with you and Tanis, if you
want me, that is?" He looked at Caramon a bit wistfully.

Caramon replied by reaching out and giving the kender a
hug that crushed several objects of interest and uncertain value
in his pouches.

"By the way," Caramon added as an afterthought, "what *did*
you do with the flying citadel?"

"Oh"—Tas waved his hand nonchalantly—"I gave it to
Rounce."

"The gully dwarf!" Caramon stopped, appalled.

"He can't fly it, not by himself!" Tas assured him.
"Although," he added after a moment's profound thought, "I
suppose he could if he got a few more gully dwarves to help. I
never thought of that—"

Caramon groaned. "Where is it?"

"I set it down for him in a nice place. A very nice place. It was
a really wealthy part of some city we flew over. Rounce took a
liking to it—the citadel, not the city. Well, I guess he took a liking to the city, too, come to think of it. Anyway, he was a big
help and all, so I asked him if he wanted the citadel and he said
he did so I just plunked the thing down in this vacant lot.

"It caused quite a sensation," Tas added happily. "A man
came running out of this really big castle that sat on a hill right
next to where I dropped the citadel, and he started yelling
about that being his property and what right did we have to
drop a castle on it, and creating a wonderful row. I pointed out
that his castle certainly didn't cover the entire property and I
mentioned a few things about sharing that would have helped
him quite a bit, I'm certain, if he'd only listened. Then Rounce
starting saying how he was going to bring all the Burp clan or

something like that and they were going to come live in the citadel and the man had a fit of some sort and they carried him away and pretty soon the whole town was there. It was real exciting for a while, but it finally got boring. I was glad Fireflash had decided to come along. He brought me back."

"You didn't tell me any of this!" Caramon said, glaring at the kender and trying hard to look grim.

"I—I guess it just slipped my mind," Tas mumbled. "I've had an awful lot to think about these days, you know."

"I know you have, Tas," Caramon said. "I've been worried about you. I saw you talking to some other kender yesterday. You could go home, you know. You told me once how you've thought about it, about going back to Kendermore."

Tas's face took on an unusually serious expression. Slipping his hand into Caramon's, he drew nearer, looking up at him earnestly. "No, Caramon," he said softly. "It isn't the same. I—I can't seem to talk to other kender anymore." He shook his head, his topknot swishing back and forth. "I tried to tell them about Fizban and his hat, and Flint and his tree and . . . and Raistlin and poor Gnimsh." Tas swallowed and, fishing out a handkerchief, wiped his eyes. "They don't seem to understand. They just don't . . . well . . . care. It's hard—caring—isn't it, Caramon? It hurts sometimes."

"Yes, Tas," Caramon said quietly. They had entered a shady grove of trees. Tanis was waiting for them, standing beneath a tall, graceful aspen whose new spring leaves glittered golden in the morning sun. "It hurts a lot of the time. But the hurt is better than being empty inside."

Walking over to them, Tanis put one arm around Caramon's broad shoulders, the other arm around Tas. "Ready?" he asked.

"Ready." Caramon replied.

"Good. The horses are over here. I thought we'd ride. We could have taken the carriage, but—to be perfectly honest—I hate being cooped up in the blasted thing. So does Laurana, though she'll never admit it. The countryside's beautiful this time of year. We'll take our time, and enjoy it."

"You live in Solanthas, don't you, Tanis?" Tas said as they

mounted their horses and rode down the blackened, ruined street. Those people leaving the funeral, returning to pick up the pieces of their lives, heard the kender's cheerful voice echo through the streets long after he had gone.

"I was in Solanthas once. They have an awfully fine prison there. One of the nicest I was ever in. I was sent there by mistake, of course. A misunderstanding over a silver teapot that had tumbled, quite by accident, into one my pouches. . . ."

Dalamar climbed the steep, winding stairs leading up to the laboratory at the top of the Tower of High Sorcery. He climbed the stairs, instead of magically transporting himself, because he had a long journey ahead of him that night. Though the clerics of Elistan had healed his wounds, he was still weak and he did not want to tax his strength.

Later, when the black moon was in the sky, he would travel through the ethers to the Tower of High Sorcery at Wayreth, there to attend a Wizard's Conclave—one of the most important to be held in this era. Par-Salian was stepping down as Head of the Conclave. His successor must be chosen. It would probably be the Red Robe, Justarius. Dalamar didn't mind that. He knew he was not yet powerful enough to become the new archmage. Not yet, at any rate. But there was some feeling that a new Head of the Order of the Black Robes should be chosen, too. Dalamar smiled. He had no doubt who that would be.

He had made all his preparations for leaving. The guardians had their instructions: no one—living or dead—was to be admitted to the Tower in his absence. Not that this was likely. The Shoikan Grove maintained its own grim vigil, unharmed by the flames that had swept through the rest of Palanthas. But the dark loneliness that the Tower had known for so long would soon be coming to an end.

On Dalamar's order, several rooms in the Tower had been cleaned out and refurbished. He planned to bring back with him several apprentices of his own—Black Robes, certainly, but maybe a Red Robe or two if he found any who might be suitable. He looked forward to passing on the skills he had acquired, the knowledge he had learned. And—he admitted to himself—he looked forward to the companionship.

But, first, there was something he must do.

Entering the laboratory, he paused on the doorstep. He had not been back to this room since Caramon had carried him from it that last, fateful day. Now, it was nighttime. The room was dark. At a word, candles flickered into flame, warming the room with a soft light. But the shadows remained, hovering in the corners like living things.

Lifting the candlestand in his hand, Dalamar made a slow circuit of the room, selecting various items—scrolls, a magic wand, several rings—and sending them below to his own study with a word of command.

He passed the dark corner where Kitiara had died. Her blood stained the floor still. That spot in the room was cold, chill, and Dalamar did not linger. He passed the stone table with its beakers and bottles, the eyes still staring out at him pleadingly. With a word, he caused them to close—forever.

Finally, he came to the Portal. The five heads of the dragon, facing eternally into the void, still shouted their silent, frozen paen to the Dark Queen. The only light that gleamed from the dark, lifeless metallic heads was the reflected light of Dalamar's candles. He looked within the Portal. There was nothing. For long moments, Dalamar stared into it. Then, reaching out his hand, he pulled on a golden, silken cord that hung from the ceiling. A thick curtain dropped down, shrouding the Portal in heavy, purple velvet.

Turning away, Dalamar found himself facing the bookshelves that stood in the very back of the laboratory. The candlelight shone on rows of nightblue-bound volumes decorated with silver runes. A cold chill flowed from them.

The spellbooks of Fistandantilus—now his.

And where these rows of books ended, a new row of books began—volumes bound in black decorated with silver runes. Each of these volumes, Dalamar noticed, his hand going to touch one, burned with an inner heat that made the books seem strangely alive to the touch.

The spellbooks of Raistlin—now his.

Dalamar looked intently at each book. Each held its own wonders, its own mysteries, each held power. The dark elf walked the length of the bookshelves. When he reached the end—near the door—he sent the candlestand back to rest upon the great stone table. His hand upon the door handle, his gaze went to one, last object.

In a dark corner stood the Staff of Magius, leaning up against the wall. For a moment, Dalamar caught his breath, thinking perhaps he saw light gleaming from the crystal on top of the staff—the crystal that had remained cold and dark since that day. But then he realized, with a sense of relief, that it was only reflected candlelight. With a word, he extinguished the flame, plunging the room into darkness.

He looked closely at the corner where the staff stood. It was lost in the night, no sign of light glimmered.

Drawing a deep breath, then letting it out with a sigh, Dalamar walked from the laboratory. Firmly, he shut the door behind him. Reaching into a wooden box set with powerful runes, he withdrew a silver key and inserted it into an ornate silver doorlock—a doorlock that was new, a doorlock that had not been made by any locksmith on Krynn. Whispering words of magic, Dalamar turned the key in the lock. It clicked. Another click echoed it. The deadly trap was set.

Turning, Dalamar summoned one of the guardians. The disembodied eyes floated over at his command.

"Take this key," Dalamar said, "and keep it with you for all eternity. Give it up to no one—not even myself. And, from this moment on, your place is to guard this door. No one is to enter. Let death be swift for those who try."

The guardian's eyes closed in acquiescence. As Dalamar walked back down the stairs, he saw the eyes—open again—framed by the doorway, their cold glow staring out into the night.

The dark elf nodded to himself, satisfied, and went upon his way.

———

The Homecoming

T hud, thud, thud.

Tika Waylan Majere sat straight up in bed.

Trying to hear above the pounding of her heart, she listened, waiting to identify the sound that had awakened her from deep sleep.

Nothing.

Had she dreamed it? Shoving back the mass of red curls falling over her face, Tika glanced sleepily out the window. It was early morning. The sun had not yet risen, but night's deep shadows were stealing away, leaving the sky clear and blue in the half-light of predawn. Birds were up, beginning their household chores, whistling and bickering cheerfully among themselves. But no one in Solace would be stirring yet. Even the night watchman usually succumbed to the warm, gentle influence of the spring night and slept at this hour, his head slumped on his chest, snoring blissfully.

I must have been dreaming, thought Tika drearily. I wonder if I'll ever get used to sleeping alone? Every little sound has me wide awake. Burrowing back down in the bed, she drew up the sheet and tried to go back to sleep. Squinching her eyes tightly shut, Tika pretended Caramon was there. She was lying beside him, pressed up against his broad chest, hearing him breathe, hearing his heart beat, warm, secure. . . . His hand patted her on the shoulder as he murmured sleepily, "It's just a bad dream, Tika . . . be all gone by morning. . . ."

Thud, thud, thudthudthud.

Tika's eyes opened wide. She *hadn't* been dreaming! The sound—whatever it was—was coming from up above! Someone or something was up there—up in the vallenwood!

Throwing aside the bedclothes and moving with the stealth and quiet she had learned during her war adventures, Tika grabbed a nightrobe from the foot of her bed, struggled into it (mixing up the sleeves in her nervousness), and crept out of the bedroom.

Thud, thud, thud.

Her lips tightened in firm resolve. Someone was up there, up in her new house. The house Caramon was building for her up in the vallenwood. What were they doing? Stealing? There were Caramon's tools—

Tika almost laughed, but it came out a sob instead. Caramon's tools—the hammer with the wiggly head that flew off every time it hit a nail, the saw with so many teeth missing it looked like a grinning gully dwarf, the plane that wouldn't smooth butter. But they were precious to Tika. She'd left them right where *he'd* left them.

Thud, thud, thud.

Creeping out into the living area of her small house, Tika's hand was on the door handle when she stopped.

"Weapon," she muttered. Looking around hastily, she grabbed the first thing she saw—her heavy iron skillet. Holding it firmly by the handle, Tika opened the front door slowly and quietly and sneaked outside.

The sun's rays were just lighting the tops of the mountains, outlining their snow-capped peaks in gold against the clear, cloudless blue sky. The grass sparked with dew like tiny jewels, the morning air was sweet and crisp and pure. The new bright green leaves of the vallenwoods rustled and laughed as the sun touched them, waking them. So fresh and clear and glittering was this morning that it might well have been the very first morning of the very first day, with the gods looking down upon their work and smiling.

But Tika was not thinking about gods or mornings or the dew that was cold upon her bare feet. Clutching the skillet in one hand, keeping it hidden behind her back, she stealthily climbed the rungs of the ladder leading up into the unfinished house perched among the strong branches of the vallenwood. Near the top she stopped, peeping over the edge.

Ah, ha! There *was* someone up here! She could just barely make out a figure crouched in a shadowy corner. Hauling herself up over the edge, still making no sound, Tika padded softly

---

across the wooden floor, her fingers getting a firm grip on the skillet.

But as she crossed the floor, creeping up on the intruder, she thought she heard a muffled giggle.

She hesitated, then continued on resolutely. Just my imagination, she told herself, moving closer to the cloaked figure. She could see him clearly now. It was a man, a human, and by the looks of the brawny arms and the muscular shoulders, it was one of the biggest men Tika had ever seen! He was down on his hands and knees, his broad back was turned toward her, she saw him raise his hand.

He was holding Caramon's hammer!

How dare he touch Caramon's things! Well, big man or no—they're all the same size once they're laid out on the floor.

Tika raised the skillet—

"Caramon! Look out!" cried a shrill voice.

The big man rose to his feet and turned around.

The skillet fell to the floor with a ringing clatter. So did a hammer and a handful of nails.

With a thankful sob, Tika clasped her husband in her arms.

"Isn't this wonderful, Tika? I bet you were surprised, weren't you! Were you surprised, Tika? And say—would you really have wanged Caramon over the head if I hadn't stopped you? That might have been kind of interesting to watch, though I don't think it would have done Caramon much good. Hey, do you remember when you hit that draconian over the head with the skillet—the one that was getting ready to rough up Gilthanas? Tika? . . . Caramon?"

Tas looked at his two friends. They weren't saying a word. They weren't *hearing* a word. They just stood there, holding each other. The kender felt a suspicious moisture creep into his eyes.

"Well," he said with a gulp and a smile, "I'll just go down and wait for you in the living room."

Slithering down the ladder, Tas entered the small, neat house that stood below the sheltering vallenwood. Once inside, he

---

took out a handkerchief, blew his nose, then began to cheerfully investigate the furnishings.

"From the looks of things," he said to himself, admiring a brand-new cookie jar so much that he absent-mindedly stuffed it into a pouch (cookies included), all the while being firmly convinced that he'd set it back on the shelf, "Tika and Caramon are going to be up there quite a while, maybe even the rest of the morning. Perhaps this would be a good time to sort all my stuff."

Sitting down cross-legged on the floor, the kender blissfully upended his pouches, spilling their contents out onto the rug. As he absent-mindedly munched on a few cookies, Tas's proud gaze went first to a whole sheaf of new maps Tanis had given him. Unrolling them, one after another, his small finger traced a route to all the wonderful places he'd visited in his many adventures.

"It was nice traveling," he said after a while, "but it's certainly nicer coming home. I'll just stay here with Tika and Caramon. We'll be a family. Caramon said I could have a room in the new house and— Why, what's that?" He looked closely at the map. "Merilon? I never heard of a city named Merilon. I wonder what it's like. . . ."

"No!" Tas retorted. "You are through adventuring, Burrfoot. You've got quite enough stories to tell Flint as it is. You're going to settle down and become a respectable member of society. Maybe even become High Sheriff."

Rolling up the map (fond dreams in his head of running for High Sheriff), he placed it back in its case (not without a wistful glance). Then, turning his back upon it, he began to look through his treasures.

"A white chicken feather, an emerald, a dead rat—yick, where did I get that? A ring carved to look like ivy leaves, a tiny golden dragon—that's funny, I certainly don't remember putting that in my pouch. A piece of broken blue crystal, a dragon's tooth, white rose petals, some kid's old worn-out, plush rabbit, and—oh, look. Here's Gnimsh's plans for the mechanical lift and—what's this? A book! *Sleight-of-Hand*

Techniques to Amaze and Delight! Now isn't that interesting? I'm sure this will really come in handy and, oh, no"—Tas frowned irritably—"there's that silver bracelet of Tanis's again. I wonder how he manages to hang onto anything without me around, constantly picking up after him? He's extremely careless. I'm surprised Laurana puts up with it."

He peered into the pouch. "That's all, I guess." He sighed. "Well, it certainly has been interesting. Mostly—it was truly wonderful. I met several dragons. I flew in a citadel. I turned myself into a mouse. I broke a dragon orb. Paladine and I became close, personal friends.

"There were some sad times," he said to himself softly. "But they aren't even sad to me now. They just give me a little funny ache, right here." He pressed his hand on his heart. "I'm going to miss adventuring very much. But there's no one to adventure with anymore. They've all settled down, their lives are bright and pleasant." His small hand explored the smooth bottom of one final pouch. "It's time for me to settle down, too, like I said, and I think High Sheriff would be a most fascinating job and—

"Wait. . . . what's that? In the very bottom. . . ." He pulled out a small object, almost lost, tucked into a corner of the pouch. Holding it in his hand, staring at it in wonder, Tas drew in a deep, quivering breath.

"How did Caramon lose this? He was so *very* careful of it. But then, he's had a lot on his mind lately. I'll just go give it back to him. He's probably fearfully worried over misplacing it. After all, what *would* Par-Salian say. . . ."

Studying the plain, nondescript pendant in his palm, Tas never noticed that his other hand—apparently acting of its own accord since *he* had quit adventuring—skittered around behind him and closed over the map case.

"What was the name of that place? Merilon?"

It must have been the hand that spoke. Certainly not Tas, who had given up adventuring.

The map case went into a pouch, along with all of Tas's other treasures; the hand scooping them up hastily and stowing them away.

The hand also gathered up all of Tas's pouches, slinging them over his shoulders, hanging them from his belt, stuffing one into the pocket of his brand-new bright red leggings.

The hand busily began to change the plain, nondescript pendant into a sceptre that was really quite beautiful—all covered with jewels—and looked very magical.

"Once you're finished," Tas told his hand severely, "we'll take it right upstairs and give it to Caramon—"

"Where's Tas?" Tika murmured from the warmth and comfort of Caramon's strong arms.

Caramon, resting his cheek against her head, kissed her red curls and held her tighter. "I don't know. Went down to the house, I think."

"You realize," said Tika, snuggling closer, "that we won't have a spoon left."

Caramon smiled. Putting his hand on her chin, he raised her head and kissed her lips. . . .

An hour later, the two were walking around the floor of the unfinished house, Caramon pointing out the improvements and changes he planned to make. "The baby's room will go here," he said, "next to our bedroom, and this will be the room for the older kids. No, I guess two rooms, one for the boys and one for the girls." He pretended to ignore Tika's blush. "And the kitchen and Tas's room and the guest room—Tanis and Laurana are coming to visit—and. . . ." Caramon's voice died.

He had come to the one room in the house he had actually finished—the room with the wizard's mark carved on a plaque which hung above the door.

Tika looked at him, her laughing face suddenly grown pale and serious.

Reaching up, Caramon slowly took down the plaque. He looked at it silently for long moments, then, with a smile, he handed it to Tika.

"Keep this for me, will you, my dear?" he asked softly and gently.

She looked up at him in wonder, her trembling fingers going

over the smooth edges of the plaque, tracing out the arcane symbol inscribed upon it.

"Will you tell me what happened, Caramon?" she asked.

"Someday," he said, gathering her into his arms, holding her close. "Someday," he repeated. Then, kissing the red curls, he stood, looking out over the town, watching it waken and come to life.

Through the sheltering leaves of the vallenwood, he could see the gabled roof of the Inn. He could hear voices now, sleepy voices, laughing, scolding. He could smell the smoke of cooking fires as it rose into the air, filling the green valley with a soft haze.

He held his wife in his arms, feeling her love surround him, seeing his love for her shining before him always, shining pure and white like the light from Solinari . . . or the light shining from the crystal atop a magical staff. . . .

Caramon sighed, deeply, contentedly. "It doesn't matter anyway," he murmured.

"I'm home."

WEDDING SONG
(A reprise)

But you and I, through burning plains,
through darkness of the earth,
affirm the world, its people,
the heavens that gave them birth,
the breath that passes between us,
this new home where we stand,
and all those things made larger by
the vows between woman and man.

ACKNOWLEDGMENTS

We would like to acknowledge the original members of the DRAGONLANCE story design team: Tracy Hickman, Harold Johnson, Jeff Grubb, Michael Williams, Gali Sanchez, Gary Spiegle, and Carl Smith.

We want to thank those who came to join us in Krynn: Doug Niles, Laura Hickman, Michael Dobson, Bruce Nesmith, Bruce Heard, Michael Breault, and Roger E. Moore.

We would like to thank our editor, Jean Blashfield Black, who has been with us through all our trials and triumphs.

And, finally, we want to express our deep thanks to all of those who have offered encouragement and support: David "Zeb" Cook, Larry Elmore, Keith Parkinson, Clyde Caldwell, Jeff Easley, Ruth Hoyer, Carolyn Vanderbilt, Patrick L. Price, Bill Larson, Steve Sullivan, Denis Beauvais, Valerie Valusek, Dezra and Terry Phillips, Janet and Gary Pack, our families, and, last but not least—all of you who have written to us.

AFTERWORD

And so, our travels in Krynn have come to an end.

We know that this will disappoint many of you, who have been hoping that our adventures in this wonderful land would last forever. But, as Tasslehoff's mother might say, "There comes a time when you have to toss out the cat, lock up the door, put the key under the mat, and start off down the road."

Of course, the key will always remain under the doormat (provided no other kender move into town), and we are not discounting the possibility that someday we might journey down this road in search of that key. But we have Tas's magical time-traveling device in *our* pouches now (fortunately for Krynn!), and there are more worlds we are eager to explore before we return to this one.

We had no idea, when the DRAGONLANCE® project was started, that it would be as successful as it has been. There are many reasons for this, but the main one, I think, is that we had a truly great team working on the project. From the writers to the artists to the game designers to the editors—everyone on the DRAGONLANCE team cared about their work and went above and beyond the call of duty to make certain it succeeded. Tracy says that—somewhere—Krynn really exists and that all of us have been there. We know this is true, because it is so hard saying good-bye.

Speaking of saying good-bye, we first realized the depth of feeling readers had for our characters and our world we had created when we received the outpouring of letters regarding the death of Sturm.

"I know Sturm doesn't mean anything to you!" one distraught reader wrote. "After all, he's just a figment of your imagination."

Of course, he was much more than that to us. Spending so much time with our characters, they become very real to us, too. We triumph with them, grieve with them, and mourn them. We did not "kill" Sturm arbitrarily. The noble Knight of Solamnia was intended to be a tragic hero from the first inception of the project. Death is a part of life, it is a part we all face and must learn to deal with—even our happy-go-lucky kender.

Sturm's death is foreshadowed in the first book by the Forestmaster, who looks directly at the knight when she says, "We do not mourn the loss of those who die fulfilling their destinies."

Sturm's brave sacrifice forces the knights to reexamine their values and eventually provides the means to unite them. Sturm died as he lived—courageously, with honor, serving others. His memory lives for those who loved him, just as the light of the Starjewel beams in the darkness. Many times, when his friends are troubled or facing a dangerous situation, the memory of the knight returns to them, giving them strength and courage.

We knew that Flint's death would have a sad impact on Tasslehoff and, indeed, we wept more for Tas when Flint died than we did for the old dwarf, who had led a rich, full life. But something in Tas changed forever (and for the better) when he lost his gruff but tender-hearted friend. This, too, was a necessary change (though Tanis would add here that some things never change—-kender among them!). But we knew that Tas would have to face a rough road in the second trilogy. We knew he would need strength and, most of all, compassion to come through it.

We always hoped we would have a chance to tell Caramon's and Raistlin's story, even when we were still working on the first trilogy. When writing the short story, "Test of the Twins," we had the vague outlines in mind of what would eventually become the second trilogy. LEGENDS grew in scope and depth even as we worked on CHRONICLES, and therefore it was quite simple to just keep traveling down the road with those of our characters who still needed us.

It was important to us to show in LEGENDS a quest that was not so much involved with saving a world as it was (as Par-Salian says) with saving a soul. Everyone believed that it was Raistlin's soul we referred to, but, of course, it was his twin's. The archmage had already doomed himself. The only thing that saves him at the end is his brother's love and that small spark of caring in his own heart that even the darkness within him cannot completely extinguish.

But now this road has brought us, as all roads must eventually, to a parting. We authors are traveling down one path, our characters another. We feel confident we can leave them now. They don't need us anymore. Caramon has found the inner resources he needs to cope with life. He and Tika will have many sons and daughters, and we would be surprised if at least one doesn't become a mage.

Undoubtedly Caramon's children will join with Tanis's one son (a quiet, introspective youth) and with Riverwind's and Goldmoon's golden-haired twins in some adventure or other. They might possibly try to discover whatever became of Gilthanas and Silvara. They might journey to the united elven kingdom, brought together at last by Alhana and Porthios, who do—after all—come to develop a deep and enduring love for each other. They may meet up with Bupu's children (she married the Highbulp when he wasn't looking) or they might even travel for a while with "Grandpa" Tasslehoff.

Astinus will chronicle these adventures, of course, even if we do not. And you who are role-playing the DRAGONLANCE games will undoubtedly come to know more about the further adventures than we will. At any rate, you will continue, we hope, to have a marvelous time in that fabled land. But we must be on our way.

We shake hands with Tas (who is snuffling again) and bid him good-bye (checking our pouches first, of course, and relieving Tas of the many personal possessions we have unaccountably "dropped"). Then we watch as the kender goes skipping down the road, his topknot bobbing, and we imagine that we can see him—in the distance—meet up with an old, befuddled wizard, who is wandering about looking for his lost hat—which is on his head.

And then they vanish from our sight. With a sigh, we turn and walk down the new road that beckons us onward.

FOR THE BEST IN PAPERBACKS, LOOK FOR THE

In every corner of the world, on every subject under the sun, Penguin represents quality and variety – the very best in publishing today.

For complete information about books available from Penguin – including Pelicans, Puffins, Peregrines and Penguin Classics – and how to order them, write to us at the appropriate address below. Please note that for copyright reasons the selection of books varies from country to country.

In the United Kingdom: For a complete list of books available from Penguin in the U.K., please write to *Dept E.P., Penguin Books Ltd, Harmondsworth, Middlesex, UB7 0DA*

In the United States: For a complete list of books available from Penguin in the U.S., please write to *Dept BA, Penguin, 299 Murray Hill Parkway, East Rutherford, New Jersey 07073*

In Canada: For a complete list of books available from Penguin in Canada, please write to *Penguin Books Canada Ltd, 2801 John Street, Markham, Ontario L3R 1B4*

In Australia: For a complete list of books available from Penguin in Australia, please write to the *Marketing Department, Penguin Books Australia Ltd, P.O. Box 257, Ringwood, Victoria 3134*

In New Zealand: For a complete list of books available from Penguin in New Zealand, please write to the *Marketing Department, Penguin Books (NZ) Ltd, Private Bag, Takapuna, Auckland 9*

In India: For a complete list of books available from Penguin, please write to *Penguin Overseas Ltd, 706 Eros Apartments, 56 Nehru Place, New Delhi, 110019*

In Holland: For a complete list of books available from Penguin in Holland, please write to *Penguin Books Nederland B.V., Postbus 195, NL–1380AD Weesp, Netherlands*

In Germany: For a complete list of books available from Penguin, please write to *Penguin Books Ltd, Friedrichstrasse 10 – 12, D–6000 Frankfurt Main 1, Federal Republic of Germany*

In Spain: For a complete list of books available from Penguin in Spain, please write to *Longman Penguin España, Calle San Nicolas 15, E–28013 Madrid, Spain*

DRAGONLANCE

The DRAGONLANCE books tell the epic tale of the fight for Krynn. If you enjoyed the book, it is the start of many adventures that can be yours in the world of Krynn. You can be Tanis or Laurana, Raistlin or Tasslehoff, or any fantastic character of your own imagination.

With the DRAGONLANCE Adventure Modules you can experience the world of Krynn for yourself.

For more information contact

Press Office
The Mill
Rathmore Road
CAMBRIDGE
CB1 4AD